# Earworms

ZACK DUNCAN

Tellwell Talent
www.tellwell.ca

ISBN
978-0-2288-7509-3 (Paperback)
978-0-2288-7510-9 (eBook)

*For Grandma.*

Ruston for decades; his family was a staple of their summer tourism boom. The Thomas family money had flowed through this town for generations. Kept the town alive. Kept sheriffs employed.

"Where's Floyd?" Thomas growled. He was taller and leaner than the sheriff, who had added to his potbelly considerably over the holidays this year.

"He's locked up," Landry said. "Sanderson, get over here. Help me out."

Alex Sanderson, a junior deputy with rusty hair and broad shoulders, sprinted over from his seat and blocked the doorway that led to the holding cell. It was a small operation, and there was only one cell. Inside that cell, Floyd Smith was lying on his back, almost catatonic.

"We just need you to remain calm," Sanderson said.

"Remain calm?" Thomas fumed. "That son of a bitch took my daughter!"

Thomas had been so busy looking for Tiffany that he had missed the call. They had found the man who had taken her. Floyd Smith. His shoe size matched the print left at the scene. He had no alibi. What he did have was a long history of trouble with law enforcement, and a motive. The Thomas family had bought up more land in Ruston. Land that once belonged to Floyd's family. Floyd was notorious for running his mouth at the local watering hole. He would drink too much and start bragging about all the things he'd like to do to those summer tourists. A few times, he had even mentioned the Thomas family by name.

*"For all the land they own, you'd think those big city fuckers would smile more often. I'd love to carve a big smile into that Thomas prick's leathery face."*

This was the same man who had been arrested countless times—by Landry and the old sheriff before him—for everything from petty theft to battery. But Floyd was a cat with more than nine lives. No matter how long he was put away for, he always seemed to end up back on the streets of Ruston with the same chip on his shoulder. The townsfolk knew Floyd well and kept their distance.

"He won't talk," Landry said. "We've tried."

"Tried what?"

"Shit that we shouldn't be telling a District Attorney," Landry admitted. "It's a small station, sir. No one around to hear his cries for help. Been going at him most of today."

"Let me see him," Thomas said. "Let me back there."

Landry and Sanderson looked at one another, weighing their options. Saying no to a man like this wasn't good for business.

"Just try not to kill him," Landry said and motioned for Sanderson to stand down. "Without him, we'll never know where Tiffany is."

Thomas pushed through the door, and the two law men followed him. The hall was dim, but at the far end, he could just make out the shape of a man behind the bars. The man was lying on his back, staring at the ceiling. He looked gaunt, his eyes falling deep into their sockets. His arms were veiny, spotted with tattoos, and his hair was stringy, tucked behind his ears.

"Floyd, you start talking right now!" Thomas shouted.

The shadow in the cell bolted upright, startled by the voice now reverberating through the concrete space.

"Who's this now?" Floyd asked, rising slowly and peering through his cell bars.

Thomas rushed at him, pulling away from Landry and Sanderson. Floyd leaned forwards, trying to get a look at his visitor, and by the time he realized the threat, it was too late. Thomas stuck his big arms through the cell bars and wrapped his hands around Floyd's neck.

"Where's my daughter?" Thomas strangled the man.

Floyd was surprisingly light, and his feet lifted off the floor.

Landry crossed his arms over his belly and watched. Floyd's nose was already bleeding from the solid smack Landry had given him. He'd also tried a few other threats. But Floyd Smith was immune to these. There was nothing you could take away from a man who had nothing to begin with.

Floyd choked and gagged, kicking his feet to try and escape the grip. Thomas looked into his eyes, watching them slowly balloon in desperation. Thomas shook him a few more times. Then, when he was certain the man's face wouldn't go a darker shade of purple, he let go. Floyd crumpled to the ground, hacking and struggling for air. He reached at his throat desperately but stopped short of touching it. It was too tender.

"Where is she?" Thomas repeated.

Floyd took a few pained breaths, and when he spoke, his voice was nothing more than a hoarse whisper.

"Fuck you."

Thomas reached through the cell bars again, but Floyd scurried away to the back of his cell.

"What did you do with her!?" Thomas raised his voice again. The echo was painful for all of them.

Thomas had a reputation for his stoic presence in the court room. They called him the Grim Reaper, both for his intimidating physical stature and for his consistency in putting criminals away for life. But his visage was falling away now.

This was his only daughter. This should never have happened. Tiffany would never have been here in Ruston if she hadn't needed space, needed to get out of the big city.

"You took her right out of her home, you piece of shit," Thomas snarled. "What did you do with her?"

Floyd glared back at him from the shadows but said nothing.

"Tried it all." Landry clicked his tongue. "Like we said. We asked him where he was the night she went missing. He said nothing. We asked him if he's seen Tiffany since she's been back in town. He said nothing. We asked him why his boot print was found at your house. He said nothing."

"He's got to say something," Thomas said, finally turning away from the cell. He tried to compose himself. He tried to think of this as work. There was always a solution.

"I don't know what's in that fucked-up head of his," Landry said, "but he ain't talking. Short of cracking his skull open, I don't know what to do."

Thomas put his hand against the cold concrete wall, needing to hold himself up as he focused on breathing. Landry may have given him an idea.

Of course, it was paint.

"Should we get started?" Janelle asked.

Max looked to his left, where his assignment editor and longtime coworker was dipping a roller into the sea. She coated its surface in the black sludge and then marched off toward the abandoned resort.

Janelle ran the roller up and down one of the crumbling walls as if trying to undo years of damage. For a moment, Max thought he could see his parents inside, standing among the greenery. It looked as though they were having an important conversation. He could see their lips moving, and he could almost hear them, but as Janelle ran her roller over the walls, they disappeared. Max would never get to know what they were saying.

"Let me help," Max said.

He stood, not feeling the effects of the heat or the alcohol. He also didn't need his trademark pair of thick-rimmed glasses. Here, on the beach, he could see just fine.

Max grabbed a second roller, which had mysteriously been left out on the beach, and went over to the black water. He stared at it for a moment. It made the beach look dystopian. He thought they should be painting the resort in a lighter shade.

Casting a glance behind him, he saw Janelle was still painting. She looked great—as always—wearing a pair of overalls with a white t-shirt underneath. She had worn this same outfit to their company BBQ last summer. Max had a picture of the two of them saved on his phone.

When Max once again faced the ocean, the sea had turned itself into a dazzling sapphire. A much prettier paint colour. He dipped his roller. She didn't see him. Max stealthily approached and dabbed his freshly-coated roller on her back.

"Max!" she shrieked, laughing. She pivoted and flung paint back at him.

She had shown up in his dreams before. This setting was unique, however. Max figured that his mind had concocted the painting scene because Janelle had asked him to help paint her new place next week. He had agreed. He was always the helpful friend. But only here in his dream did he have the courage to show her how he felt. To be more than a friend.

"Why don't we go for a swim?" Max suggested.

"But we have to finish painting," Janelle protested.

"It's done," Max said, pointing.

Janelle turned around, and the once derelict resort was now a beautiful palace. The entire building was a striking blue, matching the paint Max had on his roller. The walls looked stable once more, and the windows were restored. The villas looked modern and inviting.

Max tugged Janelle toward the beach, where the water had been mercifully restored to water again. No more paint. They paraded out waist-deep into the surf, not caring if their clothes became soaked.

Janelle shot him a playful look and then dove into the water, disappearing completely. Max watched the shape of her beneath the surface.

She remained under the water for quite a while, and suddenly, the sunlight changed. Twilight took hold, and the waves seemed to pick up. The water was murky; her shape now was just a dark blot beneath the whitecaps. Max moved closer to her, trying to grab at her and pull her up.

"Janelle!" he called out, but a wave slapped him in the face, filling his mouth with foam.

He concentrated, trying to calm the waves. Max had a gift that served him well. He was a lucid dreamer; his conscious mind was present and aware of the dream. He maintained a sense of control over the worlds he visited, able to shape them as he pleased. Very seldom did he lose control as he was now, the waves pressing him back.

*No more waves,* Max thought, and the sea subsided slightly. Janelle was still beneath the surface, her shape drifting further out. Painfully slowly, as was always the case in dreams, he waded forward. His hands caught hold of her shoulders, and he ripped her from the water.

But when he pulled her up, he found himself staring not at Janelle but at a giant black moth. The hairy beast stretched its wings and lunged at him. Max toppled backwards into the waves, raising his arms to brace himself from this monstrosity. He landed on his rear, staring up as the moth raised itself into the sky. It seemed to shrink down to a normal size before floating away, eventually disappearing altogether.

When it was gone, Max allowed the waves to push him ashore.

"What's wrong?" Janelle asked. She was behind him again, standing in her overalls and holding a paint roller.

"Did you see the moth?" Max asked.

"The phone," she said, her voice robotic.

The sun had reset itself and was once again baking the beach in an orange glow. Gulls cried out, replacing the eerie silence. The world was normal, but Janelle's eyes were distant.

"What?" Max tried to raise himself from the sand but couldn't.

"The phone!" Janelle shouted this time.

Then the entire world quaked, shattering the sea, and the sand, and the resort. Everything became black, and a piercing tone cut through it all. The sound was obscured at first, then quickly formed itself into a familiar tune: his ring tone.

Max rolled over in bed and reached for his phone with one hand, wiping sleep from his eyes with the other. He noticed the time first. Barely after 2 a.m. He should've been able to finish his dream with Janelle. Who the hell was calling him anyway?

*AUNT MELODY* was displayed across the screen. That was bizarre. She never called.

He swiped on the screen and choked out something like "Hello."

That was when Max found out that his father had passed away.

***

The organ played something that was almost familiar to Max, long melancholy notes that reverberated throughout the church. He searched his brain to see if he could place the tune. It was the best distraction he could think of. He swore he would not cry, not until this was all over and he was alone. But he could already feel his eyes welling up. He pinched his nose beneath his glasses.

The casket had been open, but Max did not recognize the man inside as his father.

The entire day had played out like a sitcom—Max was transported from scene to scene without any memory of what happened in between—only none of it was funny. He woke up in his old bedroom, having flown from Vancouver to Toronto the day before and bused the rest of the way to small-town Ontario. He got dressed in a suit he hadn't worn in years. The pants didn't sit right and hung too high. Then suddenly, he found himself outside the church, hugging old relatives he thought may have already been dead themselves. Now he was standing amongst other "presenters," waiting for his chance to say a few words.

The task of cleaning out the family bungalow awaited him when this was all finished. The house was filled with old memories and boxes that needed sorting. Max expected to toss out more than he kept.

Max and his father had such a complicated relationship toward the end, their equal stubbornness keeping them away from one another for too long. One tense conversation had been echoing through Max's mind all day. It had been a brief glimpse into his father's great disappointment in him. Max had been talking about work, and his father had cut him off.

*"You want to waste your life writing stories?" his father said with a distant voice, as if he was already*

*elsewhere. "You could be doing something important. But you're not."*

"Don't do that," Max said. "Not everybody needs to be a cop. Not everybody wants to be you."

And then silence. Many years of silence. His father's signature move, the cold shoulder. He distanced himself from his own son. The one who wouldn't follow the lineage. The one who wanted to move out west and write and carve his own path.

The worst part was it caused Max to question his own decision. It was impossible not to look at his own life and see the things his father would have hated. He was an observer. He watched people and wrote stories about what they did—always reporting on triumphs, adventures, struggles, and choices that other people made. But had he really done anything himself?

Even when they weren't speaking to one another, his father's voice was always present. It reminded him that he might have made the wrong choice.

After the initial blow up, they spoke in fits and starts. But it was never like before. His father never asked how things were. Max would come home to visit, and his mother—still alive then—would pick him up at the airport alone. His father never came. They'd get to the family home, and his father wouldn't come to the door. He just stayed in his chair. The two of them only exchanged pleasantries. No visits out to Max's place in Vancouver. No phone calls, save for the obligatory "happy birthday" call when his mother forced the man on the phone.

And then his mother got sick, and even those calls disappeared.

Eventually, Max started avoiding contact as well. The silence scared him away.

With every passing year, he feared that his father would kick the bucket before they got a chance to patch things up. And, at last, that fear had come to fruition. Unlike his mother's slow, painful decline, his father's passing was sudden. They hadn't realized that his heart had gone bad.

*Would it have killed you to call him?* Max raged at himself. After that phone call in the middle of the night, he had wondered if he bore the blame for this.

Max had always felt conflicted, somewhere between angry and brokenhearted. Those two emotions remained, even after his father left this world. In a way, his father had now won their decade-long standoff. He was able to exit stage right, while Max was the one standing here, coming back home for the funeral, being the first to crack.

*Is that "Ode to Joy"?* Max thought of the organ music that was oh so familiar. What a questionable choice that would've been for a funeral. His gaze was downward, and he could feel tears forming. He tilted his chin up to prevent himself from leaking. He scoured the horizon instead. Somber faces stared back at him. One of them was his uncle—with his father's mouth and chin. Another face was that of a cousin Max hadn't seen since grade school, but even now, he looked boyish, the same.

And then there was a face Max was sure he was imagining. A specter lurked at the back of the room, head bowed in respect, but standing away from the gathering so as not to interfere. The man was one of the tallest people in the church. His dark suit was pristine and an even deeper black than the other mourners. The man looked up and locked eyes with Max. There was a moment of understanding—and perhaps a slight nod— where condolences were silently passed on.

Max averted his gaze, forcing himself to burn a hole into the wall and avoid the rush of emotion catching up to him. He suddenly felt very exposed in standing before the church full of mourners. He felt awkward in this suit that didn't fit quite right. Max's rust-coloured hair had been brushed back with a comb in an attempt to look put together. But he felt anything but put together right now; he felt more like an exposed mess in front of judging eyes.

Soon enough, it was Max's time to speak. As he stepped up to the microphone—which whistled with feedback as he began his rehearsed words—all he could think about was the man at the back of the church. Why had he come? Max paused, creating a silence that lasted longer than it should have. He lost his place in the eulogy, his mind elsewhere.

Someone behind him mistook it for grief and murmured, "It's alright, love. Take your time."

Max tried to start up again, but his mind and his mouth weren't on the same page. He offered up a choked groan and then a quiet "I'm sorry" and stepped back. A different family member took the mic then as

Aunt Melody—the fun one who, at any other occasion, would've been holding a glass of wine—wrapped an arm around Max to console him. Max paid her no mind, instead looking across the pews, searching for the old friend who had become a stranger. But he was no longer in the room. Max felt he was imagining things.

After the ceremony, of which Max would remember very little, came the burial. The finality of it all caught up to Max, and he forced his mind to check out. He left that place entirely, pushing his thoughts to things he needed to get done. His colleagues had encouraged him to take all the time he needed. The sad truth was that the magazine would be fine without him. But Max didn't want time. Work—chasing stories—would serve as an escape, a chance to worry about the details of someone else's life.

The burial went much like his mother's: Words were said, flowers were laid, and somber hugs were exchanged. The snow made it sloppy. The cold seeped up through the soles of their shoes. And at the end of it all, Max walked back to the church alone, while most others walked side by side.

Now that the late Daniel Barker was in the ground, the congregation moved into the lobby for social hour. At any other time of the year, the beautiful park outside would've been the ideal spot to bask in the sun and reminisce. But the snow had driven everyone into the building and forced conversations into a space only big enough for half their number.

Max helped himself to the platter of sandwiches, realizing he hadn't eaten all day. But they did little for him, and the taste didn't register in his absent mind. He put his plate down and left it. He forced himself to nod politely and smile at the occasional greeting from the others. But Max was searching, his eyes busy and hoping to prove he hadn't hallucinated what he had seen earlier.

Finally, and with great relief, Max spotted his old friend across the room once again. Though it had been years, he was still recognizable as Oren West.

Max excused himself from a conversation he hadn't enjoyed and made his way over to his childhood pal. The two stood there for a moment, searching for words, and instead opted for a hug.

"I was so sorry to hear the news," Oren said, his voice deep and cool. He could've been a radio announcer or perhaps a narrator for an audiobook.

"It's nice of you to come."

"I wish I was visiting under better circumstances. But once I heard, I had to come back, thought it was important to pay my respects." Oren smiled, and Max was immediately jealous.

Oren had always been good-looking, in control, and a leader. It appeared that he had filled out and become even more striking and more gregarious than the young man Max remembered. He was easily half a foot taller than Max, who was not exactly vertically challenged himself. Oren was the kind of friend Max idolized. He always had his life together, so when he moved away for university, it was no surprise. The town they grew up in did not offer much for guys like Oren. He eventually made his way to New York and carved himself out a career south of the border.

Oren asked if he could buy Max lunch—and maybe a drink—and catch up. Max didn't even need to think about it. He wanted to escape the hushed chatter and curious eyes. They retrieved their coats from the coatroom and, without saying so much as a goodbye to his aunts or uncles, they headed for the door.

*Sorry, Mom,* Max thought, casting a glance skyward. *I just can't stay here any longer. Maybe if you were still around . . .*

They high-stepped through the snowy parking lot, trying not to stick a dress shoe into anything too deep. Max was focused on the ground, and when he heard the *bleep-bleep* of a car lock, he looked up. Of course Oren would have a nice ride.

Once inside the luxury sedan, Max looked around and couldn't help but feel like he was in a movie. A crime drama, specifically. Oren buckled up and caught the look on Max's face. He chuckled.

"I'm not surprised, but damn," Max said. "Guess being a celebrity PI pays well."

"You saw the articles, then," Oren said, putting the car in drive and taking off.

"Skimmed them," Max teased. "You're talking about the ones where you cracked Leonard Lang, yeah? Got the notorious serial killer to finally reveal where he hid the bodies? The only person to gain the trust of this real life Hannibal Lecter? Cause those are the ones I read."

"Yeah, well, that was one case," Oren said. "Not sure it warranted all the attention we got."

"It suits you." Max scanned the interior of the car as if appraising it. "I seem to remember you being the enforcer growing up. Always putting bullies in arm-bars and making them apologize. Looking out for smaller kids on the playground. And remember that time when my dog ran away?" Max laughed. "And we spent all night looking for footprints and clues in the woods? You made a career out of that. Farley the corgi, your first case."

Oren smiled, but it was a cheap mask. He was thinking of something else. "It's not exactly the kind of job that makes it easy to hold onto old friendships. The travel. The cases. Still, that's no excuse. I feel awful that we fell out of touch."

"You don't have to apologize," Max said, preferring not to address their fallout. He too had buried himself in work, letting old relationships die. The only difference was he wasn't making headlines or driving fancy cars. "Looks like you're doing pretty well. Congrats."

"I've learned to colour outside the lines, and that's given me some relative success." Oren bit his lip, something he had done as a kid when he was nervous. "I got lucky a while back. I inherited a secret weapon. You're a smart guy, Max. I imagine you've heard about MemCom, perhaps even written stories about it?"

The car passed a burger joint, and its neon sign fought against thick white flakes, begging them to come inside. Oren didn't turn in though.

"MemCom?" Max exhaled, thinking. "Yeah, I think so. Never wrote about it though. That's the thing cops were using a while back, right? Was supposed to be the future of fighting crime but led to a bunch of protests, then just kind of died away."

"Pretty much," Oren nodded. "Only it didn't entirely die away. The protests shut down production. Most of the units were destroyed. But a handful were held on to. And I was able to get my hands on one."

"That's pretty cool," Max said. He was unsure why they were talking about this, but he supposed he was happy to have the distraction. Then, as they passed another establishment—a bar offering cheap beer— Max asked, "Do you have a place in mind?"

"Not really," Oren said. "Haven't been back in ages. Don't recognize much."

"Me neither."

"Great," Oren said. "So next thing we see, I'll turn in there."

The way Oren said it made him feel as though this was by design, and not random at all.

Oren didn't press for more details about Max's job or why he had moved away, which was surprising because he couldn't have known much. They hadn't seen each other in almost ten years, and most of their recent correspondence had been just brief emails. Very little detail. Max expected Oren to ask more questions. Typically, Oren could listen for hours—with genuine curiosity too. It was part of what made him so likeable. He was an interviewer, a master at making you feel heard, asking you things that allowed you to brag.

Max had tried to make a living out of this same idea, leaving town eventually to become a journalist. He had catapulted himself to the West Coast, as far away as possible, and made a new home in Vancouver. He told stories about people—often stories that they didn't want told. He was good at digging and finding things. But he was only following Oren's model. Oren was better, and faster, at finding answers.

"You looked into me," Max deduced. "You know what I'm doing and where I went. You really *are* good at your job."

"I did. And unfortunately, I didn't come to town to just pay my respects," Oren admitted. "I feel awful about the timing. I wish I was back in town just to catch up, but I need you."

"You need *me*?" Max found the idea to be absurd.

"I'm working a case. We need the MemCom again. But we don't have anyone who can operate it."

"And you thought to come all the way back home to, what, ask me?" Max chuckled. "You know I'm not a cop like my dad, right? Just a writer. How could I possibly help?"

"You have exactly the skills I'm looking for," Oren said, sounding so certain. "If we can't find someone to use the MemCom device, we won't find our missing person in time. She's sixteen, Max. And the chances of us finding her alive get slimmer every day."

"Well . . ." Max thought of what the logical next question might be. "Why me? Why now?"

"Something happened to our last diver," Oren said, then he caught himself. "Sorry, *divers* are what we call the operators. Those who can use the MemCom."

"What happened?"

Oren did not answer. Max turned and waited for a reply. Oren was considering what to say. The amount of time this took made Max's stomach tighten.

"He can't perform his job anymore. We need someone. And as it turns out, you fit exactly what we are looking for."

"What are you looking for? How am I possibly the right fit?"

A sign appeared ahead on their right. *The Cuckoo's Nest.* Below the establishment's name was an illuminated plaque stating they were "f_lly licensed" and served "all d_y brea_fast."

"Perfect," Oren said, flicking on the turn signal. "I'll explain all of that here. I'm starving."

The car crunched over fresh snow as they found a parking spot right by the door.

Max had many questions swirling through his head. He couldn't wait for all of them. "No offence, Oren," Max said. "But why would I do this? If you couldn't tell from the fact that you found me at my father's funeral—the timing of it . . . I just can't. Even if I was the right guy for the job. And I'm not looking for work. I'm content with where I'm at."

"I know, Max." Oren shut off the engine. "I'm not offering you a job. I'm asking you for help. But I have something to offer in return."

Oren let that dangle for a second. Max was growing uncomfortable with the silence.

"If you help me, I can give you a chance to speak to your father again."

\*\*\*

The Cuckoo's Nest, as it turned out, had a very appropriate name. The entire place had been plastered with bird paraphernalia. The front entrance saw a person-sized robin statue welcome them with a cartoon smile and a sign asking them to please wait to be seated. The walls—wood-paneled and ancient—were covered with framed sketches and photographs of rare birds from across North America. To Max, they all looked the same—sparrows or crows or blue jays. But according to the plaques on the wall, they were each something unique and uncommon.

Max hadn't wanted to leave the car at first. He had been too stunned by Oren's offer.

"How can you say something like that?" Max had asked. Rage had built inside him, sparks turning to fire in his chest. Was this all just a big joke to Oren? "What do you mean by talk to him again? I buried him this morning, in case you've forgotten."

"It's the MemCom, Max. The device allows you to interact with moments in time. It lets you relive memories." Then, because he could tell Max was upset, he added, "Let me tell you more about the case. I will explain. Then you can decide."

Max had been clenching his fists, yet he had followed Oren inside.

Now, a quiet waitress with a polite smile guided them to their booth by the window. As they took their seats, an unseen clock announced the time with a series of bird chirps. Oren immediately grabbed the menu and chuckled to himself. He held the menu out for Max to see. The food items were all some creative spin-off of bird terms, including steak served with green beans and *a-sparrow-gus* instead of asparagus, and other worse attempts at humour.

"What have we done?" Oren chuckled, looking around at the place.

Max couldn't figure out why Oren was making such a big deal over the horrible decor. He was stalling. And Max wanted answers. He impatiently grabbed his own menu off the table, which was covered with a parrot-patterned tablecloth.

"How long are you going to make me wait? So I'm supposed to find my father in a memory?" Max asked over the menu.

Behind Oren, Max could see the bathrooms, where "Sea Gals" and "Woodpeckers" could relieve themselves. It was relentless.

"Many versions of your father exist inside my mind. I can open my mind up to you, and you will get a chance to see him by using the MemCom," Oren said. His eyes tracked the approach of the waitress, and he fell silent once she arrived.

She poured them each a cup of coffee. Max thanked their server and waited for her to walk out of earshot before speaking.

"I don't understand it."

"Give it time. You will."

"Who's this missing person?" Max changed topics. Too many questions. "How am I supposed to help her?"

"The missing girl is Tiffany Thomas," Oren explained. "You may have heard of Robert Thomas, the Grim Reaper? The Manhattan District Attorney. There's a lot of pressure here, which is why I was called in. When the DA's kid is missing, they pull out all the stops.

"Their family has a summer home in upstate New York, in a little town called Ruston. It's the kind of place that's not even printed on most maps. But in the summer, it gets nice weather, and it's close to Lake Ontario, and so the population doubles. Tiffany Thomas is an angry teen who ran away from home. She took off to the summer home in Ruston in order to get away from her dad and stepmother. Travelled via bus, and the ticket was paid for with her father's credit card. She texted them on the way, too. So they knew where she was headed."

"It's February, Oren," Max said.

"I'm aware. The summer home is shuttered up all winter, making it the perfect place for an angsty teen to get some space. She had the keys, opened up shop, and made herself comfortable. Couple of the locals recognized her, knew her from summertime, and called her dad to make sure everything was okay. So we know Tiffany made it to Ruston in one piece.

"I guess the girl's mother found out—saw something on social media—and threw a fit. She demanded that Robert Thomas bring her back to town. So he and his new wife hopped in the car and drove up to collect her. When he got there, the front door was left open. The front foyer was all snowed in. The house was empty. There's been no sight of Tiffany and no contact from her ever since.

"Thomas contacted local authorities right away. Tiffany's phone was left in the kitchen. A boot print was found in the snowdrift in the foyer. It was a men's size 11."

"Can I take your order?" The singsongy voice of their waitress cut through the tense atmosphere building around Oren's story.

Max was brought back to the kitschy bird cafe, and only then did he realize that he hadn't been breathing. He relaxed, just a bit.

"I'll get the empty nester, please, over easy." Oren smiled.

Max glanced quickly at the menu in front of him, where an illustrated sparrow sat perched atop the restaurant's promise that all food was guaranteed to be cooked fresh. According to the menu, the "empty nester" was an all-day breakfast dish consisting of three eggs done your way, with a bonus scrambled eggs, toast, bacon, and home fries.

"Same," Max said. "And a beer. Anything on tap is fine."

The waitress collected their menus and departed, leaving Max and Oren face-to-face with the Tiffany Thomas case hanging in the air between them.

"And?" Max coaxed Oren to continue.

"Local police started investigating. Pretty quickly, they settled on this guy, Floyd Smith. Police brought Floyd in. Evidence was strong. Floyd's shoe size is a men's 11—same as the print. He has no alibi for the night Tiffany went missing. Even has a motive; Floyd has a reputation for getting pissed at the local bar and sharing his thoughts about out-of-towners. He doesn't care for the folks who come into town for the summer, treat the town like a trash can, and then leave. And he particularly doesn't care for DA Thomas and his family, who bought up some of Floyd's family land after he could no longer afford to keep it. It seems he decided to extract a little revenge."

"Sounds like you have your guy," Max said, genuinely confused. "Why do you need me? Why do you need MemCom?"

"Tell me what you know about MemCom, Max," Oren said.

"Not much," Max said, searching his mind for what he could recall. "Memory Communication, right? It lets you see inside someone else's mind."

Of course, he had heard about it; most had. It had been an internet sensation. It was hard to tell what was fact and what was fiction. It had sparked many heated social media debates. It inspired several new crime shows, running in prime time, all with the same premise. Then the whole idea seemed to fade away just as quickly as it had arrived. And all that was left were these poorly acted fictions.

"It's illegal now," Oren continued. "There were a lot of protests. People were upset. They thought that no one should be able to invade the privacy of someone's mind. Do you know how it works? What it does?"

Max hesitated, then shook his head. He'd mostly heard things through the grapevine that he would be embarrassed to admit to Oren. Their accuracy was questionable at best.

"Maybe you heard it was like virtual reality, right?" Oren said. "They say it's like transporting yourself into someone's memories. And walking around in them. Which was supposed to help confirm or deny alibis of dangerous criminals. It was meant to bring clarity for juries when convicting murderers. MemCom could take you inside someone's memory, theoretically proving whether they were guilty. Beyond a reasonable doubt. Beyond any doubt."

Max nodded; it was all coming back to him now.

"Floyd has been in custody for three days—that's a full day longer than you're allowed to hold someone. The law is being . . . *massaged* in the Thomas family's best interest. And yet, Floyd still has not revealed what he did with Tiffany, or even whether or not she's still alive. He's not saying much. Police can't find her. The garage Floyd worked at was empty and so was his rental unit. Tiffany went missing on Tuesday, Max. Four days ago. Even if she was alive when we caught Floyd, time is running out for her, wherever she is. If he's not willing to talk, there's only one way to find out what he's done with Tiffany."

"You're going to go inside his mind," Max concluded.

"Yes," Oren said.

Their food arrived. The eggs were hot and looked delicious. The rest of the meal was sort of colourless and sad. Oren ignored the toast and bacon and went straight for his scrambled eggs. The conversation was put on hold again as the server positioned their plates and handed over a bottle of ketchup. When she left, Max spoke first.

"Why me?"

"Remember when we were kids?" Oren asked. "The summers spent at camp, when we'd wake up before everyone else and go toss rocks into the lake? You told me about the dreams you had and the stuff you did in them. Because even though we didn't know the term for it at the time, we knew you had a special way of dreaming. You were aware that you were dreaming. And it let you shape them the way you wanted."

"Lucid dreams," Max confirmed.

For as long as he could remember, he had been one of the rare few on the planet who experienced frequent lucid dreams. In fact, Max couldn't remember ever having a "normal" dream, which made him even rarer.

When his mind slipped off into a dream state, play time began. Lucid dreamers always know when they're dreaming. Therefore, they know they can bend the rules of the dreamworld. They can choose to fly if they want. Just like any other dream, it all feels real enough. But unlike most dreamers, a lucid dreamer knows that consequences don't exist. And they know that the dreamworld is malleable.

"Only people who experience lucid dreams are able to use the MemCom," Oren explained. "A diver needs to present that potential or else, once they enter someone else's mind, they don't know which way is up. I've tried it. It feels like you're having a nightmare. You can't control yourself, and your body doesn't respond to you. You end up at the mercy of whatever is happening inside that foreign mind. You won't be able to make sense of what you see. Things may harm you, and you feel stuck. A lucid dreamer, on the other hand, can enter another person's memories and choose where they go. They can navigate and make choices."

"So you need me because of my lucid dreaming." Now Max knew the truth. "How . . . how do you not have anyone else for this? Another investigator that can also lucid dream?"

"Not easy to find," Oren said, now starting in on his toast.

"You came here just to recruit me . . ." Max wasn't hungry after all. He hadn't touched his plate.

"Unfortunately, yes," Oren admitted. "And time isn't exactly on my side. We need someone *now*. If I knew anyone else who had lucid dreams, I would've started there. But I don't have a lot of options, Max. I really am sorry."

Max looked out the window for the first time. The parking lot was caked in snow and muck. The cars were all soiled from the salt and the slush. Winter depressed him. That was why he had moved away after school. He had chosen a milder climate, leaving the harsh winters behind in childhood memories. Now, seeing the snow made him feel like a kid again. And like a kid, he was learning something new and terrifying about the world that would change him forever.

"This is incredibly important, and also incredibly confidential," Oren said. "Most folks aren't receptive to the idea of the MemCom. Including the Sheriff's Department in Ruston County. The fact that we are going there, and that we are using the MemCom, has to be kept quiet. Only you and my partner know about this. Even the Thomas family, who hired us, think we are just really good, or really lucky, investigators. They don't know about our secret weapon."

For a moment, they let the restaurant din take over. Oren took another bite of his meal. Then Oren set down his fork and leaned in.

"I need you, Max. I can't find someone else with your . . ." He hesitated for a moment. ". . . *ability* on such short notice. Tiffany Thomas needs you, too. And I know you will want a chance to see your father again. If you do this for me, I will give you that chance."

Max couldn't bring himself to look at Oren, as though eye contact would've allowed him to see right inside his mind. Oren knew what he was doing. Max had amends to make with his father. Their last conversation would haunt him for the rest of his life. Oren was holding this over Max's head, baiting him into taking the assignment.

Max knew it was bait. Yet the bait looked so damned enticing.

"Ok," Max resigned.

He was able to glance momentarily at Oren, who was grinning, then averted his gaze to somewhere beyond, staring at the five-foot-tall statue of the gleeful robin at the front door.

Max would have to postpone cleaning out the bungalow. But that was something he didn't want to do, anyway. He would need to get ahold of his team at work and take some extra time off. But he had plenty of time to spare. They had been encouraging him to take more bereavement and were shocked when Max only asked for a couple days.

"I'll do it," Max said. Maybe this was all meant to be part of his grieving process.

"Do you want to try it?" Oren asked.

Curiosity had taken hold of Max now. Of course he wanted to try. This was no different than skydiving. You went up in the plane because you wanted to try it. But it didn't make it any easier when it came time for your turn to jump.

Max nodded, wiping the sweat from his palms on his pants. He hoped he wouldn't regret this.

"Good." Oren patted the table, ready to rise. "The MemCom is an incredible piece of technology. It does all the hard work for you. But it can be incredibly challenging to navigate someone else's brain. If you're okay with it, I'd like to take you somewhere nearby where you can test it out."

"Sure."

"Want to finish your meal first?" Oren asked.

"Are you kidding?" Max downed the last of his beer but left the plate—and the horrible food—untouched.

With that, they stood up, Oren tossed a generous tip on the table, and they left the Cuckoo's Nest.

***

It turned out that "nearby" was actually *quite* close. They travelled just two blocks before Oren pulled the car over next to a park. He shut off the engine and then looked at Max. There was nothing special about this park. Snow had covered whatever features it normally had. A man walked his dog along a path and around the bend to their right. A few streetlamps dotted the side of the lawn, and further down, the trees took over.

"What is this?" Max motioned out the window.

"This is the best part about MemCom." Oren grinned.

He pulled something out of his jacket pocket. It was small and got lost in Oren's large hands. He fumbled with it a bit, attempting to pull whatever it was out of a white case. He retrieved a small piece of metal and plastic and held it between his fingers. Max thought he recognized it straight away.

"Wireless earbuds," Max said. It was a small, polished earpiece, same as the kind Max used for listening to music. "I have some of those at home."

"Not the same, Max." Oren held the piece a little closer, but only for a moment. Then he withdrew it quickly, cat-like, and placed it in his ear. "While you're wearing this, you're connected to the MemCom." He shook the little white case the earpiece came from, indicating it was more than just a metal shell. "You're *this* close to placing yourself inside the mind of another."

"That's the MemCom?" Max leaned in. "I thought they were huge machines like desktop computers, or bigger."

"They *were*," Oren said, still unable to wipe the smirk from his face.

Max wanted to hear everything he had to say, so he hung on Oren's every word but hated him for it.

"They called the first models the Octopus because of all the cables you had to hook up to both parties. The diver and subject had to be in a lab. They were crude machines, and the memories were displayed differently. But the newer models are amazing pieces of technology. This one was a prototype of the latest update, before things were shut down. It has worked well enough for us. We've been using it since we started. So long as you have the base station, you can connect by simply wearing this earpiece."

Oren flicked open the case, revealing where the earpiece had been pulled from. It was triangular in shape, about the size of a matchbox, and with an aluminum frame painted white.

"That can't be it," Max said, incredulous. Though he had to believe it.

As kids, Oren always seemed to be the first one to know things. And it was always revealed to be true. Oren had a preternatural sense for hunches; Max often wondered if his friend could somehow glimpse the future.

"That's it, Max." Oren pulled the piece from his ear and passed it to his old friend. "Sorry, but I promise that my ears are clean."

Max inserted the device into his left ear and waited for something to happen. He paused, holding still and rigid as if he might get a shock, and then he took it out of his ear after nothing came of it.

"How do you . . . you know . . . choose who you're spying on?"

"Don't call it spying." Oren frowned. "Makes it sound like we're the bad guys. Like we're doing something wrong."

"Aren't we?"

"Maybe," Oren admitted. He looked out the front of the car. The man and his dog had finished their walk and were now returning across the snowy walkway. "I imagine some of what you see might be terrible. It may be private. And in those moments, it will be hard not to feel like an invader."

Max just looked at Oren, waiting for the part of his speech that made this all okay.

"If you asked me what I'd do to save a child's life, Max," Oren said, his voice heavy, "I'm not sure there would be a limit."

Max found himself hoping for a reason not to accept Oren's offer. But he wasn't getting that.

"You've used it before, this device?" Max asked. "You said you tried it."

"Yes, but only briefly. And it didn't go well," Oren shook his head. "I'm not a lucid dreamer. But Charlie—that's our old diver—told me stories about his dives. He saw things in the mind that changed him." Oren turned in his seat, the look on his face deadly serious. "Max, I wouldn't have asked you to do this if it wasn't incredibly important," Oren said. "We can save a life. But I also need to be honest with you. Misusing this device is incredibly dangerous. I will do everything I can to properly prepare you. But any warnings not heeded could be . . . well . . . fatal."

"Is that what happened to Charlie?" Max replied.

"You'll find out what happened to Charlie," Oren promised. "That's our next stop. But first, you should try the device out. It's an easy test. And I need to know you can use it before we leave town."

"So you don't waste your time," Max said. "If I end up being a bust."

"You won't be." Oren poured on some of his classic charm. "I know you're the one I need."

"You never answered me," Max reminded Oren, holding up the earpiece and waving it in front of Oren's face. "How do you select a target?"

"That's the fun part." Oren smirked yet again. "Look." He turned his attention to the car's console, selecting a music app from the touch screen and cranking the volume up. Something moody and mellow and heavy on bass—that Max had never heard before— filled the car. Oren motioned back to the earpiece.

"It uses sound waves," Oren said. "Originally, they were using white noise, you know, something consistent. But they found it also works perfectly fine with music. And why not have a little fun?"

"Music?" Max inserted the device, feeling uncertain.

"Yes," Oren continued. "As long as you and your subject are listening to the same thing, whether it be a white noise frequency or the same song on the radio, you'll be able to jump into their mind. There's a small sensor on the earpiece. If you place your index finger on it for three seconds, the piece activates, and it'll jump into the next nearest mind."

"What happens if there are other people around?" Max asked.

"Good question," Oren said. "That gets messy, yeah. The device could send you into the wrong mind. It's happened before, and it's a legitimate risk. That's why this was never approved for use in the field. It was meant to be used one-on-one in a controlled environment. If there are other minds listening to the same sounds, you have no control over where you're going. It's a sort of cross-contamination."

Max found this device to be terrifying. He couldn't comprehend what it meant to find yourself in the wrong mind. He imagined it was like a nightmare. Except he could control his nightmares.

This entire exercise was about to happen outside of Max's home court. He wouldn't be calling the shots. The rules would all be different. It felt like a losing recipe.

"So . . . how am I supposed to test it?" Max asked.

"There's someone else listening to the same song as you, isn't there?" Oren raised his eyebrows.

Max foolishly found himself looking around the car for a third participant. It was just the two of them.

"You don't mean . . ."

"Your first dive is going to be into my mind," Oren confirmed with his trademark grin.

\*\*\*

There were more rules than Max would remember all at once. Oren shared only the most important ones with him.

Time was different. Seconds slowed down into minutes. Oren was going to let Max wander around for what felt like five minutes. This meant that he would pull Max out after a couple seconds in the car. For the diver, it would be five minutes in the mind.

When Max was more experienced, he would be able to pull himself out, but for now, Oren said he would trigger the exit so that Max didn't get stuck longer than they intended.

"So if I'm in there for a minute, a real minute, it will feel like an hour?" Max tried to digest the time change.

"It's more complicated than that," Oren said. "Time accelerates exponentially. If I left you inside for thirty seconds, it would feel like an hour. If I left you in for an hour, it would feel like many weeks had passed. If I left you in for a day, it would feel like a lifetime."

"But when you pull me out . . ." Max pieced it together. "It will only have been a fraction of that time that has actually passed."

"Correct. You can experience a lot in mind-time, given just a few seconds of real time. If you were in there too long, however, your mind might not be able to tell the difference. It's like you're aging mentally but not physically."

"So." Max bit his lip. "You promise you'll pull me out then?"

What Max wanted to do was throw the device out of the car window. *No way I'm doing this.* And he wanted to run. Just get away from Oren and his mind machine. But this actually required more will power than staying put. And where would he run to? Max wasn't exactly excited to get back to his father's bungalow and clean out his things. Nor was he particularly looking forward to a long flight home with his thoughts. This was a distraction from his world, if nothing else.

After they covered the rules about time, Oren shared some other tips. The MemCom would reconstruct Oren's memory of their trip into the Cuckoo's Nest. Oren could guarantee that's where Max would end up because he would be consciously recalling it as Max began his dive. If Max were to dive into an unsuspecting subject, however, he could land anywhere in their mind and would need to find his way to the desired memory.

The reconstruction of this moment would be like a virtual world in which Max could move about and interact. There were boundaries; he would get to experience those firsthand. But even though Oren had only seen the Cuckoo's Nest from his vantage point, the reconstruction would stitch together a world that Max could move around in and view from any vantage point. He would not be locked into Oren's eyes. As such, he would be moving as a facsimile of himself. He would be given an avatar. He would have hands and legs, and he would feel as if he were whole.

"It's a lot like virtual reality," Oren explained. "You'll be able to interact with the world around you. Though it's best if you don't upset too many items; you want to keep the memory intact. Both for accuracy and to avoid upsetting the subject's mind."

*Terrifying,* Max thought.

He had played enough video games to understand what Oren was saying. But that didn't ease the anxiety. The lack of control—the out-of-body exposure—still shook him.

"There's no more reason to delay," Oren said abruptly. He turned his attention back to the console.

Oren still had his sense of humour, and it appeared as he chose Boston's "Peace of Mind" as their soundtrack. The song came to life and filled the car with strumming, followed shortly by the purr of the bass.

"Jesus." Max exhaled heavily.

When he and Oren had spent entire summers at camp together, they would often depart from the group and do their own activity. One summer, Oren had found a high cliff towering over the lake. He had told Max it was safe to jump because the water was plenty deep. Max had stood on the edge and looked down. From up there, it hadn't looked too bad. The water had cast a deceiving illusion that the fall wasn't too far. But something inside of Max had known it was too high. Self-preservation had kicked in. He shouldn't jump.

Oren was adventurous. He had leapt without fear and crashed into the rippling green lake below. From the water, Oren had called out to his friend that it was safe. Max had stood on that precipice, wondering if he would believe in Oren until the day he died—even if such a day came prematurely because of said belief.

Presently, in the passenger seat, Max stood on that same precipice, with his hand hovering near the earpiece. He pressed his index finger against it, counting to three in his mind. He counted too quickly, and as he hit *three,* he turned to look at Oren. He wanted to tell him he was wrong. That the device didn't work. But just as Oren and Max locked eyes, everything went blurry and Max felt himself lurch forwards, as if someone had pushed him off the ledge.

Max left the car. Everything went momentarily black. Then all sense of motion stopped abruptly, and Max found himself inside the front door of the Cuckoo's Nest.

\*\*\*

"I am in Oren's head," Max had to remind himself.

His conscious thoughts felt like they were floating, as though they may drift away if he didn't actively try to hold on. He had to be careful, or he might forget he was in a memory, and not the real place. Max was stunned by how real everything felt.

Even though it was sort of soft—bright and dreamy around the edges—the world was vivid, textured and real. Everything was there. Everything made sense. Max swore he could even smell eggs cooking, hear the din of people chatting, and feel his own weight as he stood in the foyer.

The five-foot robin statue greeted Max yet again. As Max studied it, he realized that something was off. Certain features were blurry. Max blinked, thinking something was stuck in his eye. But it didn't help. The robin itself was crystal clear; Max even reached out and touched it. It felt like cold plastic. But the sign the robin held looked as though Max was peering at it through water.

Even with the blurriness, Max could roughly make out what the sign read and was surprised. He recalled the robin holding a sign that read "Please wait to be seated." But through the hazy details on this version of the sign, Max thought he could make out the words "Please seat yourselves." Had the memory gotten it wrong?

Max surveyed the rest of the diner and noticed a similar effect on certain corners of the space. The kitchen was entirely blurry, just a tangle of light that could've been a child's kaleidoscope. And the faces of many of the patrons at the tables were gone, as if they had been smudged away by an eraser. The faceless people terrified Max. They acted as one might in a restaurant; they grabbed their forks and spoons and made dining motions. But none of them had any real features.

This made it easy, however, for Max to spot himself. Only he and Oren had real faces, and they stood out at their booth, crisp images compared to the slightly out-of-focus patrons at the other tables. Max walked toward the booth in awe. The memory version of him looked like a perfect replica. He was sitting there across from Oren, checking out the menu. Max was quite flattered at the vision Oren had of him; he certainly seemed to have better posture and a healthy glow here in Oren's mind.

Max crouched so that he was at eye-level with his clone. It was like a mirror that didn't do as it was told. Max recognized every hair on his head, every crease around his eyes, and the deep blue irises inside. But this reflection did not do as he did; instead, it was on autopilot, recreating the moment.

Max was encroaching on their space at the table, yet his re-creation did not see him. It was as though he was invisible, viewing the world as a ghost.

Oren chuckled, and Max nearly fell backward with shock. The sound was clear and hyper-realistic. That laugh was Oren's. This strange memory version of Oren was a dead ringer too. But as Max inspected Oren's face, he noticed the eyes weren't human. They were deep, metallic orbs that seemed alive with energy, like an ocean of thought crashed around inside his skull.

"What have we done?" Oren laughed. Max remembered this moment and a chill ran down his spine. It was the strongest sense of déjà vu he had ever encountered. Déjà vu wasn't quite the right term though because this *did* happen before. And it *was* happening again.

Max remembered the bathrooms and the witty signs he had read over Oren's shoulder. He turned to see if they were there, too. But that corner of the restaurant was dark and clouded over with that same blurry effect that all the faces had.

"How long are you gonna make me wait for all the details?" Clone Max asked.

"Many versions of your father exist inside my head. I can open my mind up to you, and you will get a chance to see him," Clone Oren replied.

Suddenly, Max felt something bump into him from behind. The force wasn't strong, but it caught him off guard, and he staggered forward, collapsing against the booth and knocking over the pepper shaker. He cringed and tried to gracefully straighten himself up. When he turned around, he saw the waitress. She had walked to her predetermined spot next to their table, and apparently Max had been in the way.

"Sorry," the waitress said to Max.

He panicked. Did she see him? As quickly as she had made her apology, her attention was turned back to the table, and she began pouring out the coffees exactly as she had in real life. She seemed to be back on autopilot, but for a moment, she had deviated from the script. Max felt his heart race. He placed his fake hand over his fake chest, looking down for the first time and seeing his own virtual form. He was dressed as he was when he sat in the car with Oren, though he seemed to exist at a lower resolution than the world around him.

Max could feel a heartbeat as he rested his hand on his chest. Or at least, he imagined he could. This level of detail was incredible.

The server finished pouring coffees, and Clone Max thanked her. She then returned to the blurry kitchen. Max brought his attention back to the booth where the virtual versions of him and his friend sat and was horrified to see Oren looking right at him with those metallic eyes. Max went cold, and his heart was now racing even more. He felt threatened, and suddenly he did not recognize his dear friend. Oren felt foreign and dangerous.

"Who's this missing person? How am I supposed to help her?" Clone Max interrupted.

With that, the stalemate had ended, and Clone Oren's attention went back to the conversation, continuing the dialogue. It was a perfect reenactment of the afternoon's events.

Max wanted to get away. He turned without hesitation and dashed for the far end of the restaurant. He was desperate to check out any other part of this memory. He decided he would head for the bathrooms and see what the blurry detail was like up close. This part of the re-creation was dark, more like a dungeon, and as Max neared the corner, it seemed to swallow any of the light from the clearer parts of the restaurant. A true black hole. Behind him, he could still see the booth where his clone was carrying on a conversation.

Facing the bathrooms once again, Max proceeded. There was a door there, but all other detail ceased to exist. Darkness and that horrible blurry film covered every surface. Max couldn't tell if there were even walls or a ceiling in this space. The floor disappeared beneath his feet. The door itself was barely there, a chalk drawing on the sidewalk after a heavy rain. The witty signs ("Sea Gals" and "Woodpeckers") that Max had seen before were nowhere to be found.

He wanted to know what was behind this door. Would Oren's mind have made something up? Or was this where the memory ended? Surely, it had to end somewhere.

The door handle felt solid enough as Max turned it. He pushed the door open, and it swung without resistance. A light filled the space, but like everything else, it was unfocused. Max couldn't tell what he was looking at. He had to step forward; he had to go through the door. He broke the barrier and entered the light, and Max was suddenly transported to a new place.

\*\*\*

Max was outside now. Only, it couldn't have been outside the restaurant. The sun was out, it felt hot, and everything was green. It was summertime. He needed to shield his eyes from the brightness of the sky. It overwhelmed him, and he couldn't quite see. But soon his eyes adjusted.

He was in a backyard. The house in front of him was plain, at least from the back, and looked shuttered up against this scalding hot afternoon. To Max's left was a patio with a neat patio set, chairs all tucked in, and a BBQ tucked away beneath its cover. To the right, the yard backed up onto a street, with just a white picket fence separating the two. It dawned on Max that he knew this home. It was a place he had visited many times in his youth.

Max noticed movement and found a young boy in the far corner of the yard, tossing a baseball in the air, as high as he could, and then catching it himself as it fell. Max recognized this boy, too, though it had been decades since he had seen him this way. Young Oren smiled, his childish innocence glowing through the joy he took from this simple activity. Max could hear the smacking of the ball hitting Oren's glove and was taken back to his own childhood.

"Hey, mister," Young Oren said. "What are you looking at?"

Max was startled. His mouth hung open, and he thought of what to say. Could Young Oren see him too? Oren was looking in his direction, having paused his game. Max couldn't think of anything to say and stood there, stupidly, in the sun. Then a voice chimed in from somewhere behind Max.

"Just watching you play with your ball," a voice said.

Max glanced behind him and saw a stranger standing at the white picket fence. His car was parked on the side of the road. The man's eyes stood out, deep set and dark black, like voids in his skull. The rest of the man's face was attached loosely, and once again blurry, like a child had sketched a portrait.

Max stepped aside, getting out of the crossfire.

"Why?" Young Oren asked the man.

"Because I like playing ball too," the strange man said.

His outfit was changing constantly, as if Oren's mind couldn't recall it. Was it a white shirt? No, a beige shirt. No, a beige jacket. Ok, it was a jacket, but wasn't it grey? The man's clothes flickered like television channels.

The landscape darkened. Max checked overhead for storm clouds, but there were none. Instead, the sides of the world were just disappearing, being replaced with black walls and forming a tunnel. There was now just a thin chute of light connecting Young Oren and this stranger. Max stood in the shadows off to the side. His head rocked back and forth as they spoke, as if watching a tennis match.

"Do you want someone to play ball with?" the stranger asked.

"Maybe," Oren said, sounding uncertain.

"I know a great park to play baseball in."

The stranger smiled. His smile was too big for his face, his lips stretching beyond his skull; he was a caricature straight from a child's nightmare. For a moment, all Max could see was this smile. The man's face seemed to grow and grow and take over the memory. It was just that monstrous smile, blotting out the sun. Then, quickly, things levelled out. Once again, the backyard was there and so was Oren, standing undecidedly.

"Come on," the Smiling Man urged. "I'll drive us. Hop in. You can have shotgun."

"I'm not allowed to ride in the front," Oren said.

"I won't tell." The Smiling Man offered a hand, as if he was going to lift Oren over the fence.

"Get the fuck out of here!" Max shouted finally.

At first, it was as though no one heard him. The man just continued to smile at Young Oren and beckoned him toward the fence. Oren, still uncertain, took a few steps forward. It seemed that Oren wanted a friend to play with. And since the man was a grown-up, Oren must have thought he could be trusted.

Max watched Oren approach the man.

"There's a good boy," the man breathed, his voice coming out like a satisfied sigh.

Max could feel the heat behind it. Oren edged on.

"Jesus, Oren!" Max shouted again. "Didn't your parents ever teach you not to talk to strangers!?" Max stepped toward the man and tried to shield him as Oren advanced, just a few feet away.

"Who the fuck do you think you are?" the stranger said, his head snapping unnaturally to the side to face Max.

His deep charcoal eyes seemed endless, like all of outer space was contained in them. Max wanted to scream.

The stranger growled at Max and then hopped up on the fence, perched like a gargoyle. He hissed and then raised a hand, which was now a claw. It grew into something twisted and knotted, like an elderly tree. Then the stranger swatted at Max, and Max had to shield his face to protect from the blow from his tree-sized talons.

Max shut his eyes tight, and the world disappeared.

\*\*\*

No blow ever came. Max was unharmed. He caught himself breathing. Once in, once out. Twice in, twice out. He was still alive.

Finally, Max opened his eyes. The version of Oren that was staring at him now was the grown-up one. The real one. With real eyes.

"Jesus, Max, what did you see in there?" Oren could tell from Max's shocked expression that he had seen more than just five-foot robins and breakfast platters.

Max blinked a couple times, gathering his senses. He was back in the car. Oren had pulled him out of the MemCom. And just in time, too.

"Where did you end up, Max?" Oren frowned, realizing that Max had encountered more than just the Cuckoo's Nest. "Did you leave the cafe? Did you go through a door?"

Max wanted to ask about the Smiling Man. He wanted to know if Oren had gone with him. But he couldn't bring himself to ask. The memory was too private. He had been wrong to go there. Until now, Max hadn't realized that he was sweating.

"I didn't think you'd be going through doors, Max," Oren said. "You aren't ready for that yet. In the MemCom, doors are how you traverse from one memory to another. Anytime you see a door, on the other side will be a different memory. It can be challenging—or damn near impossible—to sort out what doors lead to what memories. Even Charlie, an experienced diver, would take several wrong turns. It was too early for you to go rooting around through my brain."

"The restaurant was blurry," Max said.

"Parts of it, I'm sure," Oren replied. "But other parts were clear?"

"Yeah."

"Can you guess why some parts were blurry? Did it start to make sense?"

Max wasn't quite there yet. He waited for Oren to help him.

"The blurry bits were all things that the mind filled in," Oren explained. "Parts that I wasn't sure about, or maybe didn't see at all. When the MemCom builds the re-creation, the things that are most strongly remembered come through clearly. Anything that the subject isn't sure of, misremembers, or needs to guess at to fill in the blanks, remains out of focus."

"You didn't have the same view as me." Max understood. "So, everything behind you—everything from my vantage point—was just a guess."

"Right." Oren nodded. "When we're using this technology to convict suspects, it's important that we try to use evidence that comes across sharply. If the details of a memory are hazy, it can't be trusted the same way. Memories are often imperfect. Thankfully, if you know what to look for, you can tell the difference between what's true and what's not."

"You stared right at me," Max said abruptly, remembering the swirling, metallic eyes.

"My SI?" Oren asked. Max's face was blank. "An SI—short for self-image—is the representation of the mind's self in the reconstruction. In this case, the version of me you saw was more than just an autopilot carrying out the memory. The SI is a manifestation of how I view myself. And it's the portal into my schema—the way my thoughts work. Think of it like the conductor of an orchestra. If someone starts playing out of tune, it's my SI's job to correct things. If you draw attention to yourself in the memory, and the SI notices you, it may actually alert the brain that there's an intruder. It's incredibly important you don't disturb the SI."

"What happens if I do?" Max asked.

"The mind can force you out," Oren said. "It can also panic, sending you into different memories. A strong enough mind—one that knows about the MemCom, for example—might even crush your consciousness."

"Wow." Max wiped his forehead, as he was still glistening. "Thanks for telling me that *after* I signed up."

"You didn't trigger my SI," Oren said, as if this was intended to cheer Max up. "I am pretty much as educated as they come on MemCom stuff, and my mind didn't force you out. That's a good sign."

"But you saw me," Max repeated. "You looked right at me. So did the waitress. I think she spoke to me when she bumped into me."

"That's not as dangerous," Oren dismissed this. "If one of the reconstructed subjects notices you, they may behave differently, deviate from their line in the song, but it doesn't set off alarm bells in the mind the same way the SI does. So long as everyone can find their way back into the timing of the orchestra, you're fine. Just don't go out of your way to disturb the people in the memory. Sooner or later, the SI will catch on. It knows when things are out of place. If you had repeatedly blocked the waitress, preventing us from getting our food, I'd have caught on that this wasn't the way the memory should look. The SI would sense an intruder, and it would flush you out."

"Guessing that isn't just a quick exit?" Max asked.

"I've only known one person to get flushed out," Oren said grimly. "And it wasn't exactly a positive experience. We're tampering with the mind, Max. Yours is exposed here, too. You don't necessary want to hit eject with your own thoughts still linked to the MemCom. There's a lot that can go wrong."

Max sighed. Perhaps he shouldn't have signed up for this so willingly.

"Fuck you, Oren," Max said, forcing himself to smile so it sounded less harsh. "You knew I would say yes. You knew I would try this thing, no matter what."

"It's been a long time," Oren said and then paused, changing tones to something more positive. "I'm glad to see that you haven't changed all that much."

"What's next?" Max asked.

Oren pulled out of their parking spot and quickly made a U-turn.

"Hey look, it stopped snowing," Oren pointed out.

The sky had shown some mercy, and the relentless flurry had subsided. Now the sun was even attempting to poke through the overcast sky.

"Let's grab your things, Max."

"Good," Max said. "I don't want to stay here any longer than necessary."

Their journey started off with some casual catch-up, then became silent. Max spent this time wondering about the memory he had found in Oren's head, and whether or not Oren had gone with the Smiling Man.

Max wished he had never opened that door.

*** 

The airport terminal was quiet. Only a handful of passengers were still waiting around for flights. The winter daylight had disappeared, and it felt much later than it actually was. Through the windows, Max watched ground crews scurrying back and forth in the snow. Despite their work, the video board above Max's head revealed several yellow "delayed" icons next to departure times.

They were sitting in Chicago's O'Hare Airport, waiting out their layover. Their first leg, from Toronto down, had passed with awkward conversation. Now, as Oren explained, they were headed to Syracuse.

Oren had just returned from the newsstand where he had purchased an eye mask and a sports drink.

"Plan on catching some sleep?" Max asked him.

"This is for you." Oren handed over the eye mask. It was thin and cheap-looking. "You are about to get your MemCom 101 lesson. Can't have anyone gawking. So, this is your cover."

Max surveyed the terminal. Across from them, an elderly woman was reading a magazine. Beyond her, a couple was trying to get their infant child to stop fussing. A few other passengers strolled past while barely looking up from their phones.

Oren pulled out his own phone, flipped through his contacts, and then passed it to Max. He also retrieved a white earbud from his pocket and stuffed it into Max's ear.

"This one is actually just an earbud," Oren said. "Not the MemCom. It's connected to my phone."

"What's happening?"

"You're going to have a video chat with Aria and get up to speed."

Before Max could ask any more questions, a face popped up on the phone screen. The lighting was low, and the angle of the phone was awkward. The woman on the other end appeared to be in her mid-thirties, with glasses perched on her nose. Her hair was pulled back in a messy bun.

"Hi, you must be Max," she said, her voice low. She was fidgeting, adjusting the phone and looking over her shoulder at something.

"Hi . . . yes . . ." Max glanced at Oren for some sort of explanation.

"She's part of the team. She's in New York right now," Oren whispered.

"Hi Max, nice to meet you. I'm Aria." She was still moving the phone around, and must have been bumping against the microphone, because all Max heard was rubbing and banging. "Sorry, I'm just getting set up here. We have to be quick. Obviously, by now you know that we're not supposed to be putting a spotlight on what we're doing."

"Right." Max watched as she finally spun the camera around to reveal what she was doing.

"Max, this is Charlie," Aria said.

The phone screen showed a man lying on his back in a hospital bed. There was a cat resting on his lap, but when Aria came closer with the camera, the cat leapt away gracefully. It was gone so quickly that Max was sure he had imagined it.

The man in the hospital bed looked frail, woefully thin, and ashen. He was hooked up to several monitors, and the sound of laboured breathing and rhythmic beeps came through the call. The left side of the man's face was etched with a large, hooked scar.

"Charlie was our partner, a fellow investigator. He was our MemCom diver. He wouldn't have liked having visitors, but, well, he doesn't get much say on the matter anymore."

Max shot Oren a nasty look. The man who Max was replacing looked to be on his death bed. This was as foreboding a sign as Max could imagine.

"What happened to him?"

"Charlie is in a coma," Aria said. "He had an accident. But don't worry. He's still swimming around in there, and he's going to be your trainer. He probably knows more about the MemCom than anyone. So, you're learning from the best."

"How?" Max asked, a little too loudly, then lowered his voice. "Sorry, I don't mean to be insensitive, but . . ."

"It's okay." Aria turned the camera back around to her face. Her eyes looked kind, understanding. "You are going to enter Charlie's mind. You dive in there, and you can learn all he knows about MemCom in a fraction of the time. If we leave you in there for an hour or so, you'll get to see all the important bits."

"*Oof,* that feels like a long time." Max felt his palms getting sweaty again.

"Yeah, it is," Aria said. "But Oren is there to look after you. You'll feel exhausted after, like you ran a marathon. But you'll be okay. It's a lot of information to handle. And you may not be able to retain it all right away. But it will all be in your head. Like a data transfer. Pieces of it will come back to you over time, as you need it. It's really a genius method for learning things. You'll likely even pick up bits of his inner monologue along the way. Doesn't always happen, but Charlie reported this phenomenon on a few dives."

"So . . . it's *not* going to kill me?" Max's mouth was dry.

"Goodness no," Aria said. "Stay in there for a few hours and you might feel like you've been hit by a truck. But we're pulling the plug after sixty minutes or so. All you'll need are some electrolytes and some rest."

Max noticed the sports drink bottle in Oren's hand.

"What a fancy operation you run," Max sighed. He felt like he was about to skydive again. But now he wasn't even sure there was a parachute strapped to his back.

"We'll pull you out when the time is right. It's going to hit you like a tidal wave when you come back. You're kind of carrying the memories of two lives at that point. You'll feel like you've lived longer days that you actually did. Just don't panic."

"Sure, don't panic . . ." Max tried to breathe, to calm himself. But nothing was working.

"Just treat it like you're watching a movie," Aria explained. "You won't even need to worry about going through doors. It's all going to play itself out eventually. When one moment ends, another will take its place."

She flipped the camera back over to show Charlie, the skeleton with disheveled auburn hair, and Max realized how farfetched this entire premise was.

"How does this even work?" Max turned to Oren. "He's in New York. I'm here. Didn't you say we have to be careful about cross-contamination?"

"We do." Oren nodded. "That's why we are both going to play a unique series of frequencies. Aria will give Charlie an earbud, and he'll be listening to an audio file we created that no one else in the world will be listening to. You'll have the same in your right ear, and the MemCom in your left."

"You've done this before?" Max asked.

Oren grimaced. His pause forced Max's heart to skip a beat. "Aria has tested it, yes. But never quite at this distance."

"Are you kidding?"

"Please, Max, trust me," Oren said. "This is the only way to get you up to speed in time for this case. You're going to be a veteran after this. Soon, you'll be just as talented as Charlie was. And he was the best. His mind is perfectly preserved; he had hyperthymesia. You know, that one in a million condition where someone can remember every detail of every day? Ask him the weather from thirteen years ago, on a random Tuesday, and he knew it. It was fascinating; he remembered everything that ever happened to him. Which means his whole life, and all of his MemCom experiences, are an encyclopedia waiting for you."

There was that Oren charm again. The cool way he spoke. Armies would follow him into battle with just a wink. Max didn't want to let him down any more than he wanted to pass up a chance to speak with his father again.

"And there's a young woman we can save," Aria added from the phone screen.

"We need this," Oren summarized. "But if you can't go ahead, let us know now."

Parachute or not. It was his time to jump.

"Let's go," Max relented. It just now dawned on him that only this morning he had buried his father.

Aria got to work preparing Charlie. It was dark in the room, and Max wondered if she was even supposed to be in there. She worked with the cautious silence of an intruder. She placed an earbud in Charlie's ear while Oren took the phone back and readied Max. Earbud on one side, MemCom on the other. Then Oren placed the eye mask on him, and the world went dark.

"It'll just look like you're sleeping," Oren said. "I'll let you rest your head on my shoulder."

"How kind of you," Max said.

"I'm going to start the track now." Oren was calm, his voice even.

Max felt anything but.

"When the sound plays, you can hold down the MemCom button whenever you are ready."

The tune began with a high-pitched squeal. It was irritating, like a dog whistle, but Max supposed it was important that no one else was listening to something similar. Over the top of the squeal came a low tone that sounded like a gong had been rung. And then finally, a familiar tune was layered over everything else. It had been slowed down, an entirely different pitch, so it took Max a second to fully place it. When he did, he couldn't help but turn his head in Oren's direction, eye mask still blinding him, but shooting a quizzical look nonetheless.

"'Sweet Caroline'?" Max asked.

"Charlie's favourite." Oren chuckled. "He did all of his dives to this song. It'll be stuck in your head forever now. A real earworm."

Max relaxed himself back to a normal position as Neil Diamond's slowed-down voice began to sing. It was eerie, the way it had been altered.

"Whenever you're ready, Max," Oren urged.

No sense in delaying.

Max jumped. He brought his hand up to the button and held it down. He had slipped away before the first "Bah, bah, bah."

# 2. Charlie's Mind

MAX WATCHED IT ALL. THE memories flew by so fast that he was certain he was forgetting them even before they had concluded. Aria was right; he did not need to wander anywhere. He stood still and let things pass before him like a movie. He watched it all, felt it all, lived it all. He was in the shadows through every one of Charlie's reconstructed memories. *Pieces of it will come back to you over time.* Max had to remind himself of Aria's words. While most of it happened too fast to comprehend at the moment, there was some of it that stuck. Max tried to relax and surrender himself to the experience, watching Charlie's life unfold . . .

\*\*\*

A young boy—a toddler—was playing in a barn, grabbing bits of straw off the floor and raising it to eye level. He inspected it, then dropped it, watching it flutter to the ground before moving on and trying the routine again with a different handful of straw.

The boy meandered through the barn, in and out of the empty stalls that once held horses. When he found straw that looked appealing, he picked it up and gawked. What he did not see, was the horse—a brown filly— who had been left behind in the stable that day.

The boy sauntered on uncertain legs until he rounded the corner into the horse's domain. Here, his eyes locked in on something shiny in the straw. A coin. No, a necklace. No, a diamond. The shape transformed the way a lava lamp dances. It was unclear, but it had caught the boy's eye nonetheless. He had to grab it.

The horse sensed the boy behind her and was displeased. The boy barely had time to notice the horse, and hear its shriek, before the leg kicked out and connected with his jaw.

\*\*\*

A slightly older boy, perhaps ten years old, stood in a living room adorned with beat-up leather sofas and a box full of toys in the corner. The boy had a long scar along his right cheek that hooked down toward his neck, beneath his ear, in a ghastly *U* shape.

"What do you see?" the boy with the scar asked.

His younger brother was staring at the ground, where stuffed animals were laid out in a chaotic parade.

"They killed Monty, Sheriff Charlie," the younger brother declared.

He stomped around, pretending to look important, mocking the adults in his life. A stuffed rabbit sat in the centre of the display, a kitchen butter knife lodged in its back. Stuffing sprawled out onto the floor.

"Who are the suspects, Ty?" Young Charlie quizzed his brother.

There was a teddy bear sitting suspiciously under the sofa. There was the fluffy blue unicorn perched on the coffee table, looking down at the scene. A couple of stuffed pigs that neither boy had cared for were scattered around the body. And two dolls that had belonged to their older sister were having a tea party nearby.

"I don't know," Little Ty pushed out his lower lip.

Charlie broke from his character temporarily to bend down, more on level with his younger sibling.

"Just think, kay?" Charlie said. "It's like the detective novels we read. Gotta look for evidence."

Little Ty furrowed his brow and made a show of looking around. He had in his hand a little magnifying glass, and he put it to his eye as if this would change everything.

"Ah hah!" Ty shrieked at last.

"What is it?"

"It's the dollies," Ty said. "They got spoons and forks from the kitchen, but they don't got any knifes."

"That's cause they never needed any," Charlie said.

"Well then what about Ted E. Bear?" Ty tried. "You know. Cause bears don't like rabbits. They eat them."

"Yeah, but nobody ate Monty the Rabbit," Charlie pointed out. "Just stabbed him."

Ty studied the plush crime scene again, looking frustrated.

"Ty," Charlie said with a smile. "Sometimes you have to look where you least expect it. It's not always right under your nose." With that, Charlie pointed to their black cat, who was snoozing near the window. Tucked under the cat's paw was a tuft of stuffing. Caught red-handed.

"It was Domino!" Ty screamed, and then burst out into laughter.

Charlie followed suit, and soon the two of them were giggling and attacking their poor bewildered cat with kisses and hugs.

\*\*\*

Charlie was sitting on a cloud. Its white surface was fleecy, and it kept him warm as he sat cross-legged and looked down on the world. From this height, his house was just a brown stain the size of his pinky nail. He could see the school down the way, and he could see buses and cars sliding along the road no differently than his toys rolled along their tracks. The cloud was rising higher, drifting further away, and Charlie knew soon it would be time to fly back home.

But before he got the chance, a scream sent shockwaves through the world. His house shattered, the cloud melted away, and the edges of the world collapsed in on him. Charlie woke up.

"What is it?" Charlie said, swinging his feet down from the top bunk. He hopped to the floor nimbly and crouched by his little brother's side. Ty was screaming himself awake from another nightmare. From the subtle glow of their night-light, Charlie could see the panic in his eyes.

"Oh, Charlie," Ty said as he started to recognize his whereabouts. The look of terror on his face subsided and was slowly replaced with embarrassment. "It was . . . It was a monster."

"There are no monsters," Charlie assured him.

He put his arm around his brother, rubbing his back, which was damp. It appeared that they had been through this routine many times before.

"I checked, remember?"

Ty panted, eyes darting around to make sure they were safe. "But it was scaly, with sharp teeth."

"It's just a nightmare, Ty," Charlie said. "No monsters."

They were quiet a moment. The house creaked, somewhere down the hall, and Ty jumped a little. Charlie continued rubbing his back.

"How come you don't ever have nightmares like me?" Ty said finally, his breathing under control.

"I have special dreams, remember?" Charlie said. "I told you, I can always tell when I'm asleep. So, I just fly around and stuff."

"I want dreams like that," Ty pouted. "I don't want to see monsters."

"Well, maybe if you try to breathe nice and slow— like we talked about—and think about floating on clouds, you'll get to join me in my dream."

"Really?" Ty asked.

"Really," Charlie said, although he sounded unsure.

Charlie went to the kitchen to get his brother a glass of water, but when he came back, Ty was already asleep. Charlie set the glass down and climbed back into his bunk. He lay on his back a while and stared at the ceiling.

\*\*\*

A slightly older Charlie—twelve or thirteen—was seated at his desk, staring at the clock and willing the second hand to move faster. The look on his face said, "I'm bored." He paid no mind to the world around him. The chalkboard with its scribbled reminders, the walls with the student-crafted art, and the windows that looked out on a playground.

Charlie's teacher—a tall woman with hair pulled back in a tight bun—was handing back tests with scores scrawled across them in red ink. When she got to Charlie's desk, she plunked down the stapled booklet. A giant red 100 stared back at him.

"See me after," she whispered to him, before moving on.

Charlie groaned inwardly. *This is too easy.* Charlie's words rang out across the memory, his inner monologue reaching Max's ears like the voice of God in a stage play.

The boy who sat behind Charlie had his test back now and was leaning over Charlie's shoulder to compare.

"You got another 100?" The boy gasped. "Ah man, you must be cheating."

"I'm not cheating," Charlie said.

After a beat, the boy suggested, "Well, maybe you can help me cheat then?"

"Alright class," the teacher said, projecting her voice in a singsongy way that Charlie seemed to take offence to. *It's condescending.* "That's it. Those of you who scored less than fifty, remember that you can see me any time after class for extra help. You only have one test left to get those scores up before finals."

And then the bell was ringing, mercifully. Charlie stood and tried to leave, but his teacher caught his arm.

"I said to come see me."

The other kids all left, and Charlie found himself standing at the front of the room beside the boxy, generic desk that all teachers were given.

"You've gotten perfect scores on every test I've ever given you, Charlie," the teacher said.

"I'm not cheating." Charlie avoided eye contact, perhaps feeling defensive. When at last he glanced at his teacher's face, he saw that she was smiling. *I don't think I've ever seen her smile before,* Charlie's monologue revealed his thoughts.

"I know you're not cheating, Charlie," she said. "Even kids who cheat aren't this smart. Have you ever given any thought to why these tests are so easy for you?"

Charlie seemed to be caught off guard. He thought he was going to get in trouble, but this was something else entirely. He shrugged. "They just are."

"When I ask you to write out your answers," she continued, "you recite the words back to me as if straight from the textbook. Every time."

"So?"

"Can you remember what we talked about on the first day of class, back in September?"

"Photosynthesis," Charlie said.

"And what about after that, the second week of school?"

"You weren't here. We had that substitute, Mrs. Williams," Charlie said.

"What about Tuesday, October 16?"

"That was the day we started ecosystems," Charlie said.

Charlie's teacher was still grinning, as if she had been making a joke and was just waiting for him to get the punch line.

"Have you ever heard of eidetic memory?" she asked.

"No."

"What about hyperthymesia?"

"No."

"Well, if you had read about it, you certainly would never forget," she said. "That's because I believe you have both, Charlie. A photographic memory—an eidetic memory. You can recall things perfectly accurately even after having only seen it once. But that's only half of your gift.

"Hyperthymesia means you remember everything that's ever happened to you. Every detail. Perfectly preserved in your memory. That's why I imagine these tests are so easy for you. And why you're so bored with school. I'm asking you the obvious. It would be like asking the other kids what colour the chalkboard is as it sits right in front of them."

"So . . . what do I do with it?" Charlie asked, meanwhile thinking, *I knew it! I've always been smarter than these kids. They always miss the obvious. I always thought they were dumb, but I guess I'm just a step above*

"I think we need to give you some new material," his teacher told him. "Some unique challenges. Some new books to read. Let's see how far that mind of yours can go."

\*\*\*

The kids in Charlie's classroom were older, some of them were sprouting new beards while others were sprouting new breasts. But Charlie himself wasn't much older than the day he had been told about his abilities.

Charlie's teacher had given him the terminology, a diagnosis of sorts. This gave him confidence, at least, and so he could push himself more. Now he found himself in classes with kids four or five years his senior.

This classroom was much the same as the last. The only noticeable difference was that now, as the teacher handed back graded papers, the students who glanced over Charlie's shoulder were on the cusp of graduation.

"Seriously? Another one?" the young man behind Charlie scoffed. "Boy genius strikes again."

"Can you write mine next time?" the young woman next to Charlie asked, her voice sincere.

"He's touched, gotta be, no one is that smart without having some sort of magical powers," another young man chided.

Charlie didn't say anything. *While these kids chase after one another for make out sessions and drink cheap beer on weekends, I grow smarter,* Charlie thought. *I don't need a social life.*

"Quiet down." The teacher—this one a bald man with tiny glasses perched on his fat nose—tried shushing the class as he walked back to the front. "We have a special presentation for you all today. A friend of mine has agreed to come in and give you all a talk on forensics. Come in, Peter."

A man in a tweed jacket entered the classroom. He had a salt-and-pepper beard, and he surveyed the students with beady eyes.

"Peter works at the crime lab downtown, and, well, I'll let him take it from here."

"Thank you." Peter offered a small smile and placed his bag down on the desk at the head of the room. "How many of you have seen those crime shows on TV?"

"Oh my god, do you have a body in there?!" the boy behind Charlie shouted.

The class filled with laughter.

"No, no body," Peter said, unfazed by the laughter. "And if you *have* seen those television shows, I want you to forget about them. Crime scenes are never like that. There is no magical tool that enhances images like they have in the show. No machines that magically tell you who did it just because you found a hair."

"Tyler found a hair the other day," another boy chimed in. "On his balls. First one."

More laughter.

"Shut up," a boy said, presumably Tyler.

"Enough," the teacher scolded, though with limited authority.

Peter proceeded. "The real world is full of crime scenes that are infinitely more complex. They are full of puzzles that are sometimes impossible to solve. Solving crimes depends on biology and psychology."

Charlie appeared to be enthralled. His mouth sat agape. Every word Peter spoke was like someone had chiseled away at a fossil in Charlie's mind, and now it was finally obvious what the specimen was. Solving crimes could be a career. It was no longer just a game Charlie played with his brother and their stuffed animals. It was a real thing.

A hook had pierced Charlie then, and his path was fixed on a line from that moment.

But, for the other kids who were still laughing about pubic hair, Peter reached into his bag. "Ok, who wants to see a human skull?"

\*\*\*

The body was hung in a tree. *Even with all I've seen in two years, this is ugly,* Charlie thought. Not far behind the tree line was the city and the early morning sun. Charlie had been the first one here. *As always.*

Three men in street clothes huddled around the tree, on the active side of the police line that had been set up. Cruiser lights flickered in the distance, where they had parked, but the sun was starting to drown them out. Charlie watched these men studying the scene. The one in the middle was a broad-shouldered man with matted hair. *Detective Norman.*

"Looks like they wanted the vic to suffer," Detective Norman said in between sips of coffee, his grey moustache staining brown. "Death by hanging ain't a lot of fun."

His colleagues nodded in agreement.

"He didn't die there," Charlie interjected.

All three men turned to face him, as if unaware he had been there until now.

"Wus'that?" Detective Norman asked.

"The blood." Charlie pointed to the maroon stains in the dirt, trailing twenty feet away, where the woods connected with a side road. "That's a lot of blood. He would've bled out before being hung."

Norman looked back to his colleagues, who raised their eyebrows and averted their gazes. One chuckled softly.

"Alright, hotshot," Norman said. "Thanks for the tip."

The three men went back into their huddle, whispering and no doubt passing comments about Charlie. One looked over briefly with a smirk.

"Don't suppose you know where his shoes are?" the smirker called out.

The body was shoeless, swollen feet dangling two feet off the ground.

"Maybe make yourself useful and go find them." He gestured to the shadowed woods around them.

"They're not here," Charlie said.

They all turned yet again.

"Look at his feet. They're scuffed. Bloodied. He was forced to walk here barefoot. Killed there, where the blood is. And then hung. Some sort of message. Probably gang related, given the tattoos."

All of the men were speechless. *I've beat you to the finish line again. And yet they still tell me to bide my time and wait for a promotion. I should have your jobs.*

The three men tried to conceal their looks. They must have known that Charlie was right but did not want to be upstaged. Detective Norman stepped forwards and handed his coffee cup to Charlie.

"Get rid of this, will ya?"

Dismissal. It was easier than coming up with something smart to say.

Charlie dutifully took the coffee cup over to the cruisers, where a small trash bag had been left by one of the other officers, tucked under the car tire. *I'll throw out your trash now,* Charlie thought, *but one day, you'll be throwing out mine.*

"You're Charlie Blue."

A voice spooked him, made him turn around. Charlie noticed a tall man in a black coat—with a neatly trimmed beard and thick-rimmed glasses—looming over him like shadow.

"Yes."

"I've heard a lot about you," the man said. "My name's Oren. Care to join me on a walk?"

\*\*\*

"How will I get out?"

Charlie, now dressed casually in jeans and a sweater, was sitting in an aggressively beige hotel room with Oren. The sun had set.

"I can pull you out the first time," Oren said. "But in the future, you'll just need to find a dark corner and shut your eyes. It will feel like a light floating sensation, something pulling you up. Embrace it. And you'll resurface."

"Like scuba divers," Charlie said.

"That's why we call it diving," Oren said with a wink.

He had been nothing short of charming since they had met, an incredibly beguiling man.

Although Max had witnessed Charlie grilling Oren all afternoon, Charlie still seemed skeptical. Maybe he thought the offer was too good to be true.

It had intrigued Charlie immediately. Probably because he was so tired of putting away coffee cups instead of putting away bad guys.

Oren was also a great salesman, and he had suggested this test drive.

"And you've done this before?" Charlie asked.

"No," Oren said. "I can't. I get disoriented. Lose control. The whole thing feels like a nightmare. I don't lucid dream like you do."

This, Oren explained, was why he singled Charlie out. Apparently, word travelled. Charlie mentioned his dreams to a few colleagues while trying to play nice and socialize—something he found incredibly difficult to do. So, he defaulted to talking about himself, which suddenly grabbed attention. He mentioned his eidetic memory, his hyperthymesia. This made him a subject of lore to his fellow constables, who would ask him to recall things and then laugh and say *ahhh* as if he had performed magic.

Oren, who had been on the prowl for a partner, came across these stories while speaking with friends on the force. The bit about lucid dreaming specifically appealed to him.

"How do you know so much about it?" Charlie wondered as he ran the earpiece back and forth in his fingers. *Feels smooth. Nice weight. Intriguing.*

"Research mostly," Oren said. "There was a man who used it before I inherited it. He told me a lot from his experience. But he's gone now."

"I thought they were large machines," Charlie said, unable to take his eyes off the item in the palm of his hand. Its pristine white surface reflected the room back at him. It was designed to be very appealing, calling out to his eyes the way a diamond might.

"The first models were," Oren said. "They were large, required a lab, countless wires and cables everywhere. Called them the Octopus models. Now they're discreet. And you can dive from anywhere."

"It all feels very secretive," Charlie said.

"Has to be." Oren was setting up a portable speaker connected to his phone. "If the bad guys knew about it, they'd kick you out of their minds. When a hostile subject catches on, you can't trust anything they're thinking." Oren seemed to catch the way Charlie was surveying him and added, "I will only think happy thoughts, promise."

"Let's try it."

Charlie was deadpan, something Oren would have to get used to. By now, Max had realized that whenever Charlie was determined, he was cold. It was as if his mind was too busy to emote.

Charlie laid down on the bed. Oren had told him to get comfortable, but this was perhaps the most uncomfortable part of the entire exchange. Charlie awkwardly folded his hands across his chest.

"Do you have a song you'd prefer?" Oren asked.

"Anything by Neil Diamond," Charlie said after thinking a moment.

"Really?" Oren chuckled. He began scrolling.

"My dad used to play him when I was younger."

"Well, 'Sweet Caroline' is on here." Oren hit play, and the tune began pumping through his speaker.

"I'm ready."

"Then push the button and count to three."

\*\*\*

Domino, Charlie's now ancient cat, was perched along the windowsill, watching the humans with great interest. Domino had become a fixture in the cramped office Oren rented for them. Max had already witnessed many evenings in this office, where the three of them (Oren, Charlie, and Aria) would discuss cases long into the night. The first few were fairly benign. "Cases that kept the lights on," Oren had called them. They had not required the MemCom for any cases. Not until now.

"He stares at you like he can read your mind," Aria said as Domino's eyes tracked her. She was the third member of their tripod—another razor-sharp mind that Oren had encountered while recruiting for his team.

"Maybe he can," Charlie said, grabbing a slice of pizza from the box on the table.

It was cold, but he needed it. They'd been stuffed in this barebones office for days. The view of Manhattan out the window sparkled temptingly, especially now with the neon glow inviting them for drinking and dancing. But Charlie didn't much care for either.

Oren had lured him in with the promise of the MemCom. That first dive in the hotel room had Charlie fully immersed. He had trained in simulations when preparing to become an officer. *But this was better than any virtual reality*, Charlie thought. *It was real. And it's mine to master. No one else's.*

But they wouldn't use it straight away. They hadn't needed it for the first few cases. Yet Charlie was still treated like an equal partner.

*I'm finally useful. Not a freak show, like how they treated me on the force.* He was valued for his input and hard work even before his ability to lucid dream. He had known, though, that at some point the need would arise to use the MemCom. When that happened, Charlie would be even more valuable, and in a unique way.

Then came the Leonard Lang case.

Max sensed the electricity the moment this came into Charlie's life; this was different.

"You feel ready?" Aria asked. She glanced at the MemCom on the table.

"I believe so." Charlie wiped sauce from his lip. "It really just feels like dreaming to me."

"For most people, that can be terrifying," Aria reminded him. "We don't all have control of our dreams."

"I'm not most people," Charlie said.

Oren had treated him like a golden ticket.

Charlie took one last bite and then tossed his crust to Domino, who caught it and hopped away to hide.

"That cat is going to be sick." Aria shook her head.

"He's a hundred years old," Charlie said. "He's indestructible."

The door flung open then with such force that it rattled against the wall.

"It's done." Oren came bounding in, and intense grin contorting his face. "We're all set. They'll see us at the prison tomorrow. The warden has arranged everything."

"I can't believe he's okay with it," Aria said.

"This is Love Letter Lang we're talking about," Oren said, sitting and grabbing a slice of his own. "The guy is a notorious serial killer. You think the warden cares what we want to do with him? Besides, he knows we're trying to help the victims' families. He seemed supportive."

Both Aria and Charlie continued looking at Oren. They were waiting for the rest. With Oren, there was often something else.

"And it didn't help that he was open to some extra cash," Oren added.

"Knew it." Aria slammed the table.

"But we need to focus," Oren said. "This is the real deal. Tomorrow morning, we'll be face to face with a serial killer. One that evaded capture for years. One who took twenty-three victims in a five-year span. And one whose victims have still not been located."

"We'll find them." Charlie was focused again, his eyes still and burning holes through a wall. His voice was certain.

"Who knows what kind of mess his mind is," Oren continued. "I know you feel good about it, Charlie. But don't doubt that he may have suppressed the memories of where he hid the bodies. Or blacked out. Perhaps, he doesn't remember at all."

"Don't kid yourself," Aria teased. "You feel good about it too, Oren. You wouldn't have taken the case if you didn't think we'd find them."

"I don't know if we'll find all of them," Oren admitted. It was a departure from his usual assuredness. "But each one we do guarantees one more family will get closure."

And guaranteed a paycheque for them. But no one said it. The money was only an essential part of the transaction that ensured they could continue to work. The reason all of them were here was because they truly cared about righting wrongs. And Leonard Lang was one *big* wrong.

"Just keep in mind this isn't like diving into a practice mind, like mine or Aria's," Oren said. "This guy is dangerous. Even behind bars."

"I will be cautious," Charlie said.

Domino finished his pizza crust and leapt back onto the windowsill to watch them again.

"Do either of you remember the trial?" Aria asked. "I remember they talked a lot about how he was caught. The security cameras at the bar saw him leaving with the Aberdeen girl. And the sick bastard was blowing kisses at the camera, like he knew they were watching. And yet he didn't care. I remember that footage they showed, and it made my stomach turn. What I *don't* remember is why they called him *Love Letter*. Because of the kisses?"

"He earned that name long before that." Charlie pulled from the encyclopedia in his head. "They were referring to him as Love Letter for almost three years before they caught him. The name came from the strange notes that were showing up at news stations. He wrote them from his perspective, but addressed them to the victims, as if a secret admirer was passing along a note. *Charlotte, I noticed you from across the street. I like you. Do you like me?*"

"Gross," Aria cringed.

"Lang is all kinds of messed-up," Oren said, shuffling through documents. "When you see his history, it's not hard to imagine why. His father was never around. His mother passed away when he was thirteen. He spent time bouncing around in foster homes and landed in more than one abusive space. He ended up in a car wreck when he was eighteen, almost killed him, then he became hooked on painkillers. Depending on what you believe though, the evil side of him could have been there all along. There's a lot of dark stuff in that mind, Charlie. You're going to have your work cut out for you."

"I'm glad it's you and not me, Charlie." Aria shivered. "The kind of things you're bound to see in his head tomorrow . . . it would scar me for life."

"Nothing scares him," Oren added. Charlie smiled at them, yet he appeared to be mentally preoccupied, like he was already rehearsing every part of the next day.

\*\*\*

Aria and Oren met up with Charlie in the parking lot. The sky was a single grey sheet wrapped over the world. An early rain had soaked the ground. Fences and chains cut across the sky, reminding them where they were.

Oren's usual confidence—a confidence others were envious of—was notably absent. He was shaking as he tried to sip his coffee. His eyes were bloodshot.

"I feel the same," Aria said after she noticed his shaking hands.

Oren couldn't be bothered to make eye contact. "It all either goes up in smoke or catches fire. Either the MemCom proves to be worth the hassle, or I've wasted my time and we're nothing special."

"You shouldn't be worried. If anything goes wrong, it will affect me more than you." Charlie was a robot, monotonously giving them wisdom they didn't need. "I'm the one who would die in there."

"No one is dying," Oren said. "It's our careers I'm worried about. And those families who need us to find their loved ones."

None of them had anything else to say, so Oren sighed and led the way, across the wet pavement toward the prison doors.

They went through security, placing their items in bins and passing through the scanners. Oren was the only one with a firearm to turn in. Their IDs were checked and then checked again. Once inside, a sweaty man in an ill-fitting suit scurried down the hall to meet them.

"Mr. West," the man huffed and shook Oren's hand.

The man wore a goofy, forced grin, making a show of being friendly. He had, after all, been paid for this. He turned finally to Charlie and Aria and introduced himself as Perry Manfred, the warden.

They walked the halls together, spread out four wide. Warden Manfred hocked and cleared his throat. The gurgling sound reverberated off the concrete walls. Their footsteps clattered and created echoes too as they zagged through corridors and passed checkpoints. Guards nodded at Manfred and let them through. The warden needed two steps for every one of Oren's, and once Oren noticed, he slowed the pace of the group down. This bothered Charlie, who was anxious to get started.

"He's in the interrogation room," Manfred said. "It's been specially outfitted for your needs. Feels like we've got a real-life Hannibal Lector here. If you think you can get him to talk, all the power to you. But he hasn't revealed a thing to anyone. Not even world-class psychologists. So, I don't know how you're going to find out where those girls are."

"We have some different tactics we are going to try." Oren was nonchalant.

"I wouldn't hold your breath." Manfred shrugged. "But what you wanna do with your time is up to you."

True to Manfred's word, the room they were led to was perfect for their test. They all stepped through a door and into a large square. On the far wall was a large window—one-way glass—slightly tinted and peering into a plain space on the other side. A chair had been placed right up near the one-way glass, as close as one could get to Lang without being inside his cell.

There was a buzz in the air as the hum of the room fed back through the microphone intended for their conversation with Lang. It felt as though the dimmed fluorescents that hung above them were whispering to them.

On the other side of the glass, sitting between muted white walls, was a tall man in an orange jumpsuit. He sat in a chair that had been left out for him, gripping the arm rests with long, twisted fingers. He had slicked back hair and a ratty ponytail, and his eyes were dark and set in deep sockets.

Manfred made his way to the glass and pressed a button on the wall.

"Good morning, Lang," Manfred bellowed. "Your visitors are here. Play nice."

"Yes, Daddy." Lang smirked at the glass and blew a kiss. His eyes darted around, not able to land on one spot, uncertain of exactly where the warden stood.

"Fuck you, sick fuck," Manfred wheezed, flipping a middle finger that Lang would never see.

"He can't see in here, right?" Aria whispered to Charlie.

"No."

"You have a filthy mouth, Warden," Lang teased.

Manfred pressed the talk button, looking like he was about to say something, then noticed his guests and thought better of it.

"It's fine." Manfred waved a hand. "We are all used to him. He just likes to talk."

"Well, thank you for setting this up." Oren stepped forwards. "We don't imagine we'll be too long. But if we're successful, we'll definitely be back."

"Whatever you need." Manfred smiled.

You could almost see the dollar signs lighting up behind his eyes as the man imagined his opportunity. He shook Oren's hand quickly and then departed.

With their host gone, it was Oren's turn to press the talk button.

"Mr. Lang," Oren said. "My name is Harold Bentley." An alias. "I believe the warden told you why we're here?"

"Warden said you're the ones from that website," Lang replied, eyes still unsettled.

"Crime Truthers, that's right," Oren said, furthering their cover. "We're here to ask you a few questions about your side of the events. We have a large fan base who could be considered fans of yours. And they'd love to read a piece on your retelling of things."

Oren had appealed to Lang's desire to brag. Lang had never even come close to revealing any of his secrets to law enforcement. But he was notorious for telling stories—most of them grandiose fabrications. Given the chance to address his "fans," the murderer's face lit up.

It didn't matter what he spoke about. Or even if it was true. They only needed to make him think, make him recall things from deep in his mind, and to make him listen to "Sweet Caroline" for a few seconds.

"Well, I'm flattered. Where should I begin?"

"If you'd indulge me one moment," Oren said into the mic.

Lang frowned; he wanted to start.

"I'd like to play something for you." Oren glanced at Charlie, who nodded.

Charlie placed the earpiece in his ear and sat himself down in a chair. Aria put a hand on his shoulder and turned to face the door they had entered by, keeping a look out. Getting caught with this device carried the risk that all three of them may end up on the wrong side of these walls.

Oren tapped play on his phone, and "Sweet Caroline" once again bounced into its familiar tune. Oren was holding down the talk button and allowing it to pass through to Lang's side of the glass.

"Music?" Lang asked, dumbfounded. He looked offended, glaring at the ceiling and cringing.

Oren did not seem to care. They only needed a few moments of Lang's attention. "What the fuck is this?"

"We like to set the mood when we speak to our special guests," Oren lied. "Grant us this, and then we'll write down everything you say."

Whether Lang agreed or not didn't matter. He was cuffed. He couldn't leave. He had to listen. And Charlie was already pressing the button that would launch him into the serial killer's mind.

"So, what do you want to tell us about those women?" Oren asked, preparing Lang's mind, forcing him to think about the right topic. Lang, who had been salivating over this opportunity, dove right in.

\*\*\*

Now Charlie stood in an alley. Max felt it was pretty typical, murder-y setting. It was dark, but the taillights of a car were visible down at the far end. There was no sky; the memory had created a false ceiling over everything and blurred the details at either end of the alleyway. Lang was nowhere to be seen, so Charlie approached the vehicle. The ground was wet, as if it had just finished raining, and there was a weight to the air, the kind of humidity only a long summer could bring. There was even a smell, the kind that clings after an evening rainstorm.

The car was an old sedan, something that probably didn't start on the first turn of the key. Charlie was staring at a figure sitting in the driver's seat. Charlie walked around the side of the car, and so did Max. Now it was clear that the figure was a woman, and she was talking on the phone. She was blond, and she was done up for a big night, but her makeup was running down her face. She had been crying. Her conversation was inaudible, but it was clear she was upset. She hung up the phone.

Through the fogged windows came the muffled sound of the woman crying. After viewing earlier memories in which Charlie had reviewed the cases, Max knew this was the first victim, Claire McDaniels. They were behind a bar. Claire appeared to be intoxicated and was now trying to drive herself home. But her car wouldn't start; she had not been able to fool the breathalyzer tied to her ignition.

*Your ex-boyfriend later confirms that it was him you called,* Charlie's thoughts echoed across the alley.

Their sudden arrival made Max jump. *But he refused.* Suddenly, Claire threw her phone away in anger. It landed across the passenger seat, just out of arm's reach. She would not be able to grab it in case of emergency.

What came next seemed obvious, and gave Max a chill, even in the muggy night air. He was startled as Lang materialized from the shadows without warning. His greasy hair was pulled back, same as it was in the prison cell, but now, in the place of a jumpsuit, he wore a weathered brown leather jacket. Charlie had to sidestep as to not interfere with the scene.

Lang pulled at the driver's side door and was able to rip it open before Claire could react. She was startled too, and she screamed. But Lang's hand covered her mouth quickly. Instinctually, Claire began to reach for her phone. But she would never be able to reach it again.

There was no one else around in the alley. There hadn't been any witnesses. Lang had been able to subdue Claire. During the trial, they released dozens of receipts for a plethora of drugs that could be used for sedation. Charlie cringed as he watched Claire slip into unconsciousness. Lang then shoved her over into the passenger seat. Just moments ago, she had been on the phone. Now, he was in the driver's seat, pulling the sedan out of the alley. And Charlie was left there alone, without a ride.

"Shit," Charlie cursed and began looking around.

There was an emergency exit below a flickering light down at the end he had come from. Charlie jogged back through the puddles and over the uneven concrete. He tried the door. It didn't budge. Charlie glanced around quickly, confirming there were no other doors. *It has to be this one.* Charlie heaved again, putting his back into it. The door inched out at first, and then with a greater pull, it popped fully open.

At first, it looked like a dead end. Only darkness awaited him on the other side of the door. But Charlie knew better, and he stepped forwards without hesitation, inadvertently dragging Max with him.

\*\*\*

The darkness lifted, and Charlie was in a basement. Sun streaked through a cracked window above him. The basement was dank—something dripped somewhere—and old, beat-up boxes littered the floor.

A single streak of sunlight revealed all of the whirling dust in the air. A bare staircase that still had nails sticking out from the boards bisected the room. Someone was shouting from the staircase, then came the sound of footsteps. Moments later, a teenager with long hair covering his face descended the stairs.

"I said fuck you, Mom!" the teen shouted up the stairs. He then promptly ducked as a glass came soaring for his head and shattered against the wall. The teen then marched over toward Charlie.

Charlie sidestepped, trying to avoid any contact with Lang's teenage SI. Charlie watched as this young, pimple-faced kid who would become a serial killer dove onto a bare mattress in the corner.

Lang grabbed a soiled pillow and tossed it across the room in anger. It landed somewhere between the boxes. Charlie took in the entire scene. He was getting a firsthand look at the youth of this notorious psychopath. *If this was your bedroom, it explains why you turned out the way you did,* Charlie's thoughts cascaded down from every direction. Aside from the mattress, the only thing that even remotely resembled a teenager's room were the posters on the wall. Three of them hung next to the mattress, each with a different pinup girl on it, covering themselves with just enough to not be considered pornographic.

The footsteps overhead grew momentarily louder, and then a figure appeared on the staircase, peering down. The figure resembled a middle-aged woman, with curlers in her hair, bags under her eyes, adorned in a pink robe and slippers, lit cigarette in hand. But it wasn't *really* a middle-aged woman. The woman had snake's eyes, thin black slits in seas of topaz. Her lips were curled into a *V*, a devilish grin revealing razor-sharp fangs. Her skin was scaly and ashen.

She wasn't a woman. She was a demon.

Lang's mind had created his mother as a monster.

"If you think you're getting *anything* from me now, you're dreaming," she hissed. "If I see you upstairs anymore this weekend . . . well, I won't miss next time." She pointed to the glass shards on the floor.

*I've never encountered a childhood as horrific as this.* Charlie watched with the unwavering interest and the studious gaze a biologist might have when discovering a new species. *Fascinating.*

This morbid curiosity brought Charlie over closer to Lang's bed. The mother-demon had left, and now Charlie needed to see what Lang was up to.

Lang had rolled over and pulled out a shoebox from beside the bed. He clenched it tight to his chest for a moment, staring an angry hole into the ceiling. Then, when he seemed to have calmed down, he took the lid off the box, revealing a scorpion. The arachnid had a chestnut-coloured exoskeleton that glistened like an oil slick. Its tail hung over its head, pointed and daunting.

*An Arizona bark scorpion.* Lang's thoughts filled the basement, giving Charlie—and by extension, Max—a free biology lesson. *The only lethal scorpion in the US.*

Lang grabbed a pen and slowly lowered it into the makeshift terrarium, where dead bugs and tufts of grass had been littered. The scorpion didn't seem too pleased with this intruder, and it snatched for the pen with one of its pincers. Lang watched the scorpion grab at his pen with a dark interest. Max noted that Charlie was watching Lang with the same gaze.

"What do you think?" Lang said, his voice shattering the stillness, and his words bringing a rush of cool air into the space. It was as though he were whispering dark magic into existence. "What should we do about her?"

Charlie opened his mouth as if to answer, but then he must have realized that Lang was speaking to the scorpion.

The basement rattled away from them, a train car departing the station, and Charlie was left with the stomach-shifting feeling that came when the memory advanced. Time had been skipped, and he was thrust into the next relevant sequence of events.

Lang was still there, but now he was in a different room. A large window was covered with drapes, but slivers of daylight came in around the corners. Lang's mother had passed out on a ratty old sofa. Her cigarette was still perched in her lips, smoldering now. A bottle of pills was perched on her bosom, which was slipping out of the robe. A television—left on an infomercial for non-stick cookware—cast a dancing blue haze over the woman.

Lang was inching forwards carefully. The floor creaked beneath his feet, and every time it got too loud, he froze, cringing, and tried to move his foot to a different spot. Charlie stayed in the hallway, seemingly holding his breath as he watched Lang try to go undetected.

The shoebox was still in his hands, lid on.

The television was telling them to *"Call Now!"* The lighting changed, flickering, causing Lang's movement to strobe. He was nearing his mother and began to crouch, coming up behind the sofa and out of sight.

He peered over the top of the furniture, looking down on the sleeping demon. One hand was holding the shoebox now while the other went to remove the lid. Quietly, he placed the lid down on the ground. Then, Lang brought the shoebox over top of the woman.

"Fuck you," Lang whispered. "For everything."

Lang tilted the shoebox carefully, and the scorpion slid out. It turned, trying to stay in its home, but ultimately, gravity plopped it down with a soft thud onto the woman's chest. It landed right next to the pill bottle and steadied itself against her collarbone. The scorpion froze.

"Don't hold back," Lang told his pet.

Then he rose, backing away slowly. He turned and strode away with confidence. His job was done.

The scorpion appeared as if it was watching Lang leave. Then it spun in a semicircle, surveying its new environment. It decided it was exposed, and quickly, on eerily quick legs, it scuttled away down the woman's chest, toward her belly, burrowing itself under her robe.

Lang left the living room, through the hallway that Charlie was standing in. On his face was the same smirk that Charlie had seen the fully grown Leonard Lang wear while imprisoned, cuffed in his orange jumpsuit. Charlie pressed himself against the wall to avoid bumping into the SI.

As Lang walked past him, he studied the boy's face. Suddenly, a shriek rang out. Lang's mother screamed once. Then a second time. Then a third. Each scream was more blood-chilling and desperate than the last.

Charlie peered back into the living room. But the lights had already been turned out on this memory. The sound carried forwards, but there was nothing but a void where the sofa and the scorpion should have been. Lang's memory had only held onto the sound of the screaming. This was his trophy.

*His first kill,* Charlie realized. *Everyone had believed his mother's passing was an accident. Not that it matters much now.*

From the shadows came a sudden gust of wind. The breeze brought with it a new setting, and without notice, Charlie found himself transferred to yet another memory. The gust of wind continued, increasing in velocity. And it began to sting Charlie's eyes. The temperature had dropped noticeably, and he felt goosebumps run down his arms and legs.

Charlie stood in the midst of a cool fall morning. All around him, yellow leaves danced in the air, the breeze not allowing them to settle. Before him, sat the enormous expanse of a quarry. A circular body of water stood in the middle, waves distorting the surface. The intense wind bent all of the trees along the rocky shoreline, and teased their dying leaves out for a dip. A steep rock ledge rose on the far side of the water, looking down at Charlie. It witnessed everything.

Again, the sky was gone.

*Does this guy never look up?* Charlie wondered.

Of course, the trees and leaves were somewhat blurry. But the body that lay at Charlie's feet was crystal clear.

Claire McDaniels was much paler than in the previous memory of her. Now her eyes were fogged, lifeless. Her skin was bright, almost bleached. Had the bastard preserved her? She was stripped down to her underwear, several stab wounds obvious on her torso. Charlie looked away out of respect.

Lang's mind had come back full circle, connecting Charlie from his first kill to his first calculated murder.

Leonard Lang now stood triumphantly over his kill. He had that same hint of a smile on his face. He was silently eulogizing the girl, remembering whatever he had done to her and now saying goodbye.

When he finished the speech inside his head, Lang bent down and scooped up the body, heading to the edge where the rocks gave way into the water below.

Rigor mortis had taken hold, and Lang struggled to get a proper hold of his victim. Certainly, Charlie had seen dead bodies before and was thus accustomed to gore, yet Max noticed how Charlie seemed disturbed by this reenactment in Lang's memory

Charlie's inner monologue announced his feelings on the matter. *Lang does not deserve to have this perfectly preserved image of Claire etched in his mind. It's as though he gets to keep her in his own internal museum. Even with Claire dead and gone. And even with Lang in prison. He will always have this. Claire is imprisoned here, perpetually at the mercy of her killer. Reduced to a souvenir.*

Charlie looked away, seemingly unable to watch the rest. *I'm sorry. I'm sorry I couldn't save you. Lang has claimed the ultimate victory. He owns you now. Even after death.*

And now, he was carrying her to the edge of the water. He was sticking her in a large bag. Lang filled the bag with rocks from the quarry, meticulously placing them between Claire's legs and atop her chest and around her head. Then, when he was satisfied, he zipped the bag up—struggling once again—and eventually was able to give it enough of a heave that it toppled over the edge into the water. It was a steep drop off, and the bag quickly disappeared below the surface.

Lang was stoic for a while, surveying his work. He seemed confident in the place he had chosen, and so he made his way back to wherever he had left his car. Charlie watched Lang march back up the dirt path. Here stood a sign with an arrow pointing away from them. It was branded with the words *Terrence Quarry.*

So, Charlie now knew everything he needed to know.

He stared at the water. *Where exactly did he place her?* The waves already shattered any trace of the body that had broken the water's surface.

He clenched his fists. He crouched, pressing himself into a corner between a rock and a tree stump. He shut his eyes. Max saw him steady his breathing, as if meditating. Soon, it was as if Max's own body was also relaxed. *Seal yourself off from your senses, find the rising feeling,* Charlie narrated to himself. *Pull yourself out.* Suddenly, Max felt as if he was rising, and they were ripped from the memory. The feeling of the night air was left behind, but the chills remained.

*\*\*\**

Lang—the real one—sat before Charlie now, and he was back in his orange jumpsuit. He was grinning and telling Oren about how good it felt to stick a knife into human flesh. Both Oren and Aria were right where he had left them. It hadn't been long.

Oren turned his attention to Charlie. "And?"

Charlie just nodded. He fidgeted in his chair, looking nauseous. Aria patted him on the shoulder, trying to comfort him.

"Great," Oren said. "Let's make this asshole think we care about his story for a few more minutes, then make up an excuse to get out of here."

*\*\*\**

The air was just as cool, and the trees looked remarkably similar to the ones in Lang's memory. *This must be around the anniversary of Claire's killing*, Charlie thought.

Oren had procured a dive team for them, a favour from friends in law enforcement who also wanted to see this case resolved, and thus volunteered their time. Charlie had dutifully guided them to the right point.

Now Charlie, along with Oren, stood at the same spot Lang had years earlier and waited for the divers to find the body.

"What was he like?" Oren asked, needing to say something to pass the time.

"Reverent," Charlie said. "These memories are exhibits to him."

Hundreds of yellow leaves drifted across the water, being pushed toward them by the breeze. From these leaves, a head emerged, and for a moment, Charlie thought it may have been Claire come back from the dead. It was, of course, one of the divers. The diver looked toward Oren and flashed a signal. They'd found her and would begin to retrieve her.

"It's a long way down!" the diver shouted. "But we got her."

Oren nodded and waved. The dive team would pull her out, or whatever was left of her. There would be a relieved family to call, and a sense of closure to provide.

Charlie left Oren at the quarry. *I don't need to see the body come up. They found her. That's all I need to know.* The MemCom had worked as they'd intended it to. Lang's mind had shown the way. Charlie couldn't bring himself to celebrate, however. *Just twenty-two victims to go.*

# 3. A Town for No One

MAX HAD SURFACED FROM HIS stint inside of Charlie's mind, and he was feeling completely overwhelmed. He was drenched in sweat. He had no sense of how much time had elapsed. He started talking, but he wasn't sure he was making sense.

Oren silenced him, got him to hydrate, and then Max passed out. His sleep was dreamless. A few times Oren would wake him—like when they boarded the plane, or when Max needed to drink more—but Max was in and out of consciousness for most of their travels.

When they landed, Oren asked Max if he remembered much from the dive. Max couldn't seem to come up with an answer, though images of quarries and prisons and a cat named Domino danced through his mind. It would come, Oren assured him.

The next steps in their journey flashed by—the turbulent landing at Hancock International Airport in Syracuse, shuffling to collect their bags, making their way to the far end of the designated pick-up area where Oren said their ride would find them.

They stood outside and waited, their breath rising slowly in front of them as the night tried to claim the last of their warmth. Max lost feeling in the tips of his ears. The sky above them was the purest dark he had ever seen. No moon, no stars, no satellites. It felt like they had flown into an abyss.

"From Memorial Day to Labour Day, Ruston is alive with water sports, campers, and students," Oren said, reading from a brochure he had grabbed on their way outside.

"And it's how far?" Max asked.

"Couple hours, I'm afraid." Oren discarded the brochure. "Unfortunately, it's way out there."

He looked out into the night where there was nothing. A plane roared overhead, lost in the clouds, but at least giving them the sense they weren't completely alone.

"It's closer to the Canadian border than anything else of note. And the winters are hell. But that pamphlet said the lakes are gorgeous come July."

"Maybe we'll come back," Max mumbled.

He tried to force himself into good spirits, but his body was still trembling. He kept his sports drink bottle close.

At last, headlights found them. A vehicle was pulling up through the exhaust and the fog. Max expected a black Cadillac, something befitting of Oren's glamorous secret agent lifestyle. His guess couldn't have been further from the truth. A boxy orange jeep pulled up next to them; the round headlights and shiny front grill made it look like the car was smiling at them.

"Archie?!" Oren called out as a man emerged from the driver's side door, jeep still running.

The man was pushing seventy, and he had a bushy grey moustache and wore an aviator cap over his rusty-white hair. He had a nose that was too large for his face, and it gave his smile a cartoonish feel. He half-chuckled as he spoke in a sort of endearing, grandfatherly way. He had stuffed himself into a denim jacket that was tight around the torso.

"Lads." The man beamed. "I'm Archie. I'll be your chauffeur." He cracked himself up. "Let me grab your bags. No, leave 'em, leave 'em, you've had a long flight. I got 'em."

Oren called shotgun to Max's relief. Max wanted to shut his eyes and rest in the back.

As Archie loaded up their bags, Max made himself comfortable and asked Oren, "Where is this guy from?"

"The current sheriff put me in touch," Oren explained. "Archie is the old sheriff, now retired. Guess he's a fixture in Ruston, always taking on projects and helping out. I think the sheriff just wanted him to keep us busy while we were in town, so that we wouldn't be bugging him as much. But when I spoke to Archie, he offered to come get us at the airport."

Archie was climbing back into his seat now with a groan. "Good to get these old joints moving on a cold night like this," Archie huffed. "Everybody set? Yeah? Let's go."

"Thank you so much, Archie," Oren said. "Can't thank you enough. I know it's a long drive."

"When Landry said there were folks coming to help look for Tiffany, I felt it was the least I could do," Archie said, hands gripping the wheel as they took off. "It's not easy to get a rental 'round here either. Expensive. Plus, you have to know where you're going. And this time of year, it ain't exactly tourism season. The taxis in town all take off for the winter. So, instead, I'll be at your service for the remainder of your stay."

"That's too kind," Oren said. "But thank you. We will obviously compensate you."

"Nonsense," Archie said. "It's how an old man like me keeps busy. I like to drive. Took the Millers to the airport just the other week. I do things like this to keep myself young, you know. Helped paint the station last summer. Put the winter tires on the sheriff's truck every year. Things like that."

Max didn't catch much more. He drifted off to sleep, and the ride passed in fits and starts.

Archie was a chatterbox, and his stories were the backtrack to Max's slumber. When Max shifted back into consciousness, he caught loose pieces. To Archie's credit, his stories were, thankfully, quite good. He talked about growing up on a farm and all the dogs that he had as a kid. He recounted days as the town sheriff and reminisced about times that were simpler.

"It's a different world they're looking after now," Archie said. "I don't envy Landry one bit."

"Speaking of," Oren said. "Can I ask you about your current sheriff? He seemed a bit standoffish in our correspondence. Didn't seem to be much of a fan of our involvement. Seems like the sheriff has a thing against outsiders."

"Ah, he's not such a bad guy once you get to know him," Archie said. "The whole town has a chip on its shoulders for out-of-towners. Part of the complex we have when the cold weather hits, and business dries up, and all we're left with is the mess the summer tourists made."

"Well, hopefully, we'll get along fine with Sheriff Landry then," Oren said.

"If he gives you too much trouble, send him to me." Archie chuckled. "Not that he listens to me, or anyone. He is hard-headed, I will say that. Just do your best to mind his authority, and I'm sure you'll get on. You know, before I was sheriff, we had a hell of an old fella wearing the badge." Archie started with a bit of rhythm in his voice that suggested a new story was coming.

"Name was Cooper Tuppance. Tuppance was a widower; his dear wife, Margaret, had passed away very young. She was deeply religious, and though Tuppance never was himself, her passing changed him, and so he became a minister. Minister and sheriff, if you can believe it. Anyway, we used to have this old gentlemen's club out on the highway here, and one night, a call comes in that a fight has broken out at the club. Tuppance makes the drive out there, parks, and steps up to the front door. After a while, the bartender comes out all panicked and says, 'Sheriff, what are you doing standing there? We need your help with this brawl!' Tuppance looks at him and says, 'I'm fine right here. When they tire out and come out for a smoke, I'll grab 'em.'

"Bartender is shocked. Then he realizes, the sheriff don't wanna come inside because it's not a holy place. Our straight edge sheriff-minister didn't want to set foot inside that building of sin. So, one thing leads to another, and the story gets out. Soon enough, word around town is 'If you want to rob the bank, all you need to do is hide out at the peelers, and you'll get away with the whole thing.'" Archie then let loose a long, hoarse, smoker's laugh.

When the conversation withered, Archie turned to the radio. He tuned into a local station—his all-time favourite, he said—which played songs of a different era. They were older than anything Max could even remember his father playing. His father loved the old rock ballads, introducing his son to eclectic hits by Styx and Meatloaf—in the times when they were cordial. But this music predated all of that. And by quite some time. This music was certainly war-era. The only thing Max couldn't figure out was if it was World War I or II.

"No one listens to this anymore," Archie admitted. "But thankfully, the station is still on air. An old fella like me out in Fairfield runs it from his garage. Just keeps the thing going."

Archie hummed along to one song as they soared over the barren highway. The track sounded faded but still rich, the sound having ripened with age. Plucky guitar chords accompanied harmonic vocals from the quartet singers. It had all the elements of a peppy, old tune. But it struck Max as sad and nostalgic.

*We are but a memory, lasting 'til eternity.*
*Come here, my love, lay with me and die with me.*

A bunch of strumming and humming followed. A catchy—but somber—*doo-wop, doo-wop.*

The closer they got to Ruston, the harder Max found it to sleep. The ride felt as though it had been going on for years. Everything outside the car was white and desolate; the world had ended. Snow was being forced up from the ground and tossed about in angry circles, the wind having its way. Any trees they saw were bare and frail, looking as though they could snap at any moment. A few lonely houses speckled the sides of the highway, but they were either abandoned or in deep disrepair. Apart from that, all they saw was snow. An ocean of snow on either side of the road.

Max watched as they passed an island, floating by itself in the sea of white. A single mound of land and a few trees and shrubs poked out from what was otherwise a perfectly flat expanse. The wind broke around this island—you could see its ghost trails highlighted by the flurries—and then continued on its path across the fields.

Both Max and Oren had grown up with harsh winters. But this was something else. They had driven to the edge of the world, and winter was about to swallow them whole. Just three men in a bright orange jeep about to give way into nothingness.

When they finally did encounter a sign of civilization, all they could see were giant barns, some painted red and others painted blue or green. All of them, though, were battered from the elements and looked as though they may collapse.

Max gleaned from their earlier conversations that Oren had a cover story he shared with Archie. It was likely the same one he had told Robert Thomas, Sheriff Landry, and anyone else who asked. Oren was a missing persons specialist; he would be able to interrogate the suspect and get him to cave, revealing the location of the girl. Max was his assistant, there to observe and learn. No one would ever know that Max was wearing an earpiece in the other room, or that he was momentarily falling into a state something like sleep, and then awaking seconds later with all of the details they would need.

No one would need to know that Oren hadn't just figured it all out himself.

Even their client, the Thomas family, would need to believe they were just exceptional interrogators. No one could know about the MemCom. Oren had stressed this.

"There it is," Archie said as they came across the sign: *Welcome to Ruston. A Town For All.*

The sign looked as though it was losing its battle against the wind and the cold. The name *Ruston* was there in big block letters, white as the snow but backed by spruce that made it stand out. The part of the sign below the name—where the population should have been listed—was covered by a snow drift, and all that you could make out was the number 3.

Soon, they approached a stop sign and slowed down for the first time in hours. Max felt his stomach catch up to him then, and he realized he was hungry. From there, the road snaked between some low hills, more trees appeared around them, and the horizon started to clutter. Before long, they passed a few houses where the driveway had actually been shovelled out, and a grocery store advertising that it was open twenty-four hours.

"You staying at the Birch?" Archie asked as the road narrowed and bent toward a cluster of homes.

"Is there anywhere else?" Oren asked.

"No, I suppose not," Archie admitted.

Officially in town, Archie offered a tour as they cruised down main street, never a click over the speed limit. At this hour, there weren't many other cars on the road. Max tried to make a game of counting and capped out at two. Still, those two other vehicles proved to Max that the world hadn't ended.

On their right was the river, or so Archie said. All they could see was the steep embankment that dropped down. The river itself—a narrow and shallow one—was covered by snow drifts and shadow. Archie told them that there used to be good fishing in this water, but as of late, it had been more full of empty bottles than fish.

Both sides of the road were now lined with houses, none of them built later than 1970. Their weather-worn siding braved the wind the best it could. Most houses had blinds drawn, snow piling up on the porch, Christmas lights still up and twisted around the eaves, and flyers sticking out of the mailbox. A few homes broke the mold and attempted to keep up their property. These homes all had little signs at the door that said something like "Neighbours Are Family."

When the houses ran out, they sat at a three-way stop. This was the heart of downtown, Archie said. To the left was a well-paved road with nice houses spread out, buffered by their enormous yards. To the right was a pothole riddled lane that directed them toward flickering streetlamps and one neon "Open" sign at the lone late-night establishment.

"Out that way is where the Thomas family lives," Archie said, pointing to the nice road on the left.

"We're not going that way, though, are we?" Oren asked.

"No."

Archie steered them to the right, driving slow to avoid the potholes. There was a gas station, offering the cheapest gas Max had seen since he was a child. Two odds and ends shops adorned the left side of the street, one looking like it had been closed for years. They passed a general store and then a large strip mall lot offering all of the staples; there was a restaurant (Ruston Restaurant), a hairdresser (Ruston Barber & Cuts), and a Laundromat (Coins 4 Cleans). On the other side of the street was a veterinary clinic. Apparently, the town doctor shared this building. Max asked if it was the same person treating both dogs and people, and to this, Archie would only chuckle.

Past that was the town church—Catholic church—sitting proudly on top of the sloped road with one long stone spire. Next door sat the cemetery and a bank.

"Death and taxes," Archie laughed.

After the bank was a stretch of vacant lots. Then, at long last, the lone bright spot—the bar. It stood like a beacon on the far end of an otherwise empty plot. This bar was a dingy, two-storey building with neon lights in the windows. A white and yellow sign above the door identified this place as the Rusty Nail. Block letters, poorly arranged on the sign out front, told them the weekly specials.

> The Rusty Nail Nightly Features—
> Week of February 5
> Monday—2 for 1 Beers
> Tuesday—Country Night and Cowboy Shots
> Wednesday—Live Local Music
> Thursday—$2 Highballs
> Friday—Karaoke
> Saturday—Dollar Shots
> Sunday—$5 Dirty Marys

"Our girl went missing on country night," Oren noted.

Soon, the sign disappeared behind them, and the buildings all became more spread out.

"That's about it for downtown," Archie said as they passed the bar. "Up here's the post office, and then it's the river again. Kind of curves around us."

True enough, the road turned into a bridge after the post office and took them over a narrow stretch of frozen water. There was a park down below the bridge, with benches and picnic tables barely peeking out above the snow. Archie said there was a beautiful library down a bit further as well, and in the summer, it was a fine idea to grab a book and read it next to the river.

On the embankment, on the far side of the bridge, were some scattered homes, each with a unique design. They were skinny and tall, despite their lots being quite wide. The homes were modern, made of pale brick and glass. They didn't match what they had seen so far in Ruston. Archie turned down the street these houses were on, and they got a look from the front.

"These lots here all burned down, more than a hundred years ago," Archie explained. "In 1915, the home of the town's tinsmith caught fire. He lived on that corner, where that red house is now. The houses were all pretty close together, and they all went up real quick. They had to bring down firefighters from Canada to help put out the blaze. By the time they got it under control though, almost half the town was up in smoke. Lost twenty-five homes and a few good businesses entirely. Town hall was gone too, along with all the records that predated the fire."

"Why are the homes so narrow and tall?" Max asked. "They don't use up all the land they've got." The part of him that pulled at things until they unraveled, the part that told stories, urged him to seize on this thread.

"Superstition," Archie muttered, keeping quiet as if someone was going to hear them. "These lands have a sort of bad juju around them. After the fires and all. See, a few homes built on this same stretch years later *also* burned down. Then in the 1980s, two of the families that lived on the street went out boating together on a nearby lake. There was an accident, and both families were lost. Imagine that, two entire families. Little tykes and all. Locals started to get the idea this land was cursed. So those that built here decided to touch as little of the land as possible. The less of the land your house touches, the less the curse applies. Or so they say."

Max, who had always been a bit superstitious himself, felt like this made sense. It was as if the houses were all playing a big game of *The Floor Is Lava.*

They followed the street until it ended, streetlights and houselights fading away for darkness. Then, at last, there was a big blue sign and one lonely orange streetlamp above a sparse parking lot.

The Birch Motel.

Archie had been whistling along to another old tune on the radio as they drove, and abruptly stopped as they pulled into the lot.

"Well, now that's weird, vacancy sign's been switched off," Archie said.

Only two cars sat nearby, each with frosted windshields. One, closer to the office at the far end, was likely that of staff. Nearest them was an SUV with red writing on the side that read *County Fire.*

Across from the motel was an open field, and a nasty wind was kicking snow in, draping everything in white sheets. Behind the motel were the train tracks and a row of houses, all clinging onto the bright light from the motel's sign as shadows crept up around them.

"Look," Max said, pointing to the rooms.

The motel had a single row of rooms leading to the office. Each one of these rooms had square windows, and at least half of these windows had dark black stains around them. There had been a fire.

"Well, what in the hell," Archie muttered, putting the jeep into park. "What happened here?"

A small, round-faced woman—with hair as frosty as the snowbanks—hustled out from the office, holding her jacket closed. She high-stepped over snow drifts that had yet to be cleaned up on the sidewalk. One of the room doors she passed was open, and as she scurried past, she almost bumped into a firefighter walking out. She yelped and then continued her pace.

Archie rolled down his window as she approached, nodding to her.

"Sorry, Arch," she huffed. Her eyes only barely cleared the bottom of the window. "No vacancy. Your friends will have to stay elsewhere."

"Damn, Pauline," Archie said, dumbfounded. "What happened?"

"Just this morning some idiot nearly burned our motel down," the woman sighed. "Fell asleep with a cigarette, I figure. Spread to three adjacent rooms, then of course the rest got the water damage from the firemen."

One of the firefighters looked over, and the woman grimaced.

"Need to dry them out before I can rent them."

The smell of burning hung in the air—even with the wind assaulting them with winter chill—and Max could not imagine a pleasant night's sleep in this place. *The curse,* he thought.

"Well, jeez, Pauline." Archie exhaled, scratching his head.

"Sorry, folks, nothing I can do." The innkeeper shrugged and began to retreat. "Would love to help but . . . no vacancy."

"Is there anywhere else?" Oren asked.

"Not in Ruston," Archie said.

"Now what?" Max asked.

His eyelids felt like they had been deep-fried, and they itched and crinkled every time he blinked. He couldn't remember feeling this tired, not since he was a child and tried to pull all-nighters. He just needed a bed. Any bed.

"I've got an idea," Archie said, pulling out his phone. "Not the Taj Mahal, exactly, but nice and close for ya. Should do you for a day or two."

\*\*\*

Only two blocks away lived Stella Godby. She was a fiery woman, barely hanging on to her sixties, who took great pride in her short, perfectly coiffed hair. Her home had been a bed-and-breakfast for many years. Though she had retired it a few years back, the bedrooms were still made-up, and vacant, and on the phone, she had been thrilled to be of assistance. She, like Archie, was a Ruston lifer.

"Mr. West, Mr. Barker." She beamed at the front door after introductions were made.

She wore what to Max looked like a wool Christmas sweater with a festive red, black, and white pattern— even though the season for such sweaters had long since ended.

Her house was a pleasant little two-storey made of brick with a cheery red door and window shutters. It was one of the older homes. Not one of the post-fire rebuilds.

"How are you?" Without waiting for an answer, she reached out and hugged them both. Her arms shook with laughter as she swaddled them.

So far, this town was two-for-two in producing the happiest people Max had ever met. A strange juxtaposition with the miserable weather and dying economy.

"We can't thank you enough," Oren said. "I promise that we won't be a burden. We only need a couple nights of rest. During the day, we'll be out."

"Oh, not a burden at all," Stella laughed. Her laugh was hearty, several heavy thuds in a row, and Max found it incredibly infectious. "I'm thrilled to have the company. And when the ol' sheriff asks for a favour, you can't say no!"

She was surprisingly sturdy for a woman her age. Her hair was silver, and her face creased, yet most of the wrinkles seemed to be laughter lines. Her voice was strong, as was her smile, and Max didn't doubt she had plenty of physical strength as well.

Max and Oren brought their bags inside as Archie offered a wave from the jeep, tooted his horn, and then drove off. Stella waved at him as he went.

The house smelled of fresh bread, and Stella revealed she had been baking.

"It's how I keep myself busy now," she admitted. "The neighbours like it. Keeps them coming over for visits. Otherwise, not sure how many friends I would have." At this, she let out a belly laugh again, and Max couldn't help but chuckle along with her.

The home was small, with tight hallways, and the decor certainly hadn't been modernized. The wood panelled walls encroached upon Max as he shuffled upstairs with his bag. The home was beaten down, old bones at the end of a long life, but Stella had done her best to tend to it, dressing the windows with floral printed blinds and keeping the surfaces neatly dusted and adorned with crystal figurines. Two bedrooms awaited at the top of the staircase. Oren insisted Max take the one with the larger bed.

Max's room looked out over the backyard. He could see the motel's big blue sign in the distance. When he stood fully straight, his head almost grazed the ceiling. A neatly made bed sat up against the window, and an old wooden dresser sat at its foot. This dresser was also topped with neatly arranged crystal figurines, most of which were angels.

The bed looked comfy enough and inviting for him to lay down. But the smell of bread enticed him back down to the kitchen. He needed to address his hunger. He took a minute to throw on a fresh t-shirt and then exited his room. Oren's bedroom door was closed, and Max assumed he was already asleep. Soft music played from downstairs, the beautiful tones of Andrea Bocelli, just loud enough that Max could make out what it was.

The stairs creaked gently beneath Max's feet and betrayed his arrival before he fully entered the kitchen.

"I bet you're hungry?" Stella raised an eyebrow.

She was standing at the kitchen counter, folding dish rags and towels. The woman didn't seem put out to be up at this late hour.

Max nodded fervently. "If it's not too much to ask."

"Eat, eat. Midnight snacks are the best," Stella cooed and pointed at the table.

A stack of fresh buns sat in a basket next to a plate of butter. A tray of cinnamon raisin bread rested on the other end of the table.

"This looks amazing," Max said as he sat.

The kitchen was clearly the focal point of the home. It was the largest room in the house, and while the tile floor and backsplash were certainly dated, they were also spotless. Max swore he could actually see them sparkle. Next to the table where Max sat was a large bay window that looked out into the snowy mess outside.

"Baking really is an easy way into everyone's heart," Stella said without looking up. "And in this town, you could use every last roll, loaf, and bun."

Max thought about responding, about making conversation, but he had bit into his snack, and his stomach snarled at him. He continued to stuff his face. As it turned out, Stella was content to make the conversation herself.

"I came back here to open the bed-and-breakfast ages ago, after my first marriage ended. Homes were easy to afford. It was my pride and joy for many years. A few of the folks I knew from growing up here, and they are fine people. But there was this new bunch too. Never could really crack most of 'em. There seems to be two clubs of Rustonians: Those who are neighbourly, and those who don't have a soul. A lot of families, it seems, don't like others coming into our town, buying up our land or taking up space in our restaurants and shops. They feel like Ruston is a town for no one but themselves."

"I find that hard to believe," Max said. "I haven't had the pleasure of meeting many folks, outside of yourself and Archie, but you've all been quite hospitable so far." Max eagerly buttered himself a second bun.

"Plenty of prickly folks too," Stella said. "They're probably just all hiding for the night. Watch out for that Sheriff Landry, especially. That one's a mean sucker. He'll get all bent outta sorts if you just look at him the wrong way." Stella played absently with the dish towel she was holding. "Keep an eye out, that's all."

Max agreed that they would. He devoured another bun—it melted away on his tongue—and then immediately apologized to Stella for his gluttony.

"That's what they're for, sweetie." She smiled at him.

Finally full, Max yawned heartily, only realizing it may have been rude after the act was finished.

"Go on," Stella insisted. "Get some sleep. Don't feel like you have to keep an old woman company. I better turn off my music."

Stella stepped over to the island where an old stereo sat, and she powered it off. Max missed the calming music as soon as it was gone.

"Thank you again for the bread," Max said, standing, bones creaking. "It was amazing."

"Get some rest." Stella smiled. "There are towels in the bathroom for the both of you should you need to shower."

Max had seen the shower on his way by. It didn't look large enough for Max, let alone Oren, who was taller. But as Oren said, they weren't hoping to be here long. Max smiled at Stella and exited the kitchen, turning down the creaky hallway and feeling his way along the wall for a light switch. It felt darker than when he had descended, and he couldn't quite recall the shape of this place. His heart raced a little. The shadows always made him claustrophobic.

As Max fumbled in the dark, he was startled by the sound of another Andrea Bocelli song. Only, this wasn't coming from the stereo. Someone was singing. And their voice was magnificent. The sound was coming from behind Max, down the hall the opposite way, past the living room. He turned around and stared through the darkness, trying to see what was there.

Curious, he made his way up the hall, passing the kitchen, where Stella was turned the other way, seemingly oblivious. He slipped past undetected, cut through the living room, and into the dark corridor beyond. He was in a trance, following the music.

A door had been left ajar, and a sliver of orange light leaked into the hall.

Max crept over to the door and pressed up against it, holding his breath to ensure he didn't give away his position. He lined his eye up in the narrow strip of light, peering into the room on the other side.

He was looking at a bedroom, narrow and cramped like his. On the bed sat an elderly woman, who must've been ninety or older. Her hair was thin, just white wisps of cloud atop her skull. Her eyes were small and sunken, but twinkled in the light of the bedside lamp. She stared out into another world, seeing something that wasn't there. And she was belting out opera with remarkable confidence. Not just for a woman her age. She was genuinely an amazing singer. It felt surreal to see this frail woman in her nightgown hitting notes as powerful as Bocelli himself.

The woman did not notice that she was being watched, and so she continued on with her song. She did not move; she remained perched on the bed, almost uncomfortably stiff. She looked as though she was performing out of a sense of duty, not for enjoyment. Max continued to study her until a hand on his shoulder made him gasp, and he did his best to stifle a yelp.

Stella was behind him, shushing him with a finger to her lips.

"Don't startle her," Stella said. "She gets in these states, and it can do her harm if you interrupt. Just be quiet." She led Max away from the bedroom and back toward the kitchen.

"Who is she?" Max asked when they were far enough away.

"Donna Romano," Stella said. "Wonderful old lady who used to live on this street."

"Why is she here?"

"I took her in," Stella explained. "Her granddaughter was taking care of her. But she . . ." Stella paused, a hitch in her throat. "She took her own life. One of the darker stories this town won't tell you. The history of tragedy here." She paused again, shaking off a chill, then resumed, "After the granddaughter—Natalya— died, there was no one left to take care of old Mrs. Romano. I felt for her. She had no other next of kin, and I have no family of my own in town. So, I signed up to take her, and she's been staying in my spare room ever since.

"She's a pretty easy roommate, truthfully. Doesn't say much, doesn't do much. But she will parrot any music I play. She was an opera singer, and quite a good one. She was a star in her day. That was another life, many years ago. She's not always present; dementia has her all sorts of twisted. But when she sings, there's a glimmer in her eyes. It's nice to have around."

"Her voice is beautiful," Max said.

"I think she would thank you, if she could." Stella grinned. "If she ain't singing, she ain't talking. Bit catatonic that way."

"Sorry to have been spying," Max apologized and started making his way back to his own room.

"I should have told you both," Stella admitted. "But it's not an easy story. This town . . . sometimes, it just feels cursed."

There was that word again.

"I've heard that before," Max said.

"Yeah, well, maybe that's a story for another time." Stella pursed her lips and then winked. "We'll catch up again." Then she was shooing Max off to bed.

Max bid Stella a goodnight again, and this time was able to find the light switch. He made his way up the stairs, enjoying Mrs. Romano's singing all the way until he shut his door and could no longer hear it.

*What a strange town,* Max thought. *Fires and curses and old ladies without homes.*

Max shut off the lamp and crawled into the stiff bed. By the time he had settled, he realized how painfully dark it had become. The only illumination came from some rogue streetlight that snuck through the gap between the blinds and the wall. This intruding glow cast hideous shadows upon the crystal figurines. Max became claustrophobic yet again, no longer aware of the construction of his surroundings. The darkness felt oppressive.

Max quickly got up and opened the blinds, allowing the full stream of the streetlight to pour in. To his tired retinas, this felt like the entire sun had just been called upon. Finally able to see the outline of the dresser, the pattern of the wallpaper, and the sheets on his bed, he felt safe again. This was a familiar feeling; he had grown up *terrified* of the dark.

Even as an adult, he hadn't fully been able to shake it. He had always maintained a belief that anything could be lying in wait. That sense of childlike imagination was still strong. In fact, the more he aged, the more he felt justified in this fear; the nighttime was when bad things happened, and the dark was what concealed monsters.

Max retrieved his phone, needing a distraction. He had a new text message from Janelle.

*You can take the time you need. We're all here for you. Covering until you're back.*

He toyed with the idea of a response. Maybe to ask her how she'd been or strike up a conversation just for the company. But it all felt sort of awkward. He had nothing but grief in his life right now.

He and Janelle had been close for a while. Perhaps even on the path to becoming more than friends. But he was unsettled, uncertain of what he wanted. And now he was in the middle of nowhere, trying to find a missing person.

Instead of texting Janelle back, he scrolled across news articles and sent himself down a rabbit hole, reading old missing person reports. Seldom were there happy endings. Then, realizing what he was doing to himself, he immediately pivoted and began searching for more positive material.

When finally sleep found him, Max didn't have time to prepare himself. It overtook him quickly enough that he dropped his phone onto his chest and began to snore almost immediately.

# 4. Charlie's Muse

As Max slept, more of what he had seen in Charlie's mind came back to him. It wasn't like he was reliving it, not quite, but rather it was a sudden realization all at once. He had been through this before, when he was at the airport. Only, his brain could not process it all at once. Like an overworked hard drive. The data transfer was only continuing now that he rested.

\*\*\*

Love Letter Lang was non-discriminate in his killings. He chose men and women, seemingly at random. And the lack of pattern had made it harder for police to catch him. Charlie wondered which of the unfortunate victims he would meet next.

Oren and Aria once again accompanied him to the screening room. Lang sat firmly in his chair, same as before. He donned his same shit-eating grin.

"Why don't I get to learn more about you?" Lang asked. "I don't even get to see your face?"

"You're smart enough to understand how this works," Oren replied.

"At least tell me your *real* name."

"I did. It's Harold."

"Who's with you, Harold? Who are your friends?"

"No."

While Oren dealt with their subject, Aria helped Charlie get settled in his chair.

"You feel okay?" she asked him. "About going back there?" She looked nervously at Lang.

"I'm fine," Charlie said.

"And coming back up?" Aria said. "You're okay with getting out?"

"Same as before," Charlie confirmed. "Find a dark space, shut your eyes, like you're telling yourself it's just a dream . . . then find that rising sensation and *poof.* It's not that hard, once you've had a little practice."

"Just making sure." Aria smiled, trying to be friendly. "After that one trial, where you got stuck . . ."

"I'm more experienced than that now."

Oren had done his part, and now Lang was settled enough for them to get on with their agreement. Charlie put the earpiece in as Lang cackled.

"I can hear someone in there with you, mister. There's a lady in there, I can tell." Lang made a big show of tossing his hair, greasy strands landing on his shoulders. "I haven't been in the presence of a lady in a *looong* time. You know, I used to have a girlfriend once upon a time. I really did."

Oren looked at Aria and Charlie, upset that they had been speaking while the talk button was pressed. Charlie didn't have the patience for this. He held down his own button and departed, without so much as a goodbye.

\*\*\*

Charlie materialized somewhere he did not quite expect. It took him a few moments, but he quickly realized he was not in America. On all sides of the cobblestone road upon which he stood were authentic Irish pubs, their signs welcoming patrons in for a pint. And there were plenty of patrons. The streets were jammed with bodies, people of varying levels of intoxication trying to navigate who had right of way. The encyclopedia in Charlie's mind identified the place right away: Lang's memory had brought him to the Temple Bar area of Dublin.

An evening glow hung over everything. Soon, the streetlights would come on, but for now, there was *just* enough daylight. A long day of drinking was about to turn into a long night of drinking for the thousands who were barhopping in Ireland's tourist trap.

The faces of every person who pushed past Charlie had completely melted away, just smudged oil paintings where features should've been. Of course, Lang wouldn't remember a single detail about any of these strangers in the crowd.

Some of the pub signs were legible, their gold lettering just a fraction out of focus. But most were completely distorted. The colours of the bars kept cycling. Their walls were black, then brick red, then a mossy green. Lang couldn't make up his mind.

A medley of authentic Irish music travelled out into the street from the various bars. Boisterous fiddling, guitar, and piano, all mashed together. It was a warm melody though, and it made Charlie want to dance.

Charlie had not taken Lang for a traveller. But there he was, standing next to a woman with short cropped amber hair. Her face was completely clear. It was as if the entire world had put a spotlight on her.

She had stunning eyes; her gaze was inviting. Her cheeks were rosy, and her thin eyebrows tilted playfully as she laughed. Her laugh cut through the noise of the street, passing over Charlie like silk. It was the sweetest sound he had heard. She was tucking her hair behind her ear, bashful, seemingly moving in slow motion, and Charlie felt unable to look anywhere but at her.

*Why am I here?* Charlie thought, while observing the pair. He crept closer through the crowd. Surely, with enough bodies here, they wouldn't notice him.

Suddenly a filter was cast over the scene. It was as though someone changed sliders on an old projection machine. Everything sullied just a little bit, and the colours went out of sync. The mood felt different. Charlie noticed the buildings were drifting more out of focus now.

"But, baby," Lang was saying, "you don't mean that." He was holding flowers.

"Yes, I do!" she shouted at him. "Leave me alone!"

She had an accent; she appeared to be a local. Charlie enjoyed the way her voice sounded, even in anger.

It appeared to be a lovers' quarrel. Charlie watched with great puzzlement. Then it dawned on him; Lang had been talking about a "girlfriend" as Charlie began his dive. That must have prompted a visit to this particular memory. If that was the case, Charlie wasn't anywhere near the right spot.

Charlie continued to study the fight between Lang and his girlfriend.

In spite of himself, he was enamoured; she was quite beautiful. Charlie had—somewhat intentionally—avoided the opposite sex, as he focused on his career. But a desire for romance came alive inside of him now.

There was a glow about her; everything sparkled. Perhaps it was just the way Lang remembered her, but this rubbed off on Charlie as well.

Some of their words were lost over the din, or not committed to memory, but Charlie could tell by the way she carried herself that she was smart.

She slapped Lang suddenly, and Charlie had to admit that he was rooting for her. *Hit him again.*

Lang did not like being emasculated. His eyes grew dark. Had he already killed someone by this point in time? Charlie had no idea what year it was. Lang looked a bit younger, but it was hard to tell.

If he was already a serial killer, Charlie was fearful for this woman's life.

A crowd swirled around them. All of these faceless drones became a whirlpool that swept everything away, save for Lang and his girlfriend. Charlie completed the weird triangle, the three of them like rocks sticking out from the sea as the crowd crashed around them.

"I'm leaving." The girlfriend stormed away.

"Whatever, Kelly." Lang rolled his eyes.

*Kelly,* Charlie thought. Now he had a name. Charlie had studied the list of Lang's victims, each one imprinted in his photographic mind. There was no Kelly on that list. Though there was a possibility that she was a victim they didn't yet know about.

Kelly was leaving, Lang shouted after her, but the exact message was lost in the buzz of the crowd around them and the fiddle music wafting over from a nearby haunt. The foot traffic threatened to swallow her up; she was right on the precipice.

Charlie no longer cared about Lang. He wanted to know where Kelly was going. He needed to catch up to her and find out who she was. Charlie couldn't let her disappear without knowing how to find her in the real world. To find out if she was alive or dead.

Finding victims was their mission, wasn't it?

Charlie leapt into action and began to sprint after Kelly, jogging awkwardly across the uneven cobblestone. He almost bumped into Lang as he did, but he was able to shimmy away in time. Lang had no interest in chasing Kelly. He went the opposite way.

Charlie caught glimpses of Kelly's sparkling, amber hair through the tangled mess of bodies. It was all he had to guide him. The surge of people had grown, almost to an impossible size, and now it really was a current that dragged Charlie down. He pushed out with his arms, widened his stance, trying to resist the force of these imaginary people.

He was able to squeeze over to the side of the road where a streetlamp had just come to life. He grabbed it, using it to pull himself to safety. The lamp had a concrete slab at its base, and Charlie stepped up on this to get a better view of his surroundings.

The faceless people were moving in two directions; one stream headed north and the other south, like two lanes of traffic. Some of them danced and shouted, others were stiff and just completing an order to move along with the group. A few drones milled about at barrels that were set up as tables. Staff, also faceless, served unbranded beers to those who came close enough. The whole congregation bounced along to the melody of the unseen fiddle music.

It was as if the everything was just the throbbing body of a giant snake, slithering through the streets of Dublin.

The light was fading; the memory was likely nearing its end. Charlie scanned the crowd and finally spotted Kelly again. She was also pushing through the masses, moving counter to their flow, heading toward the Temple Bar itself.

Charlie jumped back into the chaos and fought against the flow of bodies. Faces without faces glared at him as he shoved them out of the way. All of this exposure, the contact with these drones, was risky. Charlie was facing detection by interfering with pieces of this memory.

"Please, move," Charlie willed them.

But they wouldn't, until he grabbed them by the shoulders and tossed them to the side. He turned his body sideways, cutting through groups of friends like a knife through butter. He was able to *just barely* squeeze between openings right before they closed.

Charlie contorted himself in this way, frantically trying to get closer to the Temple Bar. He was breaking his own rules. *When faced with reconstructions, act as they would.* That was the way to avoid detection. *Blend in with your surroundings. Do as the locals do.* But here was Charlie, running against the grain. It was the most Charlie had flirted with danger since taking over duties as a MemCom diver.

The cobblestone road was uneven, and his toe caught a stone. Charlie stumbled and collapsed to the ground. He immediately had to shield himself from the legs and shoes that began to trample him. In the real world, perhaps he would be beaten and bruised. It certainly felt as though he was being battered at the bottom of this sea. But this wasn't real, Charlie reminded himself, and where most dreamers were powerless, he held some power. He was a lucid dreamer, and he *knew* that all of this was just a reenactment.

He built himself up to be strong, ignored the pain, and told himself he was tougher than all of these faceless drones. And he stood. He muscled the entire stampede off him and rose. Then he began to push again. In between the shadows of strangers in front of him, he saw Kelly and her wonderful, shining hair disappear into the Temple Bar, passing through the front door, and then an anonymous bartender offered her a beer.

Charlie stiff-armed something that was supposed to be a person and knocked it sideways. Charlie ducked under the outstretched arms of a blurry man and then jumped to the left and found an open lane. He had to swing his arms like a windmill, fending off those who tried to step into this laneway. He stretched out his stride as long as he could and quickly closed in on the Temple Bar door.

The fiddle music was slowing down now, distorting into something horrible. Heads turned and stared at him as he muscled his way up to the door. Lang's mind was catching on.

*Kelly,* Charlie thought. *What is your last name? Where are you from?*

He was there now, stepping into the doorway without thinking and passing through it too easily. Charlie was disoriented as everything around him went black and then flickered back to life, another change on the projection machine.

\*\*\*

Of course, the door had brought him away from the streets of Dublin. Doors were the gateway into other memories. And as Charlie looked around now, he saw he was in a farmer's field. A large, abandoned barn stood to his left, blotting out most of the starry sky. The world was all shrouded in blackness, and the only other thing he could make out was a decrepit stone well over fifty feet away across the grass.

Kelly was not here, as she had been lost the second that she passed through the doors. Charlie sagged, having lost his chance to catch her. He did not have long to sulk though, as Lang emerged from the abandoned barn dragging a body behind him. Short raven-coloured hair. Pale skin. Long limbs. *I know your case too,* Charlie thought.

Oren must have forced Lang to change topics, and now he was thinking about murder again. Charlie was where he needed to be.

Charlie's own thoughts remained behind, still roaming the streets of Dublin as he stood there and watched the burial. Lang was remarkably more proficient this time around. He had dug a hole ahead of time. Aside from the hole, there was absolutely nothing remarkable about the spot he chose. He dropped the body in with no regard for the life it used to contain. He filled the hole. And then he began raking.

Lang raked a large area, so that the entire field was uniform, and thus the grave was indistinguishable from the rest. Then he began to sprinkle grass seed. Charlie stared with benign interest.

Lang wrapped up his moonlit gardening and left the field, nearly brushing into Charlie as he passed. Charlie hardly noticed. All he could think of was a name: *Kelly*. How many Kellys could there be in Dublin?

Before the memory could leave him behind, Charlie shut his eyes and focused on the darkness. He felt himself become lighter, rising to the surface, and he pulled himself out.

\*\*\*

"Jesus, Charlie, you really can't narrow it down for us?" Oren asked, the hot sun beating down on them and the countless men and women digging in the field.

The setting had changed greatly. The grass had grown in thick tufts, and it was impossible to tell where Lang's garden began and the existing grass ended. The search area was large enough that despite digging for hours, they had uncovered nothing but a shoebox containing hamster bones (Although, that had at least provided them with a moment's excitement).

"I'm sorry, I don't remember," Charlie said, his voice adrift.

Oren eyed him up. He could tell that Charlie's head was elsewhere. But neither Oren, nor Aria, nor anyone else had time to worry about Charlie's mental state. They had all been rocked by the news when Charlie emerged.

Lang had been travelling.

None of them knew this about their subject. And the fact that he had kept it hidden so well was stunning. Lang had spent considerable time abroad during an earlier part of his life. And now there was serious speculation that perhaps this meant he had victims overseas. Victims they did not know about.

Charlie silently prayed that Kelly was not one of them.

The team was frustrated. The sun was unseasonably warm, and the success of the first body retrieval had set high expectations. That job required divers, and it was still faster than this romp through the farmyard.

It had been hard enough to find the right field. The barn had burnt down, and the brick well was the only thing left to help mark the location. Charlie hadn't given them much to go off, and he lacked any real conviction. He had gotten sloppy, and there seemed to be some growing agitation amongst the crew. This agitation was misdirected at Oren, however, since no one knew that Charlie had been in Lang's mind.

"What makes us think it's even here?" one man shouted over to Oren.

"Lang told us," Oren said, only half lying. "It's here."

"I wouldn't believe that fucker," another man groaned. "Probably just wanted to make us dig all day."

Oren was starting to believe this as well. He glanced over at Charlie again, wondering if he had been fully honest.

As the sun dipped toward the horizon and the heat finally let up, granting them a bit of cool relief, a triumphant yell came from far out in the centre of their dig site.

"I've got something!" a woman yelled, trying not to sound too pleased.

Everyone breathed a sigh of relief when it was revealed to be the victim's body—a strange sensation that would later turn to guilt.

"Next time, let's try to take note of exactly where he buries them," Oren mumbled to Charlie, patting him firmly on the chest, not hiding his annoyance. "Now let's go inform the family."

# 5. Find a Dark Corner

MAX WAS ACCUSTOMED TO THE sun waking him, since he so often ended up opening blinds to avoid the pitch-black darkness. It was a nice way to wake up. Not like this, not like having Oren shake him.

"We have to go," Oren said, his hand on Max's shoulder. "I'm sorry."

Max rolled over and realized it was still dark out. He hated that. Nothing made one feel less rested than waking up before the dawn.

It was quarter after five, and Oren was already dressed. Max rushed through getting ready and met Oren downstairs. Oren was waiting at the front door. He was anxious; this was game day.

They stepped outside together, and the morning air punched Max in the gut. His breath hung in front of his face with every exhale. The cold was relentless, closing in on them. Max's entire body was already rigid, shoulders shrugged up to try and fight off the chills. This was quite possibly the coldest he'd ever felt.

The orange jeep was pulled up out front, headlights cutting through clouds of exhaust. The low rumble from the engine seemed to be the only sound in the world until the snow on the walkway crunched under their feet. Everything was dampened, however, by the white padding across the earth.

"Did you even get any sleep?" Oren asked as they piled in.

"Don't need much," Archie said, voice still hearty. "Coffees in the cupholders for you lads."

They thanked their gracious chauffeur and sipped on the caffeine during the short drive. The town was still quiet, night having not lifted its veil yet. They pulled up next to a squat, old building with ornate windows and impressive brickwork. Only after reading the sign above the doors did Max realize he had no idea what they were doing.

"Library?" Max asked.

"The Thomas family arranged it," Oren said as he opened his door. "We needed a better setup than the sheriff's station offered. Apparently, this was the solution."

"I'm around if you need me," Archie said as they departed. "Won't go far."

Oren and Max wandered up the walkway, cautious of the snow drifts that had been scattered like landmines. As they neared the door, a man opened it from inside and ushered them forwards. They knocked the snow off their boots as the door closed behind them.

"Gentlemen."

The man who greeted them was strikingly tall. Just like Oren. The two stood eye to eye and towered over Max. Their greeter also was dressed in a suit, with a long trench coat draped over top. His salt-and-pepper hair was gelled liberally, appearing wet. Expensive cologne hit Max's nostrils as they gathered in the foyer with the man.

"I'm Robert Thomas."

*So, this is the Grim Reaper,* Max thought. The man's face was unreadable, his posture intimidating. Max understood the reputation.

"Nice to meet you, officially." Oren shook his hand first. "I'm Oren. This is my associate, Max Barker."

Thomas barely glanced at Max, offering a flaccid handshake before returning his attention to Oren. "I've heard great things about your work on the Lang case, Mr. West."

"Thank you," Oren said. "I hope we can have the same success here today."

Max knew Oren well enough to detect the awkwardness in his voice. He was blushing inwardly.

"Yes, well, let's cut straight to it," Thomas said.

Heat blasted them from vents along both sides of the cramped foyer. Max welcomed it. Behind Thomas was another set of doors that led into the library itself. Max could see a couple shapes standing near the bookshelves. A few lights had been turned on, but for the most part, the library was dark.

Thomas cleared his throat and laid out the plan. "The space is prepared in the way you asked for it to be," he said. "Floyd Smith is inside. They've actually got him cuffed and sitting in the children's section. You'll be able to conduct your interview with him there."

"Who else is on site?" Oren asked.

"Sheriff Landry and two of his deputies, Sanderson and Bennet, or something," Thomas said, looking back at the shadows lingering beyond the doors.

"You don't mind giving us privacy while we conduct the interview?" Oren asked. "We have more success when law enforcement isn't present. With Lang, we had only myself and my associates on hand."

Thomas scratched his chin with his large hand. He looked uneasy. Clearly, he wanted to be there for the interview.

"Well," Thomas began.

He seemed to be weighing his options. He looked at Oren. He had heard so much about the man's reputation. All of Love Letter Lang's victims had been located. Thomas seemed to be waiting for the silence to break Oren. For Oren to concede. But the two men just stared at one another. Max was very uncomfortable, but he understood what Oren was doing. They needed the privacy in order to use the MemCom. Despite Thomas' position as the client, he'd need to back down on this.

"We really only need a few moments alone," Oren said. Then to add to the lie, he tacked on, "To build up trust. After that, you are free to join us and listen in."

This seemed to help ease the tension.

Thomas nodded. "I'll keep Landry and his deputy over here."

"Great." Oren grinned. "Then we should be all set."

"Make sure you find her," Thomas said.

Until now, they had only seen Thomas the District Attorney. Now, they were getting the father.

"We will," Oren said.

Max's stomach did flips at this. Oren's confidence was great, but he wasn't the one doing this for the first time. He wasn't the one tasked with entering another man's mind and finding a missing person.

"Shall we head in and meet the sheriff?"

"Buckle up," Thomas said. "The man is an asshole."

They stepped inside the library and were hit with the comforting aroma of books. Max flashed back to his childhood, spending time with his nose in any novel he could get his hands on, and the fresh scent of unturned pages. That bliss was universal.

The two shadows who had been conversing by the shelves stepped over toward them, walking into the reach of one of the few overhead lights that had been turned on. Now they could make out the sheriff's face. His hair was slicked back, and his skin was pockmarked and sun-damaged. It looked as though cigarettes had been put out on the man's face. Sheriff Landry's formidable gut bulged out, and his sheriff's uniform was untucked a little bit.

"You the PI?" the sheriff croaked.

He had a gravelly drawl. His upper lip was strangely smooth. Whereas the rest of his face had stubble, this patch was completely bald, as if burned or scarred. Little beads of sweat formed here, and he wiped them away with his thumb.

"Oren West." Oren offered up his hand.

Landry did not take it. He just eyed them both. "Sheriff Landry," Landry completed the formalities. "Sheriff more than a decade now. Ain't nobody knows this town better. This here's Sanderson." He motioned to his fellow deputy.

Sanderson had a baby face but covered it with a rust-coloured beard that matched his hair, and it was difficult to place his exact age.

"Nice to meet you both. This is my associate, Max Barker," Oren said. "He's going to help me conduct the interview."

Landry was slow in his responses. He was studying them as if they were animals at the zoo. It was meant to be imposing. Max was sure it wasn't working on Oren—he was never fazed by this sort of thing—but it made Max feel incredibly small. His presence here did not seem to register with anyone they had met so far.

"Look," Landry said, offering a dry laugh. "You really think you're going to get him to crack? We've tried everything already. More than what's legal. Now you're going to read him a fucking book, and he's going to tell you everything?"

Oren's face went cold. "We're confident, yes. We have been trying a different approach. A negotiation tactic that fosters trust. And it has worked for us in the past."

Landry coughed, something like a sputtering engine trying to come to life. When he finished, he grinned with yellow teeth. "We're all adults here," he said. "So, we don't have to worry about hurting feelings. I don't give a shit what tactics you wanna try. Go nuts. But things work different here. Just cause it *worked in the past* doesn't mean shit now. This is Ruston. Things are always different in Ruston. Just remember that this is my town. And you big city folks ain't better than us. No one wants you here, but we'll tolerate it for the Thomas family. Keep that in mind, and we'll get along. Shit, I might even send you off with a gift basket."

"I'm hoping we can make this quick," Oren said, unwavering. "I know the Thomases want their daughter home."

"Well then, let me show you to your room," Landry said with a sarcastic gesture of greeting.

He marched down the aisles, bookshelves towering on either side. They followed closely. Thomas was in the rear, speaking to Sanderson. Landry took this opportunity to lean in and whisper one last remark to Oren.

"When you find out where the body is, you let me know first," Landry said.

"We don't know she's dead, Sheriff," Oren replied. "We're hoping to find her alive."

"Right." Landry snorted.

The library was modest in size, and it wasn't long before they found the children's section. This area was actually walled off, a big glass divider separating it from the other books. In this corner, the walls were decorated with quotes, pictures from Dr. Seuss, and colourful cartoon animals. Small shreds of paper made to look like smiling worms were taped all over the shelves, each one declaring, "I'm a bookworm!" Other stickers had been arranged on the glass wall to spell out *Reading Is Where We Come to Grow.*

The glass was lightly frosted, and they could just make out the shape of a man in a chair on the other side. A third deputy—a woman in her late thirties, with a square jaw, who was yawning widely—nodded as they approached.

"You can go home now, Bennet," Landry said. "The investigators say they won't be long."

Deputy Bennet shambled away whout a word, a zombie inching through the aisles.

Landry led them around the glass divider and into the children's section, where Floyd was snoozing in his seated position. His head was tilted to one side, drool forming in the corner of his mouth. Floyd was wearing what he had been arrested in—a filthy t-shirt and jeans. Even in the absence of an orange jumpsuit, a flashback was triggered for Max. He felt as though he was looking at Leonard Lang.

"Wake up, shit head!" Landry shouted.

Floyd flinched, suddenly on high alert and scanning the room. His wide eyes were bloodshot. Oren noticed bruises on his neck and across the bridge of his nose. Small-town justice.

"These folks want a word."

"Who are you?" Floyd asked.

He looked like a cornered animal, immediately distrusting of these new humans in his habitat. His hands were cuffed behind his back, and he seemed to be tethered to the chair he was in because it shifted with him as he stretched his legs.

Oren introduced himself again and said they just wanted a brief conversation. He closed by asking Floyd if he was okay to agree to this. Floyd looked dumbfounded. It seemed like no one had been giving him much choice of anything lately. After consideration, Floyd nodded.

"We can take it from here," Oren said, dismissing Landry.

"The hell? I'm supposed to leave you alone with him?" Landry said.

"We're going to give them a few minutes." Thomas stepped in at last, as was their agreement. "We'll wait by the foyer."

"Fuck that." Landry forced one of his false laughs. "This is a homicide suspect. I'm not leaving you alone."

Again, Oren was agitated by the sheriff's assumption that Tiffany was already dead. He could see by the look on Thomas' face that he felt the same way.

"Sheriff," Thomas said. "Give them a few minutes." He stepped over to Landry and placed a firm hand on his shoulder.

Thomas could be plenty imposing when he tried. This microaggression worked.

"Five minutes," Landry said. His face was turning red. He did not like yielding control. He was the type of authority for whom power was the ultimate currency. And right now, Landry was going broke. But he was also smart enough to understand what defying Thomas would do for his department. "We'll be back."

Thomas shepherded Landry and Sanderson down the way they had come, and soon the shadows of the semi-lit library obscured their departure.

"We won't be long," Oren said, smiling at Floyd.

Max didn't like the idea of being courteous to a kidnapper. But he understood the assignment was to play good cop now.

"You and I will just have a brief conversation about the past few days. Max here will be taking notes in the other room. It's just you and I. Okay?"

"They fuckin' hit me," Floyd said. His eyes had tracked the sheriff's departure. He seemed eager to speak now that they were gone. "They fuckin' choked me and hit me and beat me. Whole town's got it out for me. Landry's always been a prick. Tryin' to lock me away for whatever he can. You've gotta tell someone what he's doing."

"I'm aware there was an interrogation," Oren said, again eying the bruises. "But if there was any abuse, I can look into reporting it."

"You need to do somethin' about 'im." Floyd locked eyes with Oren now. "He's out to get me."

"He is trying to find Tiffany, and get her home safe," Oren reminded Floyd.

"Then he's beating the wrong guy," Floyd said. "Who do *you* work for, anyhow?"

"The Thomas family hired us," Oren said. "Mr. Smith, are you saying you didn't take Tiffany? Because now would be the time to clear that up."

Floyd just stared at him. There was both defiance and defeat in his eyes, and this contradictory cocktail made him look drunk.

"You're one of 'em," Floyd sighed. "Another Thomas goon. He's as bad as Landry." Floyd motioned downward with his chin, a cumbersome motion. He seemed to be indicating the bruises on his neck. "Thomas was the one who did this."

"I can speak to the right people about the sheriff," Oren said. "And see about maybe getting you some proper representation. I heard you declined your right to a lawyer?"

"What's the point?" Floyd asked. "They all do whatever the Thomas family asks 'em to. Er'ybody in this shit town grovels at his feet."

"Well, we can get you one, someone independent," Oren tried. "But we don't have long. And first, we need to ask you a few questions, alright?"

"You're no different than them," Floyd said. "If you're on his payroll, you're just another Thomas goon."

Max expected Oren to keep arguing, to deny this, and say they weren't anything like the sheriff or Thomas. That they were the good guys. But he didn't.

"Excuse us," Oren said instead.

He pulled Max aside, and they left the children's section.

On the other side of the glass wall, Oren whispered to Max. "We need to hurry. He's losing faith in us. He's shutting down."

"What do we do?"

"Dive. Now," Oren said. "You stay here. Sit against the glass, so you're supported. I'm going back in there. But you'll be closest to him from this spot. You can travel through the glass. I'll play him something, and you should end up in his mind, not mine. I'll stay at the far side of the room."

"Then what?"

"You've got to find the memory Floyd has of Tiffany and see what he did with her. Where he took her. But be careful. This isn't like Charlie's head. Or mine. We don't know Floyd. You don't know what's running through his mind. I will try and ask questions that provoke the right memories. It'll make it easier for you to find things."

"Feels like there's a lot here for me to fuck up," Max said.

"You'll find her."

"I'm not just talking about that," Max said. "I mean, am I going to be okay? Am I gonna die in there?"

"Nah, it's only dangerous if you talk to anyone, touch anything, go through the wrong door, or can't get yourself out."

The joke didn't land. Max frowned.

"No, Max. You'll be fine."

"Ok," Max said.

His heart clattered against his chest. He was certain he was in shock. His body moved without him now. His lips spoke without consulting his brain. He didn't mean to say ok. What he actually wanted to say was *no.*

"Let's be quick," Oren said.

And with that, he was gone. Max could see his shape appear on the other side of the fogged glass. His hand moved down to his pocket, and he felt the shape of the MemCom inside. This was really happening. If it had been a dream, he would've known.

Max slouched against the wall, trying to calm himself by breathing. He retrieved the earpiece and put it in his ear. Behind him, he could hear the muffled voices as Oren asked Floyd some questions.

"Humour me," Oren was saying. "I'd like to play some music. I find it helpful."

And then it began. Oren had chosen "Bohemian Rhapsody." Now Freddy Mercury was coaxing Max to jump.

The concept of sending himself into another's mind felt too science fiction to be true. Even the inherent danger seemed fictitious. He figured he had not yet registered that his life was at stake. It was the only way Max could rationalize why he was still proceeding with things, given how much could go wrong.

What would they think when they found his body lying dead here in the library? That he'd had a stroke?

The music continued, and Max realized he better not delay any further. It was best to just jump. So, he forced himself not to think. And he reached up to press the button. He counted down in his mind.

Three.

He heard a voice somewhere far off. It sounded muffled.

Two.

"Forgot my keys," the voice was saying.

One.

The zombie deputy—Bennet—had meandered back down toward them and was bent over, picking something up off the floor. She didn't appear to see Max from where he sat in the shadows. She twirled a set of keys around her finger and turned to leave, yawning.

And that was the last thing Max saw before the world went dark.

***

The first thing Max became aware of was the jangling of keys. A ring packed with a dozen various keys hung from the car's ignition. The radio was on low, some easy rock guitar riff that he did not recognize.

Max was sitting in the back seat of a sedan. The only other person in the car was the driver, a young woman with a square jaw and a vaguely familiar face. He could see a sliver of it in the rearview mirror from where he sat.

*Where's Floyd?*

The sense of motion hit Max next. They were flying along a highway at a great speed. The world's light was fading; the sun was setting before them, casting a blinding glare. The windows were carrying frost, which had only partially been scraped away. The trees outside were dead and bare, but the ground was brown. No white stuff yet.

Max tried to scan his surroundings. The world was passing by too quickly for him to make out the finer details. There were no signs indicating where they were. And he didn't see any other cars either.

*Where the hell am I?*

The driver made a sound of agitation. She was shielding her eyes against the glare. This brought Max's attention forwards, to the dashboard. He saw a bobblehead affixed in the corner. It was a small horse with enormous eyes. The horse smiled, taunting Max as it bobbed its head along to the rhythm of the road.

Nothing Oren had taught Max had prepared him for an encounter like this. He looked for doors, but the only ones were those which lead from the safety of the car out onto the pavement. He was trapped here.

His breathing started to speed up as he became aware of the time crunch. How was he going to find answers from the back seat of this sedan? And who was the woman driving the car? Max felt his "body" here with him. He could tell his legs were too long for the seat, even with his back pressed against the seat. Much like his dive into Oren's mind, this all felt real. Max was himself, and he was whole. Which made him vulnerable.

He tried to use his re-created body to inch forwards. Maybe he could get a better look at the woman driving if he could see more of her face. He braced himself against the seat and leaned ahead.

As Max stuck his head between the two front seats, he heard a gasp. Through the glare of the sunset, he thought he saw the faint outline of a large, antlered animal. Max's blood went cold.

The driver slammed on the brakes.

Max catapulted forwards, and all of his weight launched into the front seat. He felt the windshield—or maybe his ribs—crack as he hit it, then lost all sense of direction as he ricocheted into the passenger seat, legs up. He heard tires squealing. He tried to right himself, but the car was spinning; inertia worked against him. He could only look up helplessly and see the desperate look on the driver's face as they barreled off the road.

*Make it stop.*

Max was pinned in this awkward position until the car hit the ditch. Then everything flipped. The car spun violently to the side, now fully upside down in midair.

Everything slowed.

It was as though they were travelling through a thick jelly. The car still moved but barely, an inch at a time. The memory had all but come to a halt; the taunting horse bobblehead was no longer nodding. The driver's trauma played everything back in slow motion. Yet Max was able to move at his regular speed.

This gave him a chance to act. His feet were on the ceiling, which was now acting as the floor. His shoulder and arm were lodged under the console, and he took a moment to free himself. The popping sensation in his arm was a little too real for his liking.

The driver was frozen in place, destined to carry out the remaining moments of this accident the way it had occurred. But Max had no intention of sticking around until the car hit the ground. He maneuvered himself into a position where he could reach the door handle. Beads of coffee from an overturned mug floated toward him, as if in zero gravity, obscuring his view. He brushed them away and pulled at the handle.

Feeling a bit like an astronaut, he propelled himself through the open door, pushing his way into the frozen world beyond. Gravity pulled at him suddenly, and he plummeted to the earth with a thud.

\*\*\*

The ground was hard. Max's entire body ached. But his bruises became a secondary concern when he realized that he had jumped memories. He had bailed on the car accident and wound up on a dirty carpet somewhere else.

This space was lit with a combination of incandescent bulbs and flashing red and blue streaks that sent shadows dancing across the plain, beige walls. Max recognized it right away as a motel room. And not a very glamorous one. The carpet and bedding were both a regrettable maroon pattern. The art on the wall was just a smudge of colours, not fully formed here. The television set was on but flickered nonsensical patterns. These details were not maintained.

Captured more clearly were the pair of deputies that stood in front of Max, obstructing his view. He got to his feet but was pinned between the deputies and the wall. The door to the motel room had been left open, and the cool night air was tickling Max. It actually felt good on his sore ribs.

The red and blue flicker came through the open door from a police car outside. Something had happened here. Max moved forwards, trying to peer around the deputies. But they kept adjusting, blocking his view. He crouched down, glancing between their arms as they conversed.

"What do you think happened?" one deputy said.

"What do you mean? Look at her," the other answered. "It's obvious."

Finally, Max found the gap he needed, and he saw what the deputies were looking at. A girl was hanging from a rope tied to the ceiling fan. Her body was rigid, facing away from them. Her lifeless arms and legs were exposed; she was clad only in shorts and a shirt. Her calf was decorated with a bird tattoo, but the type of bird kept changing; the beholder of this memory wasn't quite certain on which bird it was. What was far more concrete—and revolting—was the skin around the poor girl's neck, which was stained a deep purple.

The way that her toes dangled a foot off the ground made Max sick to his stomach.

The rope that the girl hung from was starting to twist, and the body was coming around to face them.

"I'll let the sheriff know it's a suicide," one deputy said and then left.

Now it was just the second deputy and Max. Max straightened, studying the face of this second deputy. He recognized her now. She was the driver of the car, probably still suspended upside down. She was also the same tired-looking deputy from the library. The one who had come back for her keys.

*I'm in the wrong mind*, Max realized.

By the time Max looked back at the body, the hanging girl had rotated completely, and her face was staring straight at him. The sides of the memory grew dark, and it was as if someone stuck a telescope in front of him. The horrific image of the girl was amplified in the memory. Her tongue stuck out from between her blue lips. Her eyes were wide and glassy. A fly had landed on her forehead and was walking in a zigzag down toward her eye, stepping right over its surface without being blinked away.

There was a low rumble somewhere beneath it all. Something wasn't right.

The dead girl's face seemed to be growing, coming straight at them with all the evil intent and unnatural speed of a poltergeist.

The face seemed to be lashing out at him, and Max stumbled backwards through the open door.

\*\*\*

Max was on his backside, looking up at the sky. His ears were bombarded with shouting, air horns, and explosions. The sky was thick with smoke, hanging low over the world and capturing all of the streetlights and fires that were burning in trashcans nearby. He was seated on a stretch of asphalt that was probably a road but was so thick with debris that it was hard to be certain.

On Max's one side was a line of riot police. They donned their dark armour, standing tensely in formation. One of the officers adjusted her headgear, and Max recognized her as the deputy from the previous memory.

On Max's other side was a swell of protestors. An angry sea of people were dressed in masks and makeshift body armour. They held signs that read: *My Mind, My Rights* and *Stop Spying, You Pervs.* Some held bricks, and sparklers, and bottles. They were chanting something nonsensical, attempting to provoke a response from the riot police.

The small stretch of ground that Max occupied was the DMZ. Soon a war was going to break out, and Max was right in the middle.

"You can't have our minds!" a man shouted, stepping forwards from the fray.

The group clustered around him roared in agreement. He planted his feet and swung a brick forwards with all his might. It cleared the neutral territory between the two groups and collided against one officer's shield with a dull *thunk*.

Max rose to his feet, needing to get out of the line of fire. But once standing, he wasn't sure what side to run to.

The police retaliated by firing a projectile of their own. A canister rolled across the pavement, sending trails of smoke rising into the air.

"Tear gas!" the brick-thrower screamed.

Half of the protestors turned to run away, and the other half summoned their courage, rushing the line of police.

A woman holding a *Memories R Sacred* sign crashed into Max and knocked him back to the ground. Half a dozen others trampled over him. He cowered. The tear gas canister was right next to Max's face, and the sting in his eyes was real. He could no longer see. His entire face felt like it was melting away. More feet hammered down on his ribs, knocking all the air from his lungs.

An explosion sounded off somewhere nearby, then another. Max could tell the sky was lighting up in red, even through his tears. Officers shouted, protestors charged, and there was a series of sickening crunches as flesh and bone were battered.

The earth started shaking beneath Max's feet. He figured this was the end; he would die at this protest.

But the shaking grew stronger, and the very fabric of the memory started to tear. Max was jostled free from the memory as if it had all been a dream.

***

"Max, come back." Oren was shaking him awake.

The world felt disorienting and at odds with itself. The weight of his body took some getting used to. His eyes still burned, and his ribs still ached. But he was back, and relieved.

"Who . . . What . . ."

"That deputy—Deputy Bennet—came back to get something and interfered with the dive," Oren explained.

Max remembered now. The zombie deputy that Landry had excused from the library. This was the same woman who had been driving the car. The same woman who was in the motel room with him. And the officer from the protest.

"That was awful," Max said.

His entire body ached. All of his injuries seemed to carry over, though they were only echoes of the pain he had experienced while in the mind.

"Not an ideal start, no, but she's gone," Oren said. "We only have a few more minutes before Thomas and Landry will get agitated and want answers. We need to hurry."

"Hurry . . . what?"

"We need to try the dive again, Max," Oren said.

Max was shocked. He had just barely survived a nightmare created by Deputy Bennet's mind. It was about as bad as one's first day on the job could go. And now Oren expected him to try again.

"You don't know what it was like in there." Max shook his head, refusing the assignment. "You said I'd be fine. And I wasn't. I almost *died*."

"It was a fluke."

"I need a break, at least," Max pleaded. His vision had returned, and he saw the urgency on Oren's face.

"There isn't time." Oren looked back down the aisles, worried about their privacy.

"What if it happens again?"

"It won't." Oren gripped Max's shoulder, trying to calm him. "That was an accident. That's all. The others have all obeyed the instruction to leave us alone. And once you're in his mind, we only need a few seconds of real-world time. It was a bad first attempt, but we'll get it this time."

"I don't think you understand." Max was stunned. "That wasn't anything like the Cuckoo's Nest with you. Things didn't make sense in there. And it happened so fast."

"It will get better," Oren said. "You're learning. It's like training. Gotta get back on that horse."

"You do it, then," Max said, frustrated.

"I wish I could. I've always wanted to. It pains me that I can't lucid dream like you." Oren gave him a reproachful look.

In spite of himself, Max felt like he was disappointing his friend, and since childhood, he had always sought the approval of others. Especially Oren. Confident, cool, Oren.

"If I could dive, I'd have done this all myself. But I really, truly need your help, Max."

"It was a riot," Max said after a breath. His ribs no longer ached at every inhale. He was collecting his thoughts. He needed to sound it out, to be talked off the ledge. "The memory had nothing to do with the case."

"It was a stranger," Oren explained. "She could've been triggered to think of that memory by something else. Or she could have been daydreaming. With Floyd, it will be different. I'll be asking him questions that guide his thinking. Deputy Bennet had no guide rails. And that's what made it unpredictable. You'll have a better shot in Floyd's head, at least of landing in memories that occurred around the time Tiffany went missing."

Max ran a hand through his hair. His fingers were ice cold, and it sent a chill down his spine. It served to wake him, to clear his head.

"It's not real," Max said.

Oren stared at him, trying to follow where he was headed.

"So, if something bad happens, I can just pull myself out. I don't need you to shake me again. Right?"

"Absolutely." Oren nodded. "Do you remember from Charlie . . . how to get yourself out?"

"Yeah, I think I do." Max recalled Charlie at the quarry. He placed himself in a dark corner, and— shutting off his senses—was able to find that rising feeling, floating out from the deep.

"Ok, you've got this," Oren said with his trademark grin. "And if anything goes off track, find a dark corner and get yourself out."

So, Max tried again.

*\*\*\**

The landing was softer.

Max—to great relief—found himself inside a relatively mundane memory. A part of him had expected gunfire, explosions, and danger. Instead, Floyd was underneath a truck—an old vintage pickup of some sort, Max was never good at identifying car models—tinkering away, his coveralls splattered in grease and oil. He appeared to be the only one in the garage, or at least, the only one in the memory.

Floyd started humming to himself. He was humming "Bohemian Rhapsody."

Though he had no lungs, not really, Max forced himself to breathe, and he relished in the fact that there was a smell. The garage had a real smell, the usual rubber and oil and sweat of any shop. The smell helped to distract from the fact that this was a simulation. Max was in a garage, something very ordinary and not at all scary. He could do this.

The bay door was open, but whatever lay beyond was lost in a sea of bright sunlight, unrealistically white and hot. Beneath the truck, it was shaded and cool, and Max crouched to see what Floyd was doing. His face was twisted in concentration, working hard on something.

"Pass that wrench?" Floyd asked and held his hand out.

Max held his breath. Had he gotten too close?

"Got it!" a voice called out.

A figure shuffled into view beside Max. The bearer of the wrench was a teenaged girl. She had a youthful, slender face and doe-like eyes. Max had seen her image before.

Tiffany Thomas.

"That's the wrong one," Floyd grunted after being handed the tool.

He tossed it back in the girl's direction, missing her. The wrench skittered across the floor. Floyd held out his hand again, expectantly.

"Sorry." Tiffany's voice was small.

She turned back to where his tools sat, laid out haphazardly in a tray, and rushed to get him the right wrench. The tools all appeared hazy, and Max couldn't tell them apart. A couple of other items around the garage seemed to be shapeshifting. A poster on the far wall that had started out as an image of a bright sports car now was displaying a bikini-clad model.

"Would ya hurry up, girl?" Floyd said. His agitation rose out from under the truck like steam.

"This one?" she asked, handing him another option.

"Damn it." Floyd slid out from under the truck. "No. It's that one, there." He grabbed the wrench himself. "That's what I get for bringing on summer help."

Tiffany stared at the ground. She was red-faced, seemingly holding back tears. Max knew Tiffany spent her summers in Ruston. And given who her father was, he imagined she would've been hard to turn away from a summer job. But Floyd didn't seem thrilled about this arrangement. Perhaps Robert Thomas had forced it on them both as a way to teach Tiffany a lesson, or to keep her humble.

Max also realized that this likely wasn't the memory he needed. If Tiffany was here, working, it wasn't the right time of year.

"Ya don't catch on quick, do ya?" Floyd said. He stared at her with his sneering face too close to hers.

She made brief eye contact, muttered something inaudible, and broke it off again.

Max felt himself tense up. His stomach was rising slowly in his chest. He did not want to be seeing this. It made him uneasy to watch this sort of verbal abuse and not do anything. Though, he wondered if he would've done anything in the real world either.

"Y'know what, get outta here," Floyd said.

"What?" Tiffany asked.

"You're just slowin' me down, so go home," Floyd said.

"But," Tiffany stammered, looking around for support. There was no one but the bikini model to look back at her. "It's only eleven."

"Call it a half day." Floyd waved a hand dismissively. "Just go."

Tiffany took a step away from Floyd and then stopped, finding a brief flash of courage that didn't exist before.

"You know, my dad—"

"Yer dad what?" Floyd interrupted. "Ya wanna play that game? Go tell yer dad. I'd love to have a chitchat with him about you and yer friends smokin' behind the shop on the weekends."

Tiffany froze.

"Yeah. That's what I thought," Floyd said. "Get outta here, and I'll still pay ya for the day. How about that? Just get outta my hair."

Tiffany turned without another word and marched out of the garage. She stepped across the beaming, bright threshold of the bay door and vanished.

*Doors,* Max thought. That was what he needed, too. He needed to get from here to February 6. Doors were the gateway to other memories. But the only door he saw was the same giant bay door that Tiffany had stepped through. Did that even count?

The world beyond the bay door was obscured in that all-engrossing white light. It smelled a bit like a summer day. It seemed like the sun could've been responsible for the light that came in the window on the far wall, as well as the bay door itself. But there was no way to tell what was out there. It all felt foreboding. There was no shape, no border, just whiteness. Max might fall off the edge of the world, for all he knew.

He wished he had asked Oren more questions. What counted as a door?

But he was here. Alone. In Floyd's mind. And in his garage. His sense of time was unreliable because he didn't understand how much time had elapsed back in the library. He needed to just act.

Max went straight toward the bay door without any further hesitation.

*Let's hope it's like a dream,* he thought. *If I start falling, I'll just wake up.*

He stepped through the door. The light engulfed him. He had just a moment to fear that this was the end before the light dimmed into something more comfortable. It had worked. He had stepped into another memory.

\*\*\*

"I've got nothin' to say to the sheriff," Floyd groaned, exasperated. "And I've got nothin' to say to you."

"You realize I'm trying to help you," Oren said. "If you can't clear yourself, you're going to go to jail. And if we can't find Tiffany, it could be for a long time."

Floyd was silent, pouting like a child. His lips were squeezed tight in an act of defiance. He stared down Oren for a bit, then switched tactics and tried to avoid eye contact altogether.

"Look, Floyd," Oren sighed. "I'm here because of the Thomas family. But I am not one of them. You can talk to me. Tell me where the girl is, and I can help you."

"I ain't done nothin' wrong," Floyd growled. "I didn't do anything to that girl."

"Then you need to tell me what you were doing on the night of February 6," Oren said.

"I was home," Floyd said, his voice lacking conviction.

"Can anyone verify this?" Oren asked.

Floyd just looked at him.

"You don't have an alibi, Floyd."

Floyd looked at the floor, seemingly conflicted on whether to say anything or continue with his silent protest. Oren couldn't tell what he was thinking, and that scared him. He needed to keep the guard rails on. He needed Floyd thinking about Tiffany.

"What we do know is that Tiffany went missing on February 6," Oren said. "But we don't know where you were. Seems like you had plenty of opportunity to do something bad. So, if that's not true, where were you, really?"

To Oren's great relief, Floyd looked up at him. He still didn't speak. His lips were pursed. His stare defiant. But there was a sparkle in his eye. He was thinking. And that was all Oren needed.

Remember, Floyd. Remember.

\*\*\*

Right away, Max knew he had entered a completely different part of Floyd's mind.

Honky-tonk music thrummed from a jukebox, and cheap green and blue lights flickered around an empty dance floor. The patrons were all crowded around the bar, a couple dozen elbows placed upon the stained surface. A woman in a plaid button-up stood behind the bar, hurrying to serve drinks. Max found himself next to her, and he felt bad for not helping.

He slipped away and tucked himself into a corner where he would not disturb the scene in any way. He surveilled the bar and spotted Floyd Smith leaning against the far side, sipping on whiskey, sporting a faded leather jacket. Floyd looked to have been here for a while, sweat forming on his brow, hair disheveled.

One country song ended and another began, this one faster and fuelled by more bass. A couple—possibly a middle-aged man and woman, though without faces, it was hard to tell—hollered and hurried their way onto the dance floor. The blurry-faced couple began to two-step. All of the other featureless patrons at the bar minded their business, staring into a void.

Floyd, however, had his gaze very much directed at something. Rather, someone.

Max tracked Floyd's eyes to the bartender. She hurried about, pouring drinks from bottles without labels. Her hair was tied back, but several strands had come loose and were hanging in front of her eyes. Her skin glowed, whereas the patrons looked like shadows. She was the star of this memory; a spotlight had been cast over, and her details were captured crystal clear. Floyd wouldn't look away.

Watching this gave Max the creeps. He had to look away, distracting himself with the way the bar came through in Floyd's mind. The space itself was remarkably well captured. Floyd must have come here often. There was a mirror behind the bar, reflecting back the bad lighting and half-empty bottles of various liquor. A jukebox huddled in the corner opposite Max, and the walls were decorated with a variety of old posters, some of which even came through in Floyd's mind. A few local bands were being promoted, and then, dangling above the dance floor, was the chalkboard listing the specials. It matched what Max had seen on their drive into town.

> The Rusty Nail Nightly Features—
> Week of February 5
> Monday—2 for 1 Beers

Tuesday—Country Night and
Cowboy Shots
Wednesday—Live Local Music
Thursday—$2 Highballs
Friday—Karaoke
Saturday—Dollar Shots
Sunday—$5 Dirty Marys

"Our girl went missing on country night," Oren had said in the car.

Clearly this was country night; the tunes had been among the most truck-lovin' and boot-stompin' that Max had ever heard. Even through the distortion of Floyd's mind, Max could make out Keith Urban's voice.

This meant that tonight was February 6. This was the night Tiffany Thomas went missing.

Max had found his spot.

Sometime later this night, Floyd was going to leave the bar and abduct Tiffany. Max just had to keep up and find out what he did and how. Max's stomach churned. Was he about to witness a murder? What the hell had he signed up for?

Max waited for something to happen, nestled in between an empty table and what looked to be a storage room. This memory didn't seem to be in any hurry. Max kept desperately looking around for a clock, feeling as though more time had elapsed than he was comfortable with. Several songs came and went on the jukebox, each one resembling a popular country tune but not quite nailing the lyrics.

The more Floyd drank, the less filled-in the scene became. Parts of the bar vanished entirely, replaced with vague dark holes, kind of like the blind spots Max got when suffering from a migraine.

A few of the patrons disappeared, then reappeared, then disappeared again, twinkling in and out like lightbulbs. There was now just one lone dancing girl on the floor, and she did this lightbulb trick as well. The music came in fits, like bad reception on a radio. The alcohol had eroded Floyd's memory.

Soon, the walls began to contract, and now the focus was entirely on Floyd and the bartender.

It felt as though an hour had elapsed, and Max began to worry that he had been in here too long. Yet he was afraid to leave, to step through another door. He needed to be patient and wait Floyd out. If he left this night, he wasn't sure he'd be able to find his way back.

Floyd turned to the person beside him, who had quickly become the only faceless patron remaining. Floyd started slurring something about the out-of-towners, and how much he hated the way they looked at him. It was incoherent and rage-fuelled. The amorphous figure next to Floyd stood up and left.

"Fuckin' you too," Floyd said with a laugh and turned back to stare at the bartender.

"Think it's time to go home, Floyd?" the bartender asked. She came over and rested her elbows on the bar, looking straight at him. "Everyone else has gone. I'd like to go too."

"Oh ya? Want me to take ya home, May?" Floyd winked.

"Yeah, great idea, Floyd." She rolled her eyes. "My dad would love that."

"Still livin' at home?"

"Where else is there to go?"

"Well, we don't have-ta go, then," Floyd said and reached into his pocket. "We can stay here."

"I'm closing up," May said.

"I can make it worth yer while," Floyd said with a grin.

He had fished out a small plastic bag and slapped it down on the bar. Inside was an unmistakable white powder.

May's eyes lit up. She was the one staring now, salivating at the cocaine the way Floyd had been at her all night.

"If my dad found out you had this . . ." she said.

"I know you're not gonna tell the cops on me." Floyd smiled. "Ya got yerself a bad streak. I remember. So, what do ya say? Wanna have a lil fun? It's on me."

In a flash, May had left her post at the bar and went to lock the front door. She shut off the neon signs in the window and drew down the curtains. When she turned back to Floyd, she had a devious look on her face.

He meticulously crafted two lines on the bar top. The room closed in even further. Now Max was standing in a void. His body seemed to have faded away; the floor was just a black hole beneath his feet. But he could see Floyd and May playing out the scene as if through a pinhole camera. The rest of their night came at him in flashes. The drugs and alcohol strobed Floyd's memory, and everything was brief, shuffled, and incomplete.

Both of them were laughing, shuffling over to the jukebox.

May poured a shot of bourbon straight into Floyd's mouth.

Another line was created; May took it gleefully.

Both of them sat on the floor, backs against the wall, bobbing along to the music.

A few times, Floyd would lean a little too close to her, and she shrugged away from him. It was clear that this relationship was solely about the substances provided.

More drinks were poured.

Another line was shared.

Floyd was urinating in the bathroom. He was alone, wobbling. He glanced down at himself, and Max had to shield his eyes to avoid being flashed.

Floyd stumbled out from the washroom, howling out a war cry. It went unanswered.

"Where are ya?" he was asking, but all that answered him was music.

Floyd procured himself another treat from his pocket. He quickly popped it in his mouth. To Max, it looked like a mushroom, though he couldn't be sure.

Still alone, Floyd moved over to the dance floor and tried to select another song from the jukebox.

The lights grew dimmer, the music louder. Heavy bass thrummed in the darkness.

The world was slower and slower to materialize now every time the scene jumped.

Small dots flashed through the world. When Max tried to look at them, they vanished like the little spots one sees in the corner of their eye.

Suddenly, the music slowed down. The pitch got deep, and everything was in slow motion. Max got a sinking feeling in his stomach. He didn't like this.

"Oh," Floyd said, and toppled to the ground. He sat there, against the jukebox, and looked up at the ceiling.

Max was beside him, the void now filled in, and he found himself standing next to an ATM in the corner that had been changing colours since the memory began.

When Max looked up to follow Floyd's gaze, he realized the ceiling had been replaced by the sky, like the roof of the Rusty Nail had been torn straight off. The sky was a kaleidoscope of colours. The stars had been replaced by vibrant purples, reds, and yellows. Triangles and squares overlapped one another, changing their shape, and rotating in tune with the music.

"Oh, that's good." Floyd giggled. His body seemed to be sinking into the floor. The jukebox had transformed itself into a big soft pillow.

The ground beneath Max's feet felt uneasy. The memory was losing its shape. The floor dropped away completely then, and everything became a sort of quicksand. Max tried to step away, but his feet were caught in this sludge that had the same colour and texture as the floor, but no solid shape whatsoever. As Max tried to pull one foot from the darkness, the other one would only sink deeper.

One moment, the room was there, with Floyd enjoying his high. Then in either a surge of light or a cascade of darkness, it was all gone. It came back moments later, like a photo being developed. The image was hard to make out at first, but then it started to take form.

Trees appeared at the edges of the room now, growing before them as if the world were in a time lapse. Branches quickly snaked their way into the kaleidoscope sky. These arms reached for the colours, swaying and thrashing with the music as if caught in some nightmarish mosh pit.

There was a screaming voice in the song that played. It was repeating *save us, save us, save us*. Max thought he was the one that needed saving. He could feel himself sinking even lower, almost up to his waist now in the mysterious black tar.

The giant jukebox pillow was floating away on the black sludge, a river having been created, and now all sound and image was streaming away from them. The lights behind the bar came alive, turning to fireflies that danced through the air toward them. Floyd stood, having no problems with the churning floor. He reached out at a firefly, trying to catch it in his hand but failing.

The fireflies bolted up into the sky, coming together to form letters and numbers with their bodies. They spelled out names that Max did not recognize nor care about. He was still sinking. His legs felt crushed by the weight of this illogical world, totally vanished beneath the floor by now.

The room grew dark; the colours shrank into themselves and hid for a moment. When they came back, all the pieces of the room raced back to where they had been before, trying their best to re-create the Rusty Nail, but not quite matching their previous places.

Floyd was on the ground, closer to the bar but not quite where he wanted to be. He reached out a hopeless hand, fighting against his swirling high and trying to grab a drink. Instead, he toppled over onto his belly.

The entire room began to spin like a carousel. Max thought he might vomit. He hated carnivals and rides, avoiding them at all costs as a child. The one time he tried the Fireball ride as an adult, it had resulted in him losing his lunch. The only thing that kept him stable now was the fact that he was lodged in the sinking floor.

The fireflies were multiplying. Their numbers doubled, then doubled again. The room was alive with burning dots. Floyd stared up at them helplessly, and then the room went dark again yet again.

The kaleidoscope sky did not return when the light came back. The ceiling was back on the bar. The strange dancing trees and fireflies had all disappeared as well. The music was still rumbling, something low and incoherent. The bar windows were aglow with the dawn, as the morning sun had come to shed light on the aftermath.

The floor finally had stopped eroding. Max fought against the tar he was stuck in. He wrenched his legs away with all his strength. Finally, one came free. He stepped out of the pit, the floor uneven, but solid.

Max's manufactured body dripped with dark sludge. The ooze poured off him in long tendrils, like syrup falling off pancakes. He tried to wipe it off, remove himself from its grip, and rush over to Floyd.

Floyd was waking up, his consciousness furthering the details in the room. The more he looked around, the clearer the setting became. Bottles lay littered on the floor, sticky messes were everywhere, and at least one glass had shattered on the bar top.

Someone was missing. Floyd seemed to become aware of this and rose to his feet. As he stood, the room spun like a top. Max dropped to all fours as Floyd's head struggled to regain its sense of balance. Floyd put his hand out against the bar, and the room eventually wobbled back into place.

Then he saw her.

Behind the bar, hidden from sight until this point, May was passed out on the ground. She was completely sprawled on her back, facing the ceiling, motionless. She had vomited in her sleep, it appeared, as drool and bile had formed on the corners of her mouth, and a rancid mess pooled on the floor.

"Oh shit," Floyd said, rushing to her side.

Max felt the same sense of panic and hurried over. Floyd had his hands on her chest, as if feeling for signs of life.

"Is she breathing?" Max asked aloud.

He did not get an answer.

The jukebox still chugged away, bass and guitar and drums crashing through the tense moment.

"Hey, hey," Floyd called out to her.

He slapped her face lightly. Her head just lolled from side to side. She didn't move. Floyd started looking around the room. He looked frantic. His eyes were searching for a way out.

May just lay there, completely limp. Her eyes were shut, and her chin tilted back. The bag of evidence was on the ground right next to her. It had obviously fallen out of Floyd's pocket at some point. Floyd kept his hands on her, seemingly torn between trying CPR or slapping her face again.

He pressed on her chest a couple times half-heartedly, clearly out of his element. Max resisted the urge to toss him aside and step in. He at least knew what he was doing. But he stopped himself. Everything he was witnessing here had already happened. It was already too late.

Floyd cursed to himself. He seemed unsure of what to do, eyes still bouncing around for a clue. He glanced momentarily at Max, but there was no answer there.

Finally, Floyd pressed hard on her chest again and leaned his face down nice and close to hers. He pressed his ear to her mouth, hoping for a sign of life.

"Jesus Christ!" May bolted upright as if she had received an adrenaline shot to the heart. Her head smashed against Floyd's—a loud crack echoed throughout the bar—and sent Floyd backwards, clutching his forehead. "What the fuck are you doing, Floyd?"

"I . . . it . . . you . . ." he stuttered. "I thought ya was dead!"

"What were you trying to do?" the woozy bartender said, sitting up.

"I was tryin' to save ya," he said, still holding his head. A goose egg was already forming. "Thought I had just killed the sheriff's daughter."

All at once Max connected the dots. *The bartender was Sheriff Landry's daughter?*

"Wouldn't that be a riot," the bartender said. She struggled to get into an upright position, but eventually pulled herself to her feet. "Floyd Smith goes to jail for overdosing the Landry girl."

"It's not funny," Floyd growled.

"Little bit." She smirked. "You'd get one hell of a sentence. Probably death sentence." She tried to stand but couldn't find the strength. "Shit. I feel like shit."

"Yeah, you was practically dead!"

Finally, she was able to dust herself off, and stood, looking out the window.

Then she looked around at the state of things, shaking her head. "It's already morning. I gotta get this place cleaned up." She wiped absently at some of the bile on her shirt. Then she shot Floyd a dirty look. "We didn't do anything, did we?"

Floyd looked down at his own clothes. "Don't think so."

Max could tell from the way May's skin glowed—while everything else in the bar seemed to be desaturated—that Floyd would have wanted to hook up with the bartender. His mind worshipped her. She was bright and beautiful even as she lay in her own vomit, her nose crusted, and her eyes rolled back. But Max could verify, since he had witnessed the entire night unfold, that Floyd had not been successful in his pursuit.

"Wan' me to help with anythin'?" Floyd asked.

"No, just get going," she said. "And don't say a fucking word to anyone. Need my dad to think I'm still clean."

"Trust me," Floyd choked out. "I won't be tellin' a soul."

"Good," May said, waving a warning finger at him. "I *will not* let him send me back to rehab. You blab, and I swear to you, whatever story my father hears will paint you as the bad guy. I'll tell him you laid hands on the sheriff's daughter, if I have to. Let him fill in the rest."

Floyd's eyes widened at this implication.

"Jesus." Floyd started to back away toward the door, hands in the air. Surrender. "I won't say anythin'. Don't get any fuckin' ideas!"

It was over, then. The world lurched forwards without warning, and Max felt like he was standing on the subway, trying to balance himself as things sped up, only to come to an abrupt stop a moment later.

The musty, stale air of the bar was replaced with the icy bite of the morning. Floyd was walking himself home. Max stood on the sidewalk, watching him pass. Floyd had to turn suddenly and wretch into the snowbank. The quiet morning was interrupted by the sounds of his hacking. Steam rose off his vomit.

Max's gag reflex was triggered, and he had to look away. It didn't make sense. If it was already morning— meaning it was February 7—where was Tiffany? It was beginning to look like Floyd had not encountered the girl at all; the window for him to be the guilty party was closing. But they had been so certain.

Max figured he better stick close to Floyd's side. He followed the suspect up the street until the memory jumped forwards again. Now Floyd was back at his house.

The place was bare. An open concept kitchen held a mismatched table and couple of chairs. A stained sofa stared at the fireplace, where a TV was set up on the ground. Floyd bypassed both of these rooms though, and he marched into the bedroom, where his tiny mattress caught him as he sank face first into his pillow.

Another lurch forwards in time.

Floyd was eating cereal on his ratty sofa, watching the small television set. A news anchor was mumbling something in gibberish, the story apparently not imprinted on Floyd's mind. By the light outside, it seemed to be later in the day. Floyd had slept in.

There was a knock at the door that startled him and made him drop his spoon. It clattered on the floor.

"Open up, Floyd!" a voice raged from outside.

Floyd, who was dressed only in his underwear, crept over to the door and put his eye through the peephole.

"Fuck," Floyd whispered and bolted for his bedroom.

Curious, Max dashed over to the door to see who was there. He leaned in, and through the peephole, he spotted the unmistakable mug of Sheriff Landry. His face was bloated and warped by the magnifying effect of the glass. He was staring back at Max, an impatient look on his face, and his hand on his holster. Behind him, Sanderson was perched in the same stance.

"That's it!" Landry shouted. Then he took a step back and started to swing his foot.

Max had to dive away from the door as it buckled inward. He slid across the floor toward the sofa just as Landry kicked his way into the home. The door rattled against the back wall, sending chunks of drywall and dust into the air. The door then bounced back to Landry, who braced it with his shoulder.

"Come on, Floyd," Landry said.

Max quickly got back to his feet. He bolted over to the kitchen, where he could hide behind the counter. He feared what Landry might do to him if he caught him in here.

Floyd had been tossing his clothes on in the bedroom and now made a mad dash for the kitchen himself. There was a back door there.

"Fuck you," Floyd blurted as he sprinted through the living room.

Landry spotted him late and tried to give chase, but his wet boots slipped on the floor.

Max crouched beside the stove and watched as Floyd came flying into the kitchen, launching himself at the back door. Landry was right behind him, gun drawn now. Floyd had to unlock the door, and this slowed him down. He turned the handle as he glanced back to see Landry closing in. It was hopeless, but he swung the door inward, his momentum now completely stalled.

Landry crashed into Floyd, sending the door back shut. The two men collided and slipped to the ground. Floyd tried to crawl away, but Landry pushed himself back up onto his knees. His gun was still clutched in his hand, and he swung the butt of the pistol down on Floyd's head.

A red flash cut through the room. Everything became really warm. The world lost its clarity and colour.

"Make this easy, you piece of shit," Landry cursed, removing his cuffs from his belt.

Floyd had no fight left in him. He lay face down on the floor, gasping for air and groaning. "Who told?" Floyd said, his voice seeming to drift into another plane. "She promised she wouldn't tell."

Landry ignored this and called Sanderson over to help. "You're supposed to be the young one," Landry said. "Do something fucking useful."

Sanderson pulled Floyd up to his feet. Floyd stared at Sanderson with wonky eyes, trying to make sense of how quickly it all happened.

"She promised she wouldn't tell," Floyd repeated.

"Yeah, yeah." Landry brushed dirt off his pants as he righted himself. He looked about the kitchen. "What a dump you live in, Floyd."

Floyd cringed, seemingly afraid that Landry was going to do something horrible.

"Sheriff," Floyd started but didn't have the words to complete the thought. "She's fine. She's fine," he said instead. "She didn't die. Please don't kill me."

"What are you on this time?" Landry asked. Then he started to look around. "Is she here?"

"No," Floyd said.

Sanderson held onto Floyd as Landry marched around, conducting a quick search. Landry went to the bedroom and the bathroom, and then he disappeared down into an unseen basement for a moment. When he returned, he seemed satisfied.

"She ain't here," Landry confirmed. "You gonna tell us where she is?"

"How should I know?" Floyd shrugged.

Landry's patience was thin to begin with, but he seemed especially agitated now. He stepped forwards and smacked Floyd in the face with the butt of his gun again, cracking his nose and causing it to bleed. Floyd cursed and shrank down, sheltering against Sanderson's side.

"Still no ideas?" Landry asked.

Floyd only whimpered.

Max was still huddled in the corner of the kitchen, watching while holding his breath. He feared Landry would look over, spot Max, and smack him around too.

"Get him to the station. Maybe we can make him talk," Landry ordered.

Sanderson started marching Floyd out toward the front.

"You're under arrest for the abduction of Tiffany Thomas," Sanderson stated as he walked Floyd away.

Landry shot Sanderson a look.

"He doesn't even deserve his rights," Landry scoffed.

"Wait, what?" Floyd seemed suddenly more alert now. He twisted, trying to get away from Sanderson. "What did you say?"

"Just get him in the truck," Landry said.

Floyd shot a look back at the sheriff, relief washing over his face. Floyd had actually been happy with this news. Landry had nabbed him for something else. He *wasn't* here about his daughter after all. Floyd wore a smile all the way out the door.

Time lurched forwards.

Now Max's claustrophobia was tested. He was huddled in a small cell with Floyd. The edges of the world were pitch-black, only a dim light from the hallway offered any relief. Floyd was lying on the paper-thin cot, still smirking. The man was actually thankful for this result over the alternative; if Landry had known about Floyd's time with his daughter, he likely would've shown up alone, and Floyd would've been dragged out in a body bag as opposed to cuffs.

Of course, Max realized how guilty Floyd looked because of this.

Suddenly, the door at the far end of the hall opened up. Even though the figure was blurred, Max recognized the man that stormed through as Robert Thomas. In Floyd's mind, he was even taller than in real life. He was a giant.

The enormous DA rushed forwards through the shadows, his gaze locked on Floyd. "Floyd, you start talking right now!" Thomas shouted.

"Who's this now?" Floyd asked, as he rose and went to the bars.

It was hard to make out Thomas's face, Max supposed, if you weren't familiar with the man. Floyd's head must've still been aching, because Max would never have sauntered closer to the bars like that.

The giant continued his approach, and now the light struck his face just right, and things came into focus. Floyd seemed to realize, because he recoiled at the last moment, but it was too late.

"Where's my daughter?!" Thomas asked as he stuck his massive hands through the bars, wrapping them around Floyd's neck.

Floyd's feet lifted off the floor.

Landry lurked in the background. He just crossed his arms over his belly and watched. Floyd choked, making wet gagging noises and trying to wrench himself free of Thomas' grip. Thomas towered over him, his dark frame befitting of his Grim Reaper title. Floyd's mind had turned him into an actual monster.

The world seemed to grow darker. Max flinched as the walls closed in. Floyd was getting tunnel vision. He was going to pass out. The cell was shrinking, and Max was forced to cram into the centre or risk fading into the void.

It was time to go. He buried his face in his hands, shutting his eyes and trying to drown out all the sound. *Dark corners,* he thought.

Thomas was shouting "Where is she?!" somewhere in the distance, but Max was already removing himself. All of the inherited knowledge from Charlie's brain was returning to him now. Max tuned everything out, focused inward, and tried to rise. His body was hit with a sense of chaotic weightlessness, and he jolted upward. It was the sensation one got when they attempted to pick up something heavy, only to find out it wasn't as heavy as they thought.

*Get me out of here.*

He felt like Dorothy, clacking his heels together. Thomas had dropped Floyd, who was now gasping for air. But Max didn't see any of this. His eyes were shut so tight they hurt. There was no making it darker.

*Get me out. Get me out. Get me out.*

\*\*\*

Max was pulled out of the darkness and found himself in the sweet stillness of the library. The floor was firm, uncomfortable against his rear. But it was a welcome feeling. He pressed his hands into the carpet, relieved to feel something real again.

He was perspiring. He rubbed his forehead with his sleeve just as Oren emerged from the children's section.

"Good, you're back," Oren said. "I figured I should check on you. It's been a couple minutes."

Max opened his mouth to say something, but hesitated, trying to catch his breath instead. Oren held out his hand and Max took it, allowing himself to get pulled to his feet. He was grateful to find that he was steady. Max could see three shapes walking toward them down the long rows of bookshelves. Landry, Sanderson, and Archie.

"How did it go?" Oren spoke quickly, realizing their window of privacy was closing.

A million thoughts swirled through Max's mind, and he wasn't sure how to make Oren understand what he had just witnessed. He tried to think of where to begin.

"He didn't do it," Max said. It was the simplest form of the truth he could come up with.

Concern clouded Oren's face. He had obviously not expected this response. "What?"

Oren had prepared himself for failure. For Max not finding the right moment. Or the thoughts in Floyd's head being too difficult to read. Or, God forbid, learning that Tiffany was already dead. But Floyd being innocent? It was the one circumstance he hadn't braced for.

"I saw him," Max said, keeping his voice low. "It wasn't him. Floyd didn't take Tiffany."

"How do you know?" Oren was looking for a reason for Max to be wrong. "Did you find the right date? Did you find her house?"

"I saw him on February 6, the whole time." Max nodded. "And the next day. Oren, trust me. He didn't do it. Someone else must have."

"You're sure?"

"He was with someone," Max said. "He has an alibi."

Oren studied Max. He was waiting for a *just kidding,* or a sign that would make this all logical.

Max didn't budge.

"Why wouldn't he have said who his alibi was?"

"Because," Max said. "He was with Landry's daughter. They were getting high. He thought that was worse. I don't think he understands the gravity of this situation; he doesn't know about Tiffany's case."

The expression on Oren's face was exactly what Max thought it would be. He felt it too. Complete bewilderment. Oren's jaw hung open.

"Landry has a daughter," Max continued, voice low, noticing how close the sheriff was. They had to close this conversation. "And Floyd was doing drugs with her, and . . ." Max wondered how much of this was important. The point was made. "Landry would kill him if he knew."

Oren turned to face their guests as they approached. He was still digesting but understood the logic. What chance did Floyd have to prove himself innocent when his alibi would earn him a worse beating than the one he was already receiving? It was starting to clear—like wipers across a dirty windshield—and Oren saw things for what they were. Floyd hadn't really said anything to prove himself guilty; he'd just refused to speak with Landry. He wasn't confessing to the crime, so much as resigning himself to the fact that if Landry wanted to put him away, he was going to do it one way or another.

Max was having the same thoughts. Growing up, his father had been quite the history buff, especially for American presidents. Max had been forced to hear a great deal about the JFK assassination, and specifically remembered his father's theories on Lee Harvey Oswald. Max's father believed that Oswald was a patsy.

Floyd Smith was Ruston's Oswald.

Only, Max had been able to see the truth. And now Oren had the responsibility to make sure they didn't punish the wrong man.

"And?" Thomas said, cutting through the silence.

The five men were all now gathered in a circle. Archie held a tray of coffees—already missing the two that Landry and Sanderson had in hand—and he offered them up to Oren and Max. They both declined.

Oren's face was grim. "Floyd didn't take your daughter," Oren said.

"What?" Thomas said. "Why . . . Why are you doing this? We don't have time."

"I hate to be the bearer of this news." Oren didn't flinch. "But it wasn't Floyd."

"What the fuck are you on about?" Landry chimed in. He stepped closer to the centre of the circle, trying to intimidate Oren.

"We cleared him," Oren said. He was trying to be as vague as possible.

"How?" Landry scoffed.

"We were able to retrace the events of that night, and we've determined that it wasn't possible for Floyd to have abducted Tiffany," Oren said.

Max's insides twisted. How were they supposed to make this story believable without telling them they had used the MemCom?

"That so?" Landry looked at Sanderson.

Sanderson just shrugged.

"What the fuck you know about it anyway? Didn't realize you were the fuckin' FBI."

"Sir." Oren turned his attention to Thomas. "I know it's not the news you were expecting. But you need to trust me. We ran the same practice that we did on Leonard Lang, and I can promise you that Floyd is innocent."

"Why? How?" Thomas asked.

"I can't go into the details," Oren said. "But we need to start looking at other suspects. I want to find Tiffany. I promise you that this is the right thing. We need to shift our focus."

"This is what you get for hiring outside help," Landry said, his voice low, a territorial dog's growl. "You should've left this to me."

Landry went to move around Oren and head into the children's section.

Oren stepped in front of him. "We have to start looking at other suspects now."

"Get out of my way." Landry pushed Oren aside. "I'm handling this case. I'm gonna bring that piece of shit back to the station and see if a little more time alone will clear his mind."

Oren shifted back to Thomas. "Sir, you must believe me. Max and I need to start looking at other potential suspects. Unfortunately, we are behind because everything to this point has been focused on Floyd. We need to start from scratch and make up for lost time."

Landry had heard enough and flew into the children's section like a rocket. From behind the glass, they all heard Floyd wince as the sheriff lifted him up. He was not gentle about it.

"I don't know what you think you know," Thomas said, getting super close to Oren's face. "But this better result in me getting my daughter back."

"I promise you, sir." Oren sounded like a broken record that was pleading for anyone to believe them. "We will find who did this. But it was not Floyd."

Max felt guilty for saying nothing.

"I paid you for one day," Thomas said. "I won't pay you another cent until my daughter is returned."

"Absolutely." Oren raised his hands. "I'm not concerned about the money. I want to help. And we need to go about this the right way."

"He's not gonna stop," Sanderson said, motioning to Landry on the other side of the glass.

He was muttering a string of cuss words at Floyd and shaking him as he tried to get him to move his feet.

"He's right," Thomas affirmed. "Landry's going to keep interrogating Floyd until the man stops breathing.

If you want to go figure out who else you think did this, that's fine. But you have twenty-four hours. By tomorrow morning, if you don't have a new suspect and the whereabouts of my daughter, we're done here. I'll figure this out with the sheriff."

Oren and Max exchanged glances. Max silently begged Oren not to agree to this. Even with the MemCom, he had no idea how to find a needle in a haystack—a missing girl in a cascade of memories, every memory from every person who could have taken her.

"Thank you," Oren said. "We'll have her in twenty-four hours. You have my word."

# 6. Charlie's Focus

MORE MEMORIES RUSHED BACK. THEY came to Max like water. They had been dammed away in some part of Max's brain, but now the dam was broken. He was flooded with knowledge, and his arid mind soaked it all in. The river that poured through Max's head was an angry crowd, swirling and rushing through the cobblestone streets of the Temple Bar.

\*\*\*

By this time, Charlie knew its movements. He found the crease between the football fans that he knew to be the best route to Kelly. He shimmied sideways, making himself small enough to get through the gap before it closed. Once on the other side, he had some breathing room, but he wouldn't have it for long.

The people flocked in two different directions, and Charlie jumped from one side to the other in time for new momentum to carry him into an alley. He had to push, jabbing one faceless drone in what should have been its eye. He had to dive, and he felt dramatic doing so, but Charlie was able to make it into this temporary refuge in time. He brushed himself off as he stood, and he counted down the seconds until she walked by.

Right on time, Kelly crossed the alleyway.

"Excuse me!" Charlie called out.

Kelly turned, seeing him and smiling.

The first time Charlie had called out to her, he was too startled by her response to act. He hadn't expected it to work. And now it was like a drug. The way her eyes lit up the first time she saw his face was intoxicating—and in here, every time was the first time. Charlie got to experience this again and again, so long as he repeated the right steps.

Charlie had been back inside of Lang's head countless of times now. Oren and the crew had unearthed more than a dozen bodies. Charlie was never in a hurry. He strolled through Lang's mind like a tourist seeing the sights. He would make this pit stop—at least once—every time he dove. He had rehearsed every moment of the memory. He knew what Lang said. He knew what Kelly said. And he knew when and how to cut across the crowd so he could run into Kelly in the alley.

It no longer even mattered if Lang was cooperating; regardless of what he was thinking, Charlie could navigate back to this spot. He felt he was starting to know Lang's mind better than his own. In truth, he could probably find the victims all in one dive and in a fraction of the time. But he chose to go through doors that led him to Kelly instead. And he wanted as many dives as possible. So, he only ever sought out one victim per visit.

Oren was none the wiser. He was always thrilled that they had a new location, and then he'd became distracted by the search to exhume the corpse. He had no idea that Charlie was dragging this out, touring around Lang's brain when he could've had all of their answers by now.

On this occasion, when the dive began, Charlie had found himself in the middle of one of Lang's murders, blood smeared on his face so thick he was almost unrecognizable. But Charlie calmly stepped away from the carnage by hopping into the bedroom closet and emerging in another familiar spot—Lang's first murder, his happy place—and then finding the familiar door that led back to Ireland.

What did it matter if he took a few pit stops? Charlie rationalized with himself. The hours he spent talking with Kelly were nothing, a minute at most in the real world. And as Charlie was rapidly learning, the limits of what you could get away with in the mind were beyond what they thought.

Kelly seemed to be a non-hostile re-creation (or a NHR as Charlie had referenced them in his notes). She was not probing for intruders, looking for reasons to eject him. There were still characters in these memories who seemed to want to cause trouble for Charlie. And Lang's SI specifically was likely not one he wanted to cross. But so far, no alarm bells had been set off when Charlie interfered with the memory by speaking to Kelly.

Charlie felt at peace, leaning against the alley wall as Kelly approached him. He knew how the first part of their conversation went. But she always seemed to have to leave after a minute. Charlie had yet to figure out how to get her to stay.

"Do you need help?" Kelly asked.

Her accent was beautiful, her voice locking Charlie entirely in the moment, the most effective form of mindfulness he had ever practiced.

"Yeah, actually," Charlie said, his lines rehearsed. "Typical lost tourist needing directions."

This had worked better than Charlie's attempt at boldness: calling her beautiful and asking her to join him for a drink. He always had success with asking her for help. She was happy to oblige.

She came over and her scent hit him. The way Lang remembered all these details was a blessing. Charlie never felt more in awe of this technology than when Kelly's perfume hit him. Every part of her was so perfectly preserved. Charlie had a hard time remembering she wasn't real.

Kelly's eyes sparkled, and she tossed her hair back over her left shoulder as she spoke to him. Her t-shirt was cut low and revealed a bit of her freckled chest. Her cheeks were rosy, her lips lightly reddened. All of the other people roaming these streets didn't even have faces, but Charlie could see the tiny pale hairs on Kelly's neck.

They spoke briefly about the bars nearby and how to get there, and then soon, their time expired. Kelly caught herself midsentence as she always would, and then she seemed to remember she had somewhere else to be. Charlie had given up on convincing her to stay;

she never did. This time, he couldn't help but feel a little brilliant for trying something new.

"Where did you meet your boyfriend?" Charlie questioned her.

"Sorry?" She wasn't sure what he was talking about.

"I'm sorry." Charlie tried to back up.

He had to explain better, seeing as she didn't really have a memory of her own. She could banter, but when it came to actually answering questions, Charlie learned that you had to be concise.

"I saw you talking with someone. Leonard. Where did you meet Leonard?"

"Oh." Kelly understood now. "I met him here in Ireland."

"Yeah? Just like in the pub?" Charlie tried to sound casual but was clearly fishing.

Kelly, being only a re-creation, did not have the capacity to pick up on such things.

"No," she said. "The cliffs. I was bringing a friend who had never been. Leonard was a tourist." Then abruptly, she said, "I'm sorry, I really must get going."

Charlie hated this part. But it was inevitable. Every visit ended with her needing to leave suddenly.

Charlie thanked her and waved, but she didn't see it. She was gone too fast. In any other circumstance, Charlie would feel like had had blown it; the conversation had been awkward, and the way it had ended was even worse. But thankfully, when he left, he would be hitting the restart button. She wouldn't remember a thing, yet he'd have gained valuable insight.

The nearest door was no good—Charlie had tried it before. So, he had to make his way back out onto the busy street. By now, things were slowing down. The memory was wrapping up, as Lang ceased to care about the details past this point. Whatever he was up to, Charlie had no idea. He only followed the Kelly part of the story, each and every time.

And it was Kelly he was thinking of as he crossed through the door to the pub, emerging in yet another dark and terrible night. Lang had this victim in two pieces. The blood on his face had been mostly wiped away, but his shirt was soaked. Charlie barely noticed. Lang tossed the two halves of the corpse into a hole just like all the others, and began to fill it in, planting grass seed, which they had learned was his calling card.

But all Charlie saw was someone who was lucky enough to date Kelly.

\*\*\*

By Oren's count, they were nearing the end of the search. Of the known victims, only a few remained hidden underground. They now knew that Lang had perfected his burial routine of finding fertile ground to bury his victims and then planting grass seeds over top. Given enough time, and enough return visits, he had perfectly manicured these areas so that no one would recognize anything out of place. Lang somehow had the luxury of time and patience, and he dug deep.

Even with knowing to look for grassy, flat areas in remote parts of the state, there was no way Oren and the team would find the remaining bodies without the MemCom.

So, Charlie had reason to go back. But soon enough, that reason would end. Once the bodies were all recovered, his chance to visit Leonard Lang would disappear forever.

As he showed up for the next dive, Charlie was wrestling with anxiety over the end of things.

"Try to be a little faster this time," Oren urged Charlie as they entered the prison with which they were now all too familiar (Oren knew three of the guards on a first name basis). "Last time, I had to talk to the bastard for five whole minutes."

"I'll try," was all Charlie could reply with. His thoughts were already lost as he was transfixed on the opportunity to see Kelly again.

Lang was excited to see them. He looked at the one-way glass the same way Charlie looked at Kelly. There was a certain lust forming. Oren was a ready ear, happy to hear all of the mad thoughts Lang could reveal. And though Oren's listening was only a show, it built a strange bond with Lang. Oren figured it may work the same way one develops feelings for their therapist; people just like to be heard and understood. To some, that could be confused with love. It always made him feel dirty when they left, though.

Charlie didn't hear any of Lang's greeting. He didn't care. He had the earpiece popped in even before the music started. *Hurry up, Neil Diamond.*

\*\*\*

Charlie was admittedly naive when it came to geography. He hadn't sought out much information about the rest of the world growing up, and so it did not live in the annals of his mind. He was forced to look up exactly what Kelly had been referencing, despite its legendary status. The Cliffs of Moher were one of Ireland's great tourist attractions, and they would be a truly stunning sight if the pictures online were to be believed. Charlie was looking forward to this being the new setting for his visit with Kelly.

It didn't take long to find the cliffs. A couple of doors, but nothing difficult. Charlie emerged from the tourist stop washrooms, nestled amongst the hills. Like most things worth seeing, the cliffs were not immune to being commercialized, and the scores of visitors needed somewhere to relieve themselves, as well as somewhere to shop for cheap memorabilia and a bite to eat.

Charlie's first impression was not much. He was annoyed by the crowd. But once he stepped away from the shops and the people licking ice cream cones, he was in awe. He saw the cliffs at a distance, straight ahead of him as they bisected the ocean and the sky. Surprising himself, he began to jog. He moved quickly to the nearest rail and craned his neck over.

The Cliffs of Moher were unlike anything he had seen—even with Lang's mind re-creating them in poor resolution, like a video that needed to buffer. For someone stuck inside of his own studies, and the minds of others, this level of infinity blew Charlie's mind. The stone walls towered over the emerald waves crashing into their base.

To Charlie's left, he got an incredible look at the scale, with the walls extending almost a mile away over an inlet. To his right, a seemingly endless staircase would bring him higher for a better view. But he stayed put and just gawked at the scene.

To call the cliffs steep wouldn't be quite right; they were perfectly ninety degrees, upright and dominant. From this vantage point, the cliffs dwarfed the ocean, something Charlie couldn't have fathomed before being here.

All of this was combined with the majesty of the open ocean. The horizon went on forever. Though on the other side, where America should have been, was certainly just a terrifying part of Lang's memory.

Tourists were sticking their arms out over the railing to grab selfies and daring photos of the drop below. Charlie backed away, his sightseeing now over. He collected himself again for the task at hand.

Charlie surveyed the crowds. No sign of Lang or Kelly. Charlie started walking up the staircase a bit. With a slightly higher vantage point, he turned and scanned again. Something immediately stood out. Nearly everyone was looking at the cliffs through their screen. Phones and iPads stuck out to capture a picture. But there was one person who was noticeably without technology. A man stood a meter or two behind the group at the railing, people-watching. The man was disguised in a green ball cap and rain jacket. Charlie thought he may not have recognized Lang if not for the way he lurked behind the crowd.

Lang was alone. That likely meant that he hadn't met Kelly yet. There was still time. Charlie continued his frantic game of Where's Waldo. He turned around to look in the other direction and collided with exactly the person he was looking for. Not one to believe in fate, Charlie's beliefs were tested. His heart came alive, and he became intoxicated.

"Oh my!" Kelly yelped as they braced against one another to keep from falling.

"Sorry about that," Charlie said, but he couldn't wipe the smile from his face. He was holding her arm, and she was holding his.

"You're facing the wrong way, you know," Kelly joked. "The cliffs are that way."

Charlie didn't have a script for this moment, it being the first time, and he felt like he stood still and silent for far too long. Finally, he noticed that Kelly was not alone. A girl with curly red hair and the most ivory skin Charlie had ever seen was giving him the stink eye.

"Let's go, Kell," the redhead announced. "I want to get to the gift shop."

To Charlie's immense joy, Kelly wasn't taking her eyes off him. He blushed.

"Go ahead," Charlie said. "She'll meet you there."

He was familiar with interacting with this background players by now. They just needed a little coaxing sometimes. The redhead departed without a word.

The re-creation of Kelly was predestined to find love in this memory. This version of her was wired for love at first sight. She was only, and always, going to be infatuated with a man on this staircase. Today, she just happened to bump into Charlie before she met Lang.

Her reaction was programmed. Charlie should have known better, if he had been thinking straight. Instead, he believed it was truly about him. She was smitten with *him.*

"I'm Charlie," he introduced himself.

"Kelly," she replied.

Charlie almost said, "I know."

The conversation started with small talk, not unlike Charlie's attempts in the alley. But those had always ended prematurely. Now, pressed up against what felt like the edge of the world, Kelly's eyes remained locked on him. He was running out of things to talk about, all the while feeling terrified that it could end in an instant.

"So, you're here to see the sights?" Kelly asked as Charlie smiled at her stupidly. "Well, what's next on your list?"

"I feel like you could probably give me a better list than whatever is on those travel sites," Charlie said. "What should I do?"

Kelly laughed softly, a reaction not called for in the moment but one that made Charlie feel faint. She leaned in to him, and once again, Charlie caught her scent. He was blissfully unaware of the man with the ponytail standing only a dozen yards away, starting to become aware that something was missing.

"Can I see your phone?" Kelly asked.

Charlie reached for it without thinking. Then his heart sank. Of course, he had no phone. He wasn't really here. None of this was real. He looked at Kelly, feeling his palms starting to perspire.

"What, no phone?"

"I'm realizing now that I've left it behind," Charlie said bashfully.

"No problem." Kelly shrugged it off. "But you'll have to give me your number, then." She handed her phone over to Charlie.

He had momentarily been ripped from the illusion. But her smile was so real. Her gaze was so real. And when Charlie grabbed the phone, it felt like the real thing. He plunged back into delusion with ease.

Charlie entered his phone number into her contacts, not thinking at all about what might happen to it. Kelly, who was following her function, found this to be lovely. Because she had to.

"Thank you," Kelly said, taking her phone back for a moment. "Have you been to Galway?"

"I haven't. Perhaps we could go together?" Charlie asked.

"It's been a while." Kelly thought about it for a second. "I suppose I could use a refresher."

She had leaned in even closer to Charlie. His heart was racing. He felt her own gravitational force pulling him in. She was real; she had weight and a physical place in this world.

"Good." Charlie's mind was on autopilot, and he would later regret the silly things he had said. "Perhaps you could be my tour guide, then?" He placed his hand on his neck, feeling the moment called for it, and the sensation of skin on skin was exactly how it should have been.

The moment ended all too quickly for Charlie.

Over Kelly's shoulder, Charlie saw motion. Lang was approaching them, ascending the steps two at a time, and the look on his face was that of a man possessed. Something inhuman stirred behind his eyes, driving his body toward a singular purpose. His eyes seemed to have lost their whites; they were dark, metal orbs reflecting everything back perfectly. They shifted around too, reminding Charlie of liquid mercury.

Charlie took a moment too long to understand the threat. This was Lang's SI. This was his watch dog in these memories. And the watch dog had spotted an intruder.

Flinching, Charlie tried to back away, but Lang had closed the gap and reached out over top of Kelly. She screamed, but then she fell to the ground and seemed to freeze in place. In fact, all of the people froze. It was only Lang and Charlie now. And Lang had his hands clamped around Charlie's shoulders.

Charlie squirmed, attempting to get his hands on Lang's and pry them off. Lang was supernaturally strong, his body feeling more like a machine against Charlie's feeble struggling. Lang brought Charlie closer, looking straight at him with these mercurial eyes that weren't eyes. Charlie tried not to look, but the more he fought, the more strength he lost.

A high-pitch squeal rose from the silence, and it was starting to split Charlie's head in two. He struggled to cover his ears but couldn't reach over Lang's bulk. He had pushed the limits and finally found the line. Charlie had interrupted the memory, stopped it from happening even. The alarm had finally been sounded, and now he was caught. He felt shame, guilty for having broken the rules, and he also felt terror for what was to come.

Lang's self-image lifted Charlie in the air, something the wiry man would have been unlikely to do in the real world. Charlie was suspended. What Lang was doing only dawned on him once he felt the breeze. Lang was holding Charlie up and over the railing, dangling him above the ocean which was a hundred feet below.

"Don't," Charlie pleaded, but the words didn't seem to come out. Only the high-pitch squeal existed.

Lang may have smiled, the tiniest hint of emotion breaking through his otherwise mechanical expression. And then, he let go.

The feeling of falling was familiar. Charlie shouldn't have been surprised how realistic things felt, not after everything else he had been through. But he was stunned, and his stomach was left behind with Lang as he fell. He was more than halfway down when he finally snapped to his senses.

Charlie shut his eyes. He brought his arms up to his ears, blotting out the squeal. He clenched his jaw and tried to focus. He wasn't falling. He was in a bad dream. He couldn't see or hear anything. It was just darkness.

*Get out. Get out. Get out.*

\*\*\*

Charlie hit the ground with a thud, winding himself and choking out a scream. He flailed, panicking, sure he was dying. But the fall didn't carry the impact it should have. He should've been smushed. But aside from a bruised elbow and shortness of breath, he realized he was fine.

He opened his eyes for the first time and saw Oren standing over him, perplexed and alarmed.

The ride away from the prison was one of the most silent and awkward car rides Charlie had experienced. Oren was furious. They rattled over highways under the overcast sky. When the ride was nearly over, he finally laid into Charlie.

"What the fuck are you doing in there!? You're losing your focus, Charlie! You are wasting everyone's time!"

Charlie had not seen Oren angered—not to this extent—ever before. It was a short blow up. Oren spoke his piece and then immediately fell silent, seething and motionless as he finished the drive home.

Now faced with the cold shoulder, Charlie missed the yelling. The worst part was Charlie did not disagree. He had lost his focus. And he was probably wasting their time. He was no long efficient with his work, the dives becoming more of a playground than a science lab. Oren had spotted it and called him out. But Charlie also knew he would not change; his focus now was on Kelly.

In fact, the only thing Charlie felt he learned from this ordeal was exactly where the line was. And that he should avoid the cliffs when he wanted to see Kelly next. The stakes were too high in that memory. He vowed to only use moments of less significance going forward.

The aftermath of the shouting frenzy still buzzed in the air, tainting the silence with an ugly weight. Tinnitus brought ringing to Charlie's ears. It seemed to be an echo of the siren in Lang's mind.

Soon, a different ringing emerged. It took Charlie a second to realize it was his phone.

Oren glanced at Charlie sideways as he retrieved the phone and checked the screen. The number was listed as unknown.

The phone chimed a few more times before Oren finally sighed and said, "Aren't you going to answer it?"

Charlie had a bad feeling as he swiped the touch screen and took the call. "Hello?" he asked, uncertain.

A robot responded in monotonous script.

"This is a TeleHub prepaid call from *Leonard Lang*, an inmate at the Northern Massachusetts Correctional Center. This call is monitored for safety and security. If you accept the call, please say *accept* now."

Charlie paused. Oren overheard and pulled the car over, suddenly invested. He glared at his colleague.

Charlie tried to wet his lips as he mustered up a meek, "Accept."

The line buzzed, and there was breathing on the other end.

"Is this Harold's friend?" a familiar, coy voice asked. The words were dripping with excitement, the speaker salivating for the response. Lang was referring, of course, to Oren's alias that they had been using to interview him.

"Who is this?" Charlie asked.

"You're the little one who follows Harold around, aren't you?" Lang knew the answer already; the question was just a game. "I miss you already. They give me one phone call a week, and I just couldn't wait to use it. How come I only get to talk to him? Why don't you ever speak? I'm dying to know."

Oren was squinting, looking at Charlie for an explanation.

"How did you get this number?" Charlie asked.

"What do you mean?" Lang seemed surprised by the question, as if it was a silly thing to ask.

"How did you get my number?" Charlie repeated.

"I . . . I've always known it," Lang said, sounding spaced out. Then there was almost an audible click as his mind snapped back into focus and he leaned back into his game. "Are we going to talk or not, Charlie?"

Charlie swallowed, trying to erase the chills that were creeping up his spine. He looked out the window at the nothingness of highway and fields around them, feeling exposed. Then he cursed under his breath and hung up the phone.

"Lang? What did he want?" Oren asked.

Charlie didn't answer. He was too busy thinking of Kelly's phone, and how he punched his phone number in without thinking twice. He had left something behind in Lang's mind. Now he felt dirty—used by the memories of a serial killer.

"What did you do, Charlie?" Oren sighed.

When it became clear that Charlie wasn't going to speak anymore, Oren put the car back into drive and offered one last warning. "I don't know what you're doing in there, but you're getting careless. I can see it when you come back. You aren't focused. Let's just wrap these last few dives up as quickly as possible so we can move on."

Then they fell back into silence. When Charlie did not want silence any longer, he turned on the radio, despite Oren's protest, and found the loudest, hardest rock station he could to fill the air with crashing drums and anything other than nothing.

Oren was incredibly worried. He could tell that Charlie jumping into another mind had altered his own. But there was no manual for this. And though Oren made a note to try and get Charlie some help—or perhaps look into getting a new diver so that Charlie could take a break—nothing could stop the damage that was coming.

# 7. Start from Scratch

MAX HATED THE FICKLE TENDENCIES of time. Never consistent, always making you crave more or hope for less.

When faced with confronting his father, usually around the holidays, Max would sit awkwardly on one sofa while his father occupied the other. The clock on the wall sat still. Yet somehow, the last fifteen years of his life slipped passed him undetected. The end came for both of his parents so quickly. It made him long for the days when they felt immortal, when their deaths were just suggestions as opposed to events of the past.

Now there was Thomas' threat: twenty-four hours to find Tiffany. Max knew it would simultaneously be the longest day of his life and not enough time.

Floyd was back in lockup. An innocent man behind bars, yet Max could do very little to prove that innocence without confessing to the MemCom they secretly possessed. Landry and Sanderson took their suspect—the wrong suspect—away, leaving the others at the library. Oren brought Max over to a table so they could break down their plan while Archie kept the DA locked in conversation.

"Looking at this case now," Oren said, "you can't be sure that Tiffany was even abducted. She could have run away."

"What makes you say that?"

"Most of the evidence was based on the fact that Floyd had no alibi and a long history of threatening the Thomas family," Oren said. "If you're telling me he is innocent—that his memory absolves him of this crime—then we really don't have anything left."

"What about the footprint?" Max asked. He recalled this from the breakdown of strikes against Floyd Smith that he received at the Cuckoo's Nest.

"There *was* a size 11 boot print with treads that somewhat matched Floyd's boot," Oren said with a shrug. "That's it. If we were investigating this case from scratch, I'd be looking at the family first. Those are the first people you want to speak with. It will also help us verify whether or not there was foul play involved, or if Tiffany just took off."

"Didn't she leave her phone behind?"

"She may have done that on purpose," Oren said. "We really don't know anything. We've taken the Thomas family's word as gospel up until now."

Oren glanced over at Thomas and then lowered his voice.

"We need to hitch a ride with him over to their house," Oren said. "On the way, you can do a dive. Gather whatever information you can. It'll be faster than conducting an interview. Time is not on our side, so we need to take advantage of the fact that things move faster in the memories."

"What am I supposed to look for?"

Max, too, watched Thomas. He was their client. An imposing man with a lot of power. Max suddenly wondered if this was a good idea. If they were found out, it would likely mean the end of their careers, at the very least.

"Look for the truth," Oren said. "See if they've been honest so far. Tiffany was here to get away. She wanted space from her family. What if there's something they haven't been telling us? That's what I need you to find."

"I hate this," Max groaned, but he stood up from the table, ready to leave. "I just need you to know that. I hate all of this."

"I'd be worried if you didn't," Oren said with a wink. "Now let's go ride in a fancy car."

Oren hadn't been kidding. Thomas wasn't thrilled about having to bring them back to the house—not after they had just told him that Floyd was innocent—but he told them to hop into his luxury SUV. Apparently, this was his winter ride. The convertible was covered up until spring. It was quite the transition, going from Archie's jeep to this beautiful leather interior with heated seats and a panoramic sunroof. Max felt like his very presence in the vehicle was tarnishing it. The way Thomas glared at him didn't help that feeling.

Oren once again took shotgun. Max made himself comfortable in the seat behind Thomas and—out of sight—fiddled with the MemCom earpiece.

"Can you think of anywhere Tiffany may have gone to hide out?" Oren said once they were on the road.

"Aren't you supposed to be telling me?" Thomas said.

"I'm wondering if she may have left the family home on her own accord." Oren tried to sound non-accusatory. "Perhaps she went missing from somewhere else? If she had a friend's place to camp out at or a favourite spot in town?"

"My daughter wouldn't just run away." Thomas' patience was being tested. "She left her phone. You know how hard it is to separate a teenager from their phone, Detective?"

"I understand," Oren conceded. There was a long, awkward silence. But Oren had been planning on this. "Let's maybe just put on some music 'til we get there, then."

"Fine," Thomas agreed. He flicked on the radio. He was a classic rock fan as it turned out.

This was Max's cue. He looked over at Oren one last time, hoping for a nod or a signal. Maybe a telepathic message that this would all be okay. But Oren was stoic. A perfect actor.

Max slouched. Thomas wouldn't be able to see him in the rearview. And if he turned around, hopefully he'd just see a slumbering man in his back seat. Rude, but not criminal, and not as horribly invasive as the truth—that Max had just been rummaging around in the man's most private thoughts and memories.

Max pushed the button and began his violation of Robert Thomas.

\*\*\*

Max opened his eyes in a fuzzy room, the corners completely obscured by darkness and lack of detail. Only the centre of the room was visible. A single lamp revealed a small bed adorned with pink sheets. In the bed, a young girl was fighting off exhaustion. Beside her, awkwardly trying to fit on the bed but without much room, was a young DA Thomas. He looked identical to the angry version Max left behind in the sunroom, only his hair was jet-black and his forehead was smoother.

"Read it to me again, Daddy," the young girl asked.

Max noticed the book in Thomas' hands. The cover was a pale red, but the words were smudged as if the ink hadn't dried before it had been picked up.

"It's late," Thomas said. "And I've already read it once."

"One more time, Daddy," the girl pleaded.

"No, Tiffany." Thomas stood, tossing the book down on the bedside table. "Goodnight."

It was a cold departure, and the young girl left alone in the room seemed distraught. Thomas made his way for the door, and just as he got there, the girl blurted out her response.

"I don't want the lights off," Tiffany fired off quickly, before her father could hit the switch and shut the door.

"Why is that?" he asked.

"I get scared." Young Tiffany pulled the covers up to her chin and offered puppy-dog eyes. "I don't like it in here."

Thomas stood there a moment, seeming to mull the problem over like a whiskey he was trying for the first time. He pressed out his chin, finally, and turned with a sigh. He flicked off the lights and shut the door behind him, abandoning Tiffany to the darkness. Unbeknownst to Tiffany, she was joined by Max in this sudden pitch-black cell.

Max stood in the corner and his mind raced with all of the things that could possibly be lurking in the shadows or under the bed. Despite being a grown man in a simulation, the dark bedroom spurred him into action; he wanted to get out of there fast.

Max jogged after Thomas, following him through the only door available.

\*\*\*

This silver-haired version of DA Thomas was sitting at the desk, reading something in a folder. Max was careful, sticking to the edge of the room, tiptoeing his way behind the desk. He tried to peer over Thomas' shoulder to see what he was reading. The pages were blank. It was strange to see Thomas so intently staring with nothing on the paper in front of him.

There was a flurry of buzzing, and Thomas dropped the folder and pulled his phone from his pocket. He looked at the screen briefly—this was *not* blank, and the word "Bitch" appeared—and then answered it with a sigh.

"What?" he asked.

"Where's my daughter?!" a woman's voice screeched from the other side.

Max could hear it clear as day. The memory seemed to amplify the phone call.

"She's with me," Thomas said.

"I know you're full of shit," the voice said. "I saw her post. She's in fucking Ruston."

Thomas sank in his chair and covered his face with a hand. "Yes, she's at the summer home," he said. "She's responsible enough. I trust her."

"You think she'd be off on her own right now if she wasn't forced to put up with that lunatic wife of yours?"

Thomas ignored this blow and waited for the rest of the rant.

"She's fucking miserable there. And she's missing time with her mother. Get her back. And get her back now. I want to see her in this city, in front of my fucking doorstep, or else we can have the custody talk again."

Thomas bit his lip, his free fist clenched, and he wheeled his chair around to face the city skyline. Max followed his eyeline, also staring out at the collection of twinkling signs, half-illuminated offices, and the glow of red taillights. Suddenly, things lurched forwards, and Max felt as though he were falling out the window, plummeting several stories to his death.

Instead, he was comfortably seated in the back seat of Thomas's SUV, where he had been mere moments earlier with Oren. Only, this wasn't the real world; he was still in the memory.

He was staring out another window, this one covered in condensation. The world was dark outside the vehicle.

Max held his breath. Thomas was driving the car, and Mrs. Thomas was dozing in the passenger seat. The radio was set to a talk program that seemed to have knocked her out. Max felt far too close to them. Surely, they would notice the stranger in the back seat. He held himself as still as possible and tried to will himself into invisibility.

The car rolled through the night with large flakes of snow shooting past their headlights, giving the illusion that they were on a rocket ship travelling through space. There was nothing but the white snow and the black night. Eventually though, they passed streetlamps fighting through the winter flurry to provide some faint orange glow to the world. A few buildings clustered together, a town, and one that Max recognized. He had been here already.

The car turned up a road that led to the outskirts of Ruston, where the average bungalows turned into the few spectacular lots that summertime folk would have abandoned by now. Even amongst these well-off summer homes, the Thomases' home stood out. Against the snowy night, the Victorian palace was lit up by soft floodlights strategically placed to make the house look even more grand. Nothing else on the street was lit up, and it made the home a beacon.

"What the fuck," Thomas cursed.

Max jumped, fearing he had been caught. But then he saw it through the window. Mrs. Thomas stirred to life in her seat, and she noticed it right away as well.

When Max was four or five, his parents brought him to a dinner party at a friend's house. They had both been drinking, so likely neither of his parents should have been driving, but they did anyway, and the three of them arrived home late. Max was sleeping in the back seat, but the car slowing shook him awake. Their home was dark, as in no lights had been left on. But even in the shadows, the entire family could right away spot that something was off. There was a foreign presence. A small hole in the front bay window, barely large enough for someone to crawl through, seemed to give the entire home a tainted appearance. Before exiting the car, Max's parents both knew there had been a break-in earlier. And Max sensed an intruder, knowing from his cartoons that a bad person had been there.

The Thomas summer home had this same type of scar. The front door had been left open in a snowstorm, which was a sight so uncharacteristic that it immediately made the house look wrong. The home seemed damaged and sickly. A fair amount of snow had already piled at the front door, and the great chandelier in the foyer was visible from the street.

The three of them sat in the car a moment, speechless. Max felt like he was a part of the experience in real time. Finally, Thomas seemed to gather his thoughts. He shut off the car, unbuckled his seat belt, and stepped out into the storm. Mrs. Thomas remained behind.

Max was relieved when things lurched forwards again. He wasn't sure he'd have been able to leave the car without exiting the memory. But these thoughts were connected together, and Thomas' mind brought him along automatically.

Max was standing in the foyer, watching Thomas enter through the French doors. Max looked down and noticed that Thomas' boot had left a print in the piling snow. Could this really be the boot print the deputies found? The lone piece of evidence that had pointed them to Floyd?

"Tiff?!" Thomas called out.

The rest of the room seemed undisturbed.

Max wondered if he would leave a boot print of his own if he stepped in the snow. Irrationally, he worried that would then frame him in Tiffany's disappearance, as if his actions here echoed in the real world. He avoided the drift, just to be safe, following Thomas deeper into the house.

The interior of the home was crystal clear. Understandably, Thomas would know every detail of this home, and therefore the memory seemed perfectly preserved, like a fossil found beneath the ice. Max remembered reading about a horse that had been discovered in Siberia. The thing was 42,000 years old, yet in the photos, it looked almost like it could have been alive. This memory had the same frozen clarity.

Max followed Thomas up the grand staircase and around to the left where the dark walls were interrupted by a series of doors leading to bedrooms. The hall was impossibly long, feeling like something out of *The Shining*. Max felt bad for dragging his soggy feet across the carpet. Thomas disappeared through one of the doors on the left, leaving the door open behind him. Max stood outside, watching cautiously. He didn't want to cross through it, as he was unwilling to lose his place.

On the other side the door was the master bedroom. The large, open space held a king-sized bed, a reading nook near the window, where the curtains were drawn, and on either side of the bed, a matching set of ornate lamps that resembled bare, winter trees. One of these tree lamps was on and angled toward a bureau in the corner, near the entrance to the walk-in closet.

Robert Thomas had the bureau pulled open. One of the drawers had been completely removed and was now sitting on the floor. He was pulling apart stacks of socks and reaching down to the bottom of it. His face seemed to relax when he grabbed hold of what treasure he was looking for. He pulled his arm out of the sock pit and in it was a handgun, a stack of bills, and a small bag containing a white powder. He stuffed these items carefully into his coat pocket, and then haphazardly forced the drawer back into place.

Max backed away from the door and pressed himself against the wall, sensing that Thomas was coming his way. Thomas sprinted back into the hallway. Max followed at a careful distance, curiously watching the man's actions. He still called out the occasional "Tiff!" into the house and opened bedroom doors to peer inside. When he finished with this floor, he hurried back down the stairs and rounded the corner into the dining room. Max watched from the staircase. Thomas shouted a few more times, was silent, and then reemerged through another door that Max didn't even realize existed.

Thomas quickly poked his head into the sunroom and then seemed convinced. He jogged back out to the car. Max moved quickly, taking the stairs two at a time and pressing himself against the front door so that he could watch Thomas without being seen.

The world was silent, the snow padding the street and the lawn. It made it all that much easier for Max to hear when Thomas pulled open the driver side door and commanded his wife to "Call the police." Thomas then retreated to the house, nearly colliding with Max.

Back in the foyer, Thomas pulled out his own phone. But it wasn't the police he dialed. The name "Josh" appeared on his screen before he held it to his face.

"Get your ass to Ruston, now," Thomas said into the phone. "Your sister is gone." A moment of silence. "I will not have my family scattered across the country if this makes it to the media. You're going to come here now and help us look like a family."

*Sister?* Max wondered.

The cold was stinging his eyes, and it brought Max back to the present. He checked his wrist instinctively, but obviously there was no watch. He was starting to feel anxious, like he had been here too long. Did he have enough? He knew Thomas had something to hide, that the footprint wasn't Floyd's, and that there was another family member in the picture. Certainly, this could be helpful for Oren.

Max figured it was the right time to leave.

He rushed back up the stairs, where the hall was offering plenty of dark corners to hide in. Max closed his eyes and found he was getting better at this already, pulling himself out with ease.

\*\*\*

Max found himself in the back seat. Thomas and Oren were still listening to music, minding their own business. No one had even missed Max as his consciousness had temporarily left the back seat. Max straightened out of his slouch, alive with nerves and ideas after what he had witnessed.

"You have a son?" Max asked, before even thinking of what he was saying.

"Excuse me?"

Max realized he should've been more careful with the information gleaned from his dive. Oren frowned at him, confirming his carelessness.

"Oh yeah," Oren said, covering for Max. "I thought I read that somewhere too. You have a son as well, correct?"

"Tiffany's half brother," Thomas said. He was not interested in having this conversation, but at least he wasn't questioning what had prompted Max to ask. "From my first marriage."

"And where is he?" Oren asked.

"Am I on trial here?" Thomas was growing more hostile. "He's here in town, helping to look for his sister, though he insists on staying at a friend's place. He chose to drive here from Chicago. Even though I offered to fly him. He's . . . different."

Max was happy when things drifted back into uncomfortable silence. He allowed it to stay that way the rest of the ride.

\*\*\*

They were offered a seat in the family dining room to do their work. Mrs. Thomas was apparently out, and Thomas promised—with heavy sarcasm—that they could start grilling her instead of him once she came back. Thomas then disappeared upstairs.

The dining room, much like the entire house, was more ornate that any summer home Max had ever been to. This would've been a significant upgrade on any home he had ever lived in. Even his wealthiest friends growing up did not have a solid oak table that sat twenty guests, gold-trimmed wainscoting, or a chandelier the size of a canoe.

Rows of windows with burgundy volets let in the early morning sunlight. Oren opened his laptop and looked at Max expectantly. Max filled him in on everything. When he revealed that the footprint belonged to Robert Thomas, Oren groaned and rolled his eyes. When Max revealed that Thomas hid a gun and some drugs, Oren just shrugged. He didn't believe it was related to the case. And he wasn't surprised; he had heard rumours about the Grim Reaper.

All of this news sparked an idea in Oren, though. His eyes were alive like they hadn't been all morning. The case was coming together in his head, and Max half-wished he could pop inside to see what was happening there.

Oren told Max to sit tight as he dug some things up. Oren's fingers clacked against the keyboard, and he seemed excited by what he was finding.

When they heard the front door open, they were surprised to see Sheriff Landry and not Mrs. Thomas.

"Where's the DA?" Landry asked them, his face displaying his trademark scowl.

"Upstairs," Oren said.

"Good." Landry stepped into the dining room without removing his soiled footwear, and Max couldn't help but cringe as he tracked filthy snow onto the hardwood. "I need you to understand somethin', West. Just 'cause he paid you to be here does not make you a cop. I still run this town. And you need to cool it with your ideas of who did or didn't take the girl. You've got shit to go on. So, stop poisoning his mind and let me do my fucking job."

"I mean no disrespect, Sheriff." Oren wasn't bothered by the sheriff puffing out his chest. Max envied that calmness. "We'll stick to our investigation, and you stick to yours. But we did have a lot of success with the Lang case. And using the same methods, we've been able to clear Floyd."

"These fucking mystery methods," Landry scoffed. "I heard about your success. I don't know what magic you worked over there. But this is a different case. And people here are built different."

"Anything we find, we will relay to you, and you can make of it what you will," Oren said. "Once we find concrete evidence, though, I will be suggesting that you release Floyd."

Landry seemed agitated; he hadn't expected Oren to go toe-to-toe with him.

"Just keep your shit over here." Landry pointed at the dining table. "And leave the police work to the pros."

"Absolutely." Oren's tone was agreeable. It made the veins in Landry's neck swell.

"So, what's your next big move then, boy genius?"

"We are following up with the family," Oren said. He clearly saw no point in lying to the sheriff. At least, to a point. "We're going to speak with Mrs. Thomas, as well as Mr. Thomas' son. We just want to make sure there's nothing we've overlooked. An ex-boyfriend, perhaps. Someone else who may have wanted to take her."

"Am I hearing this right?" Landry laughed. "You think her family did it? I've known this family a long time. Her brother—although he's a weirdo—wouldn't ever hurt her. And the stepmother and Tiffany were very close. We already explored the boyfriend angle, too, dipstick. She hasn't had one for almost a year. And the last one is still in Manhattan, accounted for. With an alibi. Which, by the way, Floyd still doesn't have."

Max tried his best to keep his poker face.

"Are," Oren said suddenly.

Both Max and Landry cocked their heads at him.

"What?" Landry asked.

"You mean, the stepmother and Tiffany *are* very close." Oren's face was stone, a serious look that gave Max chills. "You said they *were* close. She's not dead as far as I'm aware, Sheriff."

The front door creaked again, and everyone turned to see Mrs. Thomas walking in.

Mrs. Thomas seemed surprised to be faced with three men in her home. Her manicured eyebrows were slightly raised. When she laid eyes on Oren, however, they seemed to relax. She gave him a quick up and down.

"Mrs. Thomas," Oren said, rising to go and shake her hand. "I'm Oren West. Your husband hired me to help find Tiffany."

"Oh please, call me Jane," Mrs. Thomas tittered.

Max realized she was clearly smitten with his friend. She was a slight woman, face made-up, hair dyed and coiffed. The necklace she wore likely cost more than Max's entire year's rent.

"Jane," Landry said, once more trying to establish his territory. He was trying to prove his relationship with this family.

Mrs. Thomas shot him a dirty look—*not you*—and then returned her eyes to Oren. "When did you get in?"

"Last night, ma'am," Oren said. Their hands were still locked; Mrs. Thomas was unwilling to let go.

"Well, are you hungry?" She smiled. "I can grab something from the kitchen."

"Sure, a snack might be good." Oren finally retrieved his hand and returned to his seat.

"I'll fetch something," she said and then was gone.

"Sure seems like a murderer, doesn't she?" Landry rolled his eyes. "I needa find the DA." He finally kicked off his dirty boots and headed upstairs.

Quickly, Oren turned to Max and spoke in a low voice. "We have to check her out now."

"Mrs. Thomas?" Max said. "Seems like she was already checking you out."

"Her mind, Max." Oren wasn't in the mood for jokes. "This is our window. When she comes back, dive. We won't have long alone with her. See what she knows about the disappearance."

Oren was already calling up music on his phone. He chose a gentle piano ballad that fit the ambience of the dining room.

"When she walks back in, hit the button," Oren coached him. "Put your head down on the table now, so it looks like you're napping."

"I'm just supposed to be rude enough to fall asleep at her table?" Max scoffed, but nonetheless put in the earpiece and made himself comfortable.

"It's to find Tiffany," Oren said. "And I'll cover for you."

"We don't have much." Mrs. Thomas was returning now. "But I put together some cheese and crackers. Tiffany always likes these ones."

Max made eye contact with Oren quickly and then ducked his head down into his arms, holding the button.

"That's great, thank you," Oren said.

Mrs. Thomas placed the plate down in front of Oren, barely paying attention to Max. Though when she finally looked his way, she hesitated.

"What's up with him?"

"It was a long trip in, late night," Oren said, helping himself to a cracker. "Are you and Tiffany close, Mrs. Thomas?"

"Jane," she corrected him again. She swiveled away from Max, content to let the man sleep at her table so long as she had Oren's attention. "And yes, we are. She's such a sweetheart. I've often felt like I am her actual mother, you know. She doesn't spend much time with her mom. I think we've sort of replaced that bond with our own."

"That's nice," Oren said. "We certainly are doing everything we can to find her."

"Oh, I'm not worried," Mrs. Thomas said in her singsongy voice.

Oren was caught off guard. She was smiling at him, seeming very confident. Why was *she* not worried about the missing girl?

"Can I ask why not?" Oren shifted in his seat.

"I hired a psychic," she said, her smile never wavering.

Her gaze reminded Oren of *The Stepford Wives.*

She elaborated. "To reach out and find Tiffany. There are some shocking numbers about just how many missing persons have been found through psychic energy. Typically, the police do not believe the results of the search, but when they eventually find the person, it turns out the psychic was right the entire time. Really, just shocking numbers."

Oren had heard of this. Desperate families were sometimes prone to hiring any help they could get their hands on. And sometimes, psychics liked to take advantage. They offered hope when sometimes there wasn't any. But Oren did not believe in their so-called abilities. He found them to be no more than superstition.

There were footsteps on the stairs that spiralled down into the dining room. Thomas and Landry were returning.

"And what did the psychic say?" Landry asked with a smirk.

\*\*\*

Candlelight spotted the room, casting long shadows on the walls around them. Max found himself sitting in a circle with two others, centred around a small table. The room was hard to make out by the light of the tealights, but what little he could see was crowding them from packed shelves, loaded with gaudy objects. Trinkets and statues and figurines stared at them with lifeless eyes—all of them smudged together, indicating details not remembered clearly.

"Are you relaxed?" the person on Max's left asked.

He was a large man in every way. He was wide and tall, and even his head looked to be about twice the size of the lady across from him. Despite this, his voice was incredible soft, even high-pitched.

The man held out his enormous hands and invited his counterpart to hold them.

"I am relaxed," the woman across the table from him confirmed.

Max recognized her voice right away. It was Jane Thomas.

"Good," the man said, his voice a gentle mist.

Max felt far too close to them—a part of their circle—yet didn't dare move away, in case of detection. He tensed up and watched, wondering where he had ended up.

The candles lit awkward bags under the large man's eyes. Jane Thomas gave him her hands.

"You are searching for your daughter, is that right?" he asked.

"Stepdaughter," Jane Thomas corrected him.

"Yes." The man nodded, as if someone was in his ear confirming this information. "Tiffany."

"That's right."

"When was the last time you saw Tiffany?"

"Tuesday morning," Jane Thomas said. "At our home in Manhattan."

"Ok." The large man had his eyes shut tight and was shifting side to side slightly. "I'm getting something. But it's still very unformed. What is your relationship with Tiffany like?"

"We are very close," Jane Thomas said quickly. She spoke at rapid fire speed. "We get along well. We never fight. She's like a real daughter to me."

"Ok, yes, good." The man tilted his chin inward. "And she came here to Ruston."

"Yes."

"She came to get some space," the man continued. "But . . . not space from you."

"Oh good." Jane Thomas's shoulders slouched with relief.

It was as though this man had just confirmed for her that she wasn't at fault. Max had begun to piece together that this was some kind of psychic reading. He had received one once, for a story he was doing. He had gone into it full of optimism, hoping to hear something about or from his late mother. But he left skeptical, after the psychic failed to provide any accurate depictions.

"She came here to see a friend." The man exhaled slowly. His words moved like steam, rising into the room in a way that you might not detect if you weren't really paying attention. "She sought out the company of another."

"Well," Jane Thomas thought out loud, "she does have some friends in town."

"But something went wrong." The large man flinched momentarily, an electric shock. "Tiffany was . . . coaxed. I'm getting a sense she was lured."

"Oh my." Jane Thomas pulled her hands away, clasping them over her chest.

The reading continued regardless.

"Jane," the man said. Eyes still closed. "I'm seeing something dark. A shadow. A kind, older man. A gentle face. He's gesturing to her."

"That must be her grandfather!" Jane Thomas jumped in to complete the thought. "Yes, Robert's father. He passed away just a couple years ago."

"Yes, it's him," the psychic affirmed. "I'm getting a strong sense of the letter *M*."

"The letter *M*?"

"Yes, the letter *M*."

"Well," Jane Thomas thought, "Robert's brother's name was Matthew."

"And a *G*."

"His father's name was Gregory!"

"Gregory Thomas," the psychic said confidently.

"That's right, that's him!" Jane was ecstatic. "We all called him GeeGee. Or Gramps. But his name was Gregory."

"He was beckoning to Tiffany," the psychic rolled on. "He called her away from the house. She trusted him. And she went."

"Oh my goodness." Jane was white-knuckled. "You don't suppose he . . . was speaking to her from beyond the grave?"

Max almost groaned but forced himself to sit still and observe.

Her question went unanswered. The man across the table was in his trance.

"They are together now." The psychic nodded his large head. "She is with him."

"Does that mean . . ." Jane Thomas was looking for more.

"She's with her grandfather," the psychic said.

"So . . . did she . . . did she take her own life?" Jane Thomas asked. "Did Tiffany go to see her grandfather in heaven?"

"Tiffany is not far." The psychic finally opened his eyes, looking at Jane Thomas with great pity. "She loves you. She feels afraid. But her heart is full of love."

Max wasn't going to get anything of value here, he realized. He slowly backed away from the table. The chair made a sound against the floor (something he found ridiculous considering this wasn't a real chair nor a real floor). He cringed. Jane Thomas seemed to glance momentarily in his direction but then went back to the psychic.

"What should we do, Michael?"

"I think you should celebrate her," he replied. "Celebrate your daughter's life."

Max had to get out of here before Jane Thomas' head was filled with any more misguided advice. He spotted a small, dark door in the corner, beside a shelf with at least three buddha statues. He beelined and forced his way through it.

\*\*\*

On the other side, Max found a hallway. It was the same hall in the upstairs of the summer house. He had seen this before, in Robert Thomas' head. Every door was closed. At the far end of the hall, Jane Thomas was standing, thinking. There were five doors to choose from, three on Max's left and two on his right. He waited another moment to see if Jane Thomas did anything of note, and then decided he needed to keep searching. He picked a door at random.

\*\*\*

A pillow twirled through the air, flying straight at Max's head. He raised his hands and was able to catch it. It was silky, a throw pillow from a sofa.

He spotted Jane Thomas again straight away. They were in a modern living room. Floor to ceiling windows looked out over skyscrapers and bustling streets. They were in Manhattan. Jane Thomas was staring at a girl across from her. Tiffany.

Tiffany stood behind a white leather sofa, holding a pillow identical to the one Max had just caught.

"Don't be a bitch," Jane Thomas said with a cool malice that Max had not thought her capable of.

She was so flowery and prim. Her voice had been airy. But now there was a calculated sting in it as she spoke to her stepdaughter.

Tiffany shrieked and fired the other pillow at her. This one missed to the left, and Max didn't need to react.

"You can't do this," Tiffany said. Her eyes were red, tears forming, but she was doing her best to blink them away.

"Yes, I can." Jane grinned. "I'm your mother."

"No, you're not." Tiffany shook her head. "You'll never be my mother."

"Well, I'm your father's husband then." Jane shrugged. "Still means I can tell you no. You are *not* going to Paris with your friends."

"My dad already said yes," Tiffany seethed.

"That was before he and I talked," Jane said. "I just feel it's not the best thing for you right now. Your grades are suffering. Some of those friends are a bad influence. Your father can be a bit of a pushover. But we talked about it, and he agrees. You are not to go."

"I'm going," Tiffany decided. "I don't care."

"No, you won't be going," Jane said coolly. "I've already seen to it that your passport is tucked away. You won't be getting on any planes."

"You went in my room?" Tiffany's mouth hung open.

"Please, dear," Jane said. "Shut your mouth. You look like a whore."

"What did you say?" Tiffany stormed out from behind the couch, charging at her stepmother. She had her hands up as if she was going to strangle her. "You evil, psycho–"

"Whoa, hey!" Robert Thomas stepped into the room from the kitchen, colliding with Tiffany and having to do a mini pirouette to prevent them both from toppling to the ground. "What did you just call your stepmother?"

"Dad, she went in my room," Tiffany pleaded.

"Robert." Suddenly, Jane Thomas was crying. She was hunched over, hands on her knees, looking exasperated. "She threw things at me. She called me names. I'm just trying to talk to her about Paris."

"Tiffany." Robert Thomas looked at her with daggers in his eyes. "Shame on you. I thought we had discussed this. The way you treat Jane. It's not healthy."

"The way *I* treat *her*?" Tiffany scoffed.

Robert Thomas shook his head. "Well, I was on the fence about it before, but this settles it. You are definitely not going to Paris."

"Dad!" Tiffany looked back and forth between Robert and Jane. "Dad, she said . . . She called me . . ." She couldn't get the words out.

Robert Thomas was already dismissing her. He raised a hand. "Enough."

He glanced over at Jane and mouthed *I'm so sorry.*

"It's okay," Jane said with her lip quivering. "It's not your fault."

Then, when Robert Thomas looked back at his daughter, Jane's lip immediately stopped its quiver and turned into a devious smirk. She stared at Tiffany with taunting eyes.

Still holding the throw pillow, Max took a few steps backwards. This felt like enough information to set Oren off down a path. He figured he better get back to the real world and relay this finding. The apartment was bright, and the energy was still tense, so it wasn't exactly conducive to resurfacing. So, Max crouched down, burrowing beneath the coffee table. He used the throw pillow to cover his face and searched for that rising feeling in his gut.

Quickly, the sensation of the pillow in his hands evaporated, and he was left holding nothing.

***

Max poked his head up from his arms, face feeling smushed and eyelids resisting their commands. He felt like he had awoken from a long nap, though the time on his watch hadn't even advanced one minute.

"And what did the psychic say?" Landry was asking. He and Thomas were descending the staircase together. Landry then spotted Max, looking like a stunned animal, peering around the room with wild eyes. "Jesus, what happened to you?"

"He passed out," Oren said. "It's been a long trip."

"Sorry," Max said.

Thankfully, no one had been paying him much attention this entire time, and it didn't start now. The conversation proceeded without him.

"The psychic told us she was okay," Jane Thomas said, smiling to her husband.

"Michael Essence isn't police, though." Robert Thomas sighed. "He's a pseudo-celebrity who takes money to tell you what you want to hear."

"So, Michael Essence," Landry started, but cracked himself up at the name. "This psychic . . . He told you Tiffany's all good? Did he by chance also tell you where we can go find her?"

"He said we didn't need to worry about looking," Jane smiled. "She's in safe hands."

"Sure thing," Landry turned to Thomas. "Should we stop?"

"Don't be coy," Thomas said. "No. We aren't stopping."

Oren was staring at Max this entire time. When Max finally realized, and made eye contact, he tried to convey the need for privacy.

"You know," Oren said. "I think it'd help to canvas the neighbourhood a bit. Max, care to join me?"

"None of our neighbours stay here during the winter," Thomas said, gesturing back and forth with his hand. "The entire street is empty until May."

"Well, it'll still be good to get a lay of the land." Oren shrugged, and headed for the door.

Max followed him. No one pressed the issue too much. It felt perfectly reasonable to want some space from Jane Thomas. Even her husband felt this sometimes.

The temperature drop-off was dramatic as it had been all morning; Max wasn't ready to be outside again.

"What are we doing?" he asked as he pressed his chin down into his collar and buried his hands as deep into his pockets as he could.

"Talking," Oren said, guiding them away from the Thomas house.

The sun had come out and it bounced off the snow, assaulting their eyes.

"What did you see?"

Max told him everything. He recounted the interaction with the psychic—Michael Essence—and the fight between Tiffany and Jane, how stepmother and stepdaughter were not as close as everyone thought. By the time he had finished, they were down the sidewalk, near the neighbour's place—a beautiful Victorian home that was snowed in and shuttered up.

"I think it's entirely possible that Tiffany ran away, Max," Oren said. "If she wanted some space, especially after that fight, she may have come here to hide out.

And may still be hiding, if she knew her parents were coming to get her."

"You don't believe the psychic then," Max said with a wry smile.

"No."

"Where would she be?" Max asked. "She left her phone at home."

"That's true," Oren admitted. "But I think she's with a friend. And has another device."

Oren stopped, turning them around; they had gone far enough.

"I found a post on Tiffany's social media," Oren continued. "It was from early on February 7. As in, after midnight on the night she went missing. Just a blurry photo. Two girls—a selfie—in a dark room. Hard to identify. But she tagged someone in it. *NellFlix_9*. If I can find out who that is, I think we have a solid lead."

"So, are we done with the Thomas family?"

Max stared down the house, not wanting to go back in. Oren seemed to share this feeling. He agreed they should wrap up their research at Stella's, where they could be out from under the nose of the DA and the sheriff.

They asked to hitch a ride with Landry, who wasn't pleased but took them back to Stella's just in time for lunch.

*\*\*\**

The house had a different feel to it when it was bright out, Max found. Stella's tiny, cozy little kitchen was now looking out into a postcard setting in her yard and beyond. A tiny birdhouse with a snowcap on its peak was a flurry of activity, and the bare trees beyond tickled the blue sky as if painted carefully against it.

Both Oren and Max had graciously accepted some leftover shepherd's pie for lunch. Oren ate his quickly and then disappeared to his room, citing the need to focus. He told Max not to worry, and to stay and eat. Stella was thrilled to have the company and offered up more of her homemade bread as Max heaped his plate high.

"Dessert?" she asked after he finished, grabbing his plate before he could clear it himself.

"I mean, I wouldn't say no." Max grimaced. "I feel bad, eating all your food, though."

"Nonsense," Stella dismissed this. "Who's gonna eat it? Me? Mrs. Romano? No. I'll go grab you something from the fridge downstairs. I think you'll like it."

Stella vanished into the basement, and Max took this chance to pull out his phone. He finally texted Janelle back. He used work as the icebreaker, finding it too difficult to approach her with anything else.

*Have u heard of Thomas family? Manhattan DA? Town of Ruston? Might have good story for when back.*

When the message was sent, Stella had reappeared, a plate of brownies in her hands. She deposited them in front of Max.

"Now, they aren't mine," Stella admitted. "I picked them up at the church bake sale. But Marianne does make a pretty mean square."

She retreated into her part of the kitchen, wiping away unseen dirt from the stove top.

"Thank you," Max said and helped himself.

He couldn't help but feel like Stella was trying to fatten him up, luring him in with this little gingerbread house of hers, so that she could toss him in that oven.

Suddenly, a swell of Italian opera came booming toward them from the hallway. At first, Max thought Oren had put a record on, as the song was stunningly clear. But then he remembered Stella's other houseguest and realized this was a live performance.

"Ah, someone's awake," Stella said with a wink. "Up from her morning nap."

"That's beautiful," Max said.

"Really is." Stella's face soured, however. "Such a shame, what happened to her granddaughter."

"Yes, you had mentioned."

"She's not the only one, you know," Stella said.

"The only . . . what?"

"Youngin' to meet a tragic end." Stella sauntered over toward him. She leaned against the table, speaking down toward Max with severity in her voice. "Seems almost every year, something bad happens to another young woman."

"Really?" Max leaned forwards. The journalist inside him was screaming to get out, wanting to pry at the story.

"Last year, it was Natalya Romano. Poor thing was found hanging in the motel." Stella crossed herself. "That's why I've got the beautiful music now. But before her, it was Savannah Stevens. They found that poor girl in the lake. Broke right through the ice. She was such a smart one too, wouldn't have expected her to be out on the lake in the spring, when the ice is so thin."

"That's very sad."

"It's that damned curse," Stella continued. "Can't even recall them all. But before Savannah, I think it was that girl in the car accident. Found her Toyota in a ditch. Another one, some time back, was a house fire."

*Curses make good stories,* Max thought, though he knew they weren't real. People loved to pick up a story about a haunted building or paranormal high jinks. The unexplained made for the best tales, dating back to mythology, where the sun was explained to be pulled by a chariot across the sky. Max was happy to hear Stella recount these details because he felt it might make for good fodder one day; perhaps, he could sell this story to a magazine.

Max also knew that curses often had origins.

"What's the story behind the curse?" Max asked. "Why Ruston?"

"The townspeople will probably tell you it dates back to when this was a rail town," Stella recalled. "The trains that passed through here were often loaded with stowaways, in search of a fresh start. There's a popular story that a hundred years ago, a young woman was found on one of the trains, and police apprehended her. She begged them to let her pass through, saying she was on the run from someone terrible. But they took her in and tried to find out who she was.

"Eventually, an older man came into town who said he was the girl's father. Police released custody of the girl to the man. She screamed and didn't want to go. She told them that she would not leave town with this man. Police mocked her and sent her off anyway.

"A few days later, an older couple—a minister and his wife—came through town, saying they were looking for a young girl, and she had taken the train this way, through Ruston. They wanted to return her home. Well, the locals told them the girl had already been collected by her father, a few days earlier. The man and woman were devastated. They said, 'That's our daughter.'"

Max listened, unblinking, picturing the details with horror and fascination.

"No one knows who the man that came to collect the girl was. Police had written his name down in their logs, but when they went back to check, it was gone. Some say it was the boogeyman, others think it was a vampire. But there's no record of the man who made off with the young girl. The parents were, of course, devastated. Most believe that God turned his back on Ruston after that. Or that whatever foul energy came in and stole the girl away left its stain on the town."

Max felt the hair on the back of his neck standing up. Stella had paused, letting the silence of the kitchen—with Mrs. Romano's eerie singing—own the moment.

"But that's all a bunch of hullaballoo." Stella waved a hand.

Max looked back out the kitchen window, out into the postcard winter. Suddenly, though, the setting felt warped. The trees seemed to be screaming at the sky for help, and the birds were trying to hide.

***

Upstairs, Oren had settled onto the small bed he had been provided, and he was plugged away on his laptop. Stella did not have Wi-Fi—an oversight—so he switched to his phone. He was able to find profiles for someone by the name *NellFlix_9* on most of the major social media apps. None of them were set to private, so he began to snoop.

On the first couple of apps that he tried, the account was listed as inactive for the past few months. He cycled through to his third choice, however, and found that *NellFlix_9* had been using this one far more often. It listed her as active two days ago.

The profile displayed a teen girl with frizzy, light hair and dark makeup around her eyes. Her picture was obscured by a filter and only showed half of her face. Very moody, which was on brand for teenagers, Oren figured.

Oren navigated to the description page. All he found were song lyrics. He went instead to the photos page. He spotted several blurry photos, almost none of them capturing the girl's full face. Her hair seemed to change regularly, dyed blond or red or black, and she had a few different friends with her. The further back Oren scrolled, the more the photos just became dog pictures. He chose one of the selfies at random and opened it. It was tagged, again, with a song lyric. No description of who was in it or who this girl was. This was a trend that carried on for some time. As he clicked from photo to photo, there was nothing but song lyrics.

He gave up and moved on to the videos page. The first video—one that had been pinned to the page—that he loaded was just one of a Shih Tzu humping a table leg while someone holding the camera giggled. The second video, however, was far more valuable.

In it, the camera shook wildly as *NellFlix_9* tried to point the phone at someone.

"Ok, ok, go," someone off-screen said.

The camera finally landed on this second girl, who was holding a bottle. Angry music blasted in the background, but over it, you could make out laughter. The girl holding the bottle brought it up to her lips and tried to chug the beverage inside. She failed, though, forced to spit it out halfway through. Both girls shook with fits of laughter.

"You try it then, bitch," the girl holding the bottle said, holding it out.

Oren paused the video. For a moment, it was finally clear enough to see the girl. The one handing over the drink.

It was Tiffany.

Oren checked the timestamp on the video. It was from the early morning hours of February 7. Same as the photo he found on Tiffany's account. So, Tiffany had, at the very least, been alive, drinking with her friend, after Robert Thomas showed up at the family house and left his footprint in the snow.

Cycling back to the photos page, Oren felt his heartbeat accelerate. This was real. He found the clearest image he could of the girl. One where she had wavy blonde hair, dark eyes, and was leaning against a

Nirvana poster in some basement. This was the person he had to find in order to find Tiffany.

***

Oren rushed into the kitchen, finding Max and Stella enjoying opera music that seemed to be coming from the walls of the house. Oren didn't care, as he was out of breath with excitement.

"Max," he huffed. "I've got our lead."

"Who?"

Oren held out his phone, showcasing the picture of the teenager.

"Do you happen to know her?" Max turned to Stella after he checked out the photo.

Oren seemed surprised by this idea but quickly turned the screen around to face their hostess.

"Why, yes," Stella said, her voice beaming. "I know her. That's Nelly Masterson. Her family lives just on the other side of the rail crossing. Don't care much for her parents. Not the nicest people. But the few times I've run into the girl at the store, she's been quiet. Nice enough. Did she do something?"

"No," Oren said. "We just think she can help us. Do you know exactly where she lives?"

"Go through town, cross the tracks, turn left on Pine," Stella said. "White house with yellow trim. It's small, but you can't miss it."

"I'm going to call Archie," Oren said. His mouth seemed to be smiling, but it wouldn't be right for him to be happy. Max thought it looked more like his mouth was taught with adrenaline. "Get your things ready."

Max knew what he meant. He patted his pocket. The MemCom was still there. Its familiar shape brought back another tidal wave of Charlie memories, things Max thought to be lost from his dive at the airport.

# 8. Charlie's Question

"SWEET CAROLINE" STILL CHIMED IN Charlie's head. The tune always remained stuck there long after he arrived in Lang's mind. Charlie had lost count of how many times he had visited; the trips to the prison and subsequent dives weren't always a success, and by now, they had tallied quite a few more appointments than intended. This was entirely Charlie's fault. Most of the time he no longer even bothered looking for victims.

Instead, Charlie had mastered Lang's mind.

Charlie knew exactly where to find Kelly. He knew how to converse with her without setting off alarm bells. He had even started forming theories about the MemCom and how it worked. He wrote notes, intending to write an essay.

As was the case with his last handful of visits, Charlie brought himself to the beach. Lang and Kelly had come to Galway for the weekend, and they stood alone on this last picturesque stretch that separated land from sea. Kelly overlooked the grey, frothing North Atlantic Ocean. The sky was just a slightly brighter shade of grey than the water.

Unlike Kelly, Lang wasn't paying attention to the ocean. He had a different sort of sightseeing in mind. He had wandered away from his girlfriend, looking back at the street from which they had come. A Ferris wheel dotted the skyline, marking a nearby amusement park. A steady stream of people, tourists and locals alike, cluttered the grounds.

Lang was people-watching.

Charlie watched Lang saunter away across the sandy beach, a pile of dark rock walling him off from the road. He had become a scientist, studying and taking notes, following their behaviours, and then implementing his own tests to see what reactions he could get from Kelly.

Kelly existed in this memory now only because Lang was still vaguely aware of her presence, but she was not the focal point as she had been at the cliffs. She was a secondary player, and this worked in Charlie's favour.

"So beautiful," Charlie said, approaching Kelly.

Kelly turned to meet his gaze. The repeated elements were comforting, and he walked through dialogue that they'd carried out a dozen times already. To Charlie's own surprise, he had been content to rehearse the same stage play every encounter. He lost himself in it. If he said the right things, she would grow closer.

When she got to the part about liking his eyes, he grabbed her hand. The flesh was always warm to the touch. This sent a jolt of electricity across his body. This simple contact had been as far as he'd gone as of late, but he was always attempting to push his experiments further.

Charlie had invested enough hours now that he'd confidently formed a hypothesis. He believed that there were two types of reconstructed animates in the MemCom. There were hostile subjects and non-hostile subjects. Hostile subjects were the watch dogs. They were perceiving the memory and if anything fell out of place, alarms would go off. Non-hostile subjects didn't seem to be aware of any existing pattern that the memory should fit into. They weren't alarmed by changes to the order of things because they had no awareness that an order had been there before.

This should allow Charlie to interact with Kelly as much as he wished, he theorized. If Lang didn't notice him—which he wouldn't on this beach because he never turned back around—then Charlie was safe to manipulate as he pleased.

Today, Charlie would finally follow through with something he'd been intending to do for a long time. He had not left anything to chance.

To make sure his experiments were correct, he expanded the field. He began to run tests on others. Charlie had started using the MemCom on his own. He'd bring it with him to a diner near his apartment, always late at night, and he'd ask for the corner booth. He would lay his head down and listen to the tunes on the jukebox—usually 1980s pop—and play a game of roulette. He would end up in a stranger's head, someone else who happened to be in the diner that night, also listening to the jukebox.

Charlie threw caution to the wind in these experiments. He would immediately start interacting with all of the people in these memories, trying to figure out what the boundaries were, who the background players were, and whose mind he was in. He wanted to see where the line was.

And in most cases where he presented himself as a friend, he could get away with a lot. Even with the SI. Charlie could have full conversations with the SI, and if he didn't disturb things, they'd respond, even share a laugh. One night, he'd entered a memory where a sad man was sitting across from his boss, a tall man in a baggy suit. The sad man was being laid off. Charlie had put his arm around the sad man and told him, "You don't deserve this," and together, they threw items at the man in the baggy suit.

All of this led to his final experiment.

On a damp night while his corner booth window was spattered with rain drops, Charlie had entered another foreign mind. He found a background player—a man who had been on the sidelines watching a high school basketball game—and grabbed his hand. Together, they headed for the exit.

A set of double doors led from this school gymnasium out to a different memory beyond. Charlie dragged his new friend right up to the precipice. The man Charlie had grabbed had a pair of eyes but no nose or mouth. He was an incomplete rendering. His eyes watched Charlie with no real emotion. He was powerless to stop this. His script was only to sit and cheer.

"One small step," Charlie said, imagining himself to be a trailblazer.

This could be the beginning of a new understanding into this technology. He pushed through the door, pulling the semi-faced man behind him.

The scene changed. School walls melted away, becoming trees in a forest. The sky lit up, the sun cascading through the forest canopy. The sound of cheering was replaced with birds chirping. The hardness of the gym floor became a soft bed of moss and dirt. And when Charlie allowed himself to look beside him, he found the semi-faced man was still there, holding his hand, eyes seeing but not recognizing.

Charlie had successfully brought this man with him from one place to another. He waited a moment, wanting to see if alarm bells sounded. A pair of hikers walked by—one of them the SI—and Charlie crouched, pulling his guest down into the brush with him. The SI passed by without noticing them, enjoying his hike as if nothing were amiss.

It had worked.

Now Charlie could apply his theories in Lang's mind with confidence.

Back on the beach with Kelly, her standing close and their hands joined, he was ready to push the limits once more.

Holding Kelly's hand left an imprint on Charlie; it was as though they were still holding hands even as he left Lang's mind. A sort of phantom limb effect. It was all he could think about after his dives ended. She had become an obsession. But he wanted more than to just hold her hand.

And so, he kissed her.

Charlie kissed Kelly, letting his lips feel hers; they were real. After the kiss, he paused, opened his eyes, and saw her staring back at him. She seemed to be alive; her eyes glowed, and her skin was flush. No alarms had sounded, and Lang was still far away. Charlie began kissing her again.

Fireworks started going off from the amusement park next to them. Bursts of colour showered over them. The night turned temporarily into day. The side of Kelly's face was painted in sparkling light, changing from red to green to yellow.

"Come on," Charlie said, taking her by the hand.

He jogged over to the road, having scouted ahead. There was a bar nearby. Which meant there was a door. They had to watch for cars—though they didn't have fully formed shapes or a proper make or model, they still looked like they could kill you at the speed they were travelling—as they ran across the asphalt.

"Where are we going?" Kelly asked.

"On our first real date," Charlie answered.

He pulled her along, reaching the door, and pausing just long enough to enjoy the moment. He glanced back at Kelly. If this worked—*when* this worked—Charlie could finally be free to write his own scripts. He opened the door and brought Kelly across the threshold.

Twilight gave the world just enough to see by. Spiny trees lined a dirt road. A flashlight beam cut across the woods, illuminating a sign nearby: *Fairluck Campground: 2 miles.*

The man holding the flashlight was dragging a shovel in his other hand. When he got to this large sign, he placed the flashlight down on the ground and began to dig. There was no question that this was another one of Lang's burial spots. But that wasn't what Charlie cared about. He could still feel the warmth of Kelly's hand enfolded in his.

"We made it," he whispered, turning to her.

She watched him with confused eyes. She was out of her environment; there was no script for what she should be saying or doing here. To Charlie, this meant that he would get to program her.

"Let's go."

They began to walk away from Lang, marching down the dirt road. He let go of her hand just long enough to wrap his arm around her.

"Are you cold?" he asked.

The question itself wasn't as important as how she reacted. He wanted to make sure she could create new dialogue with him.

She didn't get to answer. A high-pitched squeal shot across the road, forcing Charlie to let go of Kelly and cover his ears. When he collected himself enough to turn around, he saw that Lang was staring straight at him. He had recognized a threat; he had spotted Charlie and an out of place actor.

Lang's mind was different than the strangers in the diner. He was beginning to recognize the intrusions. He knew, subconsciously, that Charlie was there, time and time again. Ever since the phone call, it was as if the two of them were playing a chess match. Charlie tried to avoid detection while interfering with pieces of Lang's memory. Lang was aware things were amiss and just couldn't quite tell why. Lang didn't *really* know what was happening, but his guard was up more than anyone else Charlie had dove on.

"Hurry!" Charlie shouted, trying to drag Kelly off the road as Lang came after them.

But Kelly was frozen again. She would not budge. Lang's mind had put everything on lockdown. The murderer inched closer to Charlie, walking with the deliberate, slow steps of a horror film baddie. The shovel was still in his arms, and he was smiling.

Charlie felt all of the air rush out of him. He had failed. Next time, he would need to use a different door. Or get off the road faster. He could come back, start from the beginning, and bring Kelly somewhere they wouldn't be found.

He tried to remind himself he had still made progress, that he had learned, and so it was not all a loss. But he still felt regret and heartache as he shut his eyes and withdrew from Lang's memory.

*** 

"Where?" Oren was asking.

Charlie was still groggy. This dive had lasted longer than intended. "Fairluck Campground, right by the sign," he said, though his voice felt like it was coming from someone else. He hadn't quite brought himself back to the present. He felt as though his soul was still with Kelly on that dirt road.

"Congratulations!" Oren clapped his hands together and then embraced Aria.

Charlie hadn't expected this. He looked up from his spot in the prison interrogation room. Then Oren came over and extended his hand to Charlie, looking for a shake.

"What?" was all Charlie could muster. He looked through the glass at Lang, who was still speaking, telling a story about something Charlie didn't understand.

"Mission complete, Charlie." Oren couldn't contain his smile. "That's the last victim. You found them all."

These words brought a weight on top of Charlie that nearly knocked the wind out of him.

"You must feel good," Oren said. "You've done it."

But Charlie didn't feel good. He was devastated. If they had found all of the bodies, if they had completed the mission, then his visits with Kelly were over. He was furious at himself. How had he lost count? How did he not know this was the last one? Charlie could have stalled. He could have not reported back the location. He could have lied.

His heart broke, and his chest was burning more than anything he'd ever felt. He had so much more to do. His experiments were not over. He was just getting close to figuring out how to get Kelly away from Lang. The realization Charlie had then, that would be buried away and never admitted to anyone, was that Kelly mattered infinitely more than the victims. To him, this mission had failed.

"Drinks after this?" Oren said. "My treat."

"Yeah, sure," Charlie said, still watching Lang.

Oren pressed his talk button and cut Lang off, telling him they had to run. They were done.

"Your visits are always so short," Lang whined. "And it takes me over an hour to do me hair and get all gussied up for you."

After lying and saying they'd be back soon, Oren practically skipped to the door. He held it open for Charlie. But Charlie had been forming a thought.

"I'll just be a minute," Charlie said, waving Oren off.

Oren, who was too overjoyed to consider that something was amiss, left with Aria. They were eager to get out to Fairluck Campground and find that last missing body. The two of them talked about the case all the way down the hall as the door closed.

Now alone, Charlie hurried over to the talk button. Without even introducing himself, he blurted out his question.

"Did you kill her too?"

Lang was startled and looked up at the speakers as if God himself had chimed in. The door behind Lang was opening and a guard had arrived to escort him out. But Charlie didn't care. He needed an answer.

"Huh?" Lang grunted.

"Did you kill her too?" Charlie repeated, manic. "Kelly. Is she one of the ones we haven't found?"

At first, Lang was perplexed. Then something clicked in his brain, and he had to smile. He brought his gaze down to the one-way mirror as Charlie watched, and somehow Lang managed to find his eyes. Charlie felt cold.

"So, you know about Kelly." Lang smirked. "Do you find her as *lovely* as I did?"

Charlie's knuckles started to tremble. Charlie smacked the talk button again, but his voice caught in his throat. He would've strangled Lang right then and there had they not been separated. The guard started unchaining Lang and standing him up, unmoved by Charlie's frantic cries.

"No, wait!" Charlie shouted into the microphone.

The guard didn't stop. He started escorting Lang away to the back door. Lang looked over his shoulder at the mirror, still smiling, blowing a kiss. He offered a quick wink and then turned away. Charlie, on the other side of the glass, was powerless to stop him.

"No, stop!" Charlie pleaded with the guard, but it did not work.

Lang was gone.

# 9. Suspects

NELLY'S HOUSE WASN'T FAR. EITHER that or the town was starting to feel smaller already. By now, Max was able to place himself on a mental map, always knowing where he was in relation to Stella's and the Thomases'.

Stella was right; the house was impossible to miss. It was a small bungalow with faded white and yellow siding, plunked neatly on the street between much larger homes.

The yard and driveway were both piled with snow. Two deep sets of tire tracks carved a line from the detached garage out to the main road. Someone had pulled out—or in—and not bothered to clear the way. They would have to high-step it over the snow to reach the front door.

"Want me to wait?" Archie asked as they departed the jeep.

"I don't think we'll be long," Oren said. "But if you have anywhere to be . . ."

"No, sir." Archie gave them a toothless grin. "I'll be right here if ya need me."

Their prints were the first ones leading up to the front door. Max found it strange that no one had gone in or out since the last snowfall. Despite their careful steps, their feet sank into treacherously deep drifts, and snow found its way down into Max's boots, soaking his socks.

The door was scratched, its paint many years old. A rusty knocker bore a single icicle, which Oren broke off. He then knocked heavily, three times.

They listened for movement. The street was still, and they could hear one another breathing. But no commotion from inside the house. Oren knocked three more times. They gave it a minute, and still nothing.

"Are you going to break it down?" Max asked.

"Break it down?" Oren smirked. "Who do you think I am? Let's go around back."

They gave Archie a polite wave as they trudged through the high snow again, the only sound in the neighbourhood coming from the crunching beneath their frozen feet. As they rounded the corner, they were forced to shield their eyes from the noon sun, bouncing directly off the ground.

With Oren leading the way, they navigated over to the rear deck. Oren pressed his face against one of the windows, trying to get a look inside. Max fell behind, distracted by the garage at the back of the driveway. It was a modest size—not quite large enough for two cars—and was just as beat up as the house, and the large bay door seemed to have buckled inward, not looking likely that it would open without some difficulty. Max's eye was drawn to the window on the side of the structure, which was fogged up. There was a considerable amount of condensation, and it seemed to be coming from the inside.

Max started walking toward the garage. There was a door beside the window, and the bottom was entirely scuffed with boot marks, in the way that someone might casually kick it open over the years.

"Do you see that?" Max called out. "The steam on the window?"

Oren squinted, fighting against the sun.

"Nice find," Oren said as he jogged over, giving Max a pat on the back.

"Someone's inside," Max posited.

Oren knocked on the side door to the garage the same way he had on the house, with three distinct thuds. It only took a few seconds and the door started opening inward. There was a momentary rush of steam as some heat escaped into the morning outside, and then Oren and Max were staring at a teenaged girl with too much eye shadow, her frizzy hair in braids, and she was wearing a dark hooded sweater several sizes too big. Her nails were painted black, and she played with them nervously as she spoke.

"Hello?" the girl said.

"Are you Nelly Masterson?" Oren asked.

She nodded slightly, cautiously.

"My name is Oren. I'm a private investigator. I'm working for the Thomas family. I believe you're a friend of Tiffany's, is that right?"

The girl nodded again.

"This is my friend Max, he's helping me. Do you mind if we speak to you for a few minutes?"

"Um, yeah, that's okay," Nelly muttered.

She stepped aside and beckoned for them to enter. Once inside, Max saw that the garage had been converted into a bedroom. The walls were unfinished, just bits of wood and insulation, but a slew of posters covered most of them. A ceiling fan and light fixture hung from the centre beam overhead. Curtains had been drawn over the window, and two heavy duty space heaters were on full blast. There was a large area rug laid out over the concrete slab beneath their feet, serving as makeshift carpeting.

In the far corner was a shabby old chest of drawers, each one refusing to close completely. Shirts and socks stuck out at odd angles. The other corner, on their right, housed a bare twin mattress on a white high-posted bed frame. A heap of pink and blue blankets were rolled up on the mattress, and the pillow had been knocked onto the rug below. A couple of cardboard boxes, a standing mirror, and a mini fridge rounded out the decor.

There also seemed to be a door leading to a small bathroom in behind the chest of drawers, but the door was only slightly ajar, so Max couldn't be sure.

"We won't be long, but do you mind if we have a seat?" Oren asked. "We'd like to make this as casual and comfortable as possible."

"Okay, sorry," Nelly said timidly.

They had seen this boisterous girl in the video, laughing and chanting. And now both Oren and Max were somewhat surprised by the mousy, shy specter who had answered the door. In the light of day, she didn't seem to possess the same rebellious nature.

Nelly apologized for the state of the room and moved quickly to clear some clothing from two chairs that Max hadn't even realized were there until that moment. Nelly slid them out into the middle of the room. She then took a seat on her bed.

Oren and Max both kicked off their boots at the entrance, being polite. Immediately, Max felt his wet socks start to solidify from the cold ground.

Max couldn't help but feel sorry for this girl. While he likely would've pushed his parents to convert the shed into a bedroom so he could get some space, he could never imagine them *actually* letting him live like this.

"Are your parents home?" Oren asked as he sat.

"No, they're never home," Nelly said.

She was quiet, tucking her face into her sweater partially as she spoke to them. It was hard to hear her over the heaters.

"My dad travels a lot for work, and my mom has been living over in Syracuse for a year now with her . . . I guess with her boyfriend."

"Who occupies the house?" Oren asked.

"No one," she replied. "Well, my dad when he's around. Otherwise, it sits empty."

"Do you ever have friends over? Maybe let them stay in the house?" Oren forced a small smile, the kind that made people open up to him.

"No." Nelly didn't even flinch at Oren's tactic. "It's gross in there. I try to avoid it if I can. I have everything I need out here."

Oren looked to Max, biting his lip. They both were thinking it; how could they pull off a dive in this setting? The space was too limited, and the seats were too awkward. Max was picking up on Oren's suspicion though. He clearly didn't trust the girl.

"I'll jump right into why we want to speak with you, if that's okay, Nelly?" Oren continued.

"Sure."

"You are friends with Tiffany Thomas," Oren stated.

Nelly seemed horrified—as if on trial—but nodded, biting her lip.

"Have you had Tiffany over here recently?"

Nelly's eyes darted from Oren to Max and then back to Oren. She looked like a cornered rabbit and was just now realizing there was nowhere her scared legs could carry her. She didn't answer the question, so Oren answered for her.

"I saw a video of you and Tiffany online," Oren said.

He withdrew his phone. He had saved the video for this instance. He played it back for Nelly, and the girl stared at the phone the entire time, mesmerized.

"Where did this take place?"

Nelly murmured her response so softly that they didn't catch it. Oren asked her to repeat herself.

"In the house," Nelly admitted.

"In the house there?" Oren pointed out the door at the home he had just been knocking at.

"Yes." Nelly sagged.

"So, Tiffany was with you in the house." Oren nodded, repeating the facts very clearly.

Max was sure there was a tactic to this, but he couldn't figure it out.

"Is Tiffany still in the house, Nelly?"

Nelly started picking at her fingernails, her hands working quickly like the nervous paws of a burrowing animal. She continued biting her lip and trying to sink into her sweater. Oren turned around, peering at the door they had entered through, as if he had the ability to see through walls.

It was frustrating, not getting answers. Max felt as though the girl shrank to someone ten years younger. It was like trying to get the truth from a little kid.

"Nelly, is Tiffany in the house right now?" Oren asked again.

Max sensed something building. The moment was escalating. There was electricity in Oren's veins. Nelly shook her head slightly but would not make eye contact.

Oren stood, hand moving to his hip, toward his holstered firearm. This alarmed Max. What did Oren think was about to happen?

Oren made his way to the door.

"Nelly, are you sure Tiffany is not inside the house?" Oren repeated, his voice louder now.

Nelly winced at the volume, staring at the ground and unwilling to reply.

Oren shot Max a glance, motioning for him to stand as well. "Let's all take a walk, okay? I'd like us to go into the house."

Oren slid his boots back on, and Max did the same. Nelly was a shell of a person, not taking her eyes off the floor as she found some old running shoes and put them on without tying the laces. Oren let Max lead the way, followed by Nelly, and then he took up the rear, shutting the garage door behind them. They all walked with half-closed eyes through the snow.

When they got to the sliding screen door at the back of the house—which was boarded over at the bottom—Oren asked Nelly if it was locked. She shook her head. Oren tried it. It stuck a bit at first, but with some effort, he was able to get it open. They all stepped inside.

What Nelly had said about the house being a mess was true. They were hit with the smell of mold and sour milk immediately. Oren tried to shield his face without being obvious and rude. Max wasn't able to remain discreet at all, and audibly gagged.

Once inside, Oren strong-armed the door shut again and searched for a light switch. The house was dark. Most of the shades had been drawn and only a small sliver of sunlight crawled in from a window above the kitchen sink. That same sink was littered with dirty dishes, most of which seemed to have green fuzz growing on them.

Oren finally found a light switch and turned it on. A single bulb above the kitchen table—also covered in dishes—flickered to life. The bulb was on for no more than two seconds before it flickered back off.

"What were you and Tiffany doing in here the other night?" Oren asked.

"Drinking," Nelly whispered, ashamed.

"Was there anyone else with you?" Oren asked.

Nelly stiffened again, not able to answer.

Oren looked at Max, making a small turn of his head, pointing at his ear. He wanted Max to be ready for a dive. Max had the earpiece handy but wasn't sure what he was supposed to do. He wasn't willing to pass out here in the middle of the filthy floor.

Oren forged on ahead, passing through the kitchen and into a living room with two dilapidated sofas. There was a tube TV in the corner, the likes of which Oren thought did not exist anymore. The carpet was scarred with cigarette burns. He passed over the carpet, intentionally stepping around the burns like a child avoids cracks on the sidewalk. He made his way to the front window and tore open the curtains. A moth flew out from behind them, dumbfounded and startled, smacking into walls and the ceiling as it tried to flap itself to safety. It left the room and Max didn't see where it ended up.

With more light, it was easier to see the decay. The walls desperately needed paint, the sofas were even older than they had first appeared to be, and the TV had a crack down the centre of its screen.

"Tiffany?!" Oren called out.

Nelly cringed at the name.

Oren noticed this and called out again.

There was no movement anywhere else in the house. Keeping his hand near his belt, Oren paced down a narrow hallway toward a couple of bedrooms. Max watched him go, seeing him move slowly around corners, reaching into a room, turning on the light, and then disappearing into the room entirely for a few seconds. He would reemerge with a disappointed look on his face and shake his head at Max.

Oren did this for all four rooms on this floor, and then returned to the living room.

"Where's Tiffany?" he asked Nelly again. "I need your help, Nelly."

Still stubborn, scared, or maybe a bit of both, Nelly only trembled and looked at the floor.

"Where was that video taken? Where did Tiffany sleep when she was with you?" Oren asked.

Then he glanced back at the kitchen and noticed there was a staircase descending into a dark basement.

"Did she sleep in the basement?"

Nelly flinched and rocked her head in what could have been a nod. Oren asked Max and Nelly to take a seat in the living room and stay put for a second. They did as instructed.

Oren went down the stairs by himself, each step creaking and threatening to give out. Oren felt for the lump of his gun on his hip, experiencing a familiar blend of nerves and heightened senses. He thought about calling out again but felt he was in a vulnerable position coming down the stairs into the blackness.

When he got to the bottom, a single white thread was hanging from the ceiling right in his face. Oren pulled it, and three bare bulbs came on, illuminating the unfinished basement. The space was large. It was also mostly empty save for an old dining set pressed up under a window, a love seat with no cushions, and a broken wardrobe left on its side. And then there was the bare mattress in the middle of the room.

Smack dab in the centre of the concrete floor was a bare mattress, sheets balled up on top of it.

There weren't a lot of places to hide, so Oren went straight for the mattress. He poked at it once with his foot. Then he crouched down to investigate further. With a quick glance at the wardrobe in the corner—to make sure no monsters were going to jump out—Oren slowly lifted the sheets off the mattress. Underneath was an unmistakable mark, dark and abstract, about the size of a baseball.

A bloodstain.

Oren dropped the sheets, rising back up quickly. His heart was racing now, and he felt his muscles tighten. He scanned the basement one more time. He peaked under the love seat. Nothing. He tried the wardrobe. Empty. Beside the wardrobe, he did find a small travel makeup bag. He glanced at it quickly but decided it wasn't relevant and moved on.

"Tiffany?" he called out, feeling a bit foolish.

There was nowhere for the girl to hide. Regardless, Oren felt like he was being watched. His skin prickled. Perhaps it was the basement itself, staring at him and daring him to figure it out.

With nothing left to find, Oren rushed up the stairs. He came back into the living room and saw Max and Nelly both sitting on separate couches, Nelly staring at the floor and Max staring at the broken TV.

"Tiffany was here," Oren said.

He looked right at Nelly, and after a beat, she finally made eye contact with him.

"Did you know she was reported missing, Nelly?"

Nelly stared at him. Her eyes glimmered with recognition. He could feel her saying *yes* even before she finally nodded.

"We need to know what happened, Nelly," Oren said. "We are here to help. Did Tiffany run away to come be here with you? Was she mad at her parents? Did she stay in the basement?"

There were too many questions for Nelly to pick one. She balled up her fists and let out a sigh.

Oren knew there was one way to get all the answers. He looked at Max and tapped his ear. Max already understood and had the earpiece out. Oren had his phone handy and queued up the video of the girls partying. In the background of the video was that bass-y, garbled tune. Oren turned the volume up to the highest his phone's tiny speakers could pump out. Even with the girls shouting overtop, the music was noticeable. This would work.

"I need you to look at this again, Nelly," Oren said, handing her the phone. He then carefully stepped away, making himself further away from Max. "Really look at it."

Max didn't hesitate. He brought the earpiece up to his right ear, the one Nelly wouldn't be able to see.

"Take a look at this again and remember that night. I really need you to tell us what happened," Oren said over the phone's rhythmic blaring.

Those were the last words Max heard before falling into Nelly's memories.

\*\*\*

Max was standing in a large, open kitchen. There were beautiful granite counter tops, a fridge the size of three normal refrigerators, and a row of windows that looked out onto a massive yard. As Max surveyed, he realized he had been here recently. He was back in the Thomas house.

The kitchen opened up onto a cozy den, where two girls sat on a sectional by the grand fireplace. He was third-wheeling on girls' night, apparently. Nelly and Tiffany were dancing and laughing. Liquor bottles and plastic cups littered the coffee table. They were playing some rap music that hadn't aged well and doing their best to get the lyrics right.

"Which one's mine?" Tiffany asked, slurring her words as she reached for a cup.

"The red one," Nelly said, then as Tiffany grabbed the wrong cup, she snorted and slapped her friend. "I said the red one. You're fucking colour blind."

"And proud of it," Tiffany said, grabbing a different cup instead and downing the contents.

The girls very suddenly disappeared from the sectional, and then they reappeared, standing and singing, to Max's immediate left. He flinched. The memory jumped forwards again, and now the girls were refilling their glasses. Nelly was dressed all in black, wrapped again in an oversized hoodie. But by the expression on her face, she appeared to be out of her shell a bit. Meanwhile, Tiffany was dressed as if she were pulled from a catalogue; she was a great advertisement for her family's wealth.

That the girls were still friends in spite of the class difference was impressive to Max.

As Nelly started to pour vodka into her glass, Tiffany froze as if she heard something. Nelly noticed and stopped pouring. Then, as one, they looked toward Max, suddenly aware of the strange man in their kitchen. Max tried not to move, thinking maybe they wouldn't see him.

"Who are you?" Nelly asked.

Max tried to think of what to say, but thankfully didn't need to answer.

Tiffany interrupted. "Drink up, girl." She clinked glasses with her friend and downed a healthy amount of her drink.

The memory jumped forwards again, and Max was spared. They were back in the living room, dancing.

"Oh shit!" Tiffany screamed suddenly.

"What?" Nelly asked.

"My stepmom just texted." Tiffany held out her phone, showing the evidence. "They're fucking coming out here."

"Now?" Nelly slumped down on the couch, staring at her drink woefully. She had barely even had a chance to enjoy it.

"She always has to make a big deal about everything," Tiffany raged. "So dramatic, coming all the way out here to bring me back."

Max moved into the shadows of the nearby breakfast nook, trying to stay out of the way as the girls began to furiously clean the mess they had made. Nelly wiped up spills while Tiffany threw glasses in the dishwasher and put the lids back on the bottles.

"Let's just go to your place," Tiffany suggested. "Take one for the road." Tiffany tossed Nelly a bottle.

The label was smudged, no letters clear enough to read, but Max could tell by the bottle and the colour that it was whiskey. Then she seemed to get an idea and ran to the pantry. She procured a paper bag and sheathed their drink in it.

"In case the fuzz show up."

Nelly seemed nervous about the idea of hosting her friend over at her place. She clammed up again but went along with what Tiffany suggested. She followed Tiffany around as they finished tidying the kitchen. At one point, Tiffany left her phone on the kitchen counter and walked away from it. Nelly went to grab it, but Tiffany stopped her.

"My dad can track that one," Tiffany said. "I'll bring my old one. It's still connected."

Next, Max was brought forwards to Tiffany's bedroom. The world rose like an elevator, leaving his stomach to play catch up. He exhaled in disbelief at the size of her room; it was the size of his condo in downtown Vancouver.

Max watched uncomfortably from the shadows as they stuffed some of Tiffany's clothes and some beauty items into a fancy leather travel bag. Then she grabbed a jacket from her walk-in closet and a pair of boots, and she made for the hallway. Nelly followed, taking massive sips from the bottle, apparently trying to get drunk fast.

From that point, the memories took on a sort of doubling effect, and Max watched them refract upon themselves. Every object—and each of the girls—had a sort of ghost trail that followed them behind a second later. Angles were warped, objects blurry, and colours inconsistent. The girls struggled to dress themselves in the foyer, having to sit on the floor to finish tying their boots. Tiffany pulled open the door and ran out into the night.

She hollered back at her friend. "Pull it shut tight! It sticks!"

Max watched Nelly struggle to get her boots on, finally standing and rushing out the door. The world tilted sideways, and Max flew into the wall, bracing himself against a family portrait. Nelly wobbled, caught the door frame, and then the world righted itself. She absent-mindedly pulled at the door handle as she ran. The door swung most of the way shut but hit the frame and bounced back open.

Max stared at the ajar foyer door and knew that in a few hours, the wind and snow would collaborate to fill this room. The drift would pile up high enough to collect a footprint from DA Thomas. He felt strangely guilty for leaving it open but knew not to interfere. Without thinking, he stepped outside, crossing the threshold of the door.

The dark night outside faded away and was replaced with bright sunlight.

*Shit,* Max thought. *The doorway rule.* He had exited via the front door and found himself in an entirely different memory. He would need to take an unexpected detour.

A pair of girls were sitting on the dock, each of them probably only twelve years old. They were easily recognizable as younger versions of Tiffany and Nelly. Tiffany was decked out in a fancy one-piece, something a twelve-year-old wouldn't pick out for themselves. Nelly was still in jeans and an oversized black hoodie, despite the beating sun and suffocating heat.

Max stood on a boat that had been tied to the one side of the dock, nicely tucked away from sight. He watched the two girls converse but noticed an older, stocky boy sauntering his way up the dock toward them.

"You come here every summer?" Nelly was asking.

"Pretty much," Tiffany answered. "You should come out on our boat sometime."

"I . . . I'm not sure." Nelly stared into the water, head down.

"It'll be fun!" Tiffany encouraged her. "Why not?"

"I can't really swim," Nelly admitted. "And I don't have any nice bathing suits."

The boy on the dock was closing in now. He had a nasty smile on his face. He was planning his words carefully—had been the entire walk up. Nelly must've known he was coming, or he wouldn't have appeared in the memory. She cringed even before he finished his first words.

"Hey, mopey!" the boy called out, walking right up behind the girls.

Tiffany turned, saw him, and rose, expecting to meet a new friend. Nelly shrank, staying where she was.

"Who's the new girl?"

"I'm Tiffany Thomas." Tiffany smiled.

"Whachu doin' hanging around with the human puddle here?" The boy pointed a chubby finger. Then to Nelly, he said, "Maybe ditch the sweater, and you'll finally get a tan."

"Her name is Nelly," Tiffany said defiantly.

The stocky boy had her by about fifty pounds and three or four years.

But Tiffany was tall and stood proud. "And she can wear whatever she wants."

"You know she wears it to hide the cuts on her arm, right?" the boy said.

Nelly buried her face into her arms. What little of her cheeks remained exposed were beet red.

"I think you should leave," Tiffany said.

"It's a public dock," the boy snarled.

"Well, you're not welcome."

The boy considered this a second and then rolled his eyes. "Fine, I have places to be anyway. Just don't get too attached to her, kay? She's probably gonna throw herself into the lake one of these days and do us all a favour."

At this, Tiffany reached her breaking point. She stepped toward the boy, who didn't realize what was happening and froze. Tiffany stuck one leg behind the boy and put her hand on his shoulder. With a confident shove, she tripped him backwards and sent him toppling into the lake.

The splash was triumphant. Nelly's mind exaggerated the height and sound, making it into a fireworks show.

The moment then replayed itself in slow motion. Tiffany glowed like a Goddess as she shoved the stocky boy into the water. It opened up, its dark clutches embracing him as his soaked face looked up in horror.

*That was a cool moment,* Max thought. But he wondered how long it was going to last. It was now replaying itself over again.

He realized the boat he stood on had a door that led down below deck. Good enough. He left the two girls to drench the bully on repeat and stepped through the tiny space, ducking his head.

\*\*\*

The heat of summer was replaced with the bleak cold of winter. The two girls, restored to their current age, walked ahead of Max. The streets were dark, an occasional streetlamp doing its best to show the way. Max found himself growing tired of the cold, longing for more memories on beaches somewhere. He had to remind himself it wasn't real, tucking his imaginary chin in and bracing against the wind.

The girls, however, seemed to have the protection of their whiskey. They laughed and danced as if they didn't feel a thing.

The walk felt long, and the funhouse mirror Max was seeing the world through made it difficult to keep up. He started feeling drunk himself. The ground seemed to warp and dip, and he tripped a couple times, thinking he needed to step higher when he didn't. Once, Nelly turned around and saw him staggering behind them. She watched like a curious bird, tilting her head, black beady eyes soaking up the view. Then she would laugh and turn to join her friend in prancing through the streets.

They didn't encounter any cars. And because of the cold and the late hour, there were no pedestrians. Conveniently, there were zero witnesses to see Tiffany Thomas marching down the street. Very much *not* missing. Not yet.

The laughter and jokes were growing distorted. Max felt as if he were listening to a record playing in reverse. Nothing made sense. The colours in this world streaked across the scene, everything moving at a slower frame rate than real life.

Max's lungs—or whatever the MemCom made him think he was breathing with—were feeling the burn by the time the memory finally lurched forwards again. They were greeted with warmth and shadows. A light clicked on. They were in the basement. The memory had started to clear up a bit. Nelly's intoxicated mind seemed more able to fill in the gaps inside her home.

The rancid smell of the home was still there. Max found this unsettling.

Nelly played some music on her phone for them to bounce along with, and then pulled out an abused-looking speaker and connected to that instead. Tiffany marched straight for the stained beige love seat over by the dining set in the corner, and she threw herself down heavily. She tossed her bag on the ground and started to untie her boots.

They drank a little more, the memory moving in fits and starts, and Max had to grab onto the wall to stop his motion sickness. The entire room was spinning now. He hadn't felt like this since he drank ill-advised tequila shots back in his sophomore year. The basement glowed a sickening mix of green and orange from the mismatched bulbs in the ceiling. The unfinished concrete provided a sad dance floor for the girls.

At one point, Nelly pulled out her phone. The numbers shifted around, floating way from the phone, and Max couldn't read the time. However, he recognized the events that happened next. He had seen it all before. On Oren's phone. And he now knew exactly where he was and what time it was.

Nelly unlocked her phone and pointed it with unsteady hands. She framed up Tiffany.

"Ok, ok, go." She hiccupped.

Tiffany had the brown-bagged bottle in her hands. The music raged, and she rocked back and forth to it. She slowly lifted up the bottle, carefully, to her lips, and then attempted to chug the remaining whiskey. She managed just a couple gulps before she was forced to spit it out. Both girls shook with fits of laughter.

"You try it then, bitch," Tiffany challenged her friend.

Nelly refused. The phone was still recording but now pointed at the floor.

"Do it!"

Nelly stopped recording and took a big swig. She also failed to down very much, but Tiffany had moved on to other things. The moment travelled ahead.

"You can sleep here," Nelly was announcing.

Clearly, Max had missed a conversation, as a mattress had been procured. Nelly was sliding it out from somewhere and dragging it to the middle of the room.

Tiffany was busy jumping on the love seat, using it like a trampoline. Max could tell what was going to happen even before it did. Tiffany took one bounce too high and smacked her head against one of the wood beams that ran across the ceiling. There was a crunch, and she fell straight down onto the sofa cushions, moaning.

"Tiff?!" Nelly cried out, things clearing up quickly.

Nelly dropped the mattress and ran to her friend. The mattress plopped to the ground, almost landing on Max's feet.

Tiffany straightened up, groggy. Her forehead was cut open and blood had started to pool on the love seat cushions. The blood was bright red, not natural at all. It glistened and glowed as if the rest of the world had lost all colour. Nelly's mind had embellished the gore.

Everything in the room—minus Tiffany and her bloodied head—started to lose its definition.

"*Ohshitohshitohshit!*" Nelly screamed and put her arm around her friend, trying to look at the cut.

"Chicks dig scars," Tiffany groaned, pushing Nelly off.

She staggered over to the mattress and laid down, smiling deliriously. Blood had streaked down her face and stained one of her front teeth, so her smile had a strange, missing-tooth appearance.

Some time later, there was a roll of paper towel out on the ground, unspooled. Tiffany was holding a few sheets to her head and seemed in good spirits. Nelly was unfolding some sheets and blankets and positioning them on the makeshift bed, working around Tiffany.

"I'm bleeding on your mattress," Tiffany said, hiccupping.

"It's an old mattress," Nelly said, tucking Tiffany in and then helping her to change the towel on her head. "It looks like it's stopping." There was a streak of cherry red across Tiffany's forehead, but nothing was flowing.

"You're a good woman," Tiffany said.

Nelly wiped some of the blood from Tiffany's forehead.

Then Tiffany rolled over, burying her face in the pillow. She spoke, but it was entirely muffled.

"Love you too," Nelly said.

Nelly walked over to the love seat and collapsed, careful not to sit on the bloodstain. She picked up the bottle of whiskey and took another large sip. The lights in the basement seemed to be dimming, the temperature rising.

The seasickness had subsided a bit for Max, but a strangled sleepiness took hold instead. The edges of the world started to vignette. The floor seemed as if it were made from silk, and everything just slid one way and then the other with such ease.

Nelly was trying to get comfortable in her seat, but she wiggled back and forth. She noticed that her friend was passed out, then looked at the staircase. She was calculating whether or not it was appropriate to head to her own bed. With a sigh, Nelly got up, re-capped the bottle, and then tossed the whiskey down onto the mattress.

"You finish it," she groaned and then made for the stairs.

She made temporary eye contact with Max as she walked by, but even with her glassy, black eyes, Max could tell they were spinning, unfocused. She brushed right past him without acknowledging him and went upstairs. Max followed, holding onto the rail since he still didn't trust his footing.

He followed Nelly out the back sliding door, and the second they crossed the threshold, they teleported into her garage bedroom. Nelly was in her undershirt, falling sideways onto the bed, not bothering to undress any further. She stared up at the ceiling a bit. Max looked around, but the room was fading, and he realized it was all about to go dark.

When it did, he tried to keep his eyes open, not willing to leave just yet.

Thankfully, he didn't have to.

The next morning came with a siren blaring. A high-pitch tone, like tinnitus but through a megaphone, seemed to be coming from everywhere. The sun that made it in through the tiny garage window was bleaching the room, ripping apart Nelly's vision and making the memory look like a faded sepia photograph. She cried out. Max felt the entirety of her hangover.

The sepia version of Nelly eventually got up and shuffled like a zombie through the garage, putting on her baggy black hoodie as she went. She shut off her alarm, and there was a small amount of relief. Max waited for the next jump, knowing that he wasn't done putting the pieces together yet. He peaked through the gap in the curtains and saw the back of the beat-up old house.

Back in the real world, he was sitting there on a sofa, probably passed out long enough that Nelly had noticed. But Oren would find a way to make an excuse. He was so close. He knew he needed to stick it out and figure out what happened to Tiffany.

Finally, Nelly's mind was finished with this scene, and the world changed.

Now Max was outside, watching Nelly high-step over the deep snow. The ringing in her ears had faded to a quiet, whining sound. Nelly covered her face with one hand, the snow still tinted like an old photograph. She made it to the sliding glass door and pulled it open with such force that she slipped in the snow and fell to one knee. She cursed under her breath and then got up. Max cautiously followed her through the door, relieved when it led them to the next chronological scene. Nelly was slipping off her boots. He was covering his nose from the smell of the kitchen.

Suddenly, Nelly stopped moving. It was as though someone hit pause. Max looked around. Was the MemCom broken?

Eventually, Nelly exhaled and muttered another curse. She had been breathlessly still, focused on the door. Max couldn't understand why. When she finally moved away from the entrance though, the hole appeared. Nelly hadn't noticed it until that moment, so it was absent from the earlier memory. But there was a giant hole in the sliding door. The glass had been smashed and was almost entirely missing from the bottom half of the frame.

Max moved to follow Nelly and heard a crunch under his feet. There was broken glass all over the floor now that hadn't been there before either. Max walked carefully—even if his feet weren't real—and made his way back into the basement. The lights weren't on, but there was enough sunlight coming from the window to show the shape of Nelly staring, dumbfounded, at the base of the stairs.

Max crept up behind her as close as he dared and realized she was looking at the empty mattress. There was no Tiffany. Her travel bag and boots were still lying next to the makeshift bed. Nelly hesitated, still watching the mattress as if it might procure her friend. Suddenly, she sprang into action and whipped her phone out from her pocket, dialing Tiffany's number.

There was a buzzing sound coming from the heap of blankets. Nelly moved forwards, treading carefully as though she might startle someone. She approached the bed with her hands up by her face and then crouched down to assess the pile. She moved one blanket to the side and revealed Tiffany's phone, lit up with Nelly's face and number on the screen. The phone buzzed a couple more times and then went dark.

Nelly seemed to shake. She stood back up and turned to the staircase. She looked right at Max.

"What happened to her?" Nelly asked, once again hyper vigilant and aware of the intruder in her brain.

"I don't know," Max answered honestly, even though every fibre of his being begged him to turn and run.

"She would never leave without her phone," Nelly sighed.

The two of them stayed there in silence a few more moments, sharing in the collective mystery. There was a strange sense of community, neither of them knowing where Tiffany was.

This reverence would be broken by another lurch in time; now Max found himself watching Nelly in the garage again. She was watching cartoons on her laptop. She was wearing the same clothes, so Max guessed it must be the same day, but he had no idea how much time had elapsed. It seemed strange that the next thing Nelly would do would be to watch cartoons. But here she was.

Eventually, Nelly switched her attention to her phone. The screen was blurred, and Max couldn't make out any of the details.

Max grew tired, feeling the effects Oren had described. *You'll feel like you've lived longer days than you actually did.* He had been through the same twenty-four hour period as Nelly, but without sleep. It was hard to believe this was only seconds—maybe a minute— back on the sofa. Max felt himself nodding off, but a sudden voice brought him back.

"I don't know where she is," Nelly was saying.

She wasn't looking at Max, just staring at the TV, but he sensed somehow that she was speaking to him anyway.

"You don't want to call the police?" Max asked.

He knew he shouldn't speak to her, but she didn't seem hostile. She almost seemed to be engaging with him. He stayed where he was, still afraid to get close, waiting for the girl to answer.

"Why call the police?" Nelly said in monotone, like someone reciting dull dialogue off a script. Her eyes remained transfixed on her phone. "They're already looking for her."

"How do you know?"

"Josh texted me," she said. "The family knows she's gone. They're worried. But if the police come here, I will get in trouble."

Max wondered if that were true. He had the benefit of knowing Nelly hadn't done anything, but what would the Thomas family think? Or Landry? He felt where the girl was coming from—she was just a child, clearly in self-preservation mode—though he still wished she would say or do something about it.

"That's him now," Nelly said.

The light outside quickly faded, the sun now barely hanging onto the horizon. The garage was lit mainly by Nelly's phone. There was a loud hum nearby—growing louder and louder—and soon Max recognized it as a car engine. The snow outside started to crunch and crackle. Nelly raced to the window.

A featureless sedan was crawling over the unkempt driveway, headlights blinding both Nelly and Max—as he stood behind her, spying. The car nosed its way right up to the garage and then shut off the engine, making it easier to see the rental plates and the young man behind the wheel.

Nelly tossed on her boots again and threw open the door, bounding outside. The memory started to close in on the sides, Nelly getting tunnel vision as she was focusing only on this visitor. Max stuck close behind her. She planted herself in the snow, waiting for the driver to emerge.

The man in the driver's seat stared her down. He had a beard, though it was sparse and wiry, a young man's first beard. His eyes were piercing green, and they seemed to glow there in the middle of Nelly's tunnel vision. After a few more moments of stillness, he finally emerged from the car and stood to face Nelly across the hood of the car. His look was serious, though not unkind.

"What are you doing here?" Nelly asked, her breath barely carrying over the evening air.

The young man took a second before countering with "Where's my sister?"

"Josh, I . . ." Nelly started but then faltered. She had all the confidence of a deflated balloon.

"Where's Tiff?" Josh repeated. "I know you were with her, Nell."

"What?" Nelly shrank into her sweater.

"I saw your post last night," Josh said. "Besides, who else in Ruston does Tiff hang out with?"

"She wanted to hang out, to get away," Nelly said.

"Yeah, I know. My whole family knows. And they're pissed off," Josh said. "She was supposed to be with her mom. They asked her to come home. She didn't. So, they came to get her, but she wasn't there. They think she was fucking abducted—leave it to Jane to cue the theatrics—but I know better. I know she was hanging out with you."

"She was here," Nelly confessed.

Josh raised his hands in feigned victory and rolled his eyes. "I know," he said. "But where is she now?"

"She's gone."

"Gone where?"

"I don't know." Nelly was welling up. "She was gone when I woke up."

For the first time, Josh started looking around, taking in the garage and the yard and the house. He stalled when he saw the broken sliding glass door.

"What happened there?" he asked.

"It was like that when I woke up," Nelly replied.

Josh seemed to soften. He was sensing that Nelly was distraught, not trying to be unhelpful. He took a few steps closer to her, trying to be comforting with his body language.

"You don't remember hearing anything?" Josh asked.

He came and put an arm around Nelly, awkwardly. She leaned fully into him and let out a single sob.

"I was . . ." Nelly swallowed, embarrassed. "I was drunk."

"So, you really don't know where she is now," Josh realized.

"No." Nelly's voice was muffled as she stuffed her face into Josh's jacket. "I'm sorry."

Josh held her a moment longer and then turned back to face the broken screen door. Then he let her go. He headed for the house, half-crouching and shining his phone light at the door. He looked studious, playing detective.

"The window is broken from the outside," Josh noticed. "Like someone was trying to break in."

"But I never locked it," Nelly said.

Josh stood and tried to open the door. It stuck. He yanked again, and it budged a tiny bit. He yanked a third time, and it finally slid all the way. Josh looked back at Nelly.

"Maybe someone thought it was locked," Josh said. He then turned back to look inside. "Jesus, you gotta clean this up." He could have been speaking about just about anything in the house but was at that moment pointing to all of the broken glass on the ground.

Nelly had just hid out in the garage all day, ignoring the problem.

"Her stuff is downstairs," Nelly blurted out.

That was their next stop, the scene whizzing past them and landing them in the basement. Max lurked in the corner and watched the two of them stamp around, a couple of amateur sleuths. Josh stared at Tiffany's things as if afraid to touch them.

"The blood was here before," Nelly explained.

She pointed out the mattress and the couch cushions. Josh's head tilted back and forth between the two.

At last, Josh moved forwards and grabbed Tiffany's phone.

"She wouldn't go anywhere without this," he stated. He quickly tried to open the phone, but a passcode prevented this. He gave up just as quickly.

"Josh, look." Nelly was trembling, pointing at the wall near where Max stood.

Max felt a pang of fear again, worried he was busted, a trespasser in this memory. But as both Josh and Nelly started to approach him, they were staring straight through him. Max stepped to his left and realized they were not interested in him at all, but rather what was behind him.

A single wall leading up the stairs had been drywalled and painted, the rest of the basement left unfinished. But this single wall was etched with four long scratch marks. These lines were all close together, four jagged lines that stretched about six inches up the side of the wall.

"What are those?" Josh said, studying the scratches. "Do you have a cat?"

"No."

Max watched as Josh traced the marks with his index finger, following the jagged lines across the wall and up until they eventually just stopped. He felt his stomach twist.

"Looks like . . . fingernails left these?" Josh guessed.

Then he looked at the ground. On the stairs was a small, pink square. Josh bent, grabbed it, and turned to reveal it to Nelly. Once Nelly laid eyes on it, it became clear what the object was.

"A fingernail," Nelly gasped.

"Fuck." Josh flinched, dropped the fingernail, feeling terrified and disgusted by what this meant.

Nelly broke down. She collapsed into a seated position on the floor and started bawling. Josh immediately switched gears and went over to console her. He wrapped her in another awkward side hug and waited for her to run out of tears. Nelly took a few moments, a couple of sharp inhales, and then was calm enough to try to speak.

She explained to him that she went to the garage and passed out. When she had gone to bed, Tiffany was lying on the mattress. Josh believed her and continued to console her. Max was realizing that Nelly had known both Thomas kids for years and had relationships with each of them.

Nelly finished her retelling of events, and the pair sat there pondering. Josh was rubbing Nelly's back with a comforting hand and twisting his lips, trying to keep a straight face as he battled with fear, sadness, and confusion. He seemed to want to play the part of the one who knew what to do, and eventually rose to his feet with a sense of urgency.

"The police are looking for her, Nell," he said. "You've got to clean this up. Or they're going to have questions for you. You don't want that."

Nelly sniffled and shook her head.

"So, we're going to get rid of those cushions and this mattress."

"It won't fit up the stairs," Nelly said.

"Well then, we'll try and remove the stain or cover it up. Stash her stuff somewhere. We gotta fix that back door too, okay? Make it like she was never here."

The ensuing actions disoriented Max and forced him to shut his eyes. The basement began to move forwards in uneven fits, different segmented actions all playing out on fast-forward as Nelly remembered bits and pieces but not full scenes. It all played out in front of Max like an old animation on a broken projector.

First, Josh took the soiled cushions and disappeared upstairs. Nelly remained behind, trying to scrub the blood out of the bare mattress with soap and water. It didn't work, so she opted to carefully drape sheets over it instead. Then Nelly stashed Tiffany's belongings in the overturned wardrobe against the wall.

The basement faded away and was replaced with the kitchen. Darkness closed in all around them. The world appeared to Max through a telescope. Nelly swept up the glass bits with a tiny broom and a plate as a dustpan. Josh seemed to have procured a drill and some wooden planks and was boarding up the broken bottom of the sliding door.

The scene flickered and now Max stood back in the garage as the two of them sat cross-legged, talking again.

"What are you going to do?" Nelly asked.

"I'm going to go find Tiff."

"The police are looking for her," Nelly said. "They'll find her."

"I don't trust Landry," Josh scoffed. "Do you?"

Nelly considered this and then gave a quick headshake.

"Where are you going to look?" Nelly's eyes sponged at Josh, trying to soak up the image of him, sensing their time together was ending and desperately trying to cling to the last moments.

She was an isolated kid, and Max felt sorry for her.

"I'm not sure," Josh said. "There are no tracks outside. It snowed all night. So, if someone was here . . . I'm just not sure."

Then their conversation ended abruptly. Or Nelly hadn't committed anything else to memory. She was looking out the same sad window where she had watched Josh pull up, but now it was in reverse. He was leaving, and she stayed at the window a long time after the car had disappeared from the driveway.

After another time jump, Nelly was still at the window, only now she was peering out carefully and watching an orange jeep pull up. Max watched himself and Oren step out and head to the front door. Max was all caught up. He turned away from Nelly, into the corner, shutting his eyes and reemerging into the present.

\*\*\*

Nelly was staring at him. Oren was standing over him. Max was lying comfortably on the couch in the living room. Someone must have taken the time to prop him into a resting position.

"You alright, Max?" Oren asked a bit theatrically.

Max felt more disoriented than he normally did coming out of a dive. But he blinked a few times, and reality came back to him. He was exhausted—both mentally and physically—but his bones were settling back into their current reality. He had been on the couch for no more than thirty seconds.

"Fine." Max smiled awkwardly.

"You really passed out on us there," Oren said.

It was a lazy lie, but Max supposed it didn't matter. Nelly felt like an ally now. After all the time he had spent in her head, he trusted her.

He also guessed that it wouldn't matter what lie they came up with. She spoke to him inside her head, and the way that she looked at Max now suggested she knew something was up. As if she remembered him being in her memories.

Max wondered if this was even possible.

"Where's Josh?" Max asked. "He came to see you. Where is he now?"

"What?" Oren said, his eyes hinting for Max to be careful. He was tense, hoping it didn't feel suspicious that Max suddenly had this information.

"Where is he?" Max repeated, staring Nelly down. He wasn't worried. A trust had been developed.

Oren was stunned. He kept looking back and forth between them, as if there were some telepathic joke he wasn't picking up on.

"There's a room above the Rusty Nail," Nelly said, chewing on one of the strings attached to her oversized hoodie. "He stays there sometimes when he comes to play shows with his band. The owners let him rent it."

"We need to ask him what he knows," Max explained. "Can you please text him, let him know to stay put? We aren't the bad guys. We aren't working with Landry."

Max could feel Oren's eyes on him. A blend of surprise and respect. Max had gone from quietly idling in the shadows of this investigation to leading the charge with Nelly, and it was working. Nelly agreed to text Josh.

That Max knew all the right things to say, all the right buttons to push, impressed Oren greatly.

Josh answered moments later, hesitant but willing to meet them if Nelly thought it was for the best. She replied back, promising it was.

Oren thanked Nelly for her time, saying they better leave. The two of them made for the door quickly, leaving Nelly in the living room. Max glanced back at her as they went, feeling pity. He wanted to stay and help her.

Oren's parting words to her were a reminder to call if she had any other information. Then they wrenched closed the sliding door, sealing her in. Finally outside and alone, Oren exhaled. They slowly walked back toward the jeep, and Max opened up.

"The stepbrother," Max said. "Josh. He helped Nelly clean up the evidence because they were worried it looked bad for Nelly. Tiffany was there. They were drinking. She cut her head. That's where the blood came from. But then Nelly slept in the garage, and in the morning, Tiffany was gone. The door was smashed in and there were fingernail marks left on the wall."

"So, she really is missing . . . again," Oren said.

"Nelly doesn't know anything else," Max said. "But Josh might."

They were nearing the jeep now. To Max, it felt like he hadn't seen Archie in years. But the man's windows hadn't even fogged up.

"That was fast," he said as Oren and Max climbed aboard. "Was it a successful stop?"

"It was." Oren grinned. "We have another stop though, if you're open to it."

"Name the place." Archie started the car.

\*\*\*

Max found Josh Thomas, Tiffany's notorious stepbrother, to be duller in person. His eyes didn't sparkle like they did in Nelly's mind. And he was a little rounder in the face. His jawline was speckled with hints of facial hair and acne. He greeted Oren and Max at an unmarked door around the side of the Rusty Nail.

They had released Archie after he dropped them off, saying they didn't know how long they'd be.

"That's fine. I've got errands to run anyway!" he told them.

Now, they were following Josh up a set of stairs.

At the top of the stairs was another plain door, through which was a bachelor apartment. The place was small, run-down, but Josh had been keeping it tidy. He had a duffel bag beside the bed, and his sticker-plastered laptop open on the dresser. A playlist was displayed on the screen. A single bay window, with condensation obscuring the view, looked out over the bar's parking lot. A bistro table with two chairs was next to the window. Josh offered them the seats as he dropped down onto the bed.

"So, Nelly says you are working for my dad," Josh began. It sounded like a trap.

"We're working to help find Tiffany," Oren said, dodging the core of the question. They were not spies for Robert Thomas. "We are only interested in the whereabouts of your stepsister."

"Sister," Josh corrected him. "She's my sister. We don't use the *step*. She's my family. Not our fault our dad's had three wives."

"I apologize," Oren said. "I have heard that you are trying to help find Tiffany? Nelly said you don't trust local law enforcement."

"No, and neither should you," Josh said. "They haven't done anything for anyone. All the accidents, all the deaths, and they barely look into them."

"Yeah, I heard about the curse," Max said.

"Curse?" Oren hadn't been around to hear Stella's tales.

"I meant to tell you about that." Max rubbed a hand on the back of his neck, wondering now if Oren might find it all silly. "There's some sort of hundred-year curse here. Every year, another young woman . . . dies."

"Not a hundred years," Josh interrupted. "That's all urban legend crap. The kids all talk about the curse. Old stories about satanic rituals and the boogeyman stealing away a girl. I don't believe in that. But in the time since Landry took over, it feels like every summer, we come back here and someone else is gone. The accidents, reported suicides, and missing person cases don't get the attention they deserve."

Oren looked to Max first, then to Josh, trying to understand where this all connected.

"Let's focus on your sister for a second," Oren said. "That's the most pressing concern. Nelly said you were digging into it. Do you happen to know anything that can help?"

"I know she's missing," Josh said. "And I've checked all the places she likes to hide out. Checked with my old band mates. We still play shows at the Nail sometimes, but they haven't seen or heard anything. She doesn't have her phone on her—not even the one my parents don't know about. So, I'm worried. I think something bad happened."

"Do you know anyone who would have wanted to hurt her?" Oren asked. "Anyone at all?"

"Tiffany only had friends here," Josh said. "Everyone liked her. The local kids, Nelly especially, they idolize her."

"What about anyone not from Ruston?"

"There's probably a few girls at her school that aren't her biggest fans." Josh shrugged. "But they'd never set foot in Ruston. And they never do anything for themselves, so unless they sent their tutors or piano teachers or private chefs out here . . . No, there's no one who would've done this."

"So where does that leave us?" Oren asked.

"You need to think about who did this to *all* the girls," Josh said. "Nat, and all the ones before."

"Natalya Romano?" Max asked.

Josh seemed surprised that Max knew the name. Oren was equally as stunned. Stella's stories were paying off.

"You knew her?"

"Yeah," Josh said. "We dated."

"Who's that?" Oren asked.

"The girl who . . ." Max started, but then caught the look on Josh's face. They had dated. There was still pain in his eyes. ". . . passed away last year."

"Alright, what did I miss?" Oren sighed, looking to his friend.

Max took a minute to catch him up on all that had been gleaned from Stella. He covered the supposed history of the curse and the details around Natalya Romano's suicide.

"It wasn't suicide," Josh said when Max was done.

"How do you know?" Oren leaned closer.

"Because Nat wasn't like that!" Josh sounded childlike, falling into a tantrum. "She wouldn't do that. Not to her grandmother. Her friends. Me."

They sat in silence as everyone weighed their options for what to say next. Oren pursed his lips, unconvinced that this was relevant information.

"Besides," Josh added, breaking the stillness. "I saw her with someone at the motel. The night she died."

"What?" Max gaped.

"Who did you see her with?" Oren interrogated.

"I don't remember. I mean, I don't know," Josh sighed. "I didn't get a good look. Just that there was someone else there. A man."

"So, you saw her with somebody," Oren said. "Did you tell the police? That Nat wasn't alone?"

"I tried." Josh sounded exhausted, as if he'd been through this entire conversation already. "They didn't care. They didn't believe me."

"What's the connection to Tiffany here, Josh?" Oren asked. "Why should Nat's story concern us now?"

"Because if someone killed Nat, they could be the same person who took Tiff!" Josh cried out.

Oren considered this a second. If someone did in fact kill Natalya last year, it was possible they were looking at Tiffany's case the wrong way. Maybe it wasn't someone close to her that took her. Maybe they should be looking at a serial offender.

"But you don't remember what you saw," Oren clarified. He glanced at Max as he said this.

Max knew the look by now. He sighed, looking at the floor. It was not carpeted. He was going to get real sore if he kept passing out on hard surfaces like this.

Josh was defeated, staring through them, recalling events that he had tried to let go of. The conversation stalled. Finally, Josh seemed to reconnect with the present, and he cleared his throat and turned away from them, hiding the tears that were forming.

"Could I trouble you for some water?" Oren asked, changing the subject.

Josh rose silently and headed for the small kitchenette. Oren, ever so casually, also stood and made a show of going over to Josh's laptop. He had perfectly positioned things now so that Max was closest to Josh, ready to dive.

"So, you were in a band," Oren said. "Can I hear one of your songs?"

*** 

The setting was familiar, but it was jammed with patrons this time. The Rusty Nail was overflowing, and Max was being jostled by the faceless crowd. A warm summer breeze flowed through the bar from the open doors on either end, but it did little to cut through the stench of beer and sweat. Heavy bass thrummed, Max feeling it in his feet. He stuck his elbows out, trying to brace himself against the dancing bodies and orient himself.

A small stage had been set up in the corner of the bar, and on it stood three young men. One—a guitarist—screamed into the microphone, covering a Green Day song Max had long forgotten about. Another had his eyes shut, banging away on the drums in a trance. And the third—holding the bass guitar and staring into the sea of dancers—was Josh Thomas.

The song concluded, and the crowd shrieked its approval.

"Thank you," the band's lead said as the cheap lighting rig dimmed, the strobes stilling. "We've got one more for ya. It's a slow song, so find yourself a partner and let's end the night with someone we love."

Drums and guitar kicked back into the scene. "Use Somebody" by Kings of Leon stirred the crowd as the anonymous shapes all began to pair up, getting close to one another and swaying gently. Max felt moved, his own memories triggered—he had danced to this song once upon a time, too. But he didn't join in. He stood there, a stationary tower, as the dancers twirled around him. He was watching Josh closely.

Josh plucked away at his strings. His eyes were down, at first, but when he raised them up to look into the crowd the memory changed. The music became gentler, as if someone had turned down the volume on the drums and the vocals. Now it was just Josh's part that Max heard. The lights and the dancing patrons also faded away, becoming soft shadows, background players in the scene.

At the forefront now, was one person. The memory spotlit a girl near the stage. She swayed to the tune but was by herself. Her eyes were locked on Josh, and his on her. The two of them were lit up like stage actors, the rest of the world now shrouded in blackness. The girl was tanned, with dark hair and brown eyes. She was quite tall, and slender, looking as though the crowd may knock her over.

Max knew that this had to be Natalya.

The music continued but was now obscured into just a series of bass notes that shook the corners of the memory. Josh stared at Natalya, and she returned his gaze. She smiled slightly, the edge of her mouth twisting up crookedly.

The moment was sweet and intimate. Max found himself incredibly uncomfortable. He turned his attention away from the lovebirds and studied the exits. One of these doors likely would bring him to the night Natalya died. It was a sickening thought. Here she was, so alive and fully of beauty. Yet her death was already guaranteed. And just a few feet away, through any one of the venue's doors, it might well be waiting on the other side.

He was staring at a ghost, he realized. That's all she was now.

The backdoor had been propped open and was letting in the sweet summer air. Max decided to try this one, if for no other reason than he needed to get out of the stuffy bar.

***

It was a perfect, pink-skied evening. The sun seemed to hang at the horizon, taking its time. The air was alive with crickets and the leftover heat from a warm summer's day. Max felt relaxed, as if whisked off to a vacation, and he was relieved to be out of the Rusty Nail.

Max stood on a long, narrow dock with wood planks that seemed to be almost brand new. The dock stretched out into a lake, which perfectly mirrored the sky and was rimmed by the silhouettes of towering trees huddled beneath the sunset. At the far end of the dock sat a young man—who also could've been a teenaged boy—and a girl who was pressed against him, resting her head on his shoulder. The couple was also carved out in a perfect silhouette.

Max peered back at the mainland, hoping to get a glimpse of where they were. But the colour from the sky did not carry that far, and where land should have been, there was only a curtain of obscurity.

"You'll come back?"

The girl's voice carried, shooting back toward Max and out across the water. Max crept closer to the couple, careful not to be seen. He didn't need to get too close, however. It was not difficult to tell who they were. They had their hands on one another in the needy way of young love. Josh's hands on her bare legs, hers rubbing his back.

"Of course," Josh scoffed. He was caressing her leg with his hand, tracing the lines of a tattoo on her calf—an owl. "Why wouldn't I come back?"

"Just . . . feels like I won't see you again," the girl said. She withdrew her hand and looked at him. "This summer was so perfect."

Max guessed this memory was a few years old. Josh's voice had cracked a bit, sounding more adolescent. Then of course, there was the fact that Natalya was still alive.

The two kissed, then Natalya abruptly departed from the embrace, and without warning, she stood and dove into the lake. The perfect mirrored surface of the water shattered into ripples. In this perfect scene, where the sky melted into the land, the entire world seemed to warp with tiny waves, as if her splash had carried all the way into the sky and beyond.

Max took a knee, grabbing on to the dock as the memory trembled around him. He felt seasick. Circles rippled both below and above him. When things finally settled again, it was as though he were walking out over a bottomless pit; the eternity of the sky was reflected perfectly in the mirrored surface of the lake. He felt suddenly exposed.

With most of the world reset, a small head bobbed above the water and Natalya beamed back at Josh.

"Aren't you going to have one last swim before you go home for the winter?" the girl beckoned. She waved her arms gracefully across the surface of the lake and pushed herself away, further and further from the dock.

"Isn't it cold?" Josh asked. He dipped a toe in the water and feigned a shiver. "Yeah, fuck that, Nat, I'm not going in there."

"Come on," she teased.

"No."

"Well, if you won't go swimming . . ." Natalya said, cutting herself off as she switched her attention to something below the water.

Her arms disappeared beneath the surface for a moment. Her smile turned into a smirk, and she bit her lip as she tried to concentrate. After a moment, her arms returned, holding something she had retrieved. At first Max, thought it was a dead fish, the way it hung limply in her hand, the water pouring off it. Then he recognized it as a bikini top.

"Will you at least go skinny-dipping?"

Once again, Max felt uneasy. He hated playing the part of voyeur, intruding on these private moments. He shielded his eyes with a hand, though it was a pointless endeavour, as he still peered around his hand to make sure he didn't miss something important. Anything could be evidence.

Josh was in the water a second later, pulling his shirt off as he dove. The world quaked yet again. The entire dock seemed to sway with the force of Josh entering the water, and Max hadn't been ready for it. He tried to keep his balance, but with everything shaking, there was no point of reference, and the dock had no handrail. He grasped at the air as he fell, but it was fruitless. Max toppled into the lake, shutting his eyes and expecting the cold embrace to suck him in.

But it never came. Instead, the feeling of falling lasted a moment too long, sending Max's heart into his throat in a panic.

Just as he opened his eyes, he felt himself hit. Sharp edges pressed up against his ribs and his arms, tearing at his imagined body. The moon—a perfect crescent— smiled down on him and started to make visible the elements of this new scene. Max had fallen into a shrub, it appeared. He was tangled among branches and vines and leaves. He was unharmed.

It took him a moment to right himself, extracting his limbs from the tangle of the bush and getting to his feet. Out of habit, Max brushed the dirt off himself as he surveyed his surroundings. To one side, there was only more woods, barely visible in the moonlight. Behind him, though, was a familiar beacon. The big blue sign identified the Birch Motel, and small specks of light from the windows lit up the path back toward town. In the summer, it looked almost pretty.

The world was smeared, sort of like wet paint. Trees became the sky, stars smudged themselves into clouds, and the motel windows were impossible to count—was that one or three? The definition from this night had been barely retained, the spine of this memory barely holding things together.

Just then, a branch snapped somewhere nearby. Max ducked and tried to find the source of the noise through the darkness. A shape was coming toward him, following an unseen path out of the woods. Holding completely still in his crouch, Max watched as the shape emerged into the moonlight. He was relieved to see that it was Josh.

Josh was staggering, unable to walk a straight line. He let loose a high-pitched hiccup that shattered the crickets' peaceful melody. Max remained out of sight, not wanting to alter anything for Josh's SI. Once Josh had passed by, however, Max tailed him, careful not to make a sound.

They made their way toward the motel, sticking to the road. Josh hit a couple potholes, dipping and stumbling but never quite falling to the ground. Max was able to avoid them, watching even as Josh paused to polish off the can of beer he had been carrying, tossing it disrespectfully through the air and into the grass.

Passing by the motel, Josh cast a glance toward the parking lot. At first, he had no reaction, but then he did an obvious—almost comedic—double take. He was staring at one of the cars.

"The fuck . . ." Josh muttered. He started to walk toward the car, squinting.

"That's Natalya's car," Max guessed.

He said it aloud, and as if Josh's mind had been working with him this whole time, Josh answered. "That's Nat's car," he said.

Josh never turned to look at Max, though. Instead, his voice swept across the parking lot like a stale summer breeze, and Max was suddenly privy to his inner thoughts. *First, she doesn't show up to the party, and now she's parked at a motel? Why is she here?*

They progressed toward the vehicle, which to Max was just a muddled mess of shadows and tires. As they got closer, the door to room number six—which was directly opposite the vehicle—opened. Both Josh and Max froze, holding their breath collectively.

A figure emerged from the motel room, heading toward the car. To Max's frustration, the figure was completely featureless. It possibly could've been male— the broad shoulders being the only hint—but the face was obscured completely, and even the relative frame seemed to be hidden, all of the details melting into the background. Josh had really not caught much.

Max wondered if this figure was going to spot them.

"That's not Nat," Josh whispered.

The figure went to the driver's side of the car and opened the door. They rummaged around for something inside and then returned to the motel room with what looked like a large bag, possibly a duffel or a backpack. For just a second, things slowed down. Through the motel room door, which had been left open, things suddenly came into focus. There was a light on in the room, and though the wedge of light between the door and the wall was slim, it stood out against the rest of the dark, obfuscated world. A bare leg on a bed. With an owl tattoo on the calf.

Josh's heartbeat had sped up so greatly that Max could hear it reverberate throughout the memory. *That's Nat on the bed.*

But who was the figure? Whoever it was quickly shut the door, closing off the scene inside the room. Just like that, it was all gone. Only smears of black and blue were left as Josh started to stagger again. Max thought he might topple over.

That vein was back in Josh's forehead. He was fighting a mixture of emotions. Max could see it on his face. He thought that chief among them was hurt. Josh must have thought his girlfriend was cheating on him.

Josh stood a moment longer, swirling around as if uncertain which direction his body wanted to go. They both stared at the darkness. The moment was then interrupted by the click of a lighter.

Josh whipped his head sideways and found the lonely orange glow of a lighter and a cigarette in near the motel office.

"Hey, Josh!" a voice called out.

A body began to materialize behind the cigarette's glow. An oily-haired kid, roughly the same age as Josh, stared at him from behind thick spectacles. He wore a nametag on his collared shirt. Max guess he worked at the motel. Night shift, by the looks of it.

With a low growl, Josh swiveled and decided to leave. He didn't reply to the kid working at the motel. He didn't go to the room to check out who Natalya was with. He just stormed off, new and intense purpose behind his steps.

"No," Max muttered, afraid to interrupt but also willing Josh to turn around. *We need to go over there and see who it is.*

Max started making his way toward the motel, jogging at first and then full out sprinting, trying to get to the motel room door before the memory faded. The moonlight was already fading when he reached the car. Being closer didn't make the details any clearer. The vehicle was still just a blob. Max raced for the motel door as the road behind him crumbled away. The kid with the cigarette disintegrated like the clouds of nicotine he was smoking. The crickets ceased their songs; all sound was erased.

Max reached out desperately. If he could only peak inside, he could solve this whole thing. He took one last lunge, pressing himself at the door before it, too, could vanish. He flung it open, hoping to rush inside and catch their culprit in the act. But the MemCom didn't work like that.

Instead, Max passed through the doorway and left the memory behind. The inside of the motel room was lost—or rather, it hadn't existed to begin with. Max flew into a dark void and found himself falling into another place. Weightlessness took hold of him momentarily, before he found himself dropped into a new memory. He plunged into something dark and wet.

Cold water wrapped around him, squeezing the air from his lungs. He fought against it, pushing himself up, but then he realized that he could touch the bottom. It was shallow here, and Max stood, studying the world around him as he wiped the water away from his eyes. It was the middle of the day now, and the lake was not the same. This body of water was massive and stretched out beyond the horizon. Both the water and the sky were grey.

Behind him was the shore and a sandy beach. Josh was there, staring out at the expanse. Beyond him, people scurried about, traffic honked and fought, and skyscrapers stretched themselves into the heavens. An entire city went about its business right here alongside the water.

Max was in Chicago, he realized. He had fallen out of the last memory and into Lake Michigan. He made his way out of the water, falling a couple times and forcing himself to crawl as his imaginary body was weighed down by the uneven footing and the waves.

Resting on his knees, Max was now very close to Josh. But Josh hadn't noticed him. He was lost in thought, staring at the lake. This lasted a moment longer before he seemed spurred by something and began to walk back toward the city. Max scurried after him.

As they made their way from the beach to the sidewalk, the grinding sounds of the city took over. Car horns and bus engines filled the air. The wind sent a chill through Max's damp body, and everything whizzed past them at an aggressive pace—cyclists, pigeons, trains.

Max did his best to keep up and track Josh as he marched his way to some destination unknown. The beautiful architecture of Chicago's skyline dwarfed them, blotting out the sky. The memory was confined by these buildings, a cage built inside of Josh's mind.

There was a chime, a ringtone, coming from Josh's pocket. He pulled out his phone.

"Yeah?" he said casually.

A wave crashed over everything.

Everything became warm and heavy, as though the humidity had been dialed up. The air was thick, and Max felt as though it was squashing him into the ground. At the same time, everything around them began to move in slow motion. The pigeons moved their wings slowly, dragging them through molasses. The birds inched upward through the air, barely flying. The people around them came to a virtual standstill. The wind stopped ruffling the newspapers and trash on the street. The cyclist beside Max rolled by at a snail's pace.

The entire memory now held an enormous weight. It was crushing Max. He was unable to move.

Josh remained in place, seemingly unaffected. From the phone in his hand, a low, sinister sound carried out across the city. The sound was everywhere all at once, reverberating off the buildings that loomed overhead, and even inside Max's skull. It was a voice like an air raid siren.

*She's gone, Josh. She's dead.*

The gravity had become unbearable. Max looked for a way out. There were doors all around him, but he wasn't sure if he'd be able to reach them. Whatever Josh's heart had experienced during that phone call had stuck with his memory of that moment, and it now pressed down with the weight of an entire planet against Max's head. His spine trembled, and his legs buckled. He tried to step forwards and found only resistance.

*It's not real,* Max tried to remind himself. *It's only a memory.*

Eventually, one foot moved. The momentum was all he needed. The weight worked in his favour now, surging behind him like a tidal wave. It thrust Max toward the nearest building—a nondescript office tower with two welcoming glass doors—and he stretched his arms out to brace against the collision.

Max pushed through the office doors. There was an immediate release, and the pressure was gone. The crush of that experience was left in a solitary place in Josh's mind. As was the feeling of damp clothes.

***

This new memory was brisk; the air had cooled off just enough to see one's breath, though a few leaves still clung to the trees that lined the street. The light was smooth, almost cinematic. There were no shadows anywhere. Max stood in front of a small brick building that may not have garnered much attention but for the steel letters arranged over the door: *Ruston Police.*

Sheriff Landry and Deputy Sanderson were standing outside, Landry squashing a cigarette with his boot and Sanderson sipping on a coffee.

"Hey!" an aggressive yell came from across the lot. Josh was closing in on them, walking with an intensity in his stride. He appeared to be looking for a fight.

"Ah shit," Landry said, shaking his head.

"Sanderson, what the hell?" Josh said to the deputy, who was gripping his coffee with two hands.

He looked sheepish, hiding behind his cup.

"Sorry, Josh," Sanderson said. "I know how close you two were."

Josh had closed the gap and was almost nose to nose with the deputy. He was red in the face, out of breath.

"Why did I hear that you called it a suicide?" Josh fumed.

"Look, Josh, I know you don't wanna hear it, but that's what it is." Sanderson shrugged. "Coroner's report was pretty clear. She was . . ." He hesitated, looking at Landry as if for permission.

Landry was smug but offered no reaction.

"She was strung up in the motel."

"So?" Josh said, his fists were balled up by his sides. "That's it? She wouldn't do that. We talked about stuff like this. All the time. She used to help her friends when they were depressed. She had plans to leave Ruston and go to college. She did not kill herself." Josh spat out these last five words like a decree.

Sanderson just grimaced and shrugged again. "Doesn't mean she wasn't messed up, Josh."

"You knew her too." Josh's anger was only increasing. "We were only two years behind you. Or did you forget? Nat was not the kind of person to take her own life."

"That's what the family always says after something like this. No one sees it coming, Josh."

"Did you even see the scene?"

"Course we did," Sanderson fired back. "I'm telling the truth. Nothing suspicious about it. No signs of any foul play."

"But there was someone there." Josh looked at Landry, hoping for a response, but the sheriff just continued to stare at him with his lips squeezed into something like a grin. "I saw her with someone."

"Who'd ya see her with?" Sanderson asked.

"I don't know," Josh said. "But she wasn't alone. Don't you fucking check the place for prints and stuff?"

"It's a motel, Josh," Sanderson said. "Whole fucking room is a cesspool of prints, hair, sperm, you name it. But nothing was out of place."

"That's bullshit." Josh had lost all composure. He was practically spitting. "You need to do better. She was with someone."

"Easy kid." Landry stepped in now. "Don't forget who you're talking to."

"Don't forget who my father is," Josh said, not backing down.

Landry's face went red at this mention. Clearly, he did not like being defied.

"You little Thomas brats," Landry sneered. "Acting like you run this place when you come up every summer. I'm sick of it. Shouldn't you be scuttling back along to the big city? It's getting cold out."

"I'm not leaving 'til I find out what happened to Nat," Josh said. He was trying his best to be bold. His voice rattled like a child's in spite of himself.

"Kid." Landry shook his head. "She hung herself. Case closed."

"I know what I saw," Josh said, sounding a little less convinced now. "She was with someone that night."

"Ok well." Landry thought it over a second. "Then she was fucking someone. *Then* she offed herself."

Max was stupefied. He couldn't believe he was hearing a grown man—let alone a sheriff—speak to a teenaged boy this way.

"We were dating." Josh gritted his teeth.

"Oh," Landry said, stuffing his hands in his pockets and turning casually back toward the station. "Probably why she killed herself then."

Max watched as the tendons in Josh's neck grew, and the vein in his forehead became pronounced. He was about to explode. Landry was already walking away, back to the doors.

"You fucking piece of—" Josh lunged at Landry, but Sanderson intercepted him, wrapping his long arms around the boy.

"Leave the police work to the police, kid," Landry said without looking back. He opened the door, and just before he stepped inside, he offered one last barb. "Go home to daddy."

"I'm gonna kill him!" Josh screamed as Sanderson wrestled him away from the door.

"Easy, Josh," Sanderson said. "Careful what you say in front of the police. I know you're hurting, but I think you should just go home. Be with your family."

Josh struggled against Sanderson's grip a little longer. Landry was gone, tucked away safely inside his little fortress. A moment later, the fight faded out of Josh, and the memory collapsed. The world tumbled forwards into another memory, giving Max that old familiar rush in his stomach.

*\*\*\**

They had returned to where it began. Max was back in that tiny apartment above the Rusty Nail, watching Josh slumped on the floor. A single lamp sat beside the bed, but the rest of the place was cast in shadows. A couple empty beer bottles decorated the kitchen table.

Josh was holding a bottle of pills, shaking it and staring at it. Max couldn't make out what they were, but he was getting the sense that they were trouble. If it weren't for the fact that he knew Josh was standing in the same room as him back in the present, he would have been concerned for the boy.

Josh poured out a handful of pills—more than one should take at once—and Max realized he had seen enough. He didn't want to witness any more of Josh's hurt. He had already gotten what he came for, and now they had their next lead. He had to get back to Oren.

Max had no shortage of dark corners to choose from as he surfaced.

***

A punk rock song was playing on the laptop when Max came to. Everything was as he had left it. Josh hadn't even seemed to notice his micro nap. It appeared that Oren hadn't noticed Max's return either. When Max spoke, both of them jumped and turned to look at him, surprised he was still there.

"You don't remember," Max said.

No one knew what he meant, they just stared.

So, he elaborated. "You don't remember who was there that night."

"What are you talking about?" Oren asked.

"Josh," Max said, making it clear who he was speaking to. "The night you saw Natalya at the motel. There was someone else there too."

Josh narrowed his eyes. He was on edge.

"You were on your way home from a party, you had been drinking," Max said. "But you saw her in the room. And someone getting out of the car and going into the room."

"How do you know this?" Josh was combative. He turned to Oren. "How does he know?"

"I'm not sure," Oren said, glaring at Max. He was not happy with Max blowing their cover.

But Max had found a thread and was going to pull at it. He felt he could get Josh to keep quiet. He had been inside his mind. He knew what made him tick, now. Max had the advantage.

"There was someone else there too, someone else who may have seen," Max said. "A kid smoking a cigarette by the office. You may not actively remember. But it's there. Buried in your memory."

At first, Josh just stared, anger and confusion clouding his eyes. But Max had connected the dots for him. His gaze eased.

"Wyatt," Josh said. "The guy who works nights at the motel. Oh my god, he was there."

"That's who we need to talk to," Max said. "Do you know him?"

"Yeah, he still works at the motel I think." Josh was speaking quickly, excited. He rushed about the apartment, looking for something. Then he paused and turned back to Max. "But . . . how do you . . ."

Josh's eyes flickered to Max's ear. Max raised his hand timidly, feeling for it. He had forgotten to remove the earpiece. There was a glimmer of recognition in Josh's face.

"We can help find Tiffany," Max said. "I hope I'm right in assuming you won't care how we need to do that."

The three of them all exchanged looks. Oren was realizing that Max may have known what he was doing; Josh was an ally.

"Where did my dad find you?" Josh said finally.

Oren changed the subject. "This guy from the motel, Wyatt? How can we find him?"

Josh looked again at Max, trying to figure him out. Max gave him a look that said: *We are on your side. We want to find Tiffany too.*

"I can take you to him," Josh said.

\*\*\*

Max sat in the back seat of Josh's car, staring out at Ruston as they passed it by, trying to ignore the smell of mold and socks that permeated the vehicle.

On the drive to the motel, Josh explained more. He hadn't seen or heard from Nat for a week leading up to that night at the motel. She had ghosted him, or so he thought. He wondered aloud now if she had been missing or with her eventual murderer that whole time.

"I kinda figured she had just been seeing someone else," he said. "We didn't hang out all week. And we were supposed to be at that bush party together. But she never came. So, when I saw her car, it just felt like she was over me. I was mad. I went back home."

Max's phone buzzed, taking his attention away from the conversation up front.

It was Janelle. She had messaged him back. Several times, in fact. He must have missed the alerts.

*Hope you're okay. Thinking of you.*

*Yes, heard of the Thomas family.*

*Should you really be thinking about stories right now, tho?*

Those were earlier. Then, the latest message.

*Ruston is an area with noted police corruption. Made headlines a while back. Just looked it up. Thomas family daughter missing? How is it all related? What are you up to, Max?*

Max paused for a moment before he replied. Instead of answering any of her questions, he sent back one of his own.

*Do you believe in curses?*

After sending that, he scrolled back up to her first message. *Thinking of you.* These words warmed him. This day had already felt like three, yet it was only midafternoon. This experience was making Max miss the comfort of his old life. The things that had once felt daunting—like starting a relationship with Janelle—he found himself missing. Comparing what he was doing here to what he had already done, Max felt like his old worries paled.

He promised himself he'd tell her he was thinking of her too. When he was back.

Josh pulled into the parking lot of the motel. The fire trucks were gone, but several rooms had stickers on the door warning against entry. As they exited the vehicle, the cold air stung against their eyes and their cheeks. Max spotted the sun hovering just behind the motel, threatening to disappear for the night. Soon it would get even colder, he realized.

They shuffled into the motel's main office with frozen faces, struggling to find room for the bulk of their coats in the tiny space. Across from them was a small, plain desk with a cat calendar standing proudly on display next to a tip jar. A vending machine hummed, occupying more space than felt necessary. Inside it were a handful of soda cans and chocolate bars, but mostly empty slots. A hidden radio was playing twangy country songs but struggled through the static of a poor signal.

The same round-faced woman who had greeted them upon arrival the previous night was behind the desk, stacking papers neatly. She looked up at them, seeking recognition, and finally settling her eyes on Josh with a smile.

"Josh," she said. "How are you?"

"Fine, thanks, Pauline," Josh spoke quickly. "I'm hoping we can talk to Wyatt. What time is he in?"

"He takes over for me after dinner." Pauline checked her watch—a frail, golden knock-off. "Will be a while yet."

"Do you think we can call him to come by the motel?" Josh asked. "These men are investigators looking for Tiffany. They'd like to talk to him."

"Oh my." Pauline gawked. She stopped fidgeting with her papers and looked at Oren with renewed focus. "What did that boy do?"

"Nothing, ma'am," Oren assured her. "He just might have some answers for us."

"Well, yes." Pauline's hands started dancing about again, this time feeling for her phone. "Let me get him to come by now. Not like he does anything anyway. That boy spends all his time in the basement with his games. He's my nephew, you know. My brother would be so disappointed."

"If he can come in that would be very helpful." Oren smiled. "Can you let him know it's time sensitive?"

Pauline called her nephew, turning her back and lowering her voice as she had the conversation. Oren and Max tried not to stare, politely shifting their gaze back outside. When the call was over, Pauline cleared her throat and faced them again.

"He's on his way," she said. "You can speak with him in here. I need to go clean one of the rooms anyway."

"Thank you very much," Oren said. "I'm also wondering if you can help us. Do you have records of who has rented rooms here, dating all the way back to last year?"

"They date back as long as we've existed," Pauline said, happy to be helpful. "I'm not so great with the computers though. So, a lot of it's on paper. Would you like me to get out my binders? What month are you looking for?"

"September," Josh said. Max noticed his cheeks were red, his teeth grinding. "You want to look at September."

"One sec." Pauline turned around to a filing cabinet and began to flip through it.

The binder for September was canary yellow. Oren yielded to Josh, letting him thumb over the pages and find the right date. He found the week that Nat had been missing and pushed the binder over to Oren with a sigh.

"It's in her name," he said.

"Right," Oren said.

He sounded like he hadn't expected anything different. It would have been pretty foolish for a murderer to rent the room in his or her own name. And not checking into this would've been exceptionally poor police work, even by Landry's standards.

"What room was it?"

"Six," Josh read off the sheet.

"Any chance we could take a look at room six?" Oren turned to Pauline.

"I'm afraid not," Pauline said. "That's one of the rooms that was damaged by the fire. It's in bad shape, and we're not to go in there. Besides, not much to see besides ash now anyway."

Max could tell Oren was displeased, though he hid it from their company well.

"Security cameras?" Oren asked. "Do you have any security cameras?"

"We have one." Pauline pointed to the ceiling.

They all turned to look, noticing a small white camera mounted in the corner, facing them, red link blinking.

"It faces the register. But if you're looking for last September, I'm afraid I don't have anything that far back."

"Did the police ever come and check it, last September?" Oren asked.

Pauline paused a moment, thinking. Her eyes lit up the moment she connected the dots.

"You mean about that suicide case?" She gasped. "Is that why you're interested in September? What could that possibly have to do with Tiffany? Or with Wyatt?"

"We can't say much, ma'am, but Wyatt is not in any trouble. We just need to know if someone has already seen the footage from last year."

"Well, no." Pauline tilted her head back and forth as if trying to shake loose a memory. "I don't recall anyone ever asking. They checked out the room. Asked me a couple questions. But no one asked for the security camera footage. Not sure how it was relevant, seeing as she killed herself in the room."

"She didn't kill herself." Josh couldn't hold it in.

Oren put a hand on his shoulder, meaning to calm him down, but he pushed it away.

Pauline's mouth hung open. She didn't know what to say. Oren sensed that she was starting to feel uncomfortable with them all in here, and so he tried to further defuse.

"I'm going to take a walk," Oren said. "Josh, come with me."

Max waited awkwardly in the office as Oren strolled out into the parking lot. He watched as he had Josh retrace the steps he would've taken that night after the party. Josh pointed at the wooded area he had emerged from, and then they stomped through the snow on the walk up the road.

"How long have you been a private investigator?" Pauline asked, the silence finally getting to her.

"Only a couple years," Max said with a forced grin. He felt it was a better answer than the truth: just a couple of days.

Max had bought himself one of the cans of cola from the vending machine, mostly as a means of killing time. The can got stuck, which killed a blissful few extra seconds as he shook and wrenched at the machine. Pauline came over and gave it a solid smack, freeing the can. Max cracked it and took a sip, feeling like he needed the caffeine.

Oren and Josh returned when they couldn't stand the cold anymore. Max's entire body tensed the moment the door opened and the winter seeped back in. There wasn't much to say. Max could tell Oren was upset at the lack of evidence here. All that was left for them was to speak with Wyatt.

Just as Max was considering being the one to break the awkward silence, a car pulled into the motel parking lot.

"That's him," Pauline said. She gathered her coat and mitts from somewhere underneath the desk and waddled out toward the door. "I'll give you some privacy."

Oren thanked her, but she seemed relieved to be out of the office. Once she had left, the newly arrived car shut off its engine, and from the door emerged the same greasy-haired, bespectacled young man that Max had seen in Josh's memories.

Wyatt stepped inside, and Josh greeted him with a head nod.

"Wy, these guys are looking for Tiff. They have some questions for you," Josh said.

Wyatt said nothing. He didn't seem too thrilled to be there. He wouldn't make eye contact with Josh.

"Josh, would you mind giving us some extra space?" Oren asked. "Maybe just sit in the car? It'll only take a minute."

Josh hesitated, wanting to be a part of the investigation. He glanced at Oren, a pleading look in his eyes, but Oren didn't budge. Josh relented and walked out of the office.

"Hi, Wyatt, I'm Oren and this is my partner, Max," Oren said, taking charge. "Max will be listening, taking notes. Actually, Max, why don't you sit in the chair behind the desk there. Make yourself comfortable."

This would give Max the opportunity to rest his head, pop in the MemCom, and likely not even have Wyatt see him, so long as Oren could hold his attention through the questioning.

Max settled in behind the desk as Wyatt stood still, a statue whose eyes darted about curiously, unsure of what was happening.

"Are you and Josh friends?" Oren asked.

"We *were*," Wyatt said.

It was a stinging response. There was bad history there.

"What happened?" Oren asked.

"We were friends when we were little and his family would come in the summer. When I started working here, I used to give him free rooms 'cause he wanted a place to hang out with girls." Wyatt pushed his glasses up higher on his nose. "But I don't think he ever really liked me. When I stopped giving him free rooms, he stopped hanging around with me. Never invited me to his parties or anything."

"That sounds awful," Oren sympathized. "I'm sorry. Is it safe to assume you know his sister, Tiffany?"

"Yeah."

"And did you know Natalya Romano as well?"

"Yeah, I knew Nat." Wyatt swallowed. Sweat was forming on his brow.

"We actually want to talk to you about Natalya," Oren said. "Because we think it might help us find Tiffany."

"Okay."

"You work night shifts, correct? Including last year when Natalya was found in room six?"

"That's right."

"Can you tell us anything about that night?"

Wyatt shrugged. He looked over toward Max, who had just pulled the earpiece out. He quickly concealed it in his hand. Oren tried to take over the conversation again, pulling Wyatt's focus back his way.

"Did you see Josh walking home that night?"

"Yeah."

"And did you know Natalya was staying here at the motel?"

"Yeah."

"Were you here when she checked in?"

"I . . . I'm sorry," Wyatt sighed. "I didn't know what to do."

"What do you mean, Wyatt?"

"I told Landry that I saw her check in." Wyatt was trembling. "'Cause we aren't supposed to rent rooms out to friends anymore. And I didn't want to get in trouble with Pauline again."

"But you didn't see her check in?"

"No, not really," Wyatt said. "She texted me. She said she wanted a room but wanted to be discreet. So, I told her I'd unlock room six for her. I wasn't here when she showed up. But I . . ." He paused, looking at the ground. He seemed shaken. He was recounting the details of that night.

Max knew this was his chance. No greater source of truth than what was in the man's head.

The country radio station was still coming in fits and starts, but it was good enough. Max slumped himself back in the chair, so that he wouldn't fall out of it, and pressed the button.

\*\*\*

Max had barely moved. He was just outside the motel's office now, standing against the door. Wyatt was outside too, a mere six feet away. But although it was the same place, it was not the same time. Night had descended upon them. The snow was absent; leaves carpeted the ground instead. And Wyatt's bulky jacket had been removed. He stood, puffing on a cigarette, in just his tucked-in, collared shirt.

This was all familiar; Max had seen it recently from Josh's perspective.

A car pulled into the parking lot, Natalya's car. Wyatt's vision was much clearer than Josh's, and so the scene was no longer obscured. The moon and the stars lit up the woods beyond the motel, and a couple orange lamps hung over the parking lot as the car pulled into its spot right in front of room six.

The vehicle's driver cut the engine and opened their door, walking around to help the passenger out. Both their faces were veiled in shadow, even with Wyatt's stronger memory, but it appeared that the passenger was drunk or passed out, as the driver had to practically carry them to the motel room.

Wyatt let out a long exhale, smoke rising into the night. The way he lurked, watching, made Max feel uneasy. Yet he joined him in it, needing to see who was going to emerge from the car.

A sudden snapping of branches caught Wyatt's attention. He turned his head and saw a silhouette stumbling up the road. This would be Josh, right on cue. Max ignored this, and tried to remain diligent, focused on the car.

As he watched, though, the corners of the world began to shrink. A wave of darkness—a black hole—rushed in from beside the motel and began to swallow up all of the light. Max cursed internally, willing it to stop. But the darkness took over; soon, the motel scene was too shrouded, and it was impossible to make out the shapes ambling toward room six. Josh's drunk staggering had taken centre stage instead.

Wyatt's focus had shifted.

Max stood at the edge of the scene, straddling the shadows and the light, waiting for the curtain to be lifted like a horse in the starting gate. Finally, Wyatt's gaze wandered back over to the motel, just in time to see the driver heading back out of the room. The door was open slightly, though from this vantage point, Max couldn't even see the tattooed leg that he had spotted before in Josh's mind.

It was unclear how Natalya got into the room. But the rest, Max had seen before. The driver returned to the car, retrieved a bag, and marched back into room six. Then the door closed.

"Goddamn it," Max said under his breath. *So, Wyatt didn't see anything conclusive either.*

The motel grew dark and hazy again, Wyatt's focus rotating back to the drunk man on the road.

"Hey, Josh!" Wyatt said between puffs.

The drunken shadow paused, looking his way. Wyatt could now clearly make out Josh's face. His eyes were glazed over, unsteady. He was clearly hammered. He did his best to try and recognize the man standing before him, but Josh never responded. His face was red, veins bulging as he attempted to keep his rage suppressed. Josh eventually just kept on his way, heading on the road back into town.

Now with Josh gone, Wyatt stared back at the motel. Unlike before, when the memory collapsed, Max found himself still very much at the scene of the crime. He wondered if he should approach the motel room again to try and get a glimpse inside. But before he could make up his mind, Wyatt made it for him. The night clerk tossed his cigarette butt aside and started walking over to room six. Max followed him.

For a long moment, Wyatt stood outside the motel room door, completely immobilized by thought. He looked as though he might kick the door down and barge inside. There was a mixture of lust and envy on his face. He seemed to be imagining what was happening behind the door, which stood there as his nemesis, the barrier between him and what he wanted. It was taunting him.

Wyatt loitered a moment longer before there was a noise from behind the door: a loud thud followed by a gasp or a muffled yell. Now Wyatt was swayed into acting. He crept forwards, dropping down onto one knee. He pushed his face near the door. He was spying, and it was not lost on Max that this was what he himself had been doing all day.

The motel was outdated, a surprise to no one who saw it, and the doors still had actual keyholes. Wyatt retrieved a fresh cigarette from his pocket, lit it up, and lined his eyes up with the keyhole. He had fully crossed the line into voyeurism.

Max knew that whatever he saw in there was likely going to help answer a lot of questions. But he was frozen by a momentary surge of fear. Whatever lay on the other side of that door was bound to be horrible. His resolve for witnessing awful things was waning. The powerlessness he felt at not being able to save someone like Natalya from her fate—only to be able to watch it happen again and again—made Max feel small. He became desperately lonely and wanted to crawl out of the memory immediately.

The cigarette embers reflected in Wyatt's thick glasses. Their soft orange glow was so real. The entire night was—everything from the crisp air to the way the leaves crunched under foot. Up until now, Max had been constantly trying to remind himself that it *wasn't* real, that he could stomach all of this because it was a re-creation, a facsimile that he was able to relive because of stolen technology.

This was the first—but wouldn't be the last—time that Max actually started to doubt this line of thinking. Maybe it *was* real. All of the pieces of this world existed, but they were just stuck here on a loop. Why did this have to be any less than what he considered to be the real world? In this way, what if Natalya remained alive because she still existed in Josh's mind, jumping off the dock into the pristine lake water. What if Max's dad was still alive somewhere in his own head?

Without realizing it, Max was starting to follow in Charlie's footsteps down a path that would change his view of reality.

This thought spurred Max into action. He needed to do something—anything—to help the girl that was on the other side of that door.

Max knelt next to Wyatt.

"Can I take a look?" he asked Wyatt.

He was gentle, not disruptive, careful not to be too reckless with the rules. But now Max had seen some success in interacting with SIs and was feeling confident.

Wyatt's SI, much like the real person, didn't say anything. He just slid over so that Max could gain access to the keyhole.

Max felt dirty and perverse as he shut one eye and pushed his nose up against the cool door. On the other side, he saw movement. The room was dim. The only light seemed to be coming from the television, blue and red flashes intermittently streaking across the walls. Two humanoid shadows were on the bed. The flashing light turned them into strobing silhouettes, and the small keyhole made it impossible to catch more than a partial section of movement at any given time.

The two figures writhed on the bed. What they were doing could have been sex. It could also have been murder.

The television flickered white, and Max caught a glimpse of pale skin, fingers pressed deep against it. But he couldn't tell if what he saw was an arm or a leg or a neck.

Max tried to crouch lower and get a look of their faces. But the keyhole wouldn't allow it. Every so often, the two shadows would struggle and drop, and then he could see the outline of hair, but there was not enough detail to even differentiate Natalya from the stranger. Max felt like was watching an old, badly damaged film projected on the side of a burning building. It was all kaleidoscopic nonsense.

Frustrated, Max stood. He needed to find out who this stranger was. It was the piece of the puzzle they had yet to collect. He tried the door handle, but it was, of course, locked.

"Do you have the keys?" he asked Wyatt.

Wyatt, always phantom-like with his movements, quietly retrieved a key ring from his belt and handed the master to Max. Max thrust the key into the door where his eye had been peering just moments earlier. He moved quickly. Without even pulling the key back out, he twisted at the handle and then pushed the door inward. It swung open easily and banged against the inner wall, bouncing back in Max's face and causing him to push it open a second time.

Careful not to step through the threshold in case it took him to another part of Wyatt's mind, Max stood and stared, waiting for his eyes to adjust to the dark graininess of the motel room.

But of course, they never would.

Wyatt had not witnessed anything substantial that night. His memory contained no detail of the stranger or of Natalya. And so, to Max's great horror, he found himself face to face with two human-like creatures that lacked faces, skin, or any definition.

The two shadow creatures turned their heads—or what should have been heads—toward him, realizing they had been interrupted. Their heads were the darkest shade of black he'd ever seen. But their forms were inconsistent. They shifted around, impossible to stare at, like the spots one gets in their vision during a headache.

Both figures rose, their bodies seemingly composed of the analog snow from an old television set. They writhed and vibrated even as they held still. Their forms were slender, bony, and their arms hung at their sides like broken tree branches. Intermittently, these branches would become flesh, a human leg or a human arm flickering into existence and then vanishing just as quickly.

A piercing screech began to fill the air.

This was a familiar alarm to Max—Oren's lessons coming back to him. This was the warning of a cornered animal. The sound sent ripples through Wyatt's mind. Windows cracked. The skin on Wyatt's face seemed to be blistering from sound waves like radiation.

The two hostiles started creeping toward Max, their arms now raising toward him, trying to pull him in with gnarled fingers. Max took a step back and tripped on Wyatt's leg. He hit the ground with a thud—that incredibly real ground.

The grainy hands kept coming at him.

He shuffled backwards across the sidewalk, scraping his hands on the cement.

The bodies of his pursuers cast their own glow, each of them its own flickering nightmare. Max kicked himself away, realizing they had stopped their advance. But now their arms were growing longer and longer, able to chase him no matter how fast he moved. They shot out at him like tentacles, inches away.

Finally, Max got his weight under him and was able to stand. The fingers were clawing right at his face as he turned, nicking his cheeks. He bolted away, same as the kid who raced up the stairs for fear of monsters grabbing their ankles. He couldn't tell if he imagined these shadow hands scraping the back of his neck or if they were actually pulling at him. He forced it from his mind.

The motel sign was wobbling, threatening to topple over. Max thought he could see the vine-like fingers that pursued him coiling their way up the post and pulling it down. There wasn't anywhere they couldn't reach. Soon, they'd have him, too, likely keeping him in this memory forever. Suffocating him.

Max ran for the parking lot and beyond, where the town was dark and deserted. As he did, he shut his eyes and clamped his hands over his ears. *Get me out of here,* he thought. He tried not to think of the cold fingernails tickling his hair and beckoning back into that motel room.

He pressed himself into his own mind, shutting out the demons behind him and eventually—thankfully— he pulled himself out.

\*\*\*

The screeching had turned into country music. Max found himself back in the office, propped in the chair with his head against the window. He hadn't fallen over, and he hadn't been noticed. Wyatt was just beginning to speak; Max hadn't been gone more than a couple of seconds. Despite how long this day had felt for him, it was still barely past three o'clock.

". . . feel really bad about it," Wyatt was saying. "I know I shouldn't have. But I liked her first. She shouldn't have been Josh's. Or anyone else's. So . . . I guess that's why I watched."

"What did you see?" Oren was asking.

"I . . . I think . . ." Wyatt was stammering.

Because he didn't know what he had seen. Max knew that now. The view through the keyhole was too obscured.

"She was with a guy."

"You didn't see who it was," Max said aloud.

Oren looked at him, surprised that he was back. Wyatt gave a slight head tilt in Max's direction but didn't fully look over. He nodded.

"I came back into the office after a bit," Wyatt said. "And just read my book. I couldn't tell who she was with. I never saw anyone leave the room. And the next day, the police found her inside. There was never any mention of another person in there, so I just kept my mouth shut."

"Why wouldn't you say something, Wyatt?" Oren was agitated. It was mostly rhetorical, however, as it wouldn't help them now either way.

"It wasn't my business." Wyatt shrugged. "People often show up to do shady stuff at the motel. I'm sorry. I know it was wrong not to speak up before."

"We should get going," Max said to Oren, signalling he had seen all there was to see.

"If you think of anything else, let us know," Oren said curtly, then made for the door.

Once free, Max unloaded his findings. "There was someone in the room with Natalya," he said. "I couldn't make out who it was. But there was something happening in that room. It looked like it could've been violent. Either way, someone was with her the night before she was found hanging."

"That text is bothering me too," Oren said. "Wyatt said that Natalya texted him to set up the room. But according to Josh, she had been quiet all week. That message could've come from someone else using her phone."

The sky was rapidly losing its light, a rich navy blue chased the sun down behind the horizon. Max watched his breath rising toward it.

"What's our next move?"

Before Oren could answer, Josh emerged from the car in a panic.

"We have to go check on Nelly," he said.

"Why?" Oren asked.

"I got a voice message from her, back when we were talking," he said. "I didn't check it until just now. It's a bunch of strange noises, sounds like she's in trouble."

He played it for them. The clip was only four seconds long, but during that time, they heard what sounded like heavy breathing, scraping and rubbing, glass breaking, and the phone hitting the floor.

"I've tried calling her back three times, and there's been no answer," Josh said. "I even tried her home phone. She doesn't go anywhere. She doesn't have family in town. She doesn't have a lot of friends. She doesn't party or go to the movies. And I know she's worried sick about Tiffany. She should be answering my calls."

Oren agreed to a detour. As they jogged back to the car, they had to pass by room six. Max couldn't help but feel like the demons were still lurking inside, waiting for him. A chill crept down his spine, and he was certain it was their fingers, wrapping around him and dragging him back into the darkness.

# 10. Memory Lane

THE HOUSE WAS EMPTY. As was the garage. Both were unlocked, so they'd had a look around. At first, there didn't seem to be anything amiss, and Oren was very much doubting foul play. But on the voice recording, they'd heard broken glass, so they kept looking. It was Max who had decided to peak under the bed. A lamp had been smashed and then haphazardly hidden under the bed. Small pieces of glass were visible on the rug, once he looked with a flashlight up close.

Next, it was Josh who made a discovery. Nelly's signature oversized, black hoodie. It was laying on the bed. Not in and of itself a ghastly find, but when Josh told them she didn't go anywhere without it, they could not dispute this. Max had seen the girl wear that hoodie everywhere, even in her memories.

"Something bad has happened," Josh said before storming outside.

Now Josh was pacing on the driveway, distraught. Oren was trying to calm him, get him back inside, if for no other reason than because it was freezing outside. The winter sun had made its early exit, and the twilight glistened with a layer of frost; it coated every parked car on the street, every window of every house, and every lamppost.

"There has to be a sign," Josh was babbling. "Look. Tire tracks! They're bigger than the ones from my car." He pointed out toward the street.

"We were here earlier, that's where we parked," Oren said, dismissing this.

There really was nothing concrete.

"What do we do?" Max asked from the door to the garage. He was tucked halfway inside, trying to stay warm.

"It's circumstantial at best," Oren admitted. "We don't know that she's missing."

"But what do you think?"

"I think he's right," Oren said as he watched Josh pace. "Something bad happened."

"So, what, now we have two missing girls to find?" Max had to tuck his hands into his pockets, as the cold air was numbing them, even with the space heater working overtime in the garage behind him.

"Yep," Oren said with a sigh. "I think we need to alert Landry. Although, it's not going to be easy to declare another missing person, especially when she hasn't been gone more than a couple of hours."

"Jesus," Max said with a shiver.

Just then, his phone buzzed. Janelle had responded. *We make our own curses.*

*Cryptic,* Max thought, *but highly accurate.* He worried now that even with the MemCom, they had no chance to solve these cases. It felt like they were always one step behind. This valuable tool wasn't quite the leg up they had hoped it would be. All Max was doing was verifying that the quality of police work in this town was poor.

He answered Janelle with a request, asking if she was able to look up all of the missing person headlines, suicide headlines, and tragic accident headlines that came out of Ruston. He thought this might be valuable. And Janelle was a phenomenal researcher.

"Let's go," Oren said at last.

Josh was tiring. He had stopped pacing and was just staring skyward. "Where to?"

"The station." Oren started walking.

Max shut the garage door and followed.

"To report Nelly missing. And to find out what else has been missed with these cases over the years. I think if we're going to find Tiffany and Nelly, the clues will be in what happened to every girl before them."

\*\*\*

"Kids run away all the time." That was what Landry said. He immediately dismissed everything Oren tried to tell him. And when he saw Josh standing there in the vestibule to the sheriff's station, he audibly groaned.

"You been letting that Thomas boy jerk you around?" Landry scoffed.

Sickly fluorescent lighting hummed above their heads. Landry, Oren, and Max stood in the station, near the front desk, while Josh waited in between the pairs of front doors. He had told Oren he didn't want to speak with the sheriff, for fear of what he might say.

The station was a ghost town. That they had found Landry here seemed like a stroke of luck. Everyone else appeared to have punched out at sundown.

"I know it's unusual," Oren said, "to report someone missing so suddenly. But there are signs of foul play."

Max knew that Oren was hyperbolizing a bit. There was a broken lamp and a hoodie on a bed. Not much else. Though with a bit of context, this did point at trouble.

"Well, we'll be sure to keep an eye out," Landry said.

"I think we need to take this seriously," Oren pleaded. "We likely have a serial offender. Any evidence from Nelly's disappearance can help us find Tiffany."

"My priority is the Thomas girl," Landry said. "Who, by the way, we still don't know anything about. She could've run away too. Maybe the girls took off together. In case you haven't noticed, Nelly Masterson does not have a powerful family like Tiffany does. Very few people are going to care. I have limited resources as it is. This is just the way it goes."

"I am not even asking you to do anything," Oren said. "Let Max and I look into it. We just need to see the files you have for Natalya Romano."

"What the fuck for?" Landry puffed his chest out, immediately defensive.

They were questioning his police work. *Which shouldn't be a surprise,* Max thought.

"There's reason to believe it wasn't a suicide," Oren said.

Voices were raised, and Max could tell that Josh was hearing every word. The doors were not that thick. He was standing behind the glass, staring at the floor, but Max saw the vein in his forehead bulging again.

"Is that what he told you?" Landry chuckled. "I knew you were gonna be trouble. Let's not forget you ain't real detectives, boys. So, you wanna come in here and question my entire department based off, what, the word of a fucked-up kid? Because he's sad his girlfriend died?"

"No one is questioning you or your department." Oren tried to remain calm. "But we need to see what evidence has been collected. And time isn't really on our side here. Please, let us have a look at what you have."

"Well, I won't be doin' any such thing." Landry crossed his arms. "You need to stop letting dipshit out there poison your brains. He wasn't there, at the motel. I was. The girl's neck was fucking nearly black where she hung herself. Plain as day what happened there."

Josh came bursting through the door into the lobby. He was fuming, steam practically rising from his ears. Oren sensed trouble and moved to try and block him, but Josh was too quick, too strong, and he pushed Oren forwards, into Landry.

"She didn't kill herself!" Josh raged. "Any half-decent sheriff would've fucking known that. Archie would've known that when he wore the badge."

"That old fart?" Landry chuckled. "You wanna go back to him wearing the badge? Be my guest."

"Let's all calm down," Oren said, arms spread, keeping Landry on one side and Josh on the other. He had Josh by the scruff of his jacket but didn't dare take the same hold of the sheriff.

Max was frozen, panicked, unsure of how to help.

"He's a fucking coward," Josh said, spit flying from his lips. "He won't show you anything 'cause he knows he fucked up."

"Watch your mouth." Landry wore a shit-eating grin, eyes taunting Josh. "The only reason I haven't locked you up yet is 'cause I'm worried you'll off yourself like your girlfriend did."

Max felt what was coming next even before it happened. Josh shook free of Oren's grip and sidestepped away from Oren. Oren tried to get back in front of him, to block him, but Josh had psyched him out and gone back the other direction. Now he had a clear shot. Landry's smirk disappeared from his face just as he too realized what was about to occur.

Josh wound up and swung. His fist connected perfectly with Landry's left cheek, sending the sheriff tumbling into the desk. Max knew it was deserved—the goading Josh had endured would've driven anyone to the same reaction—but he also immediately understood the severity of what had happened.

A silence overtook the station. Landry was keeled over a moment but was laughing. He righted himself then, looking proud. The entire side of his face was bright red, already swelling, and his lip was bleeding, but his smile was back. He had gotten what he wanted.

"That's the end of you, shit-for-brains," Landry said.

\*\*\*

The station didn't have more than one cell. Since Floyd Smith was still occupying that space—because to Landry and the Thomas family, he was still the likely guilty party—Josh had been cuffed and left in the break room. Deputy Bennet—she of the wrong-mind dive— was called in to help control things and keep an eye on Josh while Landry sorted this out.

"He's under arrest for assaulting a sheriff," Landry said, his front teeth stained in blood. He was holding an ice pack to his cheek now.

Robert Thomas had been called down to the station and stood towering over Landry with a look of resignation. He knew his son had stirred up his own trouble, and this was the price to pay. He was disappointed.

Oren and Max watched awkwardly. The four of them stood out in the main lobby of the police station, out of earshot for Josh as they discussed his future.

"Can't have this sort of recklessness 'round here." Landry made a show of tenderly tapping his swollen cheek with the ice pack, acting as if it stung.

"I know, I know." Thomas sighed. "Believe me. I take this seriously. We'll be having a rather firm discussion. What do you want to do about him?"

"Bennet can take him to Boonville," Landry said. "I want him out of my sight. Let him sit in their holding cell a couple nights. Let him cool off. Learn a lesson. If you can send him back home, we won't press it any further."

"Fair," Thomas agreed.

He certainly had the status to make this problem go away, to overrule the sheriff and get his son out of trouble. But his displeasure at this turn of events was so great that Max sensed Thomas wanted Josh to suffer at least a little bit. Josh played in a punk band. He lived in Chicago, on his own. And he drove a beat-up old car. The pieces all signalled toward Josh being a black sheep.

The conversation then turned to the investigation.

"What were you doing with Josh anyway?" Thomas asked. "Some investigators you turn out to be . . . You get my son arrested?"

"He was trying to help us find Tiffany," Oren said in an even, calculated tone.

Max had no idea how his blood wasn't boiling too. Max could barely hear anything over the rush of his own heartbeat, even now.

"How?"

"We're close," Oren lied.

Max cringed, realizing how they were the opposite of close. They had unearthed more problems, more missing girls and unsolved cases. They hadn't found a single answer.

"But we need to look at the evidence collected from some previous cases."

"Well, what are you waiting for?"

"We need the sheriff to agree to show us the evidence files," Oren said.

"Let them see the files." Thomas shrugged, looking at Landry. "Easy."

"But . . ." Landry's eyes widened. He looked like a kid who was just grounded. "They . . ."

"Is that going to be a problem?" The Grim Reaper was back. Thomas seemed to grow in size and stature, intimidating without trying. "If they need to see the evidence lockup to help find my daughter, please let them in."

Landry seemed to be weighing his options. He had got what he wanted with Josh Thomas but poking the bear when it came to the patriarch seemed a little too far. The DA and Ruston's wealthiest summer resident still— to some degree—held Landry's career in his hands.

"Fine," Landry said at last. "You can poke around until I leave for the night. Make it quick."

"What files do you need to look at?" Thomas asked.

Janelle had come through. In the time it took for them to wait for Thomas to come down to the station—while they had to shoot Josh silent, remorseful glances as he was cuffed and dragged away—she had responded to Max with a list of all the tragic headlines that had come out of Ruston. It didn't take her long, she said, as she had already started this prior to being asked. They were on the same wavelength. She had been falling down a rabbit hole regarding all things Ruston since Max had mentioned it. She couldn't get enough, she said. It was all rather mesmerizing in a dark way.

Max read from his phone, rattling off the names Janelle had sent.

"Natalya Romano, Savannah Stevens, Jackie Tyler-Parker, Beckie Smythe, Carla Rantanen, and Francis Delaware," Max listed.

Thomas's eyes widened.

"That many? Why?"

"We think there could be a common thread," Oren interjected. "That Tiffany's disappearance isn't an isolated case. That someone took her and has been taking others."

"Bullshit," Landry said.

"Tomorrow, we're going to charge Floyd with her kidnapping," Thomas reminded them. "And I'll be doing everything in my power to make him talk. A search crew from Syracuse is already checking the lake. Chase whatever fantasy you want right now. I'll be having Archie take you back to the airport tomorrow morning either way. I just hope for your sake that it's after you've found my little girl."

"We're going to find her," Oren said, once again sounding more confident than Max felt inside.

"You've got about a couple hours 'til I close up," Landry said, pulling out his keys and wandering away. "Keep up."

***

The evidence locker, it turned out, was nothing more than a closet with some boxes.

"Have fun," Landry said, shutting the door.

A single row of fluorescent bulbs flickered above their heads. Three metal shelves, all on wheels, were tossed into the closet with no logic. The boxes on these shelving units were mismatched, some cardboard and others plastic, some with lids and some without, some with dates and some without.

"Well, this will be easy." Oren sighed. "You want to look for the first three names on that list, and I'll look for the rest?"

They set about digging through the boxes, trying to determine if there were years or names that they could go by. Eventually, Max found one entire box labelled

*STEVENS*, and he pulled it aside. Savannah Stevens' case was inside.

"What are we looking for exactly?" Max asked.

"Commonalities," Oren said, still flipping through unmarked folders in one of the boxes before him. "Anything that stands out as maybe tying these cases together. Did all these girls date the same guy? Were they from the same school club? Were the circumstances around their deaths similar?"

"Not really," Max said. "Savannah drowned when she fell though the ice. Natalya died by apparent suicide. So, if there's a serial killer out there, he's making it look like accidents."

The search was exhausting. Max felt as though hours had past, although after checking his watch, he found that wasn't the case. This was nothing like the thrilling scenes in detective movies where the big *Aha!* moment comes from an evidence box. They were finding the most mundane items with even more mundane significance.

It was Oren who had the first find of any real interest.

"So, this is interesting," he said. "We know that Josh said Natalya was missing for about a week before she turned up at the motel. There's something similar with these two cases from years earlier. Although one was a car accident, and the other was an apparent drowning, both girls had been reported missing in the week leading up to these 'accidents.' Kind of strange, no?"

"That's right," Max said, frantically looking back over the items he had set aside. "Natalya's friend filed a complaint, but it didn't seem to be treated as a formal report. Savannah's mother filed a report. But again, it seems that this information was cast aside when the girls' bodies were discovered. Like these reports weren't taken into account at all."

"Feels to me like some pretty poor police work," Oren deduced.

This was the only real excitement they had in the search. After that, it went right back to a lot of reading and not very much finding. Max was growing agitated with the lack of a system, realizing he was going back through some of the same dates and cases a second time.

At one point, Max let loose a giant yawn, and Oren caught him. He felt a sudden pang of regret for having dragged his friend into this.

*** 

"You know what this reminds me of? Remember when we got detention that one time?" Oren said, jogging Max's mind. "What Grade was that . . . 7? When we had to clean out the gymnasium storage."

"Oh, yeah." Max chuckled.

Instantly, they were both thirteen again.

"We found that box of notes. Like, notes kids pass to each other . . ."

"But they had been confiscated," Oren chimed in. "Which was creepy. Who was holding on to them?"

"Obviously Mr. Young," Max said. "He probably pretended the letters were addressed to him."

"We found one in there that was about you," Oren recalled. "Someone thought you were cute."

"Probably also Mr. Young."

They both let out a belly laugh at this, feeling overtired and drunk on reminiscing. For a brief moment, Max felt something akin to joy coursing throughout his body. This wave of nostalgia was nice. An entire treasure chest of memories was opened, and they flooded him without enough time to really recount them all individually. But as a whole, they were pure happiness. Being a kid again. Less to worry about. It all reminded him of an old adage he heard once: *Things are always greener in the pastures of the past.*

Who knew, maybe one day he'd even look back on this time in Ruston fondly. Though he couldn't imagine why.

"You know," Oren said, sobering up rather suddenly. "Now is probably a good time for you to see your dad again."

Max's mouth hung open. He hadn't expected this. "Now?"

"We're alone, no one is going to catch us," Oren said.

So, they really were thirteen again, sneaking around where the adults couldn't catch them.

"Who knows what will happen tomorrow. I didn't expect to still be searching. I owe you. Take this chance, Max. Go get your closure."

Max wasn't ready. But what could he say? He didn't want to turn Oren's offer down. So, he just nodded. His mouth was suddenly very dry, and he was aware he had no idea what he was actually seeking with this moment.

Oren locked the door to the closet they were in, and Max sat on the ground against a stack of boxes.

"I've had a memory all picked out for you," Oren said, his eyes alight. "One where I remember your father well. I've got it all queued up."

"Okay."

Max was still not sure what he was going to do. The reconstructed corners of strange minds were blissful compared to the fear of seeing his dead father again. Max had become really good at watching from the shadows; this was the only way he knew how to interact in the MemCom. He ran through his mind for what he should do, or say, and couldn't quite land on anything.

Numb, he inserted the earpiece, staring at the floor and hoping for an idea.

Oren played a song on his phone. He chose "Cat's in the Cradle" and waited for Max's reaction with a smirk.

"Fuck off." Max shot him a look but was also grinning.

He pressed the button and was gone.

\*\*\*

Max felt like he was in space for a second before he gathered his bearings. Everything was dark, save for the neon streaks that speckled the blackness like stars. Neon pathways lit up all around him. The ceiling was spotted with illustrations. And the people were glowing. White shirts were especially vibrant. Because this place was illuminated with black lights.

Max then realized where he had ended up. Oren had brought him back to Monster Putt, a glow-in-the-dark mini putt venue they had frequented as kids.

The cavernous room was pitch-black, but black lights brought a glow to the neon-painted putting course. Glowing balls and putters wiggled as kids chased each other around, some playing by the rules, others not at all. Each hole was adorned with a monster; Max remembered being fond of the werewolf at hole one. Its big white eyes shone like headlights as it snarled down on those about to begin their game. A Halloween soundtrack—one that played year-round—was filling the space with Michael Jackson's "Thriller."

Max was impressed with how clear most of the memory was. Of course, they had come here often. So, it made sense that the big ogre at hole nine was perfectly sharp. The ogre was animatronic, and its head and arms moved disjointedly as a robotic cackle rang out. A smoke machine worked overtime, and artificial screams came from hole thirteen, adorned with false tombstones.

Only the patrons seemed to be missing any detail. Whatever other kids had been present on this day were now entirely faceless entities. Oren's mind did not fill them in. They might as well have been ghosts, floating around with their glowing putters.

To Max's immediate right was the neon mummy statue that guarded the seventeenth hole.

"Putt, if you dare," it taunted, the audio looping from a speaker.

This challenge required golfers to hit the ball up a ramp that was actually a pyramid. Max had perfected the hole in one on this particular hole.

To Max's left was the reason he was here. It just so happened that Young Max and Young Oren were on the final hole. And Max's father was playing with them. He was currently lined up over his ball, ready to hit. He was aimed at the large clown head that unnerved Max even to this day. The clown's eyes were deranged, pointing in different directions. Its hair was fire and glowed a bright orange against the black wall. If you hit the ball into the clown's mouth, it disappeared, and your round was over. If you missed, the clown would laugh at you, and you would try again.

The three of them looked so youthful and happy. Max recognized himself and Oren from school photos through the years. His father, on the other hand, he did not seem to remember. He was fit, his hair dark—not grey—and his skin less weathered. Max seemed to only remember the man who retired and had taken up the bottle.

"Alright, boys." Max's father grinned as he aimed his shot. "One-handed, watch this."

"No way." Young Max laughed. His teeth were purple in the glow.

"Ten bucks says you miss," Young Oren joined in. He wore the brightest white t-shirt.

Confidently, Max's father whacked the ball and raised his arms in celebration even before the shot was finished. Of course, the shot went straight into the clown's mouth.

Both boys groaned. They made a show of their exasperation, but both couldn't stop smiling.

"I don't have ten bucks," Oren said.

"Ah, shoot," Max's father said. "Then, I'll tell you what. If one of you also gets it in, I'll erase your debt *and* buy ice cream."

"Deal!" they screamed in unison.

Young Max went first, lining up his shot carefully. He squinted, trying to see where he was pointed, then he swung with all his might. He hit it a little too hard, and the ball veered off course straight into the wall. The clown laughed maniacally, the sound that was always loud enough to draw attention from other golfers. Young Max stared at the floor, embarrassed.

"You were too strong." Max's father knelt beside him then, arm on his son's shoulder.

This was a moment Max had not stored in his own memory. He watched in awe.

"You don't always need to hit your hardest, Max. Sometimes, you just need a little touch."

"I just wanted ice cream," Max pouted.

"It's ok," Max's father consoled him. "You know why? You have good friends. And I bet you Oren gets it in."

Oren, who had been listening to the comments about touch, stepped up and feathered his ball straight into the clown's mouth.

"See," Max's father said as Oren jumped up and down. "Have faith in your friends. You're a team."

"So, we get ice cream?!" Oren shrieked. He ran over and bumped Max on the arm.

Max broke from his sour mood.

"Yes, ice cream." Max's father held out his hand. "Give me your clubs and go meet me at the counter. Pick out your flavour."

Both boys raced off, and then it was just Max's father left alone, standing there with their clubs and watching the boys run away.

This was Max's chance. He was there on the eighteenth hole with his dad. Something that hadn't happened in twenty years. And something that shouldn't have been possible now.

Where Max was standing, it looked as though his father was staring straight at him. Behind him, monsters cackled and moved their robotic arms through the smoke. His face, although much younger, still had the same eyes. Ones that Max remembered looking to for protection as a kid when he was scared. In the middle of the night, when he swore he saw something in the dark corners of his room, his father would come to the rescue. It was these eyes that steadied Max's nerves. But it was also these same eyes that looked so disappointedly at adult Max when he had made choices that didn't fit his father's vision.

Right now, Max couldn't tell what his father's eyes were telling him. They were tinted purple from the black lights. But were they disappointed? Or were they telling him it was okay?

Oren had selected this moment specifically. He obviously remembered Monster Putt well, so the setting would be clear for Max. But also, this one moment in time would leave Max alone with his father. He was free to say something. He should say something.

But he couldn't.

The memory would end soon. Oren had left already and was lining up for ice cream. Max would need to move on too. But he didn't know what to say. All of the terrible later years came back to him then, and this innocent version of his father transformed.

He was reminded of the man who let milestones pass without a word. Max had sent his first published articles to his parents to read. His mother showered him in accolades. His father said nothing. Max had come home for a visit one year. He ran into his father's oldest friend, the best man at his wedding. The two of them went golfing together weekly.

"Max!" his father's friend had exclaimed, excited to see him. "How are you? What are you up to in Vancouver?"

All those years away. All those articles sent to his parents. And Max's father had neglected to mention anything about his son—even to his closest friend. Max could tell there was no pride there. And that damaged Max. He felt like the zombie mannequins that decorated the corners of the Monster Putt. He felt hollow.

Now it was impossible for Max to see anything but those years of suffering when he looked at this re-creation of his father. And he couldn't bring himself to step forward.

"Max," his father said then.

The words were so unexpected. Max shivered. He panicked and took off. Perhaps he was just calling out after his son in the memory, but the fact that his father was looking right at him and saying his name made Max jolt.

Max made for the nearest door, which happened to be an emergency exit. He rushed past the Dracula that spun its head around with glowing red eyes, pushing his way through, just needing to be somewhere else. As he moved through the exit, Max looked back over his shoulder. His father was still standing there, but slowly the smoke seemed to be taking over the room as the memory faded away.

"Sorry," Max murmured, and then it was all gone.

\*\*\*

He was somewhere else. An adjoining memory Oren had held onto. Although, this one did not include Max.

It was, however, a very familiar setting. Oren was standing in Max's childhood living room, now a young man. The old, beat-up furniture, brown carpet, and window overlooking the front street were all exactly as they should've been. But the art on the walls was wrong; Oren clearly didn't remember. The paintings—ocean landscapes that Max's mother had been fond of—were smudged, hazy. And they were all hung on the wrong wall. They should've been over by the fireplace.

Max's father was there too, seated in his usual spot by the television, feet up on the coffee table. This version of Max's father looked a lot more like how Max remembered him. Oren stood in front of the man, looking nervous.

"Sit, sit," Max's father said, and Oren sat on the sofa. "So, how's the big city?"

"It's been great," Oren said. His tone implied that he was just exchanging pleasantries, avoiding the main point. "Just back visiting my sister. Thought I'd come say hi. How's Max?"

"Busy with his new life in Vancouver," Max's father said, vague and short. "Been out there yet?"

"No, no, I haven't." Oren's gaze was all over the place, distracted. He was stalling.

"So, how's the force? Any promotions?" Max's father was teasing, but his eyes were bright with genuine interest.

He had never asked Max about his articles with this same fervour.

"That's actually what I wanted to talk to you about," Oren said.

He was playing with his hands, fidgeting in a way Max had never seen. Nervous. Not the usual confident Oren.

"I'm actually leaving. Going in a different direction. I want to become a private investigator."

"A PI?" Max's father said in a way that was hard to read.

Oren cringed, bracing himself.

"Wow, I think that's great."

"You do?"

"Yeah, good for you." Max's dad smiled. "Going off on your own. It's not easy. But it sounds like a fun challenge."

"I have to admit," Oren said with a relieved laugh. "I thought you'd be disappointed. You have always been a sort of father figure to me. I wasn't sure if leaving the more traditional law enforcement route would be something that you . . ." Oren didn't finish, trying to find the right phrasing, but Max's father cut him off anyway.

"Of course not." Max's father waved a hand. "Look, no police force is perfect. There are plenty of bad apples out there. This way, you get to be your own boss. You get to do what's right but without the bureaucracy. I commend you for trying this out."

"Thank you," Oren said. "You've always been so good to me. It's a big part of the reason that I want to do this. I think of the work you've done in your career, the stories you've shared, and it makes me want to be part of that. Helping people."

"Well, I'm flattered," Max's father said before letting loose a wheezing cough and temporarily clutching at his chest. Max knew now that his father had been unwell for some time but hidden it.

"But listen, no one is perfect. Not in any line of work, this one included. Not police officers, and not private investigators. I've met a lot of bad apples in my time. I just want you to keep that in mind, kay? They're not all good guys. And don't you dare treat them as such. Not even cops are above the law, Oren."

"Good advice," Oren said, though Max could tell he was already glazing over it.

For Max, however, these words stuck. The initial hurt of watching his father and best friend have the moment that he always craved was put on pause. Something else rose up inside Max, starting in his spine and then crawling like fire up his neck, sparking in his head. This advice from many years ago, it was here for a reason.

*Not even cops are above the law.*

Was this really the piece they'd been missing the whole time?

Max couldn't wait to get back and tell Oren. The whole case was starting to make sense to him now.

Adrenaline surged through his body like never before, and he felt like he could scream.

Without further delay, Max shut his eyes and pulled himself out.

\*\*\*

"Oren," Max said, pulling himself to his feet. He needed to pace himself. He was full of a new energy, a sort of determination. "We've been missing something."

"What's that?" Then Oren looked concerned. "What did you see in there? Did you leave the Monster Putt?"

"I did. I had to," Max said. "I couldn't go through with it. I couldn't speak to him. I went through the door."

"Where?"

"My living room," Max said. "You were there, talking to my dad."

Oren frowned, uneasy with Max snooping. He was also feeling uncomfortable because he knew that Max had a strained relationship with his father.

"I'm sorry."

"Don't." Max raised his hand. There wasn't time for this. He could feel upset later. "It's okay. Your mind had held onto a memory. It held onto something my dad said. Like subconsciously, you knew this the whole time."

"Knew what?"

"It's been bothering me," Max said. "Why are the police here so incompetent? Why does it feel like they're blocking our every move? What if they have something to hide?"

Oren squinted, starting to track where Max was going but allowing him to finish.

"We also keep hearing about this curse. Josh said it feels like the town has been cursed for about ten years, ever since Landry took over as sheriff. What if that isn't a coincidence?"

"Why abduct Nelly? Why abduct a second person?"

"That's the other thing," Max added. "The whole town thought Floyd had done it. The real captor would've been off the hook. Floyd was arrested, and he was going to get away with it! Then you and I determined that Floyd was innocent. Only the people at the library that morning would've known that. There's no logic to taking another girl unless . . . unless the real captor *knew* that we had cleared Floyd. And he had something to hide. Maybe he knew we had spoken to Nelly, and so he was covering his tracks."

Oren remembered how Landry had lost his cool in the library when they'd tried to tell him Floyd was innocent.

"You said we were looking for commonalities," Max continued, though he lowered his voice. "All of these missing girls have met tragic ends after Sheriff Landry came onto the scene."

The room felt still. Both of them were afraid to move.

"One person had control of all these investigations," Oren agreed. "One person could have tampered with all of the evidence." He looked around at that disorder in the room. The boxes lacking details and dates and names.

"So," Max said but didn't finish his thought.

Both of them remained silent, afraid to say it out loud. They were about to poke the bear from inside its cave. They imagined he might be able to hear them through the walls if they uttered it aloud. It was dangerous—even taboo—to accuse a member of law enforcement. But Max's father had left this hint for them from beyond the grave.

The pieces fit.

"We have one more dive," Oren said at last. "This is going to be a difficult one."

# 11. When the Pieces Fit

OREN LAID OUT THE PLAN, along with several deviations. By the end, Max felt like he had come out of a football huddle with Tom Brady, and he was just praying he didn't drop the pass. First, they had to catch Landry before he left for the evening.

They departed from the evidence locker and found Sheriff Landry at his desk, already putting on his jacket and shutting off his computer monitor.

"Time's up," Landry growled. "Hope you found what you were looking for 'cause we're done here."

Doing his best to ignore the hatred he held in the pit of his stomach for the sheriff, Oren sheepishly asked for a favour. They needed a lift. This was the part of the plan Max felt would derail things before they even got going. From the car, the two of them could safely operate the plan. Oren would ride shotgun, distracting the sheriff with conversation. Meanwhile, from the back seat, Max could feign fatigue and have a nice little nap. The drive would give them plenty of time.

"The hell for?" Landry asked.

"Max is feeling unwell," Oren said.

They both had agreed it was okay to throw Max under the bus.

"We need to get back to Stella's, where we're staying. And we don't have Archie anymore this evening."

They hadn't exactly tried to call their driver, but the lie would hold.

"Oh yeah?" Landry suspected something, but grinned. He knew something they didn't. The look on his face terrified Max. He was about to call their bluff. "I can drive *him* back there, then. But you didn't hear?"

"Hear what?"

"DA wants to talk with you." Landry pointed a finger at Oren. "He's waiting outside."

Landry was evidently taking great pleasure in this; Oren was in trouble with the Grim Reaper.

"I'll drive your sick buddy home," Landry said. There wasn't much pushback because he was celebrating. "Enjoy your chat."

Max and Oren looked at one another. This was not the plan. They were about to be separated. But they couldn't well walk it back now. Oren did his best to impart a confident look, trying to signal to Max that it would be okay.

"Sure, thank you," Oren said. "Max, go get some rest."

Max wanted to scream, "But how am I supposed to do this alone?!" But he couldn't say anything. He had to just nod. He was on autopilot. *Get into the car with the sheriff. Invade his brain. Everything will go horribly wrong.*

"Well, don't keep him waiting." Landry patted Oren on the back, giddy to be sending him off to the berating he was likely to get. Then he turned to Max. "My truck's around back."

***

From the passenger seat of Sheriff Landry's truck, Max adjusted himself so that he could lean his head on the cold, hard window. He had slipped the earpiece carefully from his pocket already and positioned it in his right hand, which was tucked up by his neck acting as a sort of pillow. It would be easy to discreetly slide it in his ear.

This wasn't ideal, him in the front seat instead of the back, but Landry had insisted. Another deviation from the plan that Max numbly had no choice but to oblige.

"You can put on music, if you want," Max said, trying to appear friendly.

The car had been uncomfortably silent as their drive began.

"Won't bother me."

"It's fine," Landry said back, his voice low and hoarse.

"You don't listen to anything while you drive?" Max prayed for the man to put something on. He needed this.

"Just the road," Landry said.

Now Max didn't even have music for the dive. How was he supposed to work the MemCom without them listening to the same music? Max looked around a bit. He considered turning the radio on himself, but Landry caught him eying up the radio and shot him a dirty look.

"What's your deal?" Landry said. "Why you always so quiet?"

"I'm new," Max said. "Just following Oren's lead."

"*Hmff*, and what's his deal?" Landry cleared his throat. "That guy hates authority, hey? Been a thorn in my side the whole time you've been in town. You better tell him to cool it."

Max searched for an appropriate response but couldn't find one.

Landry wasn't done, either.

"Thinks he's the only one who wants to find that girl." Landry chuckled. "Ain't nobody in town as valuable as he is. He's such a mother fuckin' saint. Do me a favour and let him know his shit stinks too."

Max didn't have an answer for this either. He just let the silence take hold. Landry was hoping for a rise, and when Max had no response, he kept glancing over, side-eying Max and trying to get a read on him.

"I've been sheriff here a long time, you know," Landry said. "I know my shit."

*About ten years, right?* Max wanted to add. *A lot of missing girls during your time.* He did not have the stomach to say it.

"What do you even call whatever it is that you do?" Landry asked.

Max thought a moment, then offered up, "Investigative assistant."

"Investigative assistant?" Landry said, then let loose a single, throaty laugh. "How'd you get into that line of work?"

This was getting too chatty. Max needed to shut it down before the ride was over if he had any chance of pulling off this dive.

"How'd you get into *your* line of work?" he retorted.

Landry raised his eyebrows, side-eying Max again. He made a guttural *hmff* sound and kept his mouth shut. He didn't feel like answering Max's questions. Conversation over.

*Thank God.*

At last, the truck was quiet. All Max could hear was the hum of the highway beneath them.

That was it.

*Just the road,* he thought. Maybe he didn't need the radio. The white noise provided by the truck over the highway could be enough. It was consistent. And with no other sounds in their vicinity, Max supposed it would work. They'd be listening to the same thing, at least. With no one else's mind nearby.

Max rested his head against the window, trying to take up a position that would make it less obvious when he lost consciousness.

Praying that Landry would not try to spark up more conversation, Max slid the MemCom earpiece into his hidden ear, keeping his head pinned to the window the best he could as the truck rattled. He lay his elbow across the window's ledge, using it to cushion his head and keep his finger on the button.

Then he shut his eyes.

*Believe I'm asleep,* Max thought. *Please, just believe I'm asleep.*

He felt exposed without Oren there, suddenly aware of the value of having someone monitoring his well-being. Even if he was only out for five seconds, that left him vulnerable to the man in the driver's seat. It left him vulnerable to a dangerous man.

Max worried what would happen if Landry were to look over, notice him slouched over, and try to wake him. Or if Landry jerked the truck to the side a little too fast on the corner, and Max's head lulled to the left, exposing the earpiece. If Landry knew about MemCom, he would recognize it right away. He would realize he was being spied on, and that it was the ultimate breach of privacy, looking through someone's thoughts.

And then what would he do?

What would he do with Max alone and unprotected in his truck?

Max wanted to stop. He desperately told himself, *don't do it*, and willed his hand to stay away from the button. This was far more dangerous than the dives they had attempted before. The setting was not in their control. Oren—his safety net—was nowhere near.

Max recognized the street they were on and knew it wasn't far now. He wouldn't get much more time. He needed to jump. And despite his brain's best intentions, it lost its argument. His finger pushed the button anyway, and Max left the vehicle.

\*\*\*

Oren had been through worse. Thomas was unhappy. Thomas raised his voice and cursed and made threats. The biggest of which was to rescind the money he had offered to pay Oren. With guys like this, it always came down to money. Even with his daughter still missing, Robert Thomas was concerned with the price he was paying for Oren's service.

Oren understood the rage. They had yet to find the girl. It was meant to be easy. With Charlie, it always had been. They had control there. Leonard Lang was obviously guilty, and he was exposed—at their mercy. But the MemCom was proving to be a more scattershot tool in the wild. They could dive all they want, as all they were doing was guessing at which minds would provide details.

Oren genuinely apologized for not having found Tiffany yet. His confidence was based off his experience. This was intended to be another quick job.

What they didn't tell Thomas was that they hadn't accounted for Ruston. They hadn't accounted for the curse that plagued this strange place.

The money was fine. Oren had no problems letting that go. If Thomas wanted to withhold their funds, so be it. Oren would pay Max for his time and take the financial hit himself. What really bothered Oren, though, was being removed from the case.

Robert Thomas had been given time to think while Oren and Max checked the evidence lockup. And time had allowed his negative thoughts to brew. He no longer wanted to wait to declare it; Oren's involvement here was done.

Thomas told him to leave town and get out of his sight. He had search crews now. Parties of people out scouring the lake. It seemed that Robert Thomas was already searching for a body. It was unlikely to find her alive after all this time, Oren could admit, but it still broke his heart. He wanted this to have a happy ending. And he wanted it to be himself that authored it.

He offered to stick around and help, free of charge. But Thomas was irate. He was a powerful man trapped in a powerless situation. And he needed the control of firing someone. He had to send Oren away. The lack of results, the out-of-nowhere theory about a serial killer, and now being present when Josh struck the sheriff were all of the strikes he needed.

Archie would come for them first thing in the morning. Oren agreed to this, in part because he hoped that Max would find what they needed by then, and this could all be set right. Oren didn't dare show his hand to Robert Thomas. It would make him seem crazy. But if they could prove that Sheriff Landry was behind all this, and possibly even recover Tiffany alive, then this tirade would be worth it.

So, Oren accepted the verbal abuse, and he took responsibility for his part in what had happened until this point. But all the while, he held onto the belief that they'd be proven right. He just needed Max to come through.

Thomas drove away from the station feeling somewhat back in control now that he had shattered Oren.

The night had taken from Oren all of the feeling in his hands and his feet. His nose was burning now with the beginnings of frost bite. He wasn't welcome back in the station, and he had nowhere to go. Across a field, however, he could make out the familiar sign of the Rusty Nail. He tucked his chin into his jacket, trying to use his breath to warm his face, and set out. He could use a drink.

\*\*\*

It wasn't immediately obvious who the boy was. The kid was lanky, a teen yet to grow into his frame, but still young enough that he hadn't needed to shave. His eyes were wide with alarm, looking around as if seeing ghosts. His dark hair was unkempt and flowed wildly in the breeze as he walked through the schoolyard.

"Hey, Eddie!" someone called out. Max scanned but could not see the source of the voice.

The dark-haired boy took off as if the voice had been a gunshot. With unnatural speed, the boy raced for the shelter of the nearby woods. A trickle of panic seemed to radiate from the ground; Max felt everything the boy felt. He sensed the urgency, and something told him to follow. Max did all he could to keep up.

The pace was difficult. The boy leapt over fallen logs, seeming to know where all the dangers lurked. Max staggered and stumbled over brambles, and even with longer legs, he could not match the boy's stride. Stumps and branches seemed to appear without warning—the memory filling them in late—and they'd catch Max by surprise, knocking him off course.

Yelling began to echo throughout the woods. Cackles and jeers without bodies attached. Impossibly, the sound was coming from everywhere all at once. The boy was trying to outrun something that Max couldn't see, but he could tell it was closing in. The woods seemed to be shrinking, closing in around them and sealing off any trace of light from the sun above.

They had travelled deep into the woods. Nothing was visible around them. Darkness crept in. They were isolated in nature.

The boy rounded a corner. Max was exhausted and bruised from his encounters with the foliage. For a moment, he lost sight of the boy completely, but as he pushed his way through low branches, he finally laid eyes on the kid's refuge.

A large, beat-up school bus was sitting rusted out between the trees. The tires were missing, leaving just a hollowed out, yellow stump with rows of seats. The bus was a faded yellow and somewhat blended in with the leaves around it. The entire front of the thing had been torn apart—engine missing and windshield smashed.

The boy had crawled his way into the abandoned bus and was now seeking a hiding spot at the back, behind the seats. Max looked over his shoulder, trying to locate the threat. There was no one around.

"Get out here, you little bitch!" someone screamed.

Max's skin prickled as he once again felt all of the boy's fear. Max too crawled inside the bus, feeling this would help. He didn't want to be exposed to whatever dangers were lurking.

Max had to duck as he entered, and he kept his head low as he wandered up the aisle toward the back of the bus. The paint was peeling from the sides of the walls, and the seats were worn and carved with initials. Dead leaves and vines carpeted the floor.

At the back, the boy was trembling, ducked down behind the last seat on the left. Max felt the urge to do the same, wanting to hide from whatever the boy knew to be coming.

"Get down, they'll see you," the boy snapped at him suddenly.

Max felt the blood rushing to his face again, embarrassed to be spotted. Max quickly dove behind the nearest seat.

The world outside of the bus was now nearly dark. It would have been impossible to see anyone approaching. Max kept his head down and focused on sounds instead. Mostly it was of the boy's heavy breathing, but there were footsteps too. First, far away. Then, all too quickly, they were right outside the bus.

A crash brought Max's heart into his throat. Someone was banging on the side of the bus.

"You in there, princess?" another voice called. This voice was threatening.

A new unseen entity now roared with laughter, coming from the other side of the bus.

The bus creaked as these two unseen tormentors scaled the sides, making their way to the roof. Max was realizing now how incredibly poor this hiding spot was.

"Come here, momma's boy," the first tormentor said. "Don't you remember what I said? 'The next time we catch you walking in our field, we are gonna kick your ass.'"

The footsteps rattled overhead, inching their way from front to back. There was nowhere to run. Max watched the boy look around for some way out of this nightmare. Seeing none, the boy desperately reached into his pocket and produced a whistle. The boy pressed it to his lips and blew, but he was shaking too violently, so his first attempted produced no sound. He collected himself then and blew again.

"What's that?" one tormentor said from above. "Momma give you a whistle?"

Both tormentors laughed.

"You know he's in love with his mom, right?" the other said.

"That's why he's always missing class."

More laughter.

The two unseen figures dropped from the top of the bus now, falling to the ground on the left. Max squinted, trying to make them out in the dim light. It was pointless. They were only shadows. They floated by like demons, their presence both vague and assuredly horrible.

Max stayed hidden as he watched. The demon tormentors climbed inside the bus now, the frame shaking as they laid heavy footsteps down. Instinctively, Max ducked as they passed by him. Their faces were dark, mostly featureless, but each had a set of glowing white eyes that were tracking the boy.

"Stand up, momma's boy," one said as they closed in on the boy.

One tormentor reached out one of its shadow arms and grabbed at the boy, catching him by the scruff of his collar. The other tormentor held a lighter, and its flame came to life now. He held it closer and closer to the young boy's face, close enough that his upper lip was beginning to singe. He seemed to enjoy watching the boy squirm.

Max watched all this while cringing. He had witnessed his fair share of bullying growing up, but always through the lens of a child just trying to keep his head down. Now that he was forced to look at it—to really look at it—as an adult, it was incredibly uncomfortable. He wanted desperately to jump in and stop it, holding back only because he knew this was a simulation.

Thankfully, he didn't need to play hero. Someone else did.

"Hey, leave him alone!" a female voice, oozing with confidence, rang out from the front of the bus.

Everyone froze and looked over to see who had spoken. The lighter fell to the ground. The sun started to pour in from all sides, the forest canopy opening up again. The sense of claustrophobia was dissipating.

A girl stood triumphantly, arms at her sides, backlit by the emerging sun. To Max, she appeared like a superhero.

"Ah, is this your girlfriend come to save you?" the lead tormentor teased.

As the light shifted, the tormentors' faces did as well. Gone were the demon eyes and masked features. Instead, they were now just two freckly teens with acne.

The saviour girl stepped closer, coming toward them and stepping into a pocket of sunlight that flowed in through a hole in the side of the bus. Now, with her face visible, Max could see that she was a good couple years older than the tormentors and the boy. She was taller, more filled out. Her eyes were lined with dark makeup. She carried a calmness and maturity that the boys did not possess. Max guessed the boys were in ninth or tenth grade. This girl looked like she was on the cusp of graduation. She had a cigarette in her hand, and she flicked it away coolly as she neared the group.

She was someone not to be messed with.

"Hey, that's Nina Banks," one freckled kid whispered. The other gasped.

"I said, leave him alone," Nina said as she marched straight toward the lead bully and gave him a cold stare.

Max was missing the context on who Nina Banks was, but he could largely piece it together. Dressed in ripped jeans and an open leather jacket that revealed a Ramones shirt underneath, she would have been revered. She would have been considered *cool*.

"Man, let's get out of here." One bully backed away. He scaled over the seat in front of him and scampered out the front of the bus.

The other, still frozen in terror, just gaped.

"Go." She feigned a blow toward him.

The kid cringed, let out a small squeal, and then took off. As he passed her, she turned and swung one of her boots into his ass, knocking him over. He then scrambled to his feet and vanished.

With the tormentors now gone, Nina turned around to face the boy hiding behind the seat. His collar was all askew, and his eyes were filling with tears.

Every detail on Nina's face was crisp. The pores of her skin, the smoky eye shadow, the tiny stray hairs on her neck that caught the sun.

"Hi," Nina said and smiled. She had one tooth on the top row that turned slightly inward and gave her a somewhat charming snaggletooth.

"Hi," the boy said back. "You're Nina Banks."

"Yeah. You're the Landry boy, right?" Nina asked.

The boy was Ed Landry, who would grow up to become Sheriff Landry of Ruston. Max supposed he knew this the whole time. Whose mind was he in, after all? But this scared, frail boy did not equate in his mind to the loud-mouth sheriff he was investigating.

"Yeah," Ed Landry answered nervously.

"I think my mom knows your family. She used to be your neighbour. I don't live with her anymore though," Nina announced. "Listen, if those kids bother you again, let me know, okay? It's tough enough as it is, in this town, with school and everything. You don't need some shits who think they run the place giving you a hard time. Trust me, in four years, those kids will be coming to you to do their math homework so they can go to fucking college."

"Ok," was all little Ed could summon.

"Come on, I gotta head home. You wanna walk with me?" She pulled him to his feet.

He stood a few inches shorter than her, looking up into her eyes through his tears. He wiped them away quickly, ashamed. He nodded, and she dusted his shirt off.

"K, let's go."

They emerged from the bus, Max tailing them. He was surprised to see a crowd had gathered outside the bus. Other school children, of various ages, were gawking at what had unfolded. Nina saw their onlookers and paused, standing before them comfortably, commanding attention.

"If any of you mess with my buddy Ed," she announced, not afraid of the spotlight. She welcomed this attention and made a show of turning to face every single one of the kids watching. "You have to deal with me. You understand? Ed's cool."

A couple kids nodded. A few murmured their agreement. Others either hid their faces from Nina or turned to leave. There didn't seem to be any objection. One boy even clapped before realizing he was alone, and then he abruptly silenced himself.

"Come on, Ed," Nina said to him.

The sun seemed to be centred solely on her now. The rest of the world was not as deserving of its light.

"I know a good spot for ice cream on the way home, too."

***

The memory jogged forwards. Max had been caught up and was now cursing himself for not trying to find a door out. When things settled again, he realized he was stuck. The only door he could see was at the far end of the store they were in, and he was blocked in by a crowd of teenagers.

Ed Landry was looking at a rack of CDs and cassettes—a throwback that made Max chuckle in spite of himself. Ed was deciding between two albums by Joy Division as Nina and some older boys rooted him on. The store was covered wall to wall with bright colours, band posters that Ed's brain had glazed over into a mosaic of shapes. A few hazy patrons roamed the adjacent aisles, but most of the detail was reserved for this one aisle for artists starting with the letter J.

"They're so good, Eddie," one boy said, his long hair covering his eyes. "Can't go wrong."

"You should get 'em both," Nina said. "I can't believe you've never listened to Joy Division. Trust me. Just get them both. It'll get you through the rest of high school."

"It got us this far," another boy chimed in.

"I don't have enough," Ed said quietly.

"Oh, don't worry about it, bud," the long-haired boy said. "We'll get 'em for you! Consider it a going away present. Another month, and you won't have us around anymore. We'll be off into the land of adulthood." He gazed upwards whimsically, selling his joke.

"You'll never be off to the land of adulthood," Nina teased, hitting the boy in the stomach.

They all laughed.

"Seriously, Eddie, grab them both. We'll pay. A parting gift for you. You need to upgrade your musical tastes, anyway."

Ed grabbed a pair of cassettes, and the long hair boy grabbed the same albums in CD format, adding these to Ed's stack.

"In case you get a CD player later," he explained.

The group followed Ed to the counter, encompassing him like a protective barrier. They were shielding him from the world. A herd of strong buffalo that protected the younger, weaker one.

As Nina and the long-haired boy shelled out some cash to pay for the CDs, another boy tapped Ed on the shoulder.

"You're coming over again Saturday?" the boy asked.

"Does a bear shit in the woods?" The long-haired boy turned, answering for Ed. "Of course, he'll be there. Eddie the Legend comes every weekend."

"I gotta see if I can beat you one last time." The first boy smiled. "You know, before graduation."

"Good luck," the long-haired boy answered again. "Eddie's a shark. Never misses a shot."

"And now he'll have good music to match those skills," Nina said, turning to provide Ed with the bag containing his new gift. "Memorize every single song, Eddie."

Ed had said next to nothing, yet this group had rallied around him like he was a sort of mascot. Or a demigod.

Max was in awe of this incredible group of kids and the way they took care of young Ed Landry. But he really needed to move along. Max finally had a gap large enough to squeeze past them, but as he tried to get by, he bumped into Nina. She fell back against the counter. Suddenly, Ed Landry was glaring at him.

Max froze. The dark, glossy eyes pointed at him like a gun. Ed's SI was warning him. *Don't mess with Nina. She is the star here.* Max didn't move again. He let the group recover, everyone once again standing where they should be.

"Come on, Eddie," the long-haired boy said. "We'll throw one on in the car on the ride back."

The kids made for the door. Max gave them a bit of a head start before rushing after them, desperate to get to the door before the memory ended. But he would never make it.

The walls of CDs and posters crumbled away and were replaced with trees and sky.

"Damn it," Max cursed. A new memory had begun.

A sparkling lake—one that looked familiar—stood before him, reflecting the dock and the trees and the clouds.

Ed was standing on the dock next to Max, looking back toward a large, rustic cabin. Max saw Nina marching toward them, blocking the way back to land. The sun once again radiated off her. Birds provided a sweet summer melody in the background, and a graceful breeze broke up the heat.

"Hey, where are your bags?" Ed asked as Nina approached.

She had a smile on, but it wasn't her big beaming one. It was a gentle one, more of a formality.

"I can't stay the night," Nina said.

"Oh," Ed said, clearly disappointed. "I thought the plan was to have a campout?"

"I know, Eddie," Nina said, sounding tired and a little condescending. "But it's a busy time. I have a large class load and need to get back tonight. Can't spend the whole weekend out here."

"It's just been so long since I've seen you," Ed said. "Months. Kinda feels like you moved on."

"Not at all," Nina said. "The guys all say hi. Everyone misses you. It's just that college is busy. You'll see when you get there. For now, just enjoy your last couple years."

"Well." Ed looked around. "How long can you stay? We can go out in the boat? Have a picnic?"

"I have a few hours before I have to head back," Nina said. "Those both sound lovely."

"Ok good." Ed smiled. "Let's take the boat out first then.

"Great."

Ed moved awkwardly toward Nina, arms outstretched. She caught on late, realizing he was going for a hug. Max used this as a chance to slide past them both on the narrow dock.

"Good to see ya, Eddie," she said, returning the hug stiffly.

Ed misread the situation though. Max saw it in his eyes. He saw the idea spark, the nerves build. Max wanted to warn Ed against it. He felt he could already predict what was going to happen.

All at once, Ed shut his eyes and moved in for the kiss. Nina saw his puckered lips coming for him and tried to move away. She pushed her arms out, blocking his advance. It was awkward. Max hated watching it. Ed opened his eyes to see why he had yet to find her lips, and he saw her staring at him with horror. She was waiting to be told it was a joke. Neither of them spoke.

Max didn't have time for any of this. He saw the door of the cabin just up the dock. He needed to get to something more relevant. He took off. Behind him, he heard the remainder of the interaction play out.

"I'm sorry, Eddie," Nina said. "I love you like a brother. I really do. I think you're a cool kid. But you're also still in high school. And I just don't see you in . . . that way."

Ed said nothing. Max refused to feel bad. He reminded himself who Ed Landry grew up to be. He just focused on the door, a freshly-painted red gateway into the cabin beyond. He reached it with large strides, pushing it open.

*** 

The police truck crunched over the caked snow road. The fringes of the windows were beginning to fog. Sheriff Landry chewed the inside of his cheek, willing this ride to be over.

Landry looked at the man next to him. This *investigative assistant*. Was the son of a bitch asleep? Sure seemed like he had passed out. Landry scoffed and considered hitting the next corner extra fast, just to let him crack his skull against the glass. But the silence was welcomed and allowed Landry time to think. Something he didn't get often in this line of business. So, he left his unwanted passenger alone.

It didn't much matter anyway. They were almost at their destination.

***

On the other side of the door, Max found himself standing on a dirt road somewhere in the countryside. A truck was barreling toward him. He raised his hands, shielding himself instinctively. The truck braked hard, kicking up dust, stopping a foot away from Max.

The driver's side door was kicked open, and from the raging dust clouds, a familiar face bounded out. This version of Landry had his uniform and considerable gut, but his hair was darker and the creases around his eyes had yet to form.

"Where is she?" Landry asked.

Max felt as though this was directed at him, but then other bodies began to materialize in the scene. An unrecognizable deputy stood a ways up the road. Separating him and Landry was a line of caution tape. The day was overcast, threatening rain. A house materialized now, forming itself from dust. It was a small bungalow, tattered and poorly kept.

Landry raced toward the house, stepping under the caution tape. The other deputy put out his hands to try and slow Landry, who was moving as fast as Max had ever seen him move.

"Sheriff," the deputy said. "I'm sorry. It's bad."

"Where is she?" Landry repeated.

Two paramedics appeared, wheeling a gurney out from the front door of the house. A woman was strapped on it. Her face was bloodied to the point of being unrecognizable. Long black hair clung to lumps of bone and flesh—a gory mess.

Landry stared at the gurney as it went by.

The paramedics became just a pair of uniforms— bodies absent—pushing this badly wounded person down the front porch. Red and blue ambulance lights flickered, but there was no source. The corners of the countryside faded to black, and everything was centred around the gurney. The police deputy was gone now too. Max stood a few feet behind Landry, watching people and objects come in and out of existence. The house grew transparent, fading almost to nothing as it held on, a ghost of itself.

Landry reached out a hand as the mystery victim went past. He was trying to reach, but the hand of the victim was being wheeled further and further, just ahead of where he could reach. Max tried to avoid looking at the face; it was too disturbing. His stomach churned. He wasn't sure if he could vomit inside the MemCom, but he was close.

An ambulance rose up from the ground now, and the paramedic uniforms opened the back, loading the gurney in as Landry lowered his hand. The doors were closed with a bang that rippled through the memory. The ambulance was shattered like broken glass, vanishing once more.

Now Landry wheeled around to the house. The police deputy appeared next to him.

"Where is he?" Landry said, now apparently looking for someone else.

"He's inside, but Sheriff, we've—" the deputy began, but the rest of his words were lost.

"Give the ambulance an escort; get it to the hospital." Landry marched toward the house.

"We can't leave you with him," the deputy tried, but he was already fading away again.

"Leave! Now!" Landry commanded.

Before Landry could reach the door to the house— one that Max was hoping to use to escape—a man walked through it, meeting Landry on the porch. The man was wearing a sleeveless top, his arms and neck carpeted with curly dark hair.

"Hi, Eddie," the man said with a crooked grin. One of his front teeth was missing.

Landry didn't answer the man. He just balled up his fist and swung as hard as he could. He hit the man square in the nose. A sickening crunch rang out and a spray of blood painted the air before landing on the ground. The man toppled over, holding his nose and screaming.

"You went too far this time," Landry said, standing over the man. His words were rumbling like the groans of a volcano. "I should've fucking locked you up the last time you hit her."

"Oh jeez, Eddie," the man choked out. He spat blood up on the porch. "It's just a misunderstanding. Every couple fights, you know that. Hell, you're divorced. And not to mention, she started it!"

Landry wound up with his leg and booted the man right in the gut. All the air rushed out of him. Landry thought about firing off a second kick but collected himself.

The man started wheezing as Landry looked down on him. He shook his head, trying to fight through his feelings and find the right words.

"You're never seeing Nina again." Landry gritted his teeth. "And jail is too soft a sentence for you."

"My pills," the man said.

He was pointing. Landry and Max both tracked his arm. On the ground now appeared a little orange bottle, prescription medication of some kind inside.

"I need my pills." The man's breathing was laboured.

"What's that?" Landry asked. His voice was light, as if speaking to a child. "You need your pills?"

Landry took a step over to the bottle. The man's arm was reaching out for them, his fingers grasping. Landry hovered over the bottle, looking back at the man. The man's eyes were like rubies, bulging and bloody. The man's nose still sent a trickle of blood down his face. *It isn't anywhere near as bloody as Nina's face when she was wheeled out on that gurney.* This thought seemed to radiate from Landry. Max felt it. Landry didn't believe justice was done.

Landry smiled down at the man—an evil smile, an arrogant smile. He slowly brought his foot over to where the pill bottle lay, and then he kicked it away from the man. The bottle rolled across the porch and dropped off the side into the dirt.

"Oops," Landry said.

The man's face was turning purple. He looked at Landry with desperation and disbelief in his eyes. *Help me,* he was trying to say, but couldn't speak. He was choking.

"Don't look at me like that," Landry said. "It's just a misunderstanding."

Landry took a step back, letting the man struggle. He started to convulse, reaching desperately for the pills that were no longer there.

Max snapped out of the trance he was in, as watching this unfold was magnetic. It was the same way one could not drive past an accident on the side of the road without turning to see the damage. He knew this was horrible, but he had to see how it played out. Finally, though, he was able to draw his eyes away from the carnage. Max left Landry there, smiling down at the dying man, as Max could bear it no longer.

The entrance to the house was right next to him. Escape was on the other side of the red door. And he needed to find the right timeline.

\*\*\*

Sheriff Landry pulled the truck up to Stella Godby's residence and gave the brakes a nice hard pump. The car jolted forwards, and his sleeping passenger slumped forwards a tiny bit, his head rolling and then falling back against the window.

"Last stop," Landry growled. He looked at Max disapprovingly, willing the man to wake and get the fuck out of his car. "Let's go, Sleeping Beauty."

A light came on in the front window, Stella peeking out at them. Landry stared back, thought about waving, then decided he didn't care to. He thrust an elbow into Max's side.

"Wake up," Landry said. "And get out of my car. I've got places to be."

But the passenger didn't wake up. In fact, he didn't even snore. And now Landry was starting to wonder if maybe the man had a stroke and died.

*I should be so lucky,* Landry thought as he leaned forwards. He unbuckled his seat belt and prepared to lean over and shake Max awake.

\*\*\*

"What size is this print?!" Landry shouted.

From somewhere deeper in the house, Sanderson called back, "Size 10 or 11!"

Max had made it. He stood once again in the foyer of the Thomas home. The door was wide open, and all of winter's strength had come blowing into the home. Snow was piled on the floor. Landry stared down at the boot print stamped in the drift.

It was the night of Tiffany's disappearance. Right about now, she'd be drinking in Nelly's basement.

Robert and Jane Thomas came to the door with Sanderson. They all looked at the sheriff. Jane Thomas was flush, her eyes darting about. She was clearly stressed. Robert Thomas looked stoic and just gave the sheriff a nod. They spoke, but their words were nonsense. Landry clearly hadn't committed anything they said to memory. The entire conversation played out like a scene on fast-forward. When it concluded, Landry said something to Sanderson and then turned to leave.

Max watched the back of Landry's head as he exited the home. The walls fell away, the house crumbling to rubble. The light was replaced with shadow, but Landry remained. Now, around him, the wintry street began to form. Landry's truck was parked in front of him, still running. The memory had folded itself into the next, Max now finding himself standing in the cold and watching Landry climb into his vehicle.

Landry shut the door and the truck immediately began to speed off. Max raced after it, having no desire to be left behind in the dregs of Landry's recollection. This was where he needed to be; he had to follow the sheriff at all costs. Max's lungs tightened against the cold air, struggling to draw breath. Max's legs were stiff, but he forced them to dash.

He struggled to get traction. For a moment, he thought it was a lost cause. The truck slowed as it prepared to turn onto the main highway. Max high-stepped over snow drifts, trying to force himself to run faster. He had limited experience with those dreams where the dreamer tried to run but couldn't actually move forwards. His lucid dreams always allowed him to move as he pleased. But he imagined this was the same sensation. He felt like he was never going to make it.

Just as the brake lights cut off, and the truck started speeding up again, Max made a desperate dive, lunging for the truck. His hands, cold as they were, gripped the tailgate. His boots became skis as the truck dragged him across the snow.

His grasp was already failing him, so Max had to act quickly. He kicked off the ground, tweaking something in his knee—though reminding himself it wasn't real—and pulling himself up onto the side of the truck. He then used what remaining strength he found in his arms to heave himself fully into the truck bed. He slammed hard into the cold surface, imaginary ribs throbbing.

He groaned but covered his mouth with his hands to stifle it. He waited for Landry to notice the stowaway, to stop the truck and beat him up. But they just kept on driving.

As the truck rattled on, Max lay on his back, breath rising as slow tendrils into the freezing air. Max put a hand on his chest, feeling for bruises. He ached. If he could feel pain like this, he wondered what else the MemCom could make him feel. Or make him think he was feeling.

The truck made a few turns, crossed the tracks, and just as Max's face was starting to numb, they slowed and hooked left. Max arched his neck and saw they were turning onto a residential road—one that looked awfully familiar—creeping by houses at a suspicious pace. Max strained through the awkward upside-down angle in the dark but was able to make out some familiar homes, including a white one with yellow trim at the far end. Max's gut twisted as he realized where they were.

This was Nelly's street.

Up ahead, just three houses down, two girls would be drinking in the basement.

Max felt his whole body tense. Something was about to happen. And when it did, would he stop it? Or could he bring himself to just watch it? He braced himself against the truck bed, expecting it to stop, uncertain of what he would do when it did. The truck kept crawling, crawling, and then suddenly, there was an earthquake. The entire memory rocked violently. Max's body shook, and a lightning bolt crackled through his brain.

The truck bed vanished, and Max felt as though he was falling.

\*\*\*

"You dead?" Landry was saying, shaking his passenger.

The truck still idled outside of Stella's house. Max jumped in his seat as if waking from a bad dream. His face smacked against the window and dislodged the earpiece, which fell helplessly to Max's feet. He looked wide-eyed at Landry, the way a gazelle would look at a lion. It took him a moment to gather his thoughts. They had arrived. Max tried to compose himself.

"How . . ." Max wanted to ask, *how long have I been out?* But he paused, not wanting to draw any unnecessary attention. It appeared it was too late for that, however.

"You were fucking unconscious," Landry said, withdrawing his arms. "The hell kind of drugs you been taking?"

"No drugs," Max said, looking down at the car floor, spotting the earpiece. "I just had a long day."

"Jesus, never seen anyone sleep like that." Landry shook his head. "Now get outta my truck."

*As long as that's all you saw,* Max thought. He tried to read Landry's face, to see if there was anything else. Any recognition of being spied on. It didn't appear that he had caught on. What little he knew of Landry told Max that this man didn't have a great poker face. If he suspected anything, Max would already be in cuffs.

Max returned his eyes to the floor, thinking about how to retrieve the MemCom.

"What are you staring at?"

"Nothing." Max looked up immediately. He unbuckled his seat belt and opened the door. Trying for one subtle motion, he bent down to retie his boot and palmed the earpiece. He straightened and stepped out into the cold. "Have a good night."

"Yeah," was all Landry said. He was watching Max with great interest, unsure of what was happening. But he did not say or do anything to stop him.

So, Max shut the door and turned to leave as fast as he could.

He felt hollow.

He had run out of time. And he had nothing concrete to show Oren. But his guts were all twisted from what he had seen. Landry was heading toward Nelly's house the night that Tiffany was abducted. He wasn't sure what they could do about it, but he needed to let Oren know. Max was sure this meant another dive, but he tried not to think about that. He wasn't sure he could handle it.

Without a plan, Max meandered up the walkway to Stella's front door. He wasn't sure what he was going to do once he got inside, but inside felt like safety. He needed the warmth and the distance from the sheriff. Max didn't look back; he just kept moving. He swore he could almost feel the tentacle-like fingers of the demons that had chased him earlier as he tried to get away from Landry's truck.

"Hey, get back here!" Landry shouted suddenly.

The interruption shook him. Max turned around slowly, and his breathing paused. He didn't move at first, then realized he was acting too suspicious. He inched back down the walkway, praying for divine intervention.

"Yeah?" Max felt rigid. He couldn't swallow. Oren was going to find him chopped up into tiny pieces in the woods somewhere.

"Tell your partner to stay the fuck out of Ruston once your sorry asses are kicked off the case!" Landry shouted at him.

After this threat, Landry rolled up the window and sped off, his truck disappearing into town.

Max exhaled but didn't start walking again until he was certain Landry was gone. Only then did Max trudge back up the walkway. He helped himself to Stella's house. The kitchen was empty; the light above the stove had been left on and was casting harsh shadows. Max sat down at the table, relieved not to have to speak with their host. With shaky hands, he sent Oren a message.

*Dive cut short. Couldn't find anything concrete. Sorry.*

It didn't take long for Oren to answer. Max's phone buzzed before he could even set it down.

*What did you see? Anything at all?*

Max considered this a moment. While he hadn't been able to locate Tiffany or Nelly, he was quite certain they at least had the right suspect.

*It's him, Oren. He was on Nelly's street that night. I didn't see what he did. But he's the guy who took them. What do we do?*

Oren didn't answer this one. Max stared at the screen for over a minute, but it never lit up. Instead, Max was left with his own thoughts and the creaking of the old house. He had nothing to do but worry.

*** 

Oren's hands and feet were numb by the time he had reached the Rusty Nail. A walk of that same distance in the summer would have been a delight. You wouldn't think twice about it. But in the hostile temperatures of Ruston's winter months, it felt suicidal. The heat of the bar was an immediate relief for Oren's frostbitten face, but it would take some time to seep into his bones and warm him fully.

Easy rock music poured out of the jukebox, though it was nearly drowned out by the banter from the patrons lined up against the bar. It was moderately busy, for a Sunday. Oren dropped himself into a booth near the door, not wanting to interact with the locals. The bartender—who would've been a familiar face to Max—walked over and asked him if he'd like a drink. Oren treated himself to a bourbon.

As the liquor brought heat to his chest, warming him from within, his phone buzzed. Max was already done and was sending him an update. Oren paused a moment before opening the message, praying that the results would be positive. He opened Max's message hoping for a conviction. Instead, he was disappointed.

The ride had ended quickly, and Max had failed to get any substantial evidence in that time. Oren couldn't help but feel bitter. He did not possess the ability to dive, but he felt that if he did, he could've found *something* in the few minutes it took to drive to Stella's. Even though he recognized this was an unfair thought, he silently criticized Max for not being able to get the job done.

Oren signalled to the bartender for another drink. Max was asking him what they should do next, and Oren was fresh out of ideas. He felt suddenly powerless. This was not something he was comfortable with feeling. Oren was always in control. He was a leader by nature. He had seen great success in his career, and even though he attempted to stay humble, the articles that were written about his work with Leonard Lang were printed out and saved at home. They made him feel successful. He had done the impossible.

Oren did not understand how to cope with professional failure. He was smarter and more athletic than most kids growing up. He was popular, charming, handsome, and sometimes, downright lucky. Some entity had blessed him with a streak of incredible fortune—at least when it came to his work. The misfortune in his personal life evened things out, as far as he was concerned. But he could distract himself from those woes with his incredible success on his projects. Whatever they were. Oren had begun to feel invincible.

Inevitably, the fall would come. Oren would not be able to charm his way out of a bind, or he'd hit an obstacle that he couldn't overcome. Perhaps this was it. He downed his second drink quickly, trying to avoid thinking about it too long. He asked for another before the bartender had even walked away.

He wasn't ready for the fall. Not so soon. Not when someone's life was at stake. Oren could not fail here. Oren had to keep moving forwards. But for the first time since they'd arrived in Ruston—really, the first time since he'd acquired the MemCom—he was uncertain what his next step would be.

He called Archie, suddenly feeling suffocated by the bar. Nothing was going to get solved in here. The phone rang a half dozen times before it went to voicemail. Another obstacle. Oren opened a map of Ruston on his phone, plotting out a course. Liquid courage spurred him on, then. When his third drink arrived, he pounded it back and rose, ready to brave the night. The walk wouldn't be bad if he cut through the park.

"You're headed back out there again?" the bartender asked.

She held up a finger, freezing him in place momentarily. She retrieved a ratty cardboard box from behind the bar and came back to his booth. "You'll lose your fingers. You're not dressed for this place. This is our lost and found. Some good stuff gets left behind here. Take something, please."

Oren was touched by her compassion, and he dressed himself up with a scarf, cap, and some bulky leather mittens before heading back out. Between these new items and his bourbons, he was feeling rather invincible.

Ruston was speckled with open spaces. Between rows of houses were large swaths of undeveloped areas. Some you could call parks, where paths, lights, and benches invited the public to gather. Others were nothing more than clusters of trees, outposts of nature that grew wildly even if confined to a small corner between a nail salon and a library. The map called this area Willamson Park, but having walked a few minutes through the darkness and virgin snow, Oren was starting to feel it was more like one of these wild corners. There wasn't a bench or lamppost in sight.

Stars had actually come out to light the way, the sky clearing enough for Orion's Belt to be clearly visible overhead. Oren watched it through his breath as he crunched through the snow, his footsteps becoming rhythmic, a concussive song. With the clear sky, however, came a drop in temperature. No more insulation from the winter clouds. Oren's eyelashes were beginning to freeze together. Each blink was becoming a workout.

Through the dead trees, he could see the orange glow of Stella's neighbourhood on the horizon. It wasn't far, but his pace—as his feet sank into the ground—would drag this journey out. A small creek bed cut through the trees, and Oren followed it, using it as his guide.

Movement caught Oren's eye suddenly, off to the left. He tried to make out the details of a dark shape through his freezing eyelids. Tiny crystals clouded his vision, and he moved to wipe them away.

On the other side of the creek bed stood a figure. This person seemed to be struggling with a large sack or piece of furniture. Oren's mind, hindered by the alcohol, couldn't fathom why someone would be trying to move furniture out in the middle of the woods.

"Hey," Oren said, watching the figure struggle, dropping their haul and then trying to drag it toward the creek. "Need a hand?" Oren stumbled forwards, trying to be helpful, but he staggered and snapped off a branch of a nearby tree.

The figure noticed him and jumped, seemingly out of panic. The figure bent over, getting a quick purchase of their cargo, then tossed it down the creek bed toward the frozen water below. After the toss, the figure turned and bolted, vanishing into the darkness. Oren, through ice crystals and steamy breath, failed to see where this person went.

Instead, he focused his gaze on the item that had been tossed down the creek bed. As it tumbled toward its eventual resting place, things began to take shape.

The object was now easier to make out against the stark white of the snow. It somersaulted a couple times before it landed at the bottom of the hill, and as it did, an arm flopped out to the side. Then another. Then, at last, two legs became visible.

The object that had been tossed was not furniture at all. It was a body.

A surge of hot panic erupted from Oren's gut then, washing away the last of his drunkenness. He began to sweat inside of his jacket, despite the bite of winter. His legs carried him down the snowbank faster than he thought he could move. At last, he dropped to his knees next to the body, fearful for what he might find.

The body had landed face down, and he tore off his mitts to get a better grip and roll it to the side. Snow caked her face, and the darkness shrouded her features. But the body in his arms was unmistakably Tiffany Thomas.

# 12. Charlie's Trip

FINDING KELLY HAD BEEN DIFFICULT. Max had witnessed the countless hours Charlie poured into his research. With only a first name to go on—and a common one at that—Charlie became lost in a helpless cycle of scanning social media and message boards. But he was resourceful. And driven. Charlie had been hunting down dead bodies in a serial killer's mind for nearly a year now. A living person could only stay hidden for so long.

In the real world, Kelly lived on a quaint farm not far outside of Galway. To get there, Charlie had to fly into Dublin and rent a car. They gave him a tiny hatchback that he felt he was too large for. He drove on winding, narrow roads through misty hills. The green was so lush, almost surreally so. He passed countless unimpressed sheep. At one point, he spotted a castle through the fog, majestic grey turrets standing guard over a lake that reflected nothing but grey. He imagined bringing Kelly there to propose to her.

During his research, Charlie had been relieved to find that she was not one of Lang's victims. His sadistic responses to Charlie in the prison were just another mind game. Kelly was very much alive. It appeared that she had taken over the family farm once her father passed away. She posted several photos of her tending to horses and sheep, as well as her cuddled up by the fire with a cat and a dog. She was living the idyllic countryside life.

It took a great deal of restraint for Charlie not to message her online. He wanted so badly to make that connection immediately. But he could never find the right words. There was no easy way to say, "I met you in a serial killer's memory." Charlie felt that broaching the subject in person would give him a better chance to explain it all. And then he could look into her eyes, and she into his.

Charlie's back was drenched in sweat, and his legs were stiff when he finally found the turn off for Kelly's farm. He cracked his knuckles and tried to control his breathing as the rental shuffled along the bumpy road, kicking up rocks. Dense trees covered both sides of the laneway, and thick green foliage blocked his view of the house until he rounded the bend. Ahead was the farmhouse, a barn, and a modest field where the animals grazed.

As Charlie parked on this long stretch of driveway that led to the farm, two horses came to the fence to check him out. They tossed their tails and greeted him with shrill whinnies. Charlie waved at them politely. He approached the house as if it too were an animal, one he was trying not to scare away.

The world seemed to pass in slow motion to him, the door never quite as near as he had hoped. His mind branched out on all sorts of wild thoughts. Was she even home? What would he do then? Should he have brought flowers? And part of him was already planning their life together. He did like that Kelly had animals, for instance; he felt he preferred their company to people anyway.

Nearing the house, he heard a click, and the front door began to open. He froze. He was stuck in an awkward middle distance, not quite on the road and not quite on the driveway. He wasn't ready; his words were not prepared.

Then she stepped outside.

"Can I help you?"

Her voice was familiar, the same soft tone and Irish accent. She had a thick wool sweater wrapped around her, trying to trap in the warmth. Charlie had been so warm in his tiny car, but the air was unmistakably damp and chilly. He felt it now.

"Hi, Kelly." Charlie tried to smile, though he felt it came out more as a cringe.

He shouldn't have led with her name. It was perhaps a bit too forthright. He needed to ease her into things. Pretend to know less than he did. He cursed himself for not being more careful.

"Do I know you?" Kelly was caught between a smile and a grimace herself. She wasn't sure how this encounter would play out.

"Not exactly," he said, approaching her carefully. "I'm familiar with your story. I studied it extensively. But you wouldn't know a thing about me, I'm afraid."

"My story?" Kelly asked. She tensed.

Charlie was still inching forwards, trying to act natural.

"Your relationship with Leonard Lang," Charlie said. He had been able to concoct a cover story that wasn't entirely a lie. "I work on a team that's overseeing a psychological assessment of Mr. Lang, and it required extensive research."

"My relationship?" Kelly was looking back into the house now, as if looking for a way out of this conversation. "What relationship is that?"

"Sorry," Charlie said bashfully. "I should be more sensitive. I imagine dating someone convicted of what he's done cannot be an easy topic of conversation."

"Dating?" At this, Kelly finally laughed.

Charlie was now close enough to the door that the smells of the house poured out, cinnamon and lavender. He thought he could smell perfume coming off Kelly, too, but it was nothing like the perfume he was used to in Lang's mind.

She clutched the door with knuckles turning as pale as the fog that clung to the treetops. But she let loose more nervous laughter. "I'm not sure what extensive research you've done. If you knew the first thing about Leonard Lang, or myself, you'd know that's ridiculous."

"The two of you spent a couple years in a relationship, while he was living here," Charlie said this as a statement of fact. But something in the back of his mind began to itch. Was that true? *Of course, it's true,* he reminded himself. *I've seen it.*

"Leonard was a psycho even before he was a murderer," Kelly said. "A friend introduced me to him while he was staying here."

Charlie thought back to the redhead she had been with when he interrupted the encounter at the cliffs.

"He proceeded to stalk me for a couple weeks. I kept running into him at different places. I always tried to be friendly; we had mutual friends. But when he started asking me for a date, I had to tell him no. When I found out, so many years later, about what he had done . . . Well, I count myself lucky not to be one of those girls."

"You . . . didn't date?" Charlie wasn't able to digest this.

"I wouldn't have dared," Kelly said. "He was horrifying. He stared. He followed me through Temple Bar when I was there visiting friends. He stalked me on the beach. He seemed to show up wherever I was. He was in Ireland all of two weeks, and he managed to find out my address, my phone number, showed up at one of my friend's flats."

"Two weeks?" Charlie shook his head. He couldn't believe what he was hearing.

Charlie knew the mind could create false memories. If you told yourself over and over again that something was true, you would start to believe it. The human mind was imperfect; hadn't everyone recalled something from their childhood a certain way, only to be instructed later in life that they had been wrong in their version of things?

Was it possible Lang's entire relationship with Kelly had been fabricated?

Of course, it was possible.

The man was a serial killer who claimed voices spoke to him. He obsessed over his victims and deluded himself into thinking *he* was somehow a victim.

Oren's words came back to Charlie then. "Once a mind has turned hostile, you can't trust anything you see in there."

But Charlie had to wonder, was it Lang's mind who had fabricated this plot? Or his own? What had he really seen?

"Look . . . who are you? I'm not sure I want you here." Kelly tensed.

"I'm so sorry," Charlie said, realizing his error and feeling such a horrible concoction of shame and guilt that he thought he might vomit.

He reached forwards, meaning to ask her for a glass of water, but he was unable to speak. His hand just hung in the air, his legs shambling forwards.

"Please leave." Kelly shielded herself with the door, ready to shut it.

*Stupid,* Charlie thought. He should have approached this all differently. He could've moved to Ireland, pretended he knew nothing about her, and charmed her over time. He should've been a stranger.

It would have been easy. He knew everything she liked from his time in Lang's brain.

He had been training. He had been learning. He had been *stalking.*

He had taken the wrong approach. But unlike his dates with her in Lang's memories, there was no more reset button. He had fucked up plenty before. But she never remembered him. Each visit was a clean slate. Finally, Charlie was left without a parachute. His only option was to try and fix this.

*But how do I know the version of her from his mind is anything like the real one?*

Charlie tried to smile, tried to show charm.

*I made a terrible assumption,* he thought. *I interviewed a serial killer and took his word for it that you were in a relationship. That doesn't change why I'm here.*

"Can I just come in? I would love the chance to speak with you."

Charlie didn't realize that he was sweating rather profusely. His scalp had started to bead the moment he heard Kelly call out the truth. He was ghostly pale and looked a bit unhinged himself.

"No, I'm going to ask you to leave again," Kelly said, shaking her head. "I'm not sure who you are or why you're here, but you're trespassing."

"I'm not trespassing, we're . . ." He wanted to say *in love*. He wanted to say *meant to be together*. "I just came to speak with you. Maybe share a cup of tea. If you don't want to talk here, that's fine. Perhaps you'll join me at the pub up the road? My treat?"

"Eamon!" Kelly turned and shouted into the house.

"Eamon?" Charlie bucked back as if he'd been shot. "No, no . . ."

*Why is she calling out for another man? She lives alone. Doesn't she?* Charlie thought back to what he had seen on social media. He hadn't ever really considered the fact that she would be anything other than alone at this farmhouse.

A man appeared in the doorway. His arms were corded and strong. He was tall, rangy, and loomed over Charlie. A thick beard covered his chin and hid his expression. Blankly, he surveyed the scene and wondered who this stranger was.

"Who is this?" Charlie asked, looking at Kelly for an explanation.

"Who is *this*?" Eamon echoed, guard up.

"I don't know," Kelly admitted.

"Look, I just . . ."

Charlie's entire body stung. He felt his heart collapse, a Jenga tower whose pieces had been pulled one too many times. He saw now that Kelly was wearing a wedding ring. He saw now that this beautiful woman had found herself a handsome husband and that her farm life was not one of solitude. Everything Charlie had assumed would happen with his arrival here was falling apart. Eamon was pulling the thread of this dream Charlie had weaved, and unravelling it all.

But really, it was his own fault, wasn't it?

Charlie had become transfixed. He had missed all the signs. He had turned into a horrible detective.

The reality hit him in the gut then. Lang never knew the real Kelly. So, the woman in Lang's mind did not exist. Not in the real world, anyway.

Charlie's head was spinning. He wanted to apologize but couldn't find the words. He stared at Kelly, willing her to read his mind, to understand his motives. Eamon didn't like the way he was looking at her. When Charlie moved closer, legs unstable, Eamon stepped forwards. It all happened so quickly. Charlie raised his hands to try and gather his balance but struck Eamon in the chest. The strong, bearded man had seen enough of this stranger at his doorstep and delivered a single, solid fist square into Charlie's nose.

Charlie toppled backwards, blood spewing, pain like fire between his eyes.

"Call the police," Eamon said to Kelly.

Charlie could hear the voice, but his world was spinning. He was getting to his feet, watching himself as if disembodied. All he could think was that he didn't want to get in any more trouble. Everything was off-kilter, images strobing by, and Charlie zigzagged his way back to the rental car.

Eamon shouted after him, something Charlie couldn't make out. *Please, please, please.* He kept saying to himself. *Don't let the big man come after me.* Charlie knew he was moving slowly. He started the car and thrust it into reverse. The world was shrinking, and tunnel vision took over. Charlie was operating on instinct. There was no way he should've been driving.

He was able to back the car out onto the main road. From there, he put the car in drive and hit the gas, spitting up dirt behind him, racing for the hills, trying to beat out the police.

He never saw red or blue lights. Never heard any sirens. He made it all the way back to the airport in Dublin, where the rental agent looked at his busted nose and the blood on his shirt and nearly gagged.

"Are you alright?" they asked.

But Charlie didn't answer. He turned over the keys and went into the airport, stopping at the bathroom to clean himself up.

Charlie had been reduced to a puddle of himself, shrunk back into a boy. One who was never good with girls, never comfortable speaking to them or going on dates.

Hyperthymesia or not, he would never remember the plane ride home. He had receded into himself. He was thinking about the earpiece he had left in a lockbox under his bed at home, and he was devising his next actions.

# 13. A Star in Her Day

F EW THINGS IN MAX'S LIFE had caught him off guard more than what he saw coming through Stella's front door that night.

When he was just a boy—in his memory, six or seven—his parents took him to the mountains for a family vacation. Bored and naive, he wandered away from their cottage and took himself down a hiking path in the early morning hours. As he rounded one bend, he came face to face with a mountain lion. The cat's yellow eyes locked in on his. Standing eye level with Young Max, it was a menacing predator.

The event was so unexpected that Young Max's brain failed to recognize the threat right before his eyes. He just stood there, seeing himself reflected in those topaz eyes, as if watching someone else's life play out on film. His father had thankfully noticed Max strolling away, so he was able to charge up behind them and scare the lion away. Max was reprimanded. His father's scolding definitely registered, unlike the encounter with the cat.

Looking back on it now, Max was the perfect prey. He was small, frail, and utterly motionless.

As Oren kicked open Stella's front door, Max felt the same way. He gawked, frozen, and he failed to process an appropriate response as Oren carried in Tiffany Thomas' body.

Max had been numbing himself with his phone, scrolling through social media and internet articles as he awaited Oren's reply. He wasn't aware that more than thirty minutes had elapsed. Still in the kitchen chair, he now dropped his phone on the table.

"Max," Oren whispered from the doorway. His face was concealed behind a scarf, eyelashes and eyebrows dusted white. "Where's Stella?"

Max didn't answer right away. He frowned, trying to understand what Oren could possibly be up to. The fact that Tiffany was in his arms felt like some sort of prank. Finally, Oren's words seemed to melt through his skull, and at least the answer to that question was simple enough.

"Asleep," Max said. His fugue state had yet to lift.

"Keep quiet," Oren said. "Help me get her upstairs."

Because following orders was easier than trying to make sense of this scene, Max grabbed Tiffany's feet and helped shuffle her into the house. She was surprisingly heavy. Max would later be impressed that Oren had been able to get her all the way here on his own.

Tiffany's body was without a jacket, or any proper winter gear. She was clad only in jeans and a sweater— the same outfit she had gone missing in. She was so cold that Max's hands were actually going numb from just holding her legs.

They worked their way up the narrow staircase that led to their bedrooms, Oren going backwards and leading the way. Halfway up, Max's awareness finally clicked back in. He was carrying Tiffany Thomas.

"Jesus!" Max stopped moving, causing Oren to nearly topple over. "Is she dead?"

"Shut up," Oren cursed quietly. "Just help me get her up."

"What happened?" Max asked, though he did start marching up the stairs again.

Oren just shot him a look as if to say, "Not now."

They did their best not to make a sound, but on the creaky stairs with the walls closing in on either side, it was a cacophony of suspicious sounds. Oren's jacket rubbed against the wall and even twisted a picture frame around, dislodging it and knocking it to the floor. Max was grunting, struggling with the weight of a human body. He hoped Stella was a deep sleeper.

When they finally made it into the bedroom Oren had been using, they placed Tiffany down on the tiny twin bed and shut the door. The wallpaper, curtains, and bedspread were all a soft pink, like cotton candy. A dresser sat near the window with framed black-and-white pictures of a man Max did not recognize. Oren shut the curtains and turned on the lamp. Both of them were out of breath, but Max had urgent questions.

"What are we doing?" he said, trying to keep his voice low, but his pounding heart sent his volume skyrocketing.

"Will you be quiet?" Oren huffed. "We can't have Stella poking around."

"Is she dead?" Max repeated his earlier question, the most imperative one.

"No," Oren said. "She's breathing. But she's unconscious, maybe drugged."

Max hadn't been able to really look at her face until now, fearing he would be staring at a corpse. He allowed himself to look, finally, and he was relieved that she appeared to just be sleeping. Her face was waxy and red from the frostbite. But there did seem to be a subtle rise and fall to her chest.

Oren went to the chest of drawers and began searching through them. He found blankets and sheets and pulled them all out, draping them over Tiffany in an attempt to warm her.

"So, what happened?"

"I think I interrupted her captor," Oren said as he tucked the blankets underneath Tiffany to form a little cocoon. "He must've been trying to dump her body in the creek. But I spotted him, and he just dropped her and took off. He didn't get to finish the job."

So, Tiffany was lucky, then. Max imagined that if Oren hadn't been there, the girl would not have been left breathing.

"Did you see him?" Max asked.

"I didn't get a good look," Oren admitted. "But based on his frame, I think it easily could've been Landry. And he wasn't with you anymore."

Max felt a wave of guilt. He had been with Landry not long before. He had a chance to solve this case.

Though what would he have done if he had found the evidence they needed? Would he have refused to leave Landry's truck? *No,* he admitted to himself. *I would've walked away all the same.*

"He must've sensed we were getting close to him," Oren deduced. "If he felt something was up on your ride, he probably went straight back to wherever Tiffany was and decided to dump her."

"What about Nelly?"

"Our window is closing," Oren said. "He's probably gone back to get her now too and . . ."

Oren didn't need to finish the thought. They both knew how it ended. He was going back to kill Nelly too.

"We need to get her to a hospital," Max said, suddenly feeling very afraid for the girl on the bed.

"We can't," Oren said.

Max was dumbfounded. For a second, he couldn't believe his friend; the one who always did the right thing was telling him they were *not* going to take Tiffany to the hospital.

"We can't bring her anywhere that Landry will find her. Or find us. He's the sheriff of this incredibly tiny town, Max. He could probably pin this whole thing on us right now. We don't have any evidence. And he's getting rid of it all as we speak."

"What are we going to do then?" Max balled his fists, finding a combative tone. "She might not be okay. She needs help."

"We will get her help," Oren said. "But first, we need to assure her safety. And Nelly's. We need to save the other girl and prove who did this."

"How?"

"You have all the details we need right here," Oren said, pointing to Tiffany. "We can find Nelly. We can find the evidence we need against Landry. It's all in her head."

"Are you serious?" Max wasn't even trying to keep his voice down anymore. "You're prioritizing the MemCom over a girl's life?"

"A few seconds of real time in order for you to dive and get what we need," Oren argued. "And you can find out where he took Nelly. It's the only way we'll be able to get to her before Landry kills her, Max."

"And then what, Oren?" Max shook his head and began to pace. "The two of us ride out there and arrest the sheriff?"

"We go and rescue her," Oren explained. "We tell the Thomas family. We tell the other deputies. We tell everyone. We can catch Landry red-handed if we hurry."

"You're delusional," Max said.

He was seeing Oren differently. The way the lamp lit him, casting ugly shadows around his eyes and nose, only contributed to this. Oren was no longer the cool and confident guy who always knew what to do. He was no longer the charmer who could talk anyone into anything. Instead, Max only saw someone who had become desperate for this to work out in their favour. He saw someone who had become obsessed with the MemCom and could only see a path forward that involved more diving, more invasion.

"We have to do this, Max."

"She needs help. We need to call Robert Thomas. He can make sure she's safe at the hospital. He can help us arrest Landry. Call in other deputies, or something."

"We will call him," Oren said. "But we have access to everything we need right now. One quick dive. And then we can save both girls."

Max reached into his pocket for his phone, deciding to call Thomas himself. But it wasn't there. It was still on the table downstairs. Max looked to the bedroom door, but Oren was blocking his path.

"It's the only way," Oren said. He was calm. His voice was low. "The only way we can save them both. If we take Tiffany to the hospital, we'll lose the ability to dive on her with all the people around. And we'll never find out where Nelly is."

"The police will stop Landry." Even as he said it, Max knew that this would be difficult.

"A few seconds." Oren held out his hands, as if Max were the wild mountain lion in need of being corralled. "Then we call Thomas. Then you can take Tiffany to the hospital while I go after Landry."

It was the fastest way out of the room. Max knew this. He could fight. He could struggle to get his phone, or he could debate with Oren. But if he just did the dive, five seconds from now, they could have their answers, and each of them could get their way. Max relented, knowing the only way to get Tiffany help now was to finish this.

"You've lost your connection to what's right and wrong," Max said, hoping his words stung. He was so utterly disappointed in his friend. "This." He retrieved the earpiece and held it accusingly. "This is wrong. This girl needs help. And we're hiding her in a bedroom, peering into her mind instead of helping."

"You are helping," Oren countered.

Max didn't bother arguing anymore. He was hollow where before he felt full. And he realized that void was left behind from the faith he used to have in Oren.

"You've lost your way." Max had relented but offered this parting shot as he inserted the earpiece. "Fuck you for being so obsessed with this thing. And, you know what? Fuck you for leaving. For bailing on me and never staying in touch. You always thought you were better than me. You knew you had little Max to tag along with you. This is just more of the same. Me following along with your stupid plan. The nerve it takes to show up to my dad's funeral and recruit me . . . Why can't you just face that it's over? You failed."

Max expected Oren to snap back. Or to argue the point. But he said nothing. And that was worse.

Oren simply retrieved his phone and played a dial tone. No music this time. Nothing fun or ambient or catchy. It was all business. Max sat on the floor, leaning against the bed. His head was only a foot away from Tiffany's. It would be a short trip.

\*\*\*

Max stood in a large field covered with fresh snow, and frosted evergreens lined the horizon. The sky was painted in a beautiful blue and pink gradient. Despite the wintry setting, it didn't feel cold.

"Momma, look!" a young girl shrieked with joy.

She was bundled in a full snowsuit, stamping across the open field in tiny pink snowshoes. As she stamped past Max, he realized this was Tiffany at around five years old.

Robert Thomas materialized in the field, looking much less burdened than the man Max had met in Ruston. He was actually smiling as he marched toward his daughter in snowshoes of his own. Tiffany's mother—her birth mother—was there too, holding Robert Thomas' hand. Everyone seemed happy. It was Tiffany's version of bliss.

Young Tiffany tried to move a little faster, but the nose of her snowshoe caught in the powder, sending her face-planting with a dull thud. Her parents froze, afraid to laugh until she was ok. Tiffany looked up, her eyebrows, eyelashes, and nose covered in snow, giving her the appearance of a girl dipped in cake frosting. All three of them burst out laughing then, and her parents came over and yanked her out of her predicament.

"Do you want hot cocoa?" Tiffany's father asked.

"Yeah!" Tiffany exclaimed.

"Okay, race you back," he said. "Winner gets the most marshmallows."

All three of them started stamping back toward Max, racing for the comfort of home. Robert Thomas and his then wife passed him quickly, but little Tiffany slowed down, lagging behind. She seemed distracted by the man in the field. She stared at Max, and as her parents raced ahead, she remained behind. Eventually, she came to a complete standstill.

"Who are you?" she asked.

Max took a chance in answering her, hoping it wouldn't unsettle the girl's mind. "A friend."

"You shouldn't be here," Tiffany said.

She looked around. The field was changing. The trees seemed to drop away behind the edges of the world, and now the field was just a white expanse in all directions. Her parents had vanished as well. A large metal door rose from the snow—looking like a bank vault you'd see in movies—protecting whatever lay beyond.

"I know, but I'm trying to help," Max said. "I want to know, what happened to you?"

"What do you mean?" the girl asked.

"Who took you?" Max pried.

Young Tiffany looked at him for a moment. Those glossy, mirrored eyes were capturing all the light in this world and throwing it back at Max. The expression that lit up her face then was of recognition far beyond what a five-year-old should've had. The voice, too, was far more adult. It was an eerie thing to witness: a child's body with an adult's words.

"We don't talk about that here." Tiffany's adolescent voice came through this younger version of herself. Her tiny body, in the pink snowsuit, stood rigid and defiant.

"Where can I find out?" Max's eyes darted to the metal door. He kept pushing, hoping he was going to get her to crack.

But Tiffany didn't budge. "We don't talk about that here," she repeated.

Max realized what was happening. Tiffany's mind had suppressed these horrible memories. Max was stuck, unable to dig into the night she was taken, or anything that had happened since.

It was called dissociation: the human brain's attempt to protect itself from overwhelming trauma. Block out a particularly harmful memory. This was what Tiffany had done. She had managed to lock away all of the memories of her abduction, making them unavailable for recall. This little girl was the guardian of the vault.

"Please, try and remember," Max insisted. "Anything you can. We're going to help you. We're going to take you back to your parents."

"Mommy?" Tiffany's five-year-old voice returned for a moment. "Daddy?"

"Yes." Max smiled, trying to appear like an ally.

"No." Now it was older Tiffany's voice coming through the guardian's lips. "Nothing happened. There's nothing to show you."

"Tiffany, please," Max said. He cast another helpless look around. No doors. Nowhere to go. "I need to see. I need to know where to go."

"We don't talk about that here!"

The sound coming from the little girl was growing. First, it was a scream, then it was something else entirely: a siren. The little girl's voice merged with the older girl's voice and became something demonic, echoing and shaking the corners of the memory.

"We don't talk . . . about *that* . . . HERE!"

The ground fractured, the snowy field splitting like broken glass. Max's arms shot out to try and steady himself, but there was nothing to hold onto. Tiffany screamed, loud and shrill, and the broken shards of this memory blew up. Everything became dust. Max began to fall, along with the snow and the sky. Pieces of the world drifted past him into the void as he tumbled. The sense of weightlessness brought his stomach into his head. He was desperate to get ahold of something, anything, but he could not.

He continued to tumble into nothingness as the fractured scenes of the winter setting now transformed into something else. It was as if a movie was being projected on these broken pieces of glass. Images, not entirely whole, materialized on the fragments. Some pieces fell at the same pace as Max and were easy to view. Others dropped in and out of his sight quickly, and he struggled to make sense of them.

He viewed slivers of moments in Tiffany's life, all of which seemingly came from over the past week. He recognized Nelly's basement and the girls drinking and singing. He recognized a scene from inside the Thomas family home as the girls hung out in the large kitchen.

But other pieces of memory that were tumbling through space with Max held darker, more obscure moments. Max watched from Tiffany's point of view as a dark shadow loomed over her in her sleep. Her arms shot out and a struggle ensued. Another fragment above Max projected the image of a rope coiled tightly around her hands. Tiffany was just staring at this rope through teary eyes, the details—every fibre—etched in her recollection.

Sounds shot out at Max from all sides. Laughter, music, breaking glass, screaming, muffled grunts, a car engine, and other unrecognizable sounds all played at once. They would grow or shrink in volume, sometimes playing over one another. Some sounds repeated, others faded out entirely. Max could barely make sense of it. Somewhere in this tangle of nonsensical decibels was a song Max thought he knew, but he couldn't decipher it. There was a catchy *doo-wop* in there. It bore itself into Max's mind. But whatever it was became lost in the rest of the sounds and sights that bombarded him. Some of the fragments that passed him in free fall even seemed to come with smells—most recognizably, gasoline.

The scenes that unfolded in this deteriorated part of Tiffany's memory were certainly glimpses of what had happened to her. But they were impossible to piece together. Max saw mostly darkness. Perhaps, she had been blindfolded or kept in a dark room. There was the sound of crying, plenty of screaming, and some pleading. They were the sounds of torture. It was no wonder she had blocked this out.

A few more visuals projected themselves on the jagged pieces around Max. A large green barn appeared, partially obstructed by a fogged window. Another scene displayed tentacle-like waves of multicoloured wires running across the floor. Elsewhere, a shadowy scene depicted what looked like Nelly wearing a blindfold.

The sensation of falling was a constant now. Max had always been terrified of skydiving. He imagined this was much the same thing. It felt as if it were going to go on forever, and his body was exhausted anticipating the collision. He had no parachute; the end of this descent was unpredictable and uncontrollable.

There was little else to be gained here. He hoped these pieces would be able to give them some sort of lead, but he knew Oren would be devastated to hear that there was no clear-cut image of Landry driving away with the girl.

Max shut his eyes and tried to turn off his senses, knowing the only way to stop falling was to get out. It took him a few tries. He kept opening his eyes to see that he was still in fact falling, broken shards right there alongside him, some new screams ringing out in the dark.

The third time was the charm. He just shut his eyes hard, and when he finally opened them again, he was back in the pink bedroom.

\*\*\*

"Call Thomas," Max said, his hands pressed firmly into the floor. He still felt like he was falling and needed the contact to ground himself. His stomach was up somewhere in his throat, and he felt as if he would vomit if he tried to stand. In the corners of his vision, he could still see falling glass, and he could still hear a faint *doo-wop* ringing in his ears.

"What did you see?" Oren asked, still ever-obsessed with the MemCom.

"Not what you hoped," Max said. "I didn't see Landry. She blocked out a lot."

"Well, did you try hard enough?" Oren's voice was cracking. His composure was fading.

"It's not there, Oren," Max said. "She's blocked it out."

"Go back in," Oren pleaded. "Try again. We can find it."

"Call Robert Thomas." Max started to stand, and he used the bed to help guide him to his feet. "Or I will." Max made for the door.

Oren stepped in front of him, though he seemed to think better of using force. Max shouldered past Oren and opened the door, heading downstairs to the kitchen.

Oren chased after him. "How are we supposed to find her? Huh? How are we supposed to find Nelly?"

"Look for a green barn," Max said. "I think he brought them both to a green barn. I think they were together. I saw Nelly blindfolded."

Max felt Oren grasping at his shoulder, trying to stop him from leaving, desperately clawing without a real plan. Max pressed on and rounded the corner into the kitchen at a jog. He came to an abrupt stop, however, when he saw that Stella was standing there waiting for them. Oren crashed into Max's back, and both of them jumped.

"Sorry for the fright," Stella said. She had a mug of hot milk on the counter that she was stirring absently. "But the two of you are awfully noisy. It was hard to sleep."

"I'm so sorry," Max said.

"I also couldn't help but overhear you say you're looking for a green barn." Stella brought the mug up to her lips and slurped some of her beverage. "Would that happen to be Eisner's place?"

"I . . . I don't know," Oren said.

"His is the only green barn I know of in town," Stella explained. "When everyone else painted theirs red, he went bright green. Never updated it. Ugly thing, if you ask me."

"That's gotta be it," Max said. "Tall, bright green, faded."

"Sounds like Eisner's," Stella confirmed.

"I need a driver," Oren said and ran back upstairs.

***

Calls were made. They were careful to contact only their allies and not place anything in to either the Ruston County Sheriff's Department or 911.

The orange jeep came to collect Oren. He had called Archie, apologizing for the late hour but explaining the urgency. The friendly ex-sheriff obliged. When he arrived, Oren rushed out to the jeep and announced that they were headed to Eisner's place.

Robert and Jane Thomas were the next to arrive. Robert Thomas had to duck in the foyer; his imposing frame barely fit in the cramped space. He barged in, nearly knocking over a coat rack. Jane Thomas followed him with wide eyes.

"Tiffany!" Robert Thomas cried out.

By now, the girl had been moved back downstairs. She seemed to be warming up—or so Max hoped—but was still unresponsive.

Thomas wrapped his giant arms around his daughter. A solitary sob rocked his body before he collected himself and stood, trying to take control. "Where's West?"

"He's gone after Nelly," Max explained.

"Where did he find her?"

"Tiffany? In the creek behind the Rusty Nail."

"We need to take her to the hospital."

"We can call an ambulance," Max suggested.

"No, no, we'll take her ourselves." Thomas had no problem scooping up Tiffany in his arms and taking her out to the family vehicle himself.

Max followed behind, feeling unhelpful. The sting of the cold on his face felt like punishment.

When Thomas had laid Tiffany down in the back seat, Jane crawled in next to her and held her head. Thomas shut the door on them and stood there, staring down at Max.

"You really think Landry did this?"

Oren had briefly shared this theory over the phone. They needed Thomas' help to make sure the sheriff couldn't cover his tracks, or worse, bring harm against Tiffany or anyone else. It was a complicated and difficult subject to share over a brief phone call that began with, "We have your daughter," but Thomas seemed receptive. The cold outer shell he had just hours prior had been replaced now that his little girl was back. He held a certain level of appreciation for Oren and was ready to entertain all of his theories. He had been right about Floyd, after all, so he must be right about this.

"Yes." Max nodded.

"That son of a bitch is going to pay for this." Thomas's voice was steady, and his face showed nothing resembling any emotion.

This made his threat more terrifying, and Max trembled a little.

"Call me when you hear from West. I want to know that he's found Nelly before we call the police and tip Landry off. But I have a friend in Syracuse who's sending a couple detectives down. They'll be able to take him in."

Max agreed to call Thomas—sensing that was what the man was looking for—but was feeling well over his head. He was struggling to keep up with next steps, who was bad and who was good, and what options they had now that they couldn't trust the local police. Max was able to mask this, and Thomas left, patting him firmly on the shoulder. Max took this as a thank you.

Back inside, Stella was setting out some baked goods on the kitchen table.

"In case you're hungry after all that."

Stella hadn't complained or even asked any questions during the entire ordeal. She helped where she could and otherwise just stood idly by. She was an incredible host, and though Max thanked her with full sincerity, he felt it wasn't enough.

A missing person had just shown up in her home in the middle of the night, and here she was, putting out banana bread.

"I'll leave you to it," Stella said. "Unless you want the company?"

"No, not sure I'm much in the mood for conversation."

"That's what I figured." Stella smiled. "A little space is what I'd need too. Got a good book I'm keen to finish, so I'll go read that in bed. Hard to imagine I'll sleep much after all the commotion."

Max was deliriously tired. He forced a smile that was a little too strained and thanked her again, then collapsed into a chair. He grabbed at a piece of banana bread, but when he felt it in his hand, his muscle memory brought back the feeling of holding Tiffany's legs in his hands, carrying her upstairs. He dropped the bread, deciding he wasn't hungry.

Max held his phone in his hand, waiting for the next word from Oren. He was simultaneously glad that he wasn't along for the ride, and anxious that he didn't know what was happening. The journalist in him wanted the scoop. But he wasn't a sheriff's deputy, nor a private investigator, and he didn't need to be the one poking around for missing girls.

*Doo-wop.*

That song was still floating around in his mind, a catchy earworm that he couldn't shake.

*How did the rest of it go?* Max wondered, trying to think back to where he had heard it before. His mother had once told him that if a song were to get trapped in your head, the only way to let it out was to sing it. It felt like an old wives' tale, but as a child, it always seemed to work. The only problem was that Max didn't have the words, just the melody. He hummed it aloud, trying to complete the lyrics, but he was unable to find them.

It bothered him to be so close, so in spite of himself, he kept humming, louder and louder. This song had appeared in Tiffany's mind. Was it relevant? He struggled as he pondered why he knew this song and why he should care about it.

A few words started to form in his mind.

"We are . . . *hmm-hmm* . . . memory," Max started to half-sing.

A catchy song, but very melancholy. He was certain he had heard it—recently, too—but at the same time, he wasn't sure he could trust his memory on this. Memory was becoming a very abstract concept to him.

He repeated this verse a couple times, then a few more words came.

"Lasting . . . eternity . . ." Max chimed.

When the next verse was completed for him, he jumped.

"Come here, my love, lay with me and die with me," the operatic voice of Donna Romano rang out from down the hall.

The elderly guest appeared to have heard Max and latched on to the song. Stella had warned him that Mrs. Romano did this; the woman grabbed onto songs and was able to belt them out despite her dementia.

Songs, it seemed, were a key back into memories that the disease had long since locked away.

Max's first thought was to feel bad for waking Mrs. Romano. She must've heard him, and her autopilot kicked in. He willed her to stop singing, not wanting to disturb Stella either, but Mrs. Romano continued on. As she kept going with the song, it jogged Max's memory as well.

"We are but a memory, lasting 'til eternity." Her voice was full and perfectly tuned. "Come here, my love, lay with me and die with me." Then came the *doo-wop,* which the woman belted out with such beautiful ease that it gave Max goosebumps.

*Frisson,* he thought.

As Max's skin stood up, a wave of shivers crawling across his spine, Max was hit with a full wave of memory. He knew where he had heard this song before.

There was one person they knew who listened to old-timey radio. The kind that played old ballads like this. This exact song had graced Max's ears a couple times since arriving in Ruston.

*Why would this song have been in Tiffany's mind?* Max crept down the pitch-black hall toward the source of the singing. Mrs. Romano was continuing with the next bit of the song now, eerie and inspiring all at once. Max tiptoed, not wanting it to stop.

"We are but a breath of breeze, flying o'er tops of trees," her voice caressed his ears.

He felt drawn to her room as if by a siren's song. There was a sliver of light visible beneath her door. As the warm, orange glow spilled out into the hall, so too did her singing.

"Come here, my love, lay with me and die with me."

Max slowly pushed her door open. Curiosity gripped him now. He didn't have the ability to stop himself. He nudged it open just enough so he could see the woman lying on the bed. She was seated upright, a couple pillows jammed underneath her to hold the angle. Her hair was whispy but still dark. Her face was heavily creased, but someone—likely Stella—had taken care to help draw her eyebrows on. She was dressed in bright purple pajamas, and she was tucked under the comforter.

Max leaned against the doorway and slowly slid down into a seated position, never taking his eyes off Mrs. Romano, who was lost in her song. *Doo-wop.* She was unaware—or at least pretending to be unaware—that she had an audience.

The song continued, and Max was able to remember what it was like in Archie's jeep when he heard the song for the first time. *Doo-wop.* But this was the same tune that had been in Tiffany's shattered memory. And because it was too bizarre a connection, Max pulled out the MemCom. The siren's song lured him in, telling him he needed to dive. It was as if Mrs. Romano invited him in. He pressed the button and obliged.

\*\*\*

Max had to shield his eyes from the spotlight. The singing didn't stop, but it was a different song now. The words were Italian, very classic opera. Max didn't understand any of it, but it gave him the same sense of frisson.

Once his eyes adjusted, he was able to orient himself. He was standing on a stage. To his immediate right was a beautiful, tall, dark-haired woman adorned in an emerald dress. Her skin was olive, her eyes a dazzling bronze. She was slender, and her arms cut lines through the air as they waved along with her singing. She was an opera singer. The spotlight was intended for her, and Max stepped out of it quickly.

Now he could see the rest of the auditorium. Three levels of seats towered high over them. Faces without much detail—all just sets of eyes and mouths—stared at them. The place was packed. The sound of the woman's singing rang out in the cavernous space, and it seemed to bring smiles to these strange background actors that watched her.

The singing woman pressed her hands to her chest as she gathered herself for an extended high note. She held this note for what felt like eternity. The sound poured out of her like warm water, Max's entire body enfolded in the song. At one point, the singer looked over to him, seemingly aware of his presence. The corners of her lips curled up in a knowing smile.

The note finally ceased. The orchestra—now Max could see them nestled in front of the stage—played its final flourish, and then the performance was over. Applause erupted from the masses encircling them. Max cringed at the volume of it. He shrank back to the far end of the stage. A lifetime of stage fright was heaping anxiety on him.

It was clear that this performer was beloved. Roses were tossed on the stage. The vague bodies and shapes in the audience all stood, hands clapping, mouths cheering and whistling.

The singer took a graceful curtsy and then waved her arms triumphantly in the air. She strode away from them, heading for the curtain behind her. She really was gorgeous. Max found himself drawn to her, even though he knew it was inappropriate to be distracted like this. But he chased after her, also eager to be away from the crowd.

She slipped behind the curtain just ahead of Max. When Max stepped backstage himself, he found her embracing an older man in a tuxedo. They were speaking Italian to one another—at least, that's what Max thought it sounded like. He didn't recognize any of their words. But they were both happy.

The backstage area was dim, a small red light gave just enough shape to things to avoid tripping, but there wasn't much to see. Even in this dim glow, however, the singer's face was clear. She was the beholder of the memory. And Max didn't have to stretch his imagination too far to see how she would many years later become the woman in Stella's spare room.

This was the opera stardom of Mrs. Romano. She was lively, lucid, and laughing. She kissed cheeks with her counterpart. A faceless person in a vest appeared with glasses of champagne for them, and they clinked glasses.

As Young Donna Romano spoke to the man in the tuxedo, Max tried to get around them. *You were just singing that song,* Max thought. *The right memory can't be far away.*

A doorway appeared etched into the wall beneath a sign that read *Uscita.* To Max, it was clearly an exit.

He glanced back one last time at Donna Romano, in her prime. She may have been lost to dementia in the present, but here she was, living out her best moments all over again. There was something immensely beautiful about the fact that this moment had been preserved so well. Max wondered if this was what Mrs. Romano thought about as she stared into space and sang in Stella's bedroom.

With that, Max stepped through the exit and emerged into something else entirely.

***

Ghost trails gave him double vision. Objects and people that weren't quite there seemed to be streaking through the room. It was as though two memories were playing out at the same time. The room was modern, open, with new furniture, but then layered over top of it was a cramped room with ornate old furnishings.

"Enough singing now, Nonna," a young woman said from the doorway.

Max stood at the foot of a bed. Lying in it was the version of Mrs. Romano he was familiar with seeing. She was older now, and frail. The bed she lay in was both a queen and a twin, with grey sheets and with a purple quilt. Max felt like he understood what was happening; the dementia was bouncing this room back and forth between Donna Romano's childhood bedroom and a more modern one.

Mrs. Romano was humming something, but she ceased. She looked at the young woman in the doorway. The young woman, too, was two things at once. Her solid form was that of a woman with short hair, dark skin, and a dress. But a ghost version, something barely there, was layered over top of her form. Its arms and mouth moved perfectly in sync with the base layer. This top version had long hair and wore a sweater and jeans.

"Cassandra?" Mrs. Romano said, her voice nowhere near as prominent as when she sang. She sounded lost and uncertain.

"No, Nonna," the figure in the door said. "It's Natalya. Your granddaughter."

Slowly, the ghost layer of the woman began to take over, and it edged out the base version. The woman in the doorway became whole, and she was entirely Natalya Romano.

"Where's Cassandra, *cara*?" Mrs. Romano asked.

"She was sick, Nonna."

Max could heard the disappointment in Natalya's voice. Like she had been through this many times before.

"She's gone."

"Be a good girl and fetch *mio sole*," Mrs. Romano said without hesitating.

"Cassandra is dead, Nonna," Natalya sighed. "You remember?"

"She makes the best *biscotti*." Mrs. Romano laughed. "You have to try one."

"Goodnight." Natalya was exasperated.

She turned to leave the room, and as she did, her sweater and jeans were replaced with a dress, her hair cropped from long to short. She became someone else, someone Mrs. Romano wanted her to be, as she walked away.

The bedroom was dark, but for the moonlight that poured in the window, and the light that came in from the hall. The door was left open, and through it, Mrs. Romano could see the woman in the dress moving about the living room beyond.

There was a lurch forwards, and Max became unsteady on his feet. The setting did not change, but the light in the hall was now off. Only the moonlight provided them with shadows. A soft blue took hold of this world. The bedspread was still ambiguous, the room's furnishings still undecided. Mrs. Romano was staring straight ahead, at the window, which was now completely frozen along the edges, the outside world obscured by condensation.

Headlights suddenly cut through the room, landing on the far wall. A vehicle's engine rumbled outside. The lights grew brighter. Beneath the hum of the engine, there was a song. It was dull at first, but then a door clicked open. The song grew louder, clearer, and Max recognized it right away.

*We are but a memory, lasting 'til eternity.*

Max rushed to the window, trying to get a look outside. But Mrs. Romano was stuck in bed. Her mind had never really seen what was out there. And so, no matter how much Max tried to wipe at the fogged window, it never cleared. He could only hear. The song continued a moment more before the engine cut out, and the radio with it. It was replaced by the sound of boots over snow.

Max held still. He did not dare breathe, only listen. The footsteps marched over to the front door. There was a knock. Down the hall, a flurry of noises. A young woman that looked somewhat like Natalya Romano cut across the living room in a robe. She disappeared around the corner. Max wanted to pursue but knew he couldn't leave the room. So, he stood at the edge of Mrs. Romano's bed, and they both listened.

They heard a door open.

Then Natalya's voice. "Sheriff?"

"You don't have to call me that anymore," a male voice.

"Sorry," Natalya said.

"I'm retired, remember?" the male voice said.

Max thought he could place it. He had heard this jovial voice before. He could practically picture the face as he spoke to Natalya.

"Right, sorry, Mr. Hinton."

"Please, that's so formal," the male voice chimed. "Archie is fine."

Max couldn't move. The weight of this realization pinned him in place.

"What's going on? Why are you here?"

"Well, it's important," Archie said. "It's about your Nonna. May I come in?"

"Yeah, sure."

The door closed. There were some footsteps.

"What is it?"

"Is she here?" Archie asked.

"She's asleep."

"And it's just the two of you," Archie said, not really asking. Just confirming.

"That's right . . ." Natalya said.

Then there was a noise Max didn't recognize.

"What are you doing?"

There was a loud bang. Then a muffled yelp. A few frantic bumps against a wall, some footsteps, and then one final loud thud.

"Shhh, quiet girl," Archie's voice was whispering. "Don't want to wake your grandmother."

That was the end of it. Max looked to Mrs. Romano. She was awake, staring into space, hearing everything but unable to do anything. There were a few more noises that Max did not recognize, and then the door was opening again.

Max did his best to track what was happening. More boots crunching over snow. A car door opened, then closed. Another opened and closed. The engine fired up. Beneath its roar, the radio continued. Again, it was muffled, but now that Max knew what it was, he could pair the melody with the words.

*Come here, my love, lay with me and die with me.*

The vehicle drove off. Max was trying to comprehend what he had just witnessed. He turned to Mrs. Romano. She was looking right at him. Her eyes were glossy but hyper-focused.

"Are you my Giorgio?" she asked, her tone naive and sweet.

"No."

"You look just like him." Mrs. Romano smiled.

Her eyes were not those of the other SI's Max had encountered. She felt present, like the old woman from Stella's spare bedroom had come back to be here with him.

"You saw me on stage."

Max's skin crawled now, but it wasn't frisson from the music.

"You were there, so shy," she said, piercing him. "Wasn't it a wonderful show? The audience was so full that night. One of the best I've ever performed to."

Mrs. Romano, who outside of this memory was catatonic and lost to dementia, was, at this moment, very aware. She knew that Max was there, in her mind, and she knew all the things he was doing and seeing. It was as though she had travelled through her own memories with him.

"Did you catch the man who took my Natalya?" she asked. "That's what you're here for, *sì*?"

Max wasn't sure how to respond. He felt as though he had crossed an invisible boundary. It was no longer spying; he was being invited in. The mind wanted him here.

Choosing his words carefully, he spoke in a hushed tone. "We're about to," he said.

"Good." Mrs. Romano exhaled and settled into her bed, making herself more comfortable.

Then it was all gone. That recognition in her eyes faded, and she spoke again with a frail, disconnected voice.

"Want to sing with me?" She began another rendition of the same melancholy tune that had been haunting this night.

*Doo-wop. Doo-wop. Doo-wop.*

\*\*\*

The song persisted as Max pulled himself from the dive. Present-day Donna Romano was still belting it out, and she was at the exact same line she had been in her memory, no less.

*This fucking song,* Max thought. Minutes earlier, he hadn't recognized it. Now that he did, it was a sinister hymn. He stood back up, shutting Mrs. Romano's door as he left. Her tune served as evidence. Max now had the real culprit. He walked stiffly back toward the kitchen.

It wasn't Landry. It was the *old* sheriff. Archie. And how had they not picked up on it?

If the supposed curse only began when Landry took over, it also meant that it began when Archie retired. The ex-sheriff suddenly with a bunch of spare time. He had also been at the library in the morning, hearing them clear Floyd's name. He had known they were speaking with Nelly. He had been alone when Nelly went missing.

Max felt clarity now, as though his eyes finally opened to their fullest. He was seeing the full picture. But this full picture also revealed a horrifying turn of events.

The man who had been responsible for all of the disappearances and deaths was now alone in a vehicle with Oren.

# 14. Charlie's Fall

OREN HAD TOLD MAX THAT all he would need to know about the MemCom would be there for him in Charlie's mind. And even though Max did not remember it straight away, the end of Charlie's story was there too. Everything that lead back to the present—to the hospital bed—had been transferred to Max, ready to recollect when it was needed.

*** 

Charlie sat in the prison parking lot, watching the sky. It was threatening a storm; low, dark clouds scraped across the sky. A few stray drops hit his windshield, promising to bring more.

Since arriving back in America, Charlie had been avoiding Oren like the plague. His partner—though it was strange for Charlie to consider him as such now that he was done with being a private investigator—was relentless. He called Charlie several times a day.

The celebrations were wrapped by now. They had found the last of Lang's victims. The press was all over it, turning Oren into a minor celebrity. *Inside the Mind of a Serial Killer: PI Makes Lang Talk.* Charlie saw Oren's name on the news as often as he saw it in his missed calls.

No doubt Oren wanted the MemCom back. Charlie wasn't going to hand it over, though.

With a broken heart, Charlie had spent the better part of two days preparing things. When he felt ready, he gave the warden a call and told him to expect a visit. Charlie arrived early and was just biding his time now until he knew the warden would be available to greet him.

His phone buzzed. Agitated, Charlie glanced at the screen, ready to silence yet another call from Oren. But the caller ID revealed a different name. It was his brother, Ty.

Ty was now an adult. He'd gone to university on a volleyball scholarship, having quickly become taller and stronger than his older brother. When Charlie had left the family home, he had more or less severed the connection he had with his brother. But Ty idolized him. He sent messages, called most weekends, and was always interested in what his brother was doing. Charlie never prioritized these calls. He sank himself into his work instead.

Guilt drove him to answer the phone then, thinking it wouldn't be such a bad thing to set things right.

"Ty," Charlie said, answering the call.

"Charlie! You answered? Hey, how are you?"

"I'm fine."

"Good, that's good," Ty said, hesitating. "I was worried about you, ya know."

"Why?"

"You missed Mom's birthday, Charlie."

Charlie sighed when he realized what day it was. It was customary for the entire family to use their parents' birthdays as an excuse to get together. With busy lives, and family spread out across the country, these were the dates the family held sacred. But Charlie hadn't acknowledged it. He hadn't even called. He had been in Ireland.

"I'm sorry," Charlie said.

"Don't apologize to me," Ty said. "You need to call mom. She kept saying it was okay because she knows how busy you are, but you know what she's like, Charlie. We're worried about you. I feel like I haven't seen you in ages."

"You don't need to be worried." Charlie was growing uncomfortable. He did not want to be having this conversation with his brother, or anyone. Not while he still had work to do.

"Okay." Ty hesitated again, not saying what he wanted to. "Well . . . I miss ya, big bro. You still doing the private investigator thing? Maybe we could get together some time, and you can tell me all about your cases. See if they're anything like when Domino murdered Monty the rabbit." He chuckled, trying to trigger nostalgia and connect with his brother.

Charlie wouldn't allow it to work. "We'll see," Charlie said. "I hope you're well, Ty. But I have to go."

"Ok." Ty sounded defeated. "Love you, man."

Charlie ended the call.

Fittingly, it started raining as Charlie stepped from his car. Charlie let the downpour matte his hair to his forehead, and he let it streak his shirt to the point of clinging to his skin. Warden Manfred met him inside, breadcrumbs stuck to the corner of his mouth that he wiped away absent-mindedly. He greeted Charlie with an out-of-breath hello.

"I didn't realize you had to come back," Manfred said. "West said you were all done."

"I just have a quick follow-up," Charlie lied.

"You know, I really am not supposed to let you in without—" Manfred began, but then paused as Charlie pulled out a stack of bills.

The man was easily influenced; Charlie had learned this from Oren. He rested his hand on the Warden's large shoulder.

"I'll have to get the guards to fetch him." Manfred collected the cash, enfolding it in his chubby hands. "You know, next time, if you just give us a little more warning, we can have him—"

"There won't be a next time," Charlie said coldly.

Manfred stopped, gave Charlie a quick up and down, thought about saying something, and then opted not to. He sensed something off about Charlie, but he had already collected his prize, and he wasn't a therapist. Why should he care?

"Also, your regular room," Manfred said. "It isn't set up."

"Anywhere is good."

"Well . . ." Manfred sighed. He ran his hands across his scalp, trying to figure out how to help. "I can put you in one of the conjugal rooms. One of the guards could wait outside. You wouldn't get your two-way mirror though."

"That's fine," Charlie said. "I just need to speak with him."

Charlie was brought to a small space that looked like a poor attempt at re-creating a hotel room. A twin bed was set in the corner beneath a barred window, and a table and two chairs were positioned on the opposite wall. A small bathroom with dirty tile flooring was set off in the corner, behind a partially closed door. Charlie waited in one of the chairs while Manfred rallied his troops.

Every second that passed felt like an eternity to Charlie. He passed the time by writing out an apology to his mother. It was a long text, one that read more like a farewell. He had to send it in two parts. Once that was done, he shut his phone off. He didn't want to hear back from her, or from Ty, or Oren, or anyone.

Charlie grew concerned that Oren would come bursting through the door and stop him. He imagined Warden Manfred tattling on him and now stalling. Charlie's palms were sweaty, and he was growing anxious. He became more and more certain that he'd get caught. Somehow, he felt like Oren could tell that he was here. Oren could tell what he was up to. And, of course, he'd shut the whole thing down.

Oren was now the enemy.

Charlie longed for Lang's mind. That was sanctuary. He just needed to get there before Oren had a chance to intercept him.

He imagined an entire argument with his partner.

*She's not real.*

*Who's to say she's not?*

*You need to move on!*

*This is all that matters now.*

But none of this would ever happen. And at long last, Lang arrived.

The guards paraded him into the room as if he were a trophy. Charlie was sizing him up, seeing him not as a man or a murderer but as a location. His mind was a place to visit. It was a sort of home. Lang was taking stock of the man before him, too, for he had never seen Charlie before. He was confused, trying to determine what was happening, but his eyes were sparkling. He was enjoying this.

The guards clasped him into his seat. Charlie watched, anticipation boiling over as they cuffed his wrists. As they went to shackle his ankles, Charlie waved his hand at them dismissively. *That will be all.*

The guards looked at one another, then back to Charlie. They shrugged.

"You want us in here?" one asked.

"No."

"Alright." One guard shrugged again. "We'll be right outside the door. Let us know when you finish up."

The guards exited, and now Charlie was finally ready to dig in. He had Lang alone.

"So . . ." Lang's lips twisted into a crooked grin. "Do I finally have the pleasure of meeting my interviewer? Is that you, Harold?"

Charlie didn't answer.

"And what happened to your face?" Lang tilted his chin, pointing at Charlie's horseshoe scar. Lang stared at it salaciously.

On his phone, Charlie queued up his favourite song, and soon "Sweet Caroline" drowned out most of Lang's soft laughter.

"This fucking song again?"

Charlie then pulled out the earpiece from his pocket. Lang's grin finally faded when he saw the device. Leonard Lang was evil, but he was not stupid. He had heard of these devices. He knew he was looking at the MemCom.

All at once, Lang seemed to realize what had been happening during these interviews. He had been violated. This particular role reversal did not sit well with him.

"You piece of shit," Lang growled, struggling against his restraints. "Have you been mind-fucking me with that thing this whole time?"

But Charlie didn't hear him. He had already pressed the button. He was already gone.

\*\*\*

This mind was a comfortable place. Charlie passed through it with the familiarity one might have with their childhood home. He didn't need to think about how many steps there were on the staircase; he could just walk. He knew every turn and every door. Soon, he was back at the beach. The waves crashed into the sand, and the wind did its best to drown out the sound. He spotted her in the usual place, hair fighting the breeze.

"Kelly," Charlie said, wasting no time. He walked right up to her with a confidence that made her blush.

"Yes?" she asked, her eyes tingling with the familiar curiosity of a first encounter.

"Come with me."

He grabbed her hand, the softness feeling right in his palm. He whisked her away then, confident in where they could hide and never be found.

\*\*\*

Lang watched, dumbfounded, as the man in front of him fell asleep. All of the precautions that should have been in place were waived by the last-minute nature of Charlie's visit. Lang should've had his legs shackled, but Charlie had passed on this, too. Lang was too slippery for these half measures to contain him. He had been practicing a technique for dislocating his wrists. He worked on this now. All he needed was one free arm.

Irate, Lang slipped his left hand free and then pulled himself free of the chair. He dove at Charlie, grabbing a thick handful of the sleeping man's shirt. They both toppled to the ground, Charlie's chair crashing backwards. Lang lay on top of him, hands finally free. He would enjoy this.

The commotion was heard outside the room. The guards—despite caring very little for the way Charlie spoke to them—longed for some excitement. When they heard the scuffle, they rushed back into the room, weapons drawn. One guard, much more tenured than his counterpart, had long fantasized about this moment. *Give me one reason,* he would think as he walked another murderer or rapist back to his cell. *Anything to pump a few rounds into this son of a bitch. That would be real justice.* Spending your days with criminals could make you miserable, or it could make you want to be the hero.

This particular guard got to play hero on this day. He fired two quick rounds into Lang's abdomen.

Lang was stunned. He rolled off Charlie and stared up at the guards. He coughed once, blood spraying the room. Then his eyes rolled back.

\*\*\*

The brain does not die at the same time the heart does. Cells and neurons in the brain can continue to function for a few minutes after the final heartbeat. When the end finally comes, brain death is marked by a final flurry of activity. This wave of electrical activity is called the *spreading depression.* Charlie had studied this relentlessly.

He knew that, along with regulating your circadian rhythm, the pineal gland released DMT—the most powerful natural hallucinogen—into the human brain while dreaming. He also knew that when you died, this gland let go of all control and granted you one final, overwhelming release. The brain just let everything out in a tidal wave—memories and dreams churned together.

Charlie had been fascinated by theories about what the brain did at the moment of death and how this surge of activity was perceived by the mind that was dying. Sitting with Kelly, he'd now be the first to witness it in real time.

He had brought her to a corner of Lang's mind that he had seen before. Lang was preoccupied with murder in the trees behind them. A small gravel lot provided a lookout over the hills, and a view of the entire forest was laid out below them. Charlie sat with Kelly on a concrete barrier that walled the parking lot off from the steep drop down the hill. The sun was rising, and the way it hit Kelly's face convinced Charlie that he had made the right choice.

There was no oxygen being pumped into Leonard Lang's brain, and perhaps that contributed to his lack of awareness. His SI was completely unaware of the meddling happening nearby. Charlie and Kelly were kissing, shirts tossed aside, hands on each other's chests and necks and arms. Charlie felt the tingle of electricity, the hairs all over his body standing on end. He thought that it was lust, at first, but soon the swell grew too great to be ignored. There was a storm in the air.

The sunrise erupted in a flood of light, Charlie wincing, as if someone had just burst into his bedroom and turned the lights on in the dead of night. Both Charlie and Kelly shielded their eyes, but only Charlie peered through his fingers to see what was coming.

A tidal wave moved across the forest, snapping trees like toothpicks. At first, Charlie was convinced it was water, a tsunami that somehow made its way inland. But the more he looked, the more he saw that the wave wasn't made up of any one thing. The wave was composed of images. Memories. Tiny bolts of electricity crackled on the skyline, following the wave across the world. The sky began to flicker like an old television set. An electrical field was tearing everything apart.

As the wave came closer, Charlie could make out individual memories. This was Lang's life flashing before his eyes. Charlie recognized the scorpion, the tormented childhood, the car accident that nearly took Lang's life, the murders, and Lang's trial. All of these were jumbled together in the spreading depression that raced toward the hill Charlie and Kelly were perched upon.

Sounds hit them first: laughter, screaming, music, and a percussive grinding noise that could have been a bone saw. The trees all around them began to flicker in and out of existence. One—which would've made a perfect Christmas tree—became a telephone pole. A small boy with greasy hair appeared in the parking lot, half of his body blurry, waiting to be rendered.

Charlie leapt to his feet, instinctively.

"What is it?" Kelly asked, as though she were unaware that anything was amiss.

"We have to run," Charlie said.

He grabbed her hand, pulling her to her feet. But she resisted. Her eyes disappeared for a moment, and when they returned, they were a different colour. The world inside Lang's head was no longer structurally sound, and Kelly was a part of that world. Her skin went cold.

Charlie was torn between the urge to flea and the urge to be with her. He *loved* her. She looked at him confused. He could not bare to see her torn apart.

The tidal wave of DMT was nearly upon them. A young boy played with toys in the sand, and the image fractured as the wave crashed upon trees and hills. As the wave frothed and churned, this scene became that of an elderly man, red in the face, removing his belt and whipping it through the air. A loud crack sounded out across the valley.

Every song that Lang had ever heard, every person that he'd ever met, every meal he'd ever ate, all flooded his brain with their sensations now. Charlie had never felt so hot and so cold at the same time. He could simultaneously recognize every tune in the fray while also not recognizing anything. His mouth was watering, salty and sour and sweet, and bombarding him.

Charlie pried his eyes away from the surge, forcing himself to look at Kelly instead. She was still there, for now. Her beauty managed to remain as everything else fell away. Charlie chose her. Whatever would happen when he was swallowed by the spreading depression was no longer a concern.

He sat back down with her on the concrete wall, feet dangling over the world. They embraced, and their lips locked. He focused only on this feeling and blocked everything else out.

Around them, pieces of Lang's life were washing up in the wave.

The sound of crashing and roaring swelled, drowning everything else out. The wave was now so close that it shook the world.

But Charlie could only hear Kelly's breathing. He listened to its rise and fall until there was no more sound at all.

\*\*\*

There is still much science has to learn about death, and brain death. No one fully understands when all of the capacity for awareness is lost.

Though the prison guard only shot Leonard Lang, both of the men in that room flatlined. Paramedics saved Charlie, but when his heartbeat came back, nothing else seemed to come with it. He remained in a coma. While there were many opinions that said the plug should have been pulled, Oren and Aria knew the eidetic memory inside his head would be a perfect imprint of Charlie's life. And one day, they may need it.

In the meantime, they hoped that Charlie was happy, wherever he ended up.

# 15. Spreading Depression

*I*T'S ARCHIE. NOT LANDRY.
*Can explain later.*
*On my way to you.*
*Stay safe.*

Max fired off a flurry of text messages to Oren. His first two attempts at calling him went unanswered. *He's just mad at me,* Max thought, willing it to be true.

He felt horrible about what he did next—though it had to be done. Max found Stella's purse resting on the kitchen counter. The burgundy leather bag was decorated with knickknacks and keychains. Max stuck his hand inside, fishing around as the guilt welled up inside him. His knuckle scraped against a key ring, and he snatched it.

The car was in the garage. It was an old station wagon that took two tries to start. Stella had taken good care of it; the seats were clean, and the dash was freshly dusted. But the thing was a beast, and it drove like a boat. Max flew out of the driveway and looped around in a semi-donut without intending too.

The roads were slick. All of the packed down snow was causing him to fishtail left and right. On top of that, the sky was opening up again and thick flakes were blanketing Ruston. As his headlights burst through the snow squall, it gave the illusion that Max was driving through a field of stars.

Max had his phone in one hand, trying to see where he was going. Eisner's Dairy Farm showed up on the map, which was a great stroke of luck. Max squinted to see what street he was on, head rattling back and forth from the phone screen to the windshield.

While struggling to make sense of his surroundings, Max missed the stop sign as he cruised toward Ruston's main drag. He looked up too late, saw the brake lights, and panicked. He stomped on the brakes, but the car spun out, as there was no traction on these roads. He was heading straight for the vehicle in front of him and the only way to avoid the collision was to crank the steering wheel the other way, forcing himself into the ditch. The station wagon plowed into the snow, nose first, and the horn began to sound.

Cursing, Max forced the door open against the snowbank. It wouldn't open all the way, and he had to make himself skinny to get out. He stood in knee-deep snow now, looking at the crumpled front of the car he had stolen. The world was a blur, the snow obscuring everything. The leftover glow from the streetlights and headlights was all there was to see by.

"What in the hell are you doing?!" a familiar voice shouted through the snow.

The driver of the truck, which was stopped at the intersection, had come out of his vehicle. The red of his taillights cast him as a demonic silhouette, the exhaust from his tail pipes rising around him dramatically.

*Shit,* Max thought as he recognized the driver.

"Is that you, Detective Sleeps-a-lot?" the man said as he came closer. Sheriff Landry was watching Max with a grim amusement in his eyes, the same way a cat might look at a wounded mouse. "The fuck you get that car?"

"I borrowed it . . . from Mrs. Godsby," Max said, though it took him two tries as the wind forced his breath back into his face.

"Pretty reckless driving." Landry was coy, sizing up an opportunity to make Max squirm. Maybe to even get him in trouble for the collision.

Max's first reaction was to cower from this man, still partially believing he could be a murderer. Landry's harsh words and gruff tone made it all that much easier to believe he was still the villain. Max had to remind himself what he had learned. They were after someone else. And this man was still the sheriff.

"I need your help," Max said. He shielded his eyes against the wind and the snow, face quickly numbing. "It's Archie. The one who took the girls."

Landry was speechless. His mouth hung open, unsure if a punchline was forthcoming. He looked at the car, then at Max, caught somewhere between confusion and frustration.

"He's with Oren now, on their way to Eisner's Dairy Farm," Max said. "Please, we have to get to them.

Oren doesn't know that it's Archie. He won't answer his phone."

"This a joke?"

"No," Max pleaded. "Sheriff, I'm serious."

"How come you know this?"

"We found Tiffany." Max cringed. This wouldn't help his case. "She's at the hospital now with her family."

"And no one told me?!" Landry's voice boomed. The snow that fluttered and landed on his jacket seemed to melt; he was hot with rage.

"We should've." Max raised his hands in surrender. "You're right. We messed this up. But I'm begging for your help now. We need to stop Archie before he can do anything . . . to Oren or to Nelly."

Something softened in Landry's face then. For a moment, Max was looking at Ed Landry, the boy Nina Banks had rescued from bullies. The boy who grew up to be sheriff. There was still a sense of justice in him. Max realized now that his own mind had coloured the sheriff entirely one way. He was inept and sour. But even a man who cursed a lot and who had been on the job long enough to lose touch with his attention to detail could be moved by the need to do what was right.

"Get in," Landry said. "Hurry."

Max followed him to the police truck, and they took off. The roads were barely visible. Max had no idea where they were or where they were headed, and he was relieved that Landry was the one driving.

*\*\*\**

The snow had started slowly but was now rising into a full whiteout.

"Tried to get the place all toasty for you." Archie smiled behind the wheel. The jeep's heat was on full blast. "Brutal night out there."

Oren thanked him. Archie had the radio on, as per usual, and cast a couple side-eyed glances at Oren to see if he was in the mood for conversation or not. Oren must have seemed a little tense because no conversation was started.

Once they had been on the highway for a few minutes, Oren's phone buzzed.

He pulled it out of his pocket with fingers that had not yet thawed. The screen revealed the caller to be Max, and Oren paused, staring. He didn't feel like having this conversation, whatever it was, right now. And not in front of Archie. Max had chewed him out enough for one night; he couldn't handle any more guilt.

Oren muted the call.

"Shame about that girl," Archie said.

"What do you mean?"

"Heard the Masterson girl's gone missing now, too," Archie said.

"Ah, right." Oren nodded solemnly.

The phone buzzed again, this time rattling against the plastic seat belt buckle. Oren rushed to silence it.

"Need to get that?" Archie asked.

Oren shook his head.

The world only seemed to exist inside of the cone of the jeep's headlights. Snowflakes flew toward them and the road vanished beneath them, but outside of this, the world was grey. Oren became mesmerized with it. Everything looked like an old television that hadn't been tuned into the right station.

The landscape they passed was hidden from them, and Oren was getting lulled to sleep by the heat and the monotony of the snow.

The phone buzzed again, this time in shorter bursts, indicating a text message. Oren's first thought was to keep ignoring it. But curiosity got the better of him.

*It's Archie. Not Landry*

*Can explain later.*

*On my way to you.*

*Stay safe.*

Oren's first reaction was confusion. He cocked his head and even turned to look at Archie, as if he could explain the cryptic message. When Archie turned to meet his gaze, Oren realized his mistake, and he tried to casually bring his gaze back to the window.

"Everything alright, Oren?" Archie asked.

He glanced at Oren's phone, and Oren quickly turned his phone face down to hide the message.

"Just hard to work with friends sometimes," Oren lied.

Archie looked at him for an uncomfortably long time, weighing his response. The silence made Oren's breath hitch, his palms growing slick. Archie finally turned his attention back to the road without uttering a word. Oren exhaled.

"You and Max go way back, that right?" Archie said at last, wearing his trademark grin.

"As far back as they go," Oren said, leaning in on this cheap small talk.

Internally, his mind was trying to decode the message from Max. *Archie is the killer? How is that possible?* Oren tried to think of what could have led him to this, believing that Max had maybe tried another dive on someone.

"Here we are," Archie said, pulling over to the left and rattling the jeep along a small road that Oren hadn't even seen until now.

The road hadn't been well maintained, and the ride was bumpy, but the jeep handled it well.

"Where do you live, Archie?" Oren asked.

"Me? I'm out a little further east. Why?"

"Didn't take you too long to get to Stella's tonight," Oren said.

Archie took a second before replying. "That's 'cause you didn't catch me at home. I was in town."

Oren nodded, signalling the end of the conversation. But inside, he was playing out all of the scenarios which made this possible. Oren had spotted someone trying to dump Tiffany's body. Then Archie had shown up at Stella's only minutes after he'd been called. When Josh reported Nelly missing, Archie had been excused to go run errands. He had been unaccounted for every time something bad happened. He also had ears on the investigation; he knew their every step.

"Oren?" Archie said.

They had stopped. He jumped in his seat when Archie reached out toward him. Then he realized Archie was just pointing out the window.

"You alright? That's it there."

"Yeah, sorry, long night." Oren chuckled.

He tracked Archie's hand and saw the big barn—albeit barely—as a shadowy mass in the white sheets of snow. Beside them were a pair of dilapidated chicken coops. One leaned on the other, pieces of wood and wire strung about.

"Wasn't half bad in Eisner's hay day," Archie said. "Abandoned now, obviously. You going to check things out?"

"Yeah." Oren prepared the collar of his jacket for the wind outside. "I'll just be a second."

"Want a hand?"

"No, no." Oren desperately wanted some space. Some time to think. "Just stay here."

Oren pushed open his door slightly. The wind caught it and ripped it the rest of the way. As Oren started to slide out of the jeep, Archie called out to him. As Oren turned to face him, he saw that Archie was pointing a dark, metal object straight at his face. His skin crawled, and his heart leapt into his throat.

"You might need this." Archie was offering him a flashlight. "Awful dark back by the barn."

"Thanks." Oren grabbed it, trying to act natural, as though he wasn't jumping at every single thing Archie did.

Oren marched off through the snow. It was difficult to walk, and he was looking down to make sure he didn't trip or step in too deep a drift. He passed in front of the jeep, the headlights making it easier to see the best path. But he also felt exposed.

*Just a little further,* he thought, *and I can pull my phone out again.* He wanted to call Max and ask what was going on. What evidence did he have? But he needed to put some distance between himself and Archie first.

Oren kept trudging through the snow, stamping fresh prints into the ground, all while Archie watched him in the beam of his headlights.

\*\*\*

The snowfall had ceased by the time they arrived. The fresh powder groaned as the truck's tires packed it into the earth. In the distance, Max could see a large barn. Landry was leaning forwards to get a better look at what was immediately in front of them.

"Looks like they were here," he said, pointing out the tire tracks in the snow. They were partially filled in by now, only faintly visible. "Ain't nobody else needs to come up this way." He paused, looking left and right. "But I don't see the jeep. Looks like they've gone by now."

Max's heartbeat had been shaking his entire body on the ride out. He sat quite literally on the edge of his seat, not buckled in but leaning on the dashboard, urging the truck to move faster. Landry, to his credit, hadn't derided him or cussed him out. He was silent, sensing the shift in Max's emotions.

"You're sure this is where they were headed?" Landry asked.

"If this is Eisner's farm," Max said. "And if that barn up ahead is green."

"It is."

Landry's truck crawled now, inching closer to two abandoned chicken coops that had been crushed by the elements. The shadows cast by the headlights made the fallen structures look like they had twisted hands reaching out across the snow, grabbing at anything, grabbing at—

"Wait, there!"

A dark mass against the white snow. Obscured tire tracks pointed them to it. The mass looked broken; it was folded at an odd angle and left, pressed into the packed snow. Landry steered in that direction, and when the truck's headlights fully illuminated that spot, the bright red was unmistakable. It was a crime scene.

"Oren!"

Max opened the door even before Landry had stopped. He made a mad dash for the body, tripping himself twice in the awkward snow.

"Wait!" Landry shouted after him, though it was helpless.

Max was crawling now, unable to stand up again, yet he kept moving forwards. His adrenaline had spiked, and though he felt the cold against his skin, it didn't deter him. On all fours, he made his way to Oren. Steam still rose off the body, but the angle of his neck and the blood in the snow suggested that he was beyond saving.

"Oren, it's me," Max said, lying down in the snow beside his friend. He felt for a pulse.

Nothing.

Max started saying to himself that this couldn't be right. He didn't know how to check for a pulse. That was it. Surely, Oren was fine. Just injured. The body was still warm. Surely, he was okay. His thoughts were spiralling and moving a thousand miles an hour. This body in front of him ceased to look like Oren. Max no longer recognized this person; he wasn't standing tall, confident and collected. It could not be his friend. This lifeless thing, impossibly fractured, would never be whole again.

Landry got out of the truck but kept his distance. He gave Max his privacy for this moment, knowing it was already too late to do anything. The man's eyes were open, lifeless orbs staring up at the sky. Landry kept a hand on his holster out of precaution, though it was also clear to him that Archie had left.

Oren's phone was still clutched in his hand, but the screen was cracked and dark. His jacket was open, folded back and exposing his dress shirt beneath. His gun holster sat empty. Max looked around, but there was no gun. Archie must have snagged it after running him over.

"What happened?" Max's voice was barely more than a whimper. His erratic breathing sent trails into the sky. He could feel his eyes watering, but the tears froze before they could fall.

There was a way to find out what happened.

Max stuffed his numb fingers into his pocket, fumbling for the metal case. Retrieving it, he grew shaky and dropped the earpiece into the snow. He had to carefully fish it out, pinching it with his finger and his thumb so as to not push it deeper into the snow.

"What's that?" Landry called from behind him.

Max ignored him.

*Why didn't you answer the phone, you fool?*

Max hadn't even gotten to say goodbye. At least, not yet. He slid the earpiece in, pulled out his phone, and found a song he and Oren had listened to as kids.

"What is that?" Landry repeated.

"Don't stop me. Just wait there. All I need is a few seconds."

"A few seconds for what?"

To Landry's surprise, Max collapsed face first into the snowbank.

\*\*\*

There was something in the distance. A certain buzzing—like the way the air tingles right before a thunderstorm—that prickled at Max's skin. He couldn't see it yet, but he knew from the lessons learned in Charlie's mind that the spreading depression would be coming soon. Max was inside a dying mind.

He didn't have long.

Max found himself inside a modern chalet, open with high ceilings and centred around a large glass fireplace. Oren was facing a window, looking out as the sunset cast pink over the world. They were in the mountains, somewhere, and a light snow was beginning to fall. The flakes appeared as rose petals in the sun's glow. But the corners of everything were growing dark, threatening to steal all of this.

This was Oren's happy place. And Max was glad, for Oren's sake, that he would get to enjoy it one last time. Max could smell dinner cooking somewhere nearby—cardamom, cinnamon, and nutmeg. The warmth of this scene enfolded him too, and he felt safe.

"Is this the best place we've ever rented?" A man appeared from nothing, walking up behind Oren and embracing him.

There was a brief hiccup in the world where the dark edges receded, the sunset growing in splendour. But it didn't last.

"I think so," Oren said. He turned around, looking deep into the man's eyes. His face was aglow in a way Max had not seen before. "Merry Christmas."

"I got you something," the man said, pulling away from their embrace.

The man was tall and dark, like Oren, but skinnier and clean-shaven.

"I didn't have time to wrap it, though."

"What is it?"

The man reached deep into his jeans' pocket and pulled out a white case, metallic and sparkling. He presented it to Oren as if it were fragile and important, hand outstretched.

"Scott . . ." Oren's mouth hung open. "Is that . . . what I think it is?"

"You said you wanted to make a difference." The man—Scott—forced Oren to take it, folding his hands over the device.

"How?"

"I may have fudged the inventory numbers at the warehouse." Scott shrugged. "I couldn't bear seeing them all destroyed. Not after all the work that went into it."

"If they find out you kept one . . ." Oren was still in awe, studying the dazzling white in his hand. ". . . won't they . . ."

"Lock me up forever? Probably. That's why we won't let anyone find out."

"I won't be able to use it," Oren realized.

"No," Scott admitted. "But we can find someone. We can teach them how."

"You have to tell me everything." Oren's expression flipped. He became a little kid on Christmas, receiving the toy he'd asked for.

The sense of static in the air changed as if shifting in the wind. It was growing in intensity. Max had to cut this history lesson short, though he was grateful to have learned about how Oren acquired the MemCom.

Max needed a door. The chalet had one lone hallway out of the living room. It was cast in shadow, the sunset not reaching this far. Max headed toward it, struggling to see through the dark. Once his eyes adjusted, his heart sank.

The hallway stretched on for quite a long way. Surely, Oren's mind was exaggerating its size. Both sides of the hall were lined with doors, roughly a dozen on the left and the right. Far too many options.

"Damn it, Oren."

Max sighed as he went for the first door on his left. It was a roll of the dice.

*** 

Through this first door, Max intruded upon a small office space adorned with clean, white bookshelves.

Oren was sitting, legs crossed, on a chaise lounge. A middle-aged woman with thin glasses was peering at him from a comfortable chair of her own.

"That must be really hard, Oren," the woman said, voice full of genuine sympathy.

"It causes me to wonder a lot," Oren replied. "If I made the right decision."

Max didn't like this. He felt immediately awkward. The space was too small, too intimate. And it became obvious very quickly that this was a therapy session. He should not be seeing this.

"I miss it." Oren half-laughed. "Never thought I would. That town felt like it was strangling the life out of us. We all wanted out. But now that I'm gone, it feels even more like home. A part of me is still there. And I'm missing out being that part. I don't get to see my family, my friends, my best friend—Max—I've left them all. And soon, they'll probably forget about me."

The therapist moved to say something in response, but Max had clapped his hands over his ears. He did not want to hear any more. This wasn't for him. And it already broke his heart. Hearing Oren sad, hearing him miss his home, was too much.

Max had no choice but to retreat the way he had come. He stepped out of this moment . . .

\*\*\*

. . . and back into the hall of a thousand doors. There was a rattling beneath his feet now, as if thunder bellowed in the distance. Max still had far too many choices. He only knew that this one door was no good.

He decided to progress in order, and so he attempted the second door on that same side.

\*\*\*

It was another small space. This one cast in a sickly green light. Max was in a hospital room. The smell of sickness and cleaner hit his nose, flooding him with horrible memories of his own.

Before him was a hospital bed, where Scott lay on his back, looking ashen and gaunt. Oren was on his knees at the side of the bed, holding Scott's hand in his, fighting back tears. There was a steady beep on the monitor next to the bed, but Max thought it sounded far too slow.

"Don't go," Oren said, his voice barely audible. "I'm not ready to do this without you."

There was no life in Scott's face. His chest didn't even seem to rise and fall with breath. These were his last moments.

Oren laid his head down a moment, touching Scott's hand to his forehead, and when he looked back up, he stared intently at the dying man's face. There seemed to be a moment where the lights in the room flickered, and then the beeps became one long tone.

Max cringed, hating seeing these private moments.

Once again, he retreated, out the way he had come. Another dead end.

\*\*\*

Was it just him or was the hallway darker now? Max glanced back toward the living room, where Oren and Scott—still alive—stood by the fireplace. The colour seemed to have drained from this moment. They existed now only in gray scale. The sunset's magic was reduced to a chalky blur.

Max was going to run out of chances. He switched sides, going for the first door on the right. This one stuck a bit, forcing him to press his weight against it before it finally gave way.

\*\*\*

The blizzard was still blowing strong. Max knew right away where he was.

The night looked and felt exactly the same. Present Day Oren was standing at Eisner's farm, stomping his way through the snow, shielding his eyes against headlights that caused the snowflakes to glimmer.

Once Oren left the cone of light, the world became dark rather quickly. He stomped a little further, toward the chicken coops, but couldn't see where he was going. He went to turn on the flashlight that Archie had given him.

It flickered once but didn't turn on. Oren smacked it once. Another flicker. Then he smacked it a second time, and suddenly, he was blinded by a powerful white beam. The light was accompanied with a great roar. At first, Max thought the light and sound had come from the flashlight. But then he saw the vehicle heading toward them and realized it was the jeep.

Oren was back in the jeep's crosshairs, and the engine was snarling as Archie pressed down on the gas, flying toward where Oren stood. Oren shielded his eyes, barely having time to make out the threat. He turned and began to sprint.

He only made it a few steps through the snow before his foot caught, sending him to one knee. The snow was too deep for running. The jeep, however, had no difficulty with this terrain. It surged forwards, picking up speed.

Oren went to his holster, attempting to withdraw his gun. He wasn't fast enough. The jeep's front grill connected with Oren and thrust him hard into the snow and the chicken coops. The tires followed, crunching over the snow and Oren together.

Max was shaken by a fiery pain that coursed through the memory. Everything went black.

***

When light returned, it was the kind of light that comes through windows in grey sheets on a stormy winter day. And this particular winter day hadn't occurred all that long ago. Max knew the place by the image of the blue jay on the wall. He was back at the Cuckoo's Nest. This was where the entire misadventure began.

Max spotted himself at the booth. Oren was there too, looking happy. The restaurant was crumbling, though. The other patrons had vanished. Now Max and Oren were the only ones. The details in the walls and floor were reduced to just a smooth brown and beige mosaic.

"What have we done?" Oren chuckled, looking around at the place.

"How long are you going to make me wait for all of the details?" the memory of Max at the booth asked, his elbows on the parrot-patterned tablecloth.

That pattern seemed to bleed into Max's arms, the line between shapes not holding true.

Max wanted to run over to this table and interrupt them.

He wanted to tell himself not to go to Ruston.

He could prevent Oren from ever getting run over if he stopped it all now.

*But you can't.* He hated this voice in his head. Rational, yet despised. *These moments aren't to be changed.* All he could do was watch, studying Oren's face, enjoying that smile for perhaps the last time.

Something pulled at Max, reminding him of the last time he was here. He had visited the Cuckoo's Nest in Oren's memories before. Back then, there was a door . . .

Max spun around. There it was again. The blurry, black door past the bathrooms.

That it was dark and hidden away was no surprise. Something haunting had lived on the other side—the man with the enormous smile who had tried to take Oren. Max's feet moved almost on their own. He found himself marching through the shadows and heading for the door. He didn't want to go back. Yet he felt like he didn't have a choice. Something made him go through that door.

Forcing his way through it, he landed, once again . . .

\*\*\*

. . . in the yard where a much smaller Oren played with his ball.

The day was bright, sunny, and idyllic.

"Hey, mister," Young Oren said. "What you looking at?"

The Smiling Man was there again on the other side of the picket fence. His features drifted, his entire being detached from reality, and his eyes seemed to stare at Oren and Max at the same time.

The entire scene played out again as Max watched in horror. The smile grew bigger, stretching beyond the confines of the man's face as he beckoned Young Oren over to the fence.

Max should have jumped in and strangled the Smiling Man. He should have forced him to get away. He knew what kind of monster he was. But that same force that drove Max toward the door now paralyzed him and forced him to watch it all again.

"Do you want someone to play ball with?" the stranger asked.

"Maybe," Oren said, sounding uncertain.

"I know a great park to play baseball in." The smile grew.

Max fought against his invisible shackles. *Get away from him.*

"Come on," the stranger urged. "I'll drive us."

The sky darkened.

"Hop in."

A bolt of lightning erupted on the horizon, but it didn't disappear. It just became suspended in the sky. Pieces of other memories began to drift past like clouds. Newspaper clippings talked about missing persons and kidnappers. Articles and pieces of research from Oren's life were falling out of his memory and stamping themselves in the sky.

"You can have shotgun."

"I'm not allowed to ride in the front," Oren said.

"I won't tell."

Max strained, trying to at least open his jaw, trying to shout. The man's smile grew into a sun-blocking monstrosity again. The eclipse pushed them into twilight, yet the air felt stale and hot. Young Oren stared at the smile in a trance. Max felt his restraints ease, just enough, and he began to shout. He tried to warn Oren. *Hey!!*

"Hey!!" His voice. Only more shrill. Higher-pitched. But the same words he mouthed now. "You shouldn't talk to strangers."

Max still couldn't move, but he darted his eyes off to the right. The voice—his voice—had come from that direction. To his great surprise, he saw himself standing on the other side of the street, staring across at Oren and at the Smiling Man. But it was himself almost thirty years ago. Max, just a kid, missing two front teeth with skinned knees and a mop of hair.

He hadn't watched this far last time he was here. This was the rest of it. This was how it ended.

"Well, hello," the Smiling Man said, trying to turn his enormous pearly whites on Young Max.

But it didn't work. Max crossed the street, looking fearless. As a kid, he was always playing outside and challenging boundaries. He wondered when he had started to become more cautious, more practical.

"We aren't supposed to talk to strangers," Young Max repeated. He spoke with confidence, as if he was an authority on the subject.

He had no idea what the actual danger was, not yet. Max was just a smart-ass who felt it was his business to tell people what to do. He parroted the lessons he remembered from school about strangers.

Though Max did not remember this exact day, he and Oren had been friends since a young age. They were neighbours as far back as Max could recall. He wondered if this was the day they had met.

"Well, I'm not a stranger," the Smiling Man tried, but he was already shrinking. He took a step back toward his vehicle.

"My mom is inside." Max pointed back at his house.

The Smiling Man looked wounded. He held out his hands in a show of innocence.

"We're just playing. No need to be scared."

"Mom!" Max called out now.

The Smiling Man's smile shriveled like a deflating balloon, all the way back to a normal size. He took another step away. The sky brightened.

Oren just watched, mouth open, as this new boy crossed the street.

"Where's your mom?" Max asked him.

Oren stared back at Max, not answering.

"Well, she should've taught you not to talk to strangers."

He was such an annoying kid. He remembered now, being a bit of a brat. An overconfident know-it-all. But that little brat had just prevented a nightmare from happening.

To Oren, this was a safely guarded memory that was tucked behind an unmarked door in the shadows of his mind. Max thought back to how standoffish Oren had seemed when Max had stumbled upon this memory in his first dive back home. It broke Max's heart to think that Oren was ashamed of this, and that he had never told Max the truth about that day. He wondered why.

It was an origin story. Not just for Oren and Max, but for the career Oren would pursue. It should have been no surprise, Max realized, that Oren was so committed to finding missing persons. This traumatic close encounter would have sparked something inside him.

And yet, to Max, this day was nothing. He hadn't even remembered it himself. To him, Oren had sort of always been there. He never remembered that first encounter. How often did one remember the start of something, especially when they didn't know it was the start of something?

This day was small, forgettable for Max. But for Oren, it was everything.

"Let's play ball in my yard," Max said. "I have a better ball than that anyway."

Oren looked down at his ball, feeling a bit embarrassed at the tattered seams, and sauntered over toward Max's yard.

The Smiling Man hadn't even gone back to his vehicle. He just vanished. He was now powerless. He was now as insignificant as this memory had been to Max. Just an ordinary day, full of summer sun, passing the ball with a friend, accented by the smell of freshly-cut grass.

No strangers. No monsters.

A crack of thunder shook the memory. Both boys jerked their heads up. They had sensed something was wrong. They stared at the sky now, fully alert soldiers of Oren's mind. This was a reenactment, and the thunder was not part of the script. The sky was fracturing, more images appearing in the clouds. None of this belonged. Neither did adult Max, and they turned their eyes on him.

They seemed to expect an explanation.

"I'm sorry," Max said, ignoring his younger self and addressing only Oren. "I'm not even sure what for. I guess, for everything."

Oren's eyes were glossy and metallic, the all-knowing orbs of the SI.

"I wish I could've stopped it." Max fought back tears. "But I *will* stop him. I just want you to know that. I'm going to stop him. I'm going to save Nelly."

There was a pause as they stared at one another. Max imagined he could see recognition in Oren's mercurial eyes, but then thunder rippled across the sky again, and both boys became distracted.

"Goodbye, Oren," Max said.

Then he turned quickly, aware of the urgency. He made for the door to his childhood home at a full sprint.

Taking a second to wipe away the tears that had fully formed, he grabbed at the knob.

\*\*\*

He was in that damned hallway again. The doors lining either side stretched into infinity. Max cast a glance back to the living room, but Oren and Scott were no longer there. The light snow that had been falling outside was now a downpour of freezing rain.

Max started running down the hall, not sure where to go next. He felt like he wasn't quite done. There was a force guiding him in the Cuckoo's Nest. That force had brought him back to the day he and Oren met, forced him to watch the entire encounter. It was trying to show him something. Max was confident this same force would tell him what door to try next.

Max continued running, the end of this space never materializing. He could have just kept going forever. Nothing around him ever changed. The charge in the air was peaking. He now received a tiny jolt every time his foot touched the ground. At last, he felt something stop him; a cold, hard hand pressed against his chest. Max was winded but progressed no further.

Motion caught his eye. There was a cat on the ground, looking up at him. It grew disinterested rather quickly and then darted for the door on the right. The door was ajar, and the cat squeezed its way inside. Max knew he was meant to follow.

One more time, he went through the door.

\*\*\*

Oren was upright and running, nothing like the still, mangled knot that had been left in the snow at the farmhouse. Max had to sidestep suddenly, as he realized Oren was running in his direction and not slowing down. They were in a narrow alley, and there wasn't much room.

"Move, move, move!" Oren shouted.

Max obliged, making himself as skinny as possible. He saw the sweat on Oren's forehead as he brushed past him. Oren motored on, pumping his arms furiously. He looked like an action movie hero; with incredible form, he sliced a path through the alley. Soon, he was gone.

Max cast a quick glance at the sky, yet there didn't appear to be one.

The only thing that kept him here was the sense that he was not done. There was still something to find. The spreading depression was close; Max could hear the swirling of all the sounds Oren had ever heard, growing like a siren in the distance. He could not see it yet, so he prayed that he would have enough time.

He took off running after Oren. In the real world, he wouldn't stand a chance. This version of him, however, was leaner and travelled very quickly on foot.

He came to the end of the alley, around the corner from where Oren had disappeared, and he realized they were now on a crowded street.

"Stop!" Oren shouted after someone.

There appeared to be a chase, but Max couldn't determine who they were after. There appeared to something or someone running, always a step ahead of

Oren. But this figure wasn't fully there, appearing only as a phantom.

They were on a downtown street, but the businesses all around them were nondescript. The buildings nearby only stood a few stories high, but further along, Max could see skyscrapers and cranes, new construction climbing toward the heavens.

The street was packed, providing hurdles for Oren and the unseen figure he was chasing. Max did his best to keep up, at first not even realizing what they were dodging. It wasn't taxis, or cyclists, or pedestrians. The objects in their way were people, for the most part, but not ones that belonged in this memory. Their shapes were jagged and hazy. It was as if they were cut out from a magazine and then pasted here like a child's school project.

Men in uniform served as pallbearers, solemnly holding an anonymous coffin as they marched up the sidewalk. They were spattered with rain, yet the rest of the street was dry.

An elderly woman sitting in a chair was crocheting, right in the middle of the road.

An entire youth football team was huddled up near a fire hydrant, quickly breaking huddle and spreading out, blocking Max's path until he could squeeze between two of the children.

Max saw himself on that street as well. To his embarrassment, this version of him was yelling and chastising Oren about being a failure.

Oren's memories had all congregated in the street, a block party for his dying mind.

Shapes in the sky were merging too. Where the skyscrapers had been, mountains now formed. Some buildings became famous landmarks—the Eiffel Tower, for instance.

Up ahead, Oren was nearing another bend in the street. The phantom he chased had already rounded the corner. Max tried to move faster, cutting in front of a group of teenagers wearing bowling shoes and cheering for something that was happening elsewhere.

Then Max saw Charlie. He was standing, studiously with his hand to his chin, looking at something Max couldn't see. The same cat from the hallway was here again, and it hopped up onto Charlie's shoulder, perching there and watching Max run. The name *Domino* floated through Max's mind.

A cluster of cows wandered into the street as Max was distracted, and he had to pivot to avoid crashing into them. This hectic obstacle course continued all the way down the street, and as Max rounded the corner where Oren and the phantom had gone, he saw this laneway congested with even more misplaced characters.

Oren was still running, already halfway down the road toward a three-storey parking structure. A rock band performed for a crowd of no one beside a dumpster on the left. A little further down, Max spotted Aria grabbing a slice of pizza, seemingly occupying the same space as a lamppost—a glitch.

Max had to remind himself that this wasn't real as he forced his lungs to swallow down gulps of air, pumping his false legs as fast as he could. Oren chased the phantom through the large gaping mouth of the parking structure. As Max himself neared the structure, he saw there was an attendant standing at the entrance. But the attendant appeared as Jack Nicholson's character from *The Shining*, one of Oren's favourite films.

A sudden whoosh of air and the sound of screeching tires made Max flinch. He pulled his arms toward his face in cowardice, freezing as he looked to the source of the noise. Two bright lights were flying toward him, and he braced for impact.

But it never came.

Archie's orange jeep was suspended in the air beside him. Max relaxed, watching as the jeep thrust itself into reverse and completed its loop over again. It was soaring through the air on repeat, an ominous fragment of Oren's last memory.

Max moved on from this fright and continued to the garage. Ignoring Jack the attendant, he crossed into the shadow. Here the world became Monster Putt again. Max's father watched as he continued his pursuit. Dracula and Frankenstein were taunting him. Glow-in-the-dark golf balls seemed to drop from the ceiling and bounce across the floor, pelting Max.

The giant glowing clown's face stood as the only way out, and Max saw Oren and the phantom pass through its mouth on their way back out into the daylight. Laughter—chiding and evil—peppered Max's ears, growing louder the closer he came. Then, popping out from the ground, came the Smiling Man. Of course, it had to be the Smiling Man.

His warped grin already inflating back to a preposterous size, he blocked Max's way forwards.

"Do you want someone—" he started to ask, but then his voice transformed, becoming Oren's. "I need you Max. You can lucid dream. Dive, Max. Dive."

Max knew he was meant to be afraid but didn't have time to feel anything. He pushed past the Smiling Man, his frame surprisingly light. Then he moved on through the clown's gaping mouth.

Max was back on a crowded street, the sun bearing down, immeasurably hot. On the horizon—marked now with skyscrapers that constantly jittered, changing location—Max could see the spreading depression coming. Electric claws scratched across the sky, devouring everything.

Beside Max, there was a bang, and he shifted his gaze in time to see the phantom figure, with its nondescript features, bump into a trash can. He dipped to one knee, then got up and kept running. Oren was right behind him, and he didn't stumble. This was peak Oren: strong, athletic, and fast. He looked like a cheetah about to pounce on his prey.

The chase had led them to a bistro on the corner, with a green awning protecting patrons from the sun as they dined at patio tables beside the busy street. They all seemed oblivious to the world ending around them.

Oren sprung forwards, knocking the phantom to the ground. The two of them fell hard, skidding across the hot pavement, their momentum only stopping when they collided with a set of tables and chairs. Patrons shrieked and fled the scene. Chairs were overturned, glasses broke, and nearby cars came to a halt to rubberneck at the chaos.

The phantom struggled, rolling beneath Oren. He now had a gun in his hand and was trying to aim it. The two battled back and forth, and eventually the gun went off, fired into the sky. The gunshot left a trail behind it, tracing a line through the world and revealing a different memory beneath it. Through the thin line in the sky, Max could see the faint images of Oren and Scott in the chalet.

The phantom tried to aim again, but Oren knocked the gun free, and it skittered away. Oren pinned the man down hard, and with great strength, he was able to get the man's arms behind his back and cuff them. People applauded as backup arrived, police cruisers surrounding the bistro. Their sirens weren't right, however; the sound seemed to be melting.

Oren stood, the man restrained at last.

Max was curious to see who it was that Oren had been wrestling with. But a crowd had formed, all trying to get a look at the action. The man was face down. Three headless deputies and Oren stood over him.

"We'll take it from here," one Deputy told Oren, though Max wasn't sure how he spoke.

Max drifted closer, pushing through the crowd.

The deputies bent over and grabbed the phantom, flipping him over to reveal his face.

It was Archie.

Memories were merging. Oren's mind had pulled Archie into something from a long time ago. The slow, dying sirens from the police cruisers became music, like an old record spinning just a little too slow.

Now the former sheriff spoke to them, words that Max had heard recently.

"No one listens to this anymore," Archie said, his eyes unfocused, his body cuffed and lying on the ground. "But thankfully, the station is still on the air. An old fella like me out in Fairfield runs it from his garage. Just keeps the thing running."

Max was hearing this for a reason. It was a clue. Oren's mind, even as it died, was helping Max figure out what to do next. There was a radio station that no one listened to. Yet Archie never went anywhere without listening to these old songs. Oren needed him to know this.

Max looked over at Oren's SI. This proud, athletic version of Oren was the one that he should always remember. Oren was looking back at him, the metallic eyes fully aware of Max's presence.

"It'll be okay," Oren said. It wasn't a part of the memory. He was speaking to Max.

Max got chills. After the shock wore off, he tried to answer.

"What?"

"I trust you," Oren said. Then he turned away.

Oren's frame shifted. He became older, dressed now in winter attire. He began to act out some other memory altogether.

The electricity in the air was overbearing. It pressed itself against the sides of Max's head. The entire world hummed.

The cast of misfits were still in the street. Oren's parents, friends, and colleagues, all strewn across the pavement in various poses, interspersed with an actor or a band that he liked at some point in time. Buildings shifted, afraid to hold still, some becoming mountains or trees. The parking facility behind them turned into the farmhouse where Oren had died, and a gust of snow flew in from the same direction. Despite the heat, the snow landed on the ground and formed a drift.

"Goodbye," Max said again.

The ground began to shake. The tidal wave closed in. Max didn't look up, but he knew it was there. In a matter of seconds, everything would be erased.

"Sweet Caroline" joined the cacophony as every sound Oren had ever heard released itself from his brain. Smells and flavours toppled down from the sky.

Max shut his eyes. The noise was awful. The pain in his head seared at his temples, and bolts of lightning struck his limbs. But he forced himself to remain in the darkness.

All of the animals, celebrities, family members, bad guys and good guys, were consumed then as the world succumbed to the electrical tsunami. Everything was gone; Oren's mind shut down. But Max pulled himself out just in time.

\*\*\*

"What the shit?!" Landry shouted. He was scared less so than angry. His voice cracked. He was still keeping half an eye on the shadows in the nearby structures.

Max awoke with a face full of snow again. He pulled the MemCom from his ear. Oren's body was still in front of him and seeing it this way again—after having just spoken to him, so full of life—made Max's stomach turn.

"What just happened to you?" Landry asked. "What is that thing?"

He high-stepped over to Max, still with his gun pointed at the chicken coops. But he held out an arm to help Max up. Max accepted it and was tugged to his feet. Now, standing face to face, Landry looked at the device in Max's hand.

"What . . ." Landry squinted. "I've seen that before somewhere."

"It's a MemCom," Max admitted.

"A . . ." Landry was starting to understand. The gears in his mind were turning, recalling what he knew of this device.

"Call Sanderson," Max said. "We have to go get Nelly before Archie does."

"What? You just passed out. Fell into the snow. Left me here in this fucking place. Thought I had two bodies on my hands."

Max didn't have time to explain. Archie would be desperate, knowing they were on to him. He was woozy, but Max pushed his way past Landry, heading for the truck.

"Do you have a radio?"

"Of course, I do," Landry said, fumbling on his belt and pulling his radio away.

"No, not that," Max said. "Like . . . FM radio. We need to tune into a station."

"In the truck . . . but . . . what are you talking about?"

"We are going to rescue Nelly."

"We don't even know where she is," Landry protested.

"I'm about to find out," Max said.

He pulled open the passenger door. He reached over to the centre console and turned on the radio. It took him a moment to scan and find the same old radio station Archie liked. Outdated music played over outdated technology.

Max was exhausted, these dives having drained him. He had lived so many more hours over the course of this day than anyone else in Ruston. Or in the world, for that matter. But he steeled himself for one more try, gathering up whatever strength he had left. He knew this last dive would be the most important.

It was dangerous. Almost impossible. *The equivalent of a great bank heist,* Max thought. The kind of thing Oren would say would never work but then would go along with anyway.

Who knew how far away Archie was by now. But Max figured there was a pretty good chance that the radio in his jeep was still on and still tuned into this station. And with so few other listeners—according to Archie—Max figured he had at least a slight chance that Archie's was the closest mind dialled into the same song. A slight chance of making this work. And a slight chance was all he wanted.

There was a possibility he'd end up in the wrong mind. He'd encountered that already. But he wasn't sure what happened if an attempted dive didn't find *any* target. He pushed these thoughts away.

"I'm going to pass out for a few seconds again," Max warned through the open truck door. "When I'm back—" *Or if I come back* "—I'll know where Nelly is. I'll know where Archie is."

"That thing lets you read minds," Landry said as though still trying to catch up. He still clutched his gun close, in awe of Max and the device in his hands. "It's the whatchamacallit . . ."

"Yes," Max said. "Call Sanderson, call for help. You probably won't even have time to explain before I'm back. Then we need to go. Fast."

The radio was playing a scratchy old track with rich vocals. It sounded like a duet.

"You can't be listening to the same thing I am," Max said. He crawled into the truck fully now. "Don't open the door, no matter what. And back away, to be safe. I'll be right back." He shut the door, leaving Landry dumbfounded.

*Please work,* Max thought. He readied the earpiece, listening to the woman on the track hold a long note. He imagined himself dressed all in black, repelling down the side of a tall building, Hollywood's version of a bank robber. The perfect heist.

In real life, though, he was just sitting in a truck, listening to a song.

He pushed the button.

# 16. The Worst Kind of Monster

RELIEF WASHED OVER MAX AS he realized he wasn't dead. He had landed somewhere. But the relief was quickly replaced with fear when he realized he was drowning.

The long-distance dive had worked, though Max had no idea whose mind he was in. Determining this would prove difficult, too. He found himself completely submerged. His lungs ached for air, but he couldn't find any. His vision was reduced to a blue haze. Something burned bright overhead, the sun, but he was ten feet below the surface. And the water was ice cold, pressing down on him and sending spikes of freezing pain through his limbs.

Bubbles streamed in front of his face as the person with him tried to scream. It was a boy. A kid of only four or five years was floating in the icy abyss, a look of horror chiseled on his icy face.

The boy was bundled up in a snowsuit that was dragging him slowly deeper. His arms grabbed out in front of him for help that wasn't there. His face had lost all colour. The water pulled him down as he struggled. Light was fading, everything becoming a shadow of itself.

Max's first instinct was to help the boy. And he kicked a few times to try and swim closer. But he quickly remembered what he was doing and where he was. He couldn't save this kid. This child's fate was already determined. And if this was a memory, and the boy was the only one here, that meant that his fate was—

The stillness of the water was disrupted, ripples and waves shaking Max from his thought. Someone else had entered their small cone of blue haze. An older boy, a teen, dressed only in pants, had plunged into this icy hell, arms outstretched in perfect diving form. The teen kicked twice, making quick ground toward the drowning boy. This teen glowed like a superhero from an action film, appearing larger than life. Of course, a child's mind would remember his saviour this way.

The Super Teen wrapped an arm around the drowning boy and yanked him up. The kid seemed to rise with ease. Super Teen hugged the kid tight and made for the surface. Max spotted a small hole in the ceiling of this place, a hole in the ice where they both had likely entered.

They ascended, and Max's imaginary lungs began to scream. He needed to breathe, so he pumped his legs and followed them up. His arms shot into the air, and he dragged himself up onto the ice. Max's face stung as cold air met his soaked skin, but the oxygen was sweet.

Super Teen had already emerged and crawled onto a thicker part of the ice. He had the drowning boy laid in his arms and was pounding his back, the boy spitting up water and hacking. Max wrapped his arms around his body, watching them and wondering whether he could die from hypothermia in someone else's thoughts.

"What were you doing out on the ice?" Super Teen asked, the drowning boy finally slowing his coughing to a manageable pace. "It's not safe here. Where are your parents?"

The no-longer-drowning boy looked up at his hero. Super Teen fit the part with his chiseled jaw and strong, corded arms. All he was missing was the cape.

The boy, his face still colourless and his hair pressed flat against his forehead, craned his head over to the shoreline. They were on what appeared to be a lake, frozen over but for the space where the child fell through.

On the one side, bracketed by naked trees, was a towering black structure. This building had spires that climbed so high into the sky that they seemed to break through the clouds. The spires spiralled and twisted on the way up, defying gravity with their sheer mass. The walls of this dark palace were so purely black that all light was absorbed by the surface. Max couldn't tell what it was made of. The only detail that stood out against the blackness was a large, silver gate.

"Is that your home?" Super Teen asked, pointing at the haunting towers. Super Teen didn't seem disturbed at all by the warped and unnatural spires. This building looked like an architectural collaboration between Dr. Seuss and Stephen King. Max figured it had to be embellished by the young boy. Nothing in the real world looked this way.

The no-longer-drowning boy did not get a chance to answer.

A deep howl rose from within the dark palace, reaching them with impossible volume. As a low, grumbling voice started to speak, a pair of red eyes appeared behind the castle's gate.

"Come home now, boy," it said.

Max felt the bass of this voice in his feet. The ice threatened to crack and send them all into the lake again.

The voice continued, so heavy that its sentences were drawn out. "Look what you've done . . . Falling through the ice . . . Shame on you . . . Get inside and tell your father what you've done."

The red eyes stared out from behind the bars, unblinking. The boy quivered and shrank back into his rescuer. Super Teen seemed painfully naive. He stood up, dragging the boy to his feet with him.

"Your mother is calling," Super Teen said with a smile.

He started walking the young boy back to the dark castle, unaware that he was guiding this child to a pair of evil, crimson eyes.

As they approached, a hand reached out from the metal bars, beckoning them closer. The nails were long and chipped, and the skin was greyer than the ice water.

"Come home . . . Archie," the echoing voice said.

Max privately celebrated. *That boy is Archie.* He was in the right spot. It had worked after all; he had managed to travel a great distance into a mind using a radio of all things. Max allowed himself a brief moment of satisfaction before returning to the task at hand. He needed to find the right memories now and guide them to Nelly.

Except, the only door in this memory was the one from which the red eyes stared.

The only way out was through that castle gate.

Super Teen walked Young Archie back to this hellish home, and Max jogged to catch up. Their walk was the slow death march of someone in a bad dream, every step seeming to take them no closer to their destination. This was good; Max wanted to get there first. He had no desire to see the outcome of this memory.

Super Teen was losing his glow. He shrank into the normal size for a boy his age. The hero complex was evaporating now that Young Archie was feeling betrayed.

Max overtook them quickly. He ran at a normal speed, leaving them in their nightmare crawl. He made his way up the slope to the base of the castle. The building grew even darker as he approached. The red eyes did not move. They just stared straight ahead, hand still beckoning.

"You better let me in, you bitch," Max huffed, gasping for cold air.

The twisted hand withdrew into the blackness. The metal bars climbed slowly, revealing a pair of feet— waxy, dead, with talons for toenails.

Max ducked his head, not wanting to see the owner of these terrifying appendages. The gate was just high enough that he could dip underneath. He took a few last shuffling steps and then slid on his knees, kicking up snow as he went. He shut his eyes as he passed through the door, praying that he wouldn't see anything but imagining what face must have been looking down at him in the dark.

Nothing happened. And then suddenly, it was bright.

\*\*\*

"You were lucky to even get one." A man in a crisp, black suit was standing outside a large truck trailer in a parking lot.

Behind them was the Ruston Police Station. A few pale streetlights came to life as the world dipped into night. Max watched things unfold from relative safety; he found himself on the far side of the parking lot. The air was cool but not cold; spring instead of winter.

Archie was there too, looking a little more like the old man Max recognized. His hair wasn't quite as greyed yet, but the rest seemed to fit. He wore the same sheriff outfit that Landry normally adorned.

"I just don't understand." Archie had his arms crossed.

Two faceless men in overalls appeared. They were each holding an end of a large machine, about the size of a table. The machine had exposed wires coiled and strapped to its side. It was partially covered in a glistening, white paint. A small monitor extended from the top, and one of the men carrying it kept whacking his chin against the screen. The men hauled the heavy beast up a ramp into the trailer. Several similar machines, along with countless boxes and crates, already sat inside.

"People don't want folks creeping around in their heads," the man in the suit said. "Especially the police."

"So, they're just going to destroy them all?" Archie asked.

"Not my call." The man in the suit shrugged. "I'm just supposed to repo them all, take them home."

"They don't understand how important these machines are," Archie argued.

"Like I said, not my call." The repo man lit a cigarette. "This Octopus unit you've got wasn't much good anyway. It malfunctioned all the time. They were a bitch to hook people up to. Be thankful you didn't have one of the nicer, newer units. The folks we took those away from bawled like babies."

The men were dropping the unit in between others of its kind in the truck now, and they were not being very careful either. They let it topple sideways, and the screen cracked. Archie flinched.

"Who was your diver?" The repo man exhaled smoke in Archie's direction.

"Me." Archie's voice was small.

"No shit." The repo man chuckled. "You can use the thing? Well, that's a first. Most places had to bring in a special officer just to use it. Not a lot of folks had the ability. Think you're the first sheriff I met that could use it too."

"Well, I was lucky, I guess," Archie moped, staring at his stolen machine as if his child were being taken away from him.

"Get to use it much?" The repo man was amused. "See anything good?"

"A few times. It's pretty quiet around here."

"Ah, right. See, you won't miss it anyway."

The repo man patted Archie on the back then and tossed his cigarette aside. He whistled to his two faceless drones and started wandering back to the station doors.

"We just gotta check your files," he said without turning around. "Make sure you weren't keeping any MemCom data. Won't take long."

"Okay."

Archie watched them head back inside the station. As soon as they were gone, his head snapped back to the truck. He clenched his hands into tight balls. Max could tell already what he was planning on doing.

Archie sprinted up the ramp into the truck's trailer. Before he went fully inside, he checked the station doors. No movement. Next, he rushed over to the machine, squatted next to it, and tried to lift. It was a struggle for one person, so he fumbled it back into the pile of machines and broken parts. It made a loud sound, glass breaking at the bottom of the pile, and he cringed.

Max glanced back toward the station. No one seemed to notice.

Archie tried again, and he was surprisingly strong for his age. He was able to lift the machine off the pile just long enough to get it free of the debris. Then he started to drag it. He held one end in both arms, the other scraping across the trailer floor. The sound was awful, but Archie didn't stop. Cables came unspooled and dragged behind the machine, flopping about like serpents.

He reached the ramp and stumbled, moving a little too quickly. Archie toppled over and lost his grip on the machine. It slid down the ramp after him, crashing to the pavement. The screen gained another crack, but surprisingly, the thing was mostly still intact.

There was still no movement at the station doors, but Archie kept eying them suspiciously. He knew he didn't have long. He got to his feet and continued dragging the machine. He brought it over to where Max stood. A row of low bushes decorated the side of the lot.

Max kept himself from view as Archie brought the Octopus unit across the pavement and stashed it in these bushes. It was a poor job, but since it was dark out, someone would need to be looking for it to notice.

Finally, the repo man and his drones reemerged from the station. Archie tried to walk toward them at a casual pace. But then, his foot struck something.

There was a green cable lying on the ground. It had fallen off the machine in the chaos. Archie bent quickly to scoop it up and tossed it off into the bushes just as the repo man started to speak.

"Seems we're all good." The repo man came over to Archie and offered his hand.

Archie shook it.

"Thanks for your cooperation. See? Told you it would be painless."

"Yeah," Archie said. He was stiff, trying not to look back to the bushes.

The repo man didn't notice anything amiss. The drones closed up the truck without even looking inside. The pile of machines and parts was so dense that Max doubted they would ever notice that thing was even missing. Unless they took inventory, maybe, but Max hadn't gotten a sense that this repo man was that committed to his work.

"Hey, at least you got to use the thing a few times," he said with a smirk as he headed toward the truck's cabin.

One of his drones opened the door for him.

"Most people never even got to try it. So long, Sheriff."

The truck roared to life, and Max was reminded to move on. He could imagine how this would unfold anyway. Archie would bring his vehicle around, load the machine into it, and get away with keeping an old Octopus model MemCom when the rest of the world was destroying theirs.

Max made sure to stay out of Archie's peripherals as he slinked toward the station doors. This was one SI he didn't want to cross.

The station doors opened easily, welcoming Max to the next corner of Archie's mind.

*** 

A scream pierced the air. Its force frightened Max.

"Quit your whining," Archie's voice answered.

Spots of colour that started as vague blobs began to take shape. Natalya Romano was lying on her back on a bed of straw. He could tell it was Natalya Romano by the tattoo on her leg. She was dressed in the same t-shirt and shorts that she was found in, hanging in the motel room.

The poor girl's face was marked with terror; her eyes were wide, and her forehead was slick with sweat, pale as a ghost. Her jaw was locked in a never-ending scream, even when she ran out of breath.

Archie was lying in the straw bed too, about six feet away from Natalya. They appeared to be in a barn. The walls were plain wood boards. They lay in a medium-sized stall that may have once held horses within the larger, empty structure.

Nat screamed again— an absolutely bloodcurdling sound. She tried to cover her face, but her arms were shackled, bound with chains and wires that all traced back to a large machine. The Octopus. Natalya was hooked up to the junky old MemCom unit that Archie had stolen off the truck.

*Is this what you're doing to all those girls?* Max kept himself hidden, out of the glow of the overhead bulb that swayed casually, the light ever moving. He forced himself to watch—to learn—though he already wanted to leave.

"I said shut up," Archie snapped. He got to his feet and kicked a bunch of straw toward Natalya. "Unless you want me to go back in there."

"No, no more." Nat forced the words out.

"Well then, keep your mouth shut. I'm done for the day."

The green and yellow and red cables that spiralled out from the giant MemCom—the tentacles of the Octopus—eventually ended in a needle. That needle was stuck in Nat's right arm like an IV. Her other arm was clamped down with a metal brace, affixed to a chain, and tethered to the MemCom unit. A thick, orange cable also snaked its way through the hay toward Nat, this one plugged into her ear.

At the far end of the stall, Archie had removed his attachment to the machine. A similar multicoloured cord of wires came his way, but these ones were linked to a headset. Thick goggles and headphones were connected to a plastic dome, similar to a helmet. Archie held this in his arms now, threatening to use it again. Nat's eyes watched the helmet in horror.

Archie placed the helmet down in the straw and walked over to Nat. She cringed as he approached, though she could not move away from him. He bent over and pulled the needle from her arm. She cried out. Archie ignored her and then set about coiling up the stretch of wires. He removed a wrench from his belt, tightening some parts that were a mystery to Max.

As he set about tending to his beloved machine— taking the time to fold the cables neatly while the girl next to it sobbed in the hay—Nat started to gather herself. Her one arm was now free, and she was clenching her fist, watching Archie while forming a plan.

Archie finished cleaning up. He set the wrench down in the straw momentarily while he crouched down to open a compartment at the bottom of the machine. Nat struck.

She flailed out with her free arm and grabbed the wrench. Then she pulled herself up into a seated position, which was awkward because her one arm was still stuck. She had just enough leash to swing the wrench at Archie.

The blow wasn't as forceful as it could have been; her seated position prevented her from making proper contact. The wrench struck Archie in the back. He cursed and turned around, face red with rage.

Archie snarled at Natalya and smacked the wrench free from her hand.

"You're going to pay for that," Archie said. He retrieved another chain with a cuff on the end of it and brought it over, shackling Natalya's free arm. "For that, we're going to do a bonus session."

"No, please," Natalya wailed, part scream and part sob.

Archie went about undoing all of his work, taking the cables back out and stretching them over to his victim.

Max watched, studying the way he did his work. He noticed the chain that was tethering Natalya was wrapped around a large stake in the ground. It would have been possible for Natalya to fling the chain upwards, sort of like a skipping rope, and get the chain to come off the stake. It wasn't tied down. But it required a specific way of pulling on the bindings, and when Archie came over to her, Natalya panicked, struggling against the chain and pulling horizontally instead of vertically. There was no way she could've known this, Max realized, because she was stuck facing one direction with her restraints behind her head.

Natalya tried to break free but couldn't, so Archie was able to once again insert the needle into her left arm with little resistance. She protested, begged, but he ignored her. The old sheriff just walked back over to his helmet at the far end of the stall.

"Where should we visit this time?" Archie asked.

"Please, no more, stop." Natalya trembled.

"Maybe something from school?"

"No, no, no."

"You're right, we've done that before." Archie lifted the helmet and started adjusting the tether.

"Stop."

"Let's do something new," Archie said, placing the goggles over his eyes. "Go somewhere we've never been."

"No more! No!" Natalya yelled with all the energy left in her body.

Max felt her fear. He had no idea what Archie was doing inside the girl's mind, what kinds of torment could be administered from within one's memory.

The rules were different in the MemCom. Obviously, Archie could inflict methods of torture not possible in the real world. The memory would be Archie's playground; with infinite time and no surveillance, there would be no limit to his evil. Archie would be in total control. Max watched with disgust, realizing that Archie was the worst kind of monster.

Max didn't care to ever find out what Archie used the MemCom for. He left his corner of the stall, making for the door. Max was getting closer to the answers, but he had more to uncover. He knew they were kept in a barn, but he just didn't know which one.

As Max crossed the barn, Archie stopped, looking at him. He was suddenly aware there was someone else here. Max picked up his pace, not giving Archie a chance to assess, and he exited the memory.

\*\*\*

Max now stood on a driveway where an elderly woman was standing beside Archie's iconic orange jeep. Archie himself was leaning casually against the hood. Behind the old woman was a lane that led back out to the highway. They were surrounded by a densely wooded area, but through the trees, Max could see a bright red barn. In the other direction, next to an open plot of land, was a tiny white farmhouse.

Max shimmied over behind the jeep so he wouldn't be spotted.

"You'd really be doing me a favour," the elderly woman said as she pulled a key ring from her purse. She dangled it out in front of her. "Minding the place is just too much work for these old bones, nowadays."

Archie had a bit more colour in his hair, and he stood a bit straighter. The sky was overcast, but the air was warm. The world was greener than the Ruston that Max was used to.

"Would be doing me a favour too, Ethel," Archie said as he grabbed the keys. "I've got plenty of things that don't fit in my place anymore. Could use that old barn for storage. So long as Mort don't mind me doing so."

"Oh, old Mort ain't likely to even know you're here." Ethel scrunched her nose and looked at the white house. "Old fart never leaves his house. His grandson comes up once in a while with groceries. But that's about all the traffic this place gets. Barn would be all yours. If you can shovel in the winter and mow in the summer, Mort and his son will leave ya alone."

"Really is a great trade then." Archie grinned. "I don't mind a little extra labour, now that I'm retired. Should keep me feeling young."

"Let me know how long that keeps up." Ethel chuckled. "Well, that barn was a beauty back in its day. Not much to it now. I think it's empty, save for a few space heaters. Handy if you want to do any work in there."

"Well, I can probably put those to good use," Archie said. "Nice to have a space to tinker in."

"Then I'm happy to hand over the keys," Ethel said. "Thanks, Sheriff."

"Not anymore," Archie reminded her, and they shared a laugh.

*Mort. Red barn. White house.* Max wondered if this was enough to go on. Surely, in a small place like Ruston, Landry would know what this place was. That quaint little red building in the trees would become the scene of Archie's atrocities. Max was sure of it. Now he just had to make sure they could get there in time.

Max was about to shut his eyes and pull himself from the memory when he noticed how quiet it had gotten.

He turned back to Archie and the old woman, and noticed they were both looking right at him.

"There's someone behind your jeep," Ethel said.

"You're the same one from the barn." Archie moved ahead quickly, treating Max like a rodent he wanted out of his house. "What are you doing in my mind?"

Max had to run. He made for the farmhouse on the other end of the field. It was closer than the barn.

"I know you're spying on me," Archie's voice bellowed across the field.

And suddenly, the ground rose up. The dirt and grass flowed like waves in the ocean, all matter now breaking apart and changing.

The waves knocked Max to his feet, making it impossible to get away.

"I know what you're doing. Get out of my head."

Archie was no longer behind Max. Now, he stood in front of him, blocking the way to the farmhouse. The trees that lined the property were growing, stretching into the sky, their branches becoming hands that reached for him, trying to throw him out of the memory like bouncers at a bar.

Archie's eyes were swirling, and that familiar molten stare bore holes in Max as the squeal of alarm rose up from the earth. The sound felt like it was splitting Max's head open.

He covered his ears but didn't look away from Archie. And Max was smiling. Because he knew why this memory was so angry, why the trees and the earth and Archie were all trying to intimidate him. And Max wasn't afraid.

Archie was the one who should be afraid.

"We're coming for you," Max told Archie.

The trees flailed, trying to grab hold of Max. Archie's eyes were boiling out of his head. The sky darkened, and everything began to shrink.

But Max didn't notice any of this. He had shut his eyes again, now confident in what he was doing. He let things melt down around him. He was getting out. And he was going to stop this monster.

\*\*\*

"I don't have time for any more questions!" Landry was shouting with urgency from outside the truck. "Just get on the road and head out east. I'll call you back when I know more." Landry glanced over and saw that Max was awake. "Jesus, he's back. Hang on, he's awake again."

Max pushed open the door, realizing he didn't have much strength yet.

"Mort . . ." Max said, each breath a challenge. "Does that name mean anything to you? Old man with a red barn and a white house."

Right away, there was recognition in Landry's eyes. He locked in on Max.

"That's Mort Grey's place," Landry said, then repeated it into his phone. "Mort Grey's place. Meet us there. And call us some goddamn backup while you're headed over. This is the real fucking deal."

Landry hung up and sprinted to the truck. Max crawled over to the passenger side, allowing Landry the driver's seat.

Max was nauseous. He felt himself shaking, weak from living several days in the span of a few seconds.

"You sure about this?" Landry asked as he started the engine and hammered the gas.

"There's a red barn," Max said. "They said it was Mort's property. Archie was looking after it. He stashed the girls there. Along with . . . some other stuff."

"And he'll be there now?"

"If he's keeping Nelly there, he'll be on his way," Max said. "We just have to hope he doesn't have time to do something to her before we get there."

\*\*\*

Sanderson was just pulling up himself as Landry and Max arrived at the long driveway into the red barn. The eastern horizon was a bluish grey that hinted at the sun's arrival. It had been a long night, and now dawn was taking over. Seeing the property in person, Max realized he knew this place from Tiffany's memory. There, the barn had been green. She was colour blind, and this had led them down the wrong path.

Landry threw the truck into park and leapt from his seat. Max reached for his winter gear, locating his cap but no gloves. *Did I leave them somewhere?* He was forced to step outside, hiding his hands in his pockets.

"Did you call the county?" Landry asked.

Sanderson nodded, rubbing sleep from his eyes.

Landry surveyed the farm. "No sign of the jeep. Maybe he didn't come here."

"We need to check the barn," Max said. "That's where he was keeping them."

"I think I ought to check in with Mort," Landry said, hand once again near his weapon. "See what he knows and get him to let us into the barn."

Sheriff Landry and Deputy Sanderson started walking over the packed snow that led to the white farmhouse.

"But what about . . ." Max trailed off, pointing at the barn uselessly.

"Stay put," Landry said. "Wait here until we've spoken with Mort."

"If Nelly is inside—"

"We'll get her." Landry shot Max a look that said, *I'm in charge here.* "Probably need the key from Mort anyway."

Max watched them go and then turned his attention to the barn. It wasn't more than thirty yards to his left. Nelly could be sitting right on the other side of that big red wall.

"What would you do, Oren?" Max asked to the silent twilight.

Knowing the answer, he marched himself toward the barn. Landry and Sanderson were far enough ahead, and they were focused on the house. They didn't even see him go.

He felt inflated by a courage he did not normally possess. This was the way Oren felt, or at least the way he acted, all the time. Max was just doing his best to make him proud. The courage extended beyond the moment, and Max felt inspired to pull out his phone, calling up his history with Janelle. He sent her a message that he should've sent ages ago.

*Dinner when I'm back?*

After he put his phone away, stashing his hands in his coat pockets to try and warm up, it dawned on him that he didn't have any means of protecting himself against whatever he found on the other side of the door.

He wondered if that should have deterred him. But it didn't.

Arriving at the barn, he tried the handle on the big sliding door. He put his entire weight into it, but the door didn't budge. *Fuck.* Landry was right. The door was locked. Max glanced back at the house. They were now just dark specks in the distance, approaching the front door. Max heard their knocks as muffled thumps across the snowy expanse.

Max tried the door one more time, but his back groaned and told him he had nothing left to give. His exhales rising in feverish trails, Max stepped back. There had to be another way in. He opted to make his away around the far side of the barn, where the building pressed against the encroaching woods.

The snow was deeper here, and his boots sank. Snow caked against his socks. As Max rounded the corner, scanning for a window or a side door, he noticed a large shape looking out of place against the trees. It would have been impossible to see from the front of the property, tucked purposefully behind trees and out of the way. Its orange paint didn't immediately register because the dawn was still too dark. Max could, however, make out the shape of the jeep.

The danger took half a second to register. But then Max's adrenaline kicked in, and it all became clear. Archie was here.

"Landry!" Max shouted, stumbling over his own boots as he tried to back up and race to the house.

He caught himself with a hand, bracing against the frosty side of the barn and scraping his palm. He left a handprint of blood in the snow as he rose and scurried back to the police truck.

Before he could round the corner, he heard the shots.

Two crisp gunshots reverberated across the open air. The echoes lingered long after the shock.

Max gasped, and then strode around the front of the barn, spotting the outline of the farmhouse on the horizon. The front door was now open; he could tell by the sliver of light that highlighted one side of the frame. There was a mass on the front porch, something lying motionless. What could have been an arm or a leg hung down from the top step. But there were no other signs of life.

Max debated his next move. Return to the truck and wait? Or rush to the house and try to help?

His decision was made for him when the voice called out.

It was muffled by the barn walls but unmistakable now that the gunshots had ceased their echoing.

"Help!" It was a scream, shrill and desperate.

Max looked at the barn doors helplessly. He willed them to open.

"Nelly?"

"Help me!"

Max rushed over. He pressed against the door, feeling powerless but trying to get as close as he could to comfort the girl imprisoned inside.

"Help is here," Max said. Then, as much for himself as for her, he added, "Don't worry."

"Please don't let him come back for me!" she cried through the door.

"I won't," Max promised.

He looked nervously back at the house. There was a crash, the sound of breaking glass, but no movement that he could see. The shadow on the front porch still hadn't moved.

"Can you open the door?"

"I'm tied up," Nelly said. "He keeps hurting me. Please make him stop."

"Try lifting the chains up," Max said, thinking back to what he saw in Archie's mind. "If you can kind of toss them over your head, they should lift off the post they're wrapped around. Think of it like a skipping rope. You can do it, Nelly. I'll try to get in somehow."

There was a brief moment of silence; Nelly was registering what he had said before she spoke again.

"He always uses the side door."

Max perked up. There was still no movement coming from the house. He thought he maybe heard a shout, or a grunt, but his ears had been ringing ever since the gunshots. He also thought he saw blood on the front porch. He wasn't sure he could trust his own senses, though.

"I'm coming," Max said.

He ran back around the far side of the barn, retracing his prints in the snow. He ran past the jeep this time and realized there was, in fact, a door. It was an average-sized door, perhaps even smaller than average. Max felt he may have to duck to guarantee he didn't smack his head. He tried the handle. The door gave, just a bit, but ultimately didn't open. He tried again, harder. It moved an inch but no further.

"It's locked too!" Max shouted, hoping Nelly could hear.

There was no answer.

Max threw his shoulder into the door, trying to re-create what he had seen in movies. It didn't work, and now his shoulder screamed with pain. He looked around, thinking there must be a hidden clue. All that appeared were the trees, the snow, and the jeep.

The jeep.

Max bolted for the vehicle. Halfway there, he heard another gunshot ring out. It startled him and sent him ducking momentarily. The pain in his palm and his shoulder had a chance to catch up to him, as did the cold in his hands and feet. He had to grit his teeth through the pain. The gunshot had come from the house again. He still had time.

Regaining his footing, Max continued on to the jeep. He tried the driver's door with his good hand. It opened. The overhead light came on and cast a yellow pallor over the seats. On the passenger side sat a key ring. It didn't just feel like luck. To Max, it just felt like part of a script. He was destined to grab the key ring off the seat and go rescue Nelly. He trudged back to the barn—slower now and sweating beneath his jacket.

Max held the key ring in his bloodied hand, using just his frozen thumb and forefinger, trying to keep anything from touching his multiple cuts and gouges. With his good hand, he began peeling apart the keys. There were seven in total. All the same size but for one small silver one.

He tried the small one first. It wasn't even close; it did not fit into the keyhole.

The next key slid in but didn't turn.

"Please help!" Nelly screamed again from inside.

Max wanted to console her, but he didn't dare speak. He had become worried at the lack of sound since the last gunshot.

Max tried the third key, struggling to get it away from its friends on the key ring. His hands shook, his vision blurred, and the cold was making his fingers useless. Same result. The key did not turn. He was beginning to feel like finding the keys wasn't good fortune at all. This was taking too long.

Still nothing but silence. Was the sky getting brighter? Or was he imagining it? He tried the fourth key. It didn't even fit in the lock. As he tried to move on to the next key, his shaky hands failed him, and the key ring slipped from his bloody grip. All seven keys plummeted into the snow.

Max cursed.

He bent over and retrieved them, but now the keys were covered in snow. They were wet. And cold. He used his shredded hand to brush them off, which stung like hell. Now he had no idea which keys he had already tried. Back to square one.

"Nelly, I'm coming," he said, trying to reassure himself.

"Please hurry!" her muffled cry came back.

Max tried a random key. It didn't fit. He moved on.

Everything was still. Max heard only his breathing and the squeal of his tinnitus. The ringing in his ears became a needle against his temples. The tone was so high, so piercing, that he felt his head might explode.

He tried another key. Wrong one.

He held his breath, trying to focus.

His heart pummeled the inside of his chest. Now, there was thumping from inside the barn. Perhaps, Nelly was banging, trying to get out. She could have been trying to get free of shackles or bindings. Or was it footsteps he heard? Max didn't dare take his gaze off the key as he tried to steady his hands and insert it into the lock. But it sounded a lot like footsteps. Crunching. It sounded like footsteps crunching against the snow.

The key slid in. Max turned it. To his relief, it rotated. The key turned, and there was a subtle click.

But now his mind flipped channels, and he realized he had definitely heard footsteps. He turned to the source of the sound, on his left.

Archie stood at the far corner of the barn, advancing through the snow. His hair stood on end, and a small dot of what might have been blood painted the left side of his forehead. He looked at Max with dark eyes. He was holding a gun.

Max stepped back, dropping to the ground as his legs went numb. His arms automatically went in front of his face.

The first shot missed. Archie fired high as Max fell. Reloading, he aimed lower and took another step forwards.

There was something crazy in Archie's eyes that Max had not registered before. He appeared hollow and soulless. Max was certain this man would take his life.

The intense gaze of the worst kind of monster stared down at him, beady black pupils reflecting what little morning light the sky offered up.

Archie huffed and pulled the trigger.

At the same moment, the barn door swung open with full force, as if coaxed by a hurricane.

Archie had been standing right next to the door, and its wooden frame crashcd into his arm. The force shattered his extended forearm, contacting just below the elbow. Max heard the crack even as the gun fired. The shot discharged but missed high and wide. The gun was sent flying from Archie's limp hand. The force of the door was great, and it continued; after buckling Archie's arm, it connected with his head as well. The blow toppled Archie into the snow.

A steady stream of blood poured from Archie's left temple. He looked up at the sky without any recognition. The shape of a person emerged from the barn. She was hunched, bracing herself against the cold. But to Max, her posture looked nothing short of triumphant.

Nelly was dressed in only an undershirt and jeans. Her was hair frazzled, and her forehead was dirty with straw and mud. Her forearms were raw with needle marks. But she was free.

Max was trying to comprehend what had happened.

Nelly must have been able to free herself following Max's advice, and then burst through the door after hearing the click and knowing that the latch was unlocked. She had no intention of waiting for anyone to step foot into her cell. She took matters into her own hands. She launched herself full speed at the door, pushing with both hands, and the thing swung out quickly.

Nelly saw Archie lying on the ground, struggling like an overturned tortoise. Max saw something in her eyes then too. She was tired of being the victim.

She stepped over Archie, who could only grasp helplessly at her legs with hands like claws. He tried to say something, but it came out as a series of wet coughs. Nelly calmly went for the gun that had landed in a snow pile. Archie tried again to flip himself. It took everything he had just to roll to his side.

Nelly cocked the gun with all the confidence of someone who had handled a weapon before.

Max could hardly believe what he was seeing. Later, he would realize he likely wouldn't have stopped her, even if he hadn't been in shock. He would never admit it to anyone, but he was glad that Nelly inflicted true justice.

That didn't make it any less horrific to witness, however.

Nelly pointed the gun and didn't even hesitate. Archie held up one of his clawed hands in a weak protest, but the first bullet passed right through his fingers and into his chest. The next two did the same.

Steam rose from the three freshly formed holes in Archie's torso, just as it did from the barrel of the gun. Nelly held the gun out in front of her for many long seconds, unsure if she should relax or not. Max finally gathered himself and climbed to his feet. He looked at Archie and knew it was over.

"He's dead," Max said. He went to Nelly, removing his coat. He wrapped it around her, coaxing her to let go of the gun. "It's over, it's over."

She let out a choked sigh, just a single gasp, and then fell against Max and sobbed silently.

The mass of all that was lost over the past twenty-four hours hadn't caught up to Max yet. But in this moment, with Nelly collapsed against him, his jacket being all that kept her warm, and his arms all that kept her from falling, he felt the weight—every pound—of the life he had saved.

# 17. Goodbye

THICK FLAKES HAD BEGUN TO fall and were already blanketing the ground. Archie's body was partially coated when help arrived—three different police cruisers, an ambulance, and an unmarked sedan all pulled in at roughly the same time. Max waited with Nelly in the warmth of Landry's truck. The girl trembled, hid under his jacket, and didn't say a word. He was too afraid to go to the farmhouse and see the aftermath.

The paramedics tended to Nelly, and the newly arrived deputies asked Max many questions. He was able to answer very few. He wasn't sure how long he sat there, speaking to one person after another. It felt like days.

He tried to put together what had transpired, watching the frantic activity. More vehicles showed up. Police tape was posted everywhere. Eventually, a friendly detective with dimples told Max that they were going to take Nelly to the hospital in Hillport, forty-five minutes up the road from Ruston.

"Just precautionary," she said. She asked Max if he'd like to go as well.

Max accepted the offer and crawled into the unmarked sedan. The last thing he saw before they departed was Archie's body being lifted away. *There goes the curse,* he thought. Archie had been the plague upon Ruston, ever since he retired—and probably, even while wearing the badge.

They patched up Max's hand at the hospital, and then he was pulled aside for more questioning.

"What I still don't understand is what led you to the barn," the detective with the dimples said, becoming less friendly the more she had to ask. She held an old-fashioned notepad in one hand, ballpoint pen in the other.

"Just a hunch." Max shrugged. He could tell that she was frustrated as he played coy.

"And you suspected the former sheriff because . . ."

"My friend Oren was with him. When he didn't answer, we went to check on him. That's when we found his body. Did anyone go back for him like I asked?"

"He's been retrieved." She sounded clinical, emotionless.

"Good." Max relaxed a little. "After that, we knew Archie had killed him. And so, we went after him."

Max had to lie. He couldn't have anyone knowing about the MemCom. He couldn't afford Oren's name being tied to a scandal. But he was very careful not to create lies that he wouldn't be able to recall later. Keep it as close to the truth as possible; some true crime documentary had taught him this.

After it was all over, when Nelly collapsed against him outside the barn, Max had realized what a horrible mess they had on their hands.

"I need your help," he had said to Nelly.

No one could find out what Archie had been doing to her, either. It would lead to more questions about the MemCom. And if the Octopus unit was confiscated, there was a chance it could fall into the wrong hands again. So, when Max had told Nelly his idea, she had been in support of it.

Nelly had grabbed one end, surprising Max with what strength she'd had left. The tangle of cables had dragged behind them in the snow. Max had lifted the bulkier side, his wounded hand protesting. The cold hadn't seemed to bother them as much, now that they'd had a purpose. They had marched the torture device into the woods and down a slight embankment. The pond was frozen over, but not too thick. It was deep enough.

The giant MemCom had crashed against the ice, punching a clean hole through its surface, and disappearing into the murky depths. Max had taken Nelly's arm, guiding her carefully back up the slope and to Landry's truck, where they could finally warm up. Fuzzy snowflakes had begun to drift whimsically down from the sky, Mother Nature promising to help cover their tracks. No one who examined Mort Grey's property would ever notice the path they had carved behind the red barn. No one would realize there was a submerged nightmare just a hundred yards away.

"And the one who shot the suspect was . . . the girl?" The detective brought Max's mind back to the present, her eyes trying to find the truth inside him.

"Yes. She broke out of the barn, the gun was knocked from his hand, and she picked it up."

Max could tell that the detective wasn't thrilled by his answers. But she had no way to disprove this version of events. Nelly had told them the same thing.

She was a brave girl. Max was impressed by her composure, after everything she had been through. As they had waited in the truck, she had told Max that she wouldn't tell anyone about his secret. And she had thanked him.

"Well, that's all for now, I guess." The detective closed her notepad.

Her eyes told him that this wasn't over. Not yet.

"I'm guessing you'll want to go visit the sheriff? He's in the room at the end of the hall."

"Landry?" Max was confused. "He's alive?"

"Both of them got real lucky," the detective said as she walked out of the room. "Just flesh wounds."

Max found Landry resting in a private room. The TV was on at a low volume in the corner, sitcom reruns flickering across the screen. Max was surprised to see Landry awake.

"I don't know what to say," Max admitted.

"Nothing needs to be said," Landry rasped, his voice a husk of its old self. "Ain't much to celebrate, and hell if I know what there is to be learned."

Max felt the same. He thought there'd be more of a sense of victory, or maybe even relief, when they finally caught their suspect. But instead, he just felt like all the air had been sucked from the world.

There was no victory, just a mitigation of future losses.

"At least that fucker's dead." Landry snorted, the closest thing to a genuine laugh Max had heard from the man. "Never liked him much anyway."

Landry shared his version of events with Max. He and Sanderson had gone to the farmhouse, calling on old Mort Grey.

"No one answered, so we tried the door," Landry groaned. "Archie was lying in wait on the other side. I dove for cover, in the sitting room, but Sanderson... he caught a bullet in the side, went down on the porch."

According to Landry, there had been an intense standoff, with he and Archie exchanging barbs, until Landry had tried to crawl into a better position in order to take a shot.

"I was on all fours in the kitchen when I found Mort's body," Landry continued. "Only just realized there was someone behind me when I felt the bullet in my back and passed out. For as close as he had been, the fucker missed the important shit." Landry proudly patted his heart and smirked.

Max let this play out in his mind, staring at the white abyss outside the window, a parking lot full of snow.

"Guess they found a box of things in the barn," Landry said in his gravelly whisper. "Things from the Romano girl. The Thomas girl. And five others. Enough to prove Archie was behind it all."

Max stuffed his hands in his pocket, staring at the ground and feeling uncertain of whether this was good news or bad news. It didn't really matter. He fidgeted with the MemCom in his pocket and looked back at Landry.

"What about . . ."

"I didn't mention anything about it," Landry said. "What difference does it make? Hunch, mind reading, it's all the same result. I still got shot. And Archie's still dead."

"So, they don't know," Max confirmed.

Landry grunted and shook his head. "Consider it my one and only gift to you," Landry said. Then he relaxed his hardened features just a bit. "And to your late partner. My condolences. So, no, I haven't told anybody 'bout what you have in your pocket. And I'll keep that to my grave."

Max was relieved. He felt he could almost respect Sheriff Landry now. He may have been unconventional, but so was Oren. Both of them, at the end of it all, had wanted the same thing.

"You used that thing on me, didn't you?" Landry finally asked.

The way Max stalled confirmed the truth.

Landry grunted, feeling violated. "Should've fucking known. What did you see?"

Max toyed with lying some more but opted for the truth.

"I thought it was you," Max said. "You were driving down Nelly's street the night Tiffany went missing. I never did see the end of that memory, though. You woke me up."

"I was doing my fucking job," Landry said but paused for a brief coughing fit. "I was checking out places I thought the girl was likely to go. Cause no one knows this town and its people better than me. I went to her friend's place. Saw Nelly Masterson staggering out to her garage from the house. No sign of the Thomas girl. Went home after that and had a fitful sleep."

Max figured this had to be the truth; Landry had nothing to gain from lying now.

Another fragment of Landry's memory occurred to Max then. He felt the need to ask, his curiosity overtaking him.

"What happened to Nina?" Max thought about the girl young Ed Landry had been in love with. The one who saved him from the bullies but, in turn, met a bully of her own.

Landry stared at Max, not answering, just studying. He was gauging what Max had seen inside his head. Instead of rage, he responded with something gentler. He became human all at once, and his eyes lit up.

"You should've stuck 'round in there a little longer," Landry said with a coy grin. "You would've seen the good stuff. Been married to Nina a long time now. Even have a daughter together."

Max was amazed at this news. The MemCom held so much potential, providing a link to the past with remarkable clarity. But the truth was still something it struggled to find.

The old Landry returned.

"Don't ever use that fucking thing on me again," he added. "You're lucky I don't have the energy to whoop your ass."

Max promised he wouldn't. A wave of uncertainty crashed over him; for the first time, he realized he no longer had anyone to guide him.

"I don't know what to do with it," Max admitted.

"It's a mind reading device," Landry scoffed. "Read some fucking minds."

\*\*\*

Two women and a young girl passed by Max on his way out of Landry's room, rushing to the man's side. His wife and daughters—one he shared with Nina, and the other being May, the bartender who inadvertently served as Floyd's alibi. It was surreal to encounter these women outside of memories.

The rest of the day dragged. Max was still not used to real world time after so much time spent in memories. He had plenty of paperwork to fill out, all things that didn't register, but he signed them anyway.

Before leaving the hospital, he ran into Robert Thomas. The man offered brief condolences, having heard about Oren. He struggled to make eye contact with Max as he offered a meager apology. Thomas said he'd happily pay Max the full amount, despite the threats. Max wasn't concerned with money. He refused payment and asked Thomas to instead look after sending Oren's body back home. The District Attorney obliged.

He learned that Tiffany was awake now, talking with her stepmother and Nelly. The family was in good spirits; their daughter was safe.

Max's phone buzzed, and he picked it up, surprised to hear Aria's voice on the other end. Aria was devastated, her voice unsteady. She asked what happened, and Max gave her the abbreviated version.

"You have to destroy it," Aria said. "We need to destroy the MemCom. We can't have any of this coming back on Oren. Or us. That thing is a nightmare. We need to let it die."

"I can do that," Max said.

"Are you sure?" Aria asked. "I want to make sure we shut this down right."

Max promised her that he'd take care of it. It didn't feel like a lie at the time.

***

The sky was growing dark again when it was finally time for Max to leave. As he waited for his ride in the lobby, the last loose end came to him. Josh was dashing through the parking lot. He had been released from his overnight holding. Josh stepped inside, and the two of them made eye contact.

"Thank you," Josh said. "For Tiff."

"You won't tell anyone?"

"My sister is safe. That's all I care about." And then, he was gone.

Deputy Bennet, whose mind Max was unfortunately acquainted with, pulled up in one of the marked trucks. Landry had arranged for her to take Max all the way back to the airport in Syracuse. Not much was said between them, aside from the usual small talk. Eventually, Deputy Bennet resorted to music to drown out the awkward silence.

Max felt nervous, like something would suddenly leap out in front of the truck and prevent him from going home. His business in Ruston wasn't entirely behind him—Max owed Stella for stranding her car in the ditch, for one—but watching it fade away in the rearview mirror was a great relief.

This town had done something to Max. He'd only been there a little more than a day, yet it felt like he stepped through a portal into another world. Somewhere behind him, the Thomas family was celebrating, soon to return home. Floyd Smith was being released, finally having his name cleared. Families were being informed of what *really* happened to their daughters.

Yet Oren's next chapter would never be written.

This guilt would've eaten Max alive all the way home, if not for the fact that he felt he was carrying a small bit of Oren with him. The MemCom provided him a gateway. There were lives inside of his pocket.

# Epilogue: The Bungalow

Before heading back to Vancouver, Max had to fly back to his hometown and finish packing up his father's things. By the time he touched down, he was already forgetting what Ruston had felt like. Did the place even exist? Perhaps the whole thing had been a bad dream. *No,* he reminded himself, *I have better control of my dreams.*

He caught a cab from the airport and watched the world pass by from the back seat.

*They say you die twice. One time when you stop breathing and a second time, a bit later on, when somebody says your name for the last time. —Banksy*

Someone had sprayed this in lazy writing on the wall beneath an underpass. It reminded Max of the great responsibility now on his shoulders.

The bungalow looked lonely, in need of companionship. The first thing Max did was shovel the snow that had built up.

He spent most of the day alone, packing boxes with things that needed to be kept, and tossing into bags and bins those which did not. He had been afraid of what he might uncover; each closet contained memories that threatened to bring him to tears. He battled mixed emotions with every item he pulled out.

One of the items Max uncovered was a ticket stub from a concert they had attended together. At the time, Max hadn't been keen on going; it wasn't his type of show. But he was glad now to have made that memory with his father. Just holding the ticket stub, Max was able to hear the music again. It lodged itself in Max's head and played on repeat as he cleaned out the bedrooms.

Max hummed the tune to himself as he continued his cleanup. He doubled back to his father's bedroom at one point, realizing he had forgotten the drawer in the bedside cabinet. He tugged on the handle, and the drawer slid out of its holding completely, crashing to the floor, catching Max off guard.

In the commotion, a stack of papers that had been housed inside were scattered about the room. Max bent over to collect them all but paused as his hands touched the sheet on top of the pile. His vision was becoming blurry.

In his hand, he held a printout of a webpage. A news article. And at the top of the article, just below the headline, were the words *Written by Max Barker.* Max crouched and retrieved the rest of the papers, already knowing what they were but needing to verify.

The drawer was full of Max's work. It seemed that everything he had ever written had been placed in this drawer. Right next to where Max's father slept. Until the day he died. The pages were weathered, too. Well-worn. Not ignored.

*Stupid old man,* Max thought. He forced himself to hold back the tears. He had sent his dad a few stories, many years ago, and never received a comment. But even after he had given up sending things, it appeared his father was still seeking them out. Finding them on his own.

"And you never could even figure out the damn printer." Max chuckled to himself.

Max finished collecting the papers. He had only just stacked them back neatly on the bed when he heard someone at the door. His solitary project had been interrupted by his Aunt Melody. His father's only sister.

She had come to help him. Or so she said. She barely lifted a finger, but Melody was always one to share a story. She had plenty to say about Max's father, good and bad. Max ended up nodding along as he tuned most of the stories out.

They migrated to the living room. Max began sealing up the boxes he had finished packing.

"You know, there's a beautiful Thomas Campbell quote that says, 'To live in hearts we leave behind is not to die.'" Aunt Melody grinned. "You know, your father carries on in you."

Max smiled to be polite because he didn't much feel like talking.

"And I suppose he'll carry on with me, at least for a few more years 'til I'm gone," Melody said with a morbid smile.

Max blinked. She was right. She had no idea *how* right.

"Do you mind if I throw some music on, Aunt Melody?" Max asked.

"Be my guest," she said. "I'll just go through some of these." She set to work on a box of trinkets Max was going to discard until she showed an interest in them.

As she worked, he retrieved his phone and called up an old album by the Eagles. It fit the mood quite well.

"You used to like the Eagles too, right?" Max asked. "Like Dad?"

"Oh yes, we used to listen to them all the time," Melody tittered. She put a hand to her lips as she thought. "You know, this one time—"

For once, Max was happy to get her talking. His hand slid down into his pocket. The familiar cold shell was still there. He had promised Aria he would destroy it. But when the time had come to discard it, he had found that he couldn't part with it. It was a key, he realized. And it unlocked treasures that Max felt he might need again one day.

Max quietly left the room, sitting down on the sofa just on the other side of the half-wall that divided the living room from the front room. Once positioned, he slid the earpiece in—an action that had become a satisfying hit.

The Eagles cooed in the background as his aunt told her story. Max relaxed and pressed the button.

\*\*\*

The house Max now stood in was even more dated than his family bungalow. This place was the epitome of the 1970s. The shag carpet beneath his feet felt like the real thing, and Max recounted days spent in his grandmother's house. This house. Only, many years later.

The house, as it stood now, was fresh—in style and newness—and music boomed through the wood-panelled basement. Two people danced in the far corner, in front of the stereo, mouthing along the lyrics as the Eagles drowned out their occasional laughter.

Though both of them were younger than Max could remember ever seeing them, these two were unmistakable as his father and his Aunt Melody. They were probably in their late twenties, both wearing horrible perms and intermittently bouncing off the couch and the floor as they performed in their drunken cover band.

The two of them had always been close friends. Max just never realized they were get-drunk-together-and-party-in-the-basement friends.

Aunt Melody—here not greyed—collapsed onto the sofa, having burnt out. Max's father carried on. The guitar solo was coming up, and he had the liquid courage to step up on the coffee table for this moment.

"No, don't," Melody cautioned through laughter. "You're a dad now, remember? Can't be taking those risks."

"Dad strength," he said with a wink.

*So, I must have just been born,* he realized. This was the version of his father that had just welcomed his son into the world.

Max's father made it through only a couple strums before the table collapsed under his weight. Wood splinters flew out in all directions, and his father toppled backwards onto his ass. His head smacked against the side of the stereo. The music stopped.

"Ow," Max's father said casually as he brought his hand up to his scalp. He tested it and then brought his hand in front of his face. When he saw the blood, slight as it was, he looked at Melody with wide eyes. "I fell."

They both chuckled.

"What the hell is going on down there?!" a voice called down from upstairs.

Max heard footsteps. More family members were in the house.

"Nothing, hun!" Max's father shouted.

"Oh, hold on." Melody rose from the sofa. She was laughing so hard that she could barely stand straight. It took her a few attempts to get her words out as she bolted up the stairs. "I'll get you something for that cut."

Max's father wasn't down long, however. He popped back up and tried to get the stereo working.

Max took this opportunity and emerged from the corner. He had been standing next to the old shuffleboard that he had played with as a kid. This basement was almost an exact replica of the one he spent time in as a child, except for the broken table and his drunken father.

"Hey, Dad," Max said.

The man stopped dancing, now facing his son. His eyes were the same as Max remembered. And there was recognition in them. Enough for Max to believe.

Then, because Max had long since needed to say this and finally close out that chapter of silence between then, he stepped forwards. He whispered, "I love you" as he hugged the re-creation of his dad. It even smelled like him. And that was all that Max would remember.

***

Max finished cleaning out the bungalow, thanked Aunt Melody for her stories—genuinely meaning it, too—and planned his trip home. Life would return to normal. Or as normal as it could be. He'd never outgrow the sudden pangs of grief, where he'd urgently miss his father, or his mother, or Oren. But his mind never let them go. It kept them alive.

Ruston began to feel like it had come from a different life entirely by the time Max and Janelle moved in together. And when their first child arrived, Max made sure that the small, metallic device was tucked away safely in his sock drawer. One day, he hoped to use it to introduce his children to their grandfather, and to Uncle Oren.

For as long as Max's mind belonged to him, he would use it to keep them alive.

And one day, that job would hopefully belong to his children.

Perhaps, this way, Max could keep them from ever dying again.

*This story is a work of fiction. Any resemblance to actual persons or events is purely coincidental.*

# Acknowledgements

THANK YOU TO MY WIFE, Mary, and to loyal, furry Ruth, for always allowing me to disappear into Ruston and for the constant inspiration and support. Thanks to my family and friends who acted as very early, and kind, editors. The music I was subjected to as a child provided plenty of inspiration for this story, so thanks are in order to my parents for having good taste. As well as for promoting my work before anything had even been published. I wish I could pretend that writing this story was easy, but it was not. It was stubborn and didn't want to get told. It took many rewrites and "dives" into memories of my own—some that provided inspiration for Ruston, and others that died on the cutting room floor. That I am getting to write an acknowledgement at all means the story has finally been told. So, thank *you*, most of all, whoever you are, for reading this.

Printed in Great Britain
by Amazon